"I mean to have you," he said, looking up at her, his voice husky with desire. Shocked, her knees trembling, she stared into his eyes for a long moment. "How dare you," she began, fighting to control the tremor in her voice.

"I sense something in you that would not object to a small lesson in love," he said softly, his voice drawing her like a magnet. "Am I right?"

Before she could answer he grasped her face in both hands, his mouth coming down hard on her parted lips. His arms went around her, pulling her closer, crushing her breasts against his hard muscled chest. She felt the length of his booted legs through her silk robe, the sinewed muscles burning her skin. The fire spread as one hand parted her robe and found her naked breast and the other pressed her buttocks into his burgeoning desire.

BRIDGE OF FIRE

Fiona Harrowe

FAWCETT GOLD MEDAL • NEW YORK

A Fawcett Gold Medal Book
Published by Ballantine Books
Copyright © 1989 by Fiona Harrowe

Library of Congress Catalog Card Number: 88-92989

ISBN 0-449-13157-2

Printed in Canada

First Edition: June 1989

Chapter I

Francisca sat spine straight in her cushioned chair, her lovely features composed. No frown marred the smooth brow, no emotion disturbed the serene dark eyes or altered the repose of the full pink mouth. In contrast, Leonor, her sister, seated uneasily next to her, twisted and turned, leaning forward every few moments to peer anxiously through the latticework of the window.

"I wish you wouldn't fidget so," Francisca said.

"I can't help it. Why don't they begin?"

"Yes," Cousin Beatriz agreed, from her chair behind them. "What do you suppose is delaying them?" A mestiza, the offspring of a distant relative and an Indian woman, Beatriz had been taken in by the girls' parents as a child and was considered one of the family.

"They will be here in due time." The palms of Francisca's hands were sweating. To sit quietly and appear serene was an agony. Only by an effort of supreme will was she able to hide her agitation. Her heart was beating so loudly against the tight bodice of her blue brocade gown, she wondered that the other two didn't hear it.

"I envy you. You're so patient," Leonor pouted.

"Not always." Francisca gave her sister a small smile.

1

Francisca, her cascading black hair tamed into curled sidepieces and brought to a jeweled and ribboned bun at the nape of her slender neck, was seventeen; Leonor, her brown, rather thin tresses tied back with a bowed ribbon, was fifteen. Beatriz was eighteen.

"If only we could go down and mingle with the people in the square," Leonor complained.

"You know that's impossible," Francisca said. "Ladies do not mingle with crowds."

"Yes, I suppose you are right," Leonor murmured with a resigned sigh.

Francisca smiled again at Leonor, thinking how easy it was to convince her fragile, high-strung sister that her position in life held certain strictures, acceptable if not enviable.

Francisca herself was not too sure genteel birth conferred such blessings. Waiting for the procession to begin, she thought how much more exciting it would be if she did not have to sit behind a shuttered window like a prisoner or a veiled Moorish princess. How would it feel, she wondered, to be someone else, a simple peasant among the crowd thronging the Great Square below? And for a few moments she imagined herself as an ordinary onlooker, a girl chattering and laughing with a friend, a plain cotton shawl over her shoulders, and straw sandals on her feet.

But she was Doña Francisca de Silva y Roche, daughter of a wealthy, aristocratic father and a patrician mother. Spanish girls of good family, even here in Mexico City, New Spain, lived sequestered lives in virtual seclusion until they married. Closely guarded, they rarely left the house without a duenna or relative to accompany them. Even on this special occasion her parents and her Aunt Juliana were in the next room, seated on the balcony with their hosts, the Orozcos.

In her childhood Francisca, like Leonor, accepted her well-ordered but restricted life. But as she grew older she began to chafe under the rules imposed upon her and often wished she were the son her father never had.

"Here they come!" Leonor suddenly exclaimed.

Beatriz clapped her hands. "Where? Where?"

Francisca pressed her face against the latticework. But all she could see was the restless multitude beneath her, and the cathedral across the square. Yet unfinished, the cathedral was nevertheless imposing in its awesome majesty, its twin spires rising high toward a cloudless blue sky. In front of the church a platform with wooden seats had been erected. These would be occupied by the prisoners accused of heresy. To the right stood a pulpit with the immense cross of the Holy Office brooding above it. From this pulpit sermons would be preached by high-ranking clergy and by the grand inquisitor himself. Afterward sentences would be pronounced upon the criminals who had betrayed the faith and sinned against Mother Church.

The year was 1649.

The girls were about to witness the concluding stages of the ritual known as *auto de fe*.

The *auto* was an act of faith, a week-long ceremony in which all Catholics were reminded by their parish priests in thunderous diatribes of the terrible doom that awaited should they stray or question the true gospel. Yet in spite of the solemn intent of the *auto*, it had engendered an air of festivity among the population. On the preceding night, in anticipation of this rare public spectacle, church bells had joyfully pealed in clashing, clanging disharmony. Windows and rooftops had been hung with colorful banners and woven rugs. Bonfires had been lit, their leaping flames illuminating the excited faces of the common folk, who welcomed a holiday to break the bleak monotony of their daily lives. Some had gathered at the gates of the prison, bringing refreshments to the honorary guards who kept vigil over the criminals. Others had gone to mass and given thanks to God that the Holy Office had protected them by routing out the blasphemers, the Protestants and Judaizers.

"Listen!" Leonor leaned her head against the grille.

The throb of drums and the piercing cries of trumpets, faint at first, became louder, stronger.

In a few minutes the procession entered the square. First to appear were the clergy carrying the standards of their parish churches draped in black. An acolyte followed ringing a bell, its low, mournful *cling-clang* hushing the crowd. Then came the robed and mitered criminals, stumbling over the cobbles, each carrying a green wax candle and a placard with his name, birthplace, and offense chalked upon it. Those with lesser charges preceded the condemned, who had committed the more heinous crimes against Mother Church.

Bringing up the rear were the *conversos*, the Judaizers or Jews who had outwardly manifested Catholicism but who still practiced their own religion in secret. The repentants among them who had become reconciled to the church would be granted the privilege of being garroted before being burned at the stake; the unrepentant would be burned alive. They were all dressed in sanbenitos, a robe reaching to the knees, on which the green cross of Saint Andrew had been sewn front and back. Their mitered headgear was painted with devils, snakes, and flames. Behind them porters bore effigies of the miscreants who somehow had escaped the long arm of the Inquisition and were to be burned in absentia.

Next came the dignitaries, the senior and junior inquisitors, the viceroy, and the inquisitorial prosecutor, a tall, hawk-nosed man, bearing the crimson standard of the Holy Office. Tasseled with silk and golden cords and fastened to a silver pole, it was capped with a gilded cross that winked and glimmered in the hot sun above the heads of the marchers.

More clergymen followed, prominent among them the white-and-black-robed Dominican order so essential in carrying out the duties of the Holy Office. And lastly, mounted on curvetting horses held tightly in check, rode men of rank.

Francisca's eyes widened as they rested on the hidalgo leading them. His horse was a handsome chestnut stallion, richly caparisoned, bridled in intricately worked silver. He sat in his cordovan saddle with an arrogance that came of an innate sense of place, his red velvet cape spread over the sleek haunches of his steed, his hand resting lightly on the sword hilted in nacre and precious gems at his side. On his head he wore a wide-brimmed cocked hat plumed in crimson and gold, the open side revealing tawny hair and the glint of a golden earring.

When he reached the spot directly under Francisca's window, he turned his face up and smiled—a flash of white teeth in a sun-bronzed face—lifting a gloved hand in salute.

"Why, that's del Castillo!" Leonor exclaimed. "Is that smile for you, sister?"

"Not at all," Francisca remarked offhandedly. "How could it be? We are too well hidden for him to see us."

But Francisca guessed Miguel Velasquez del Castillo knew she was there, watching.

They had met three nights ago. Miguel, the second son of the Marquis of Avila, nephew to the grand inquisitor of Seville, had recently arrived from that city aboard his galleon, the *Espíritu Santo*, now anchored in the port of Veracruz. He had come to Mexico City to trade his cargo of wine, oil, and mercury for silver. And since Francisca's father, Don Pedro, owned extensive mines in Taxco, Miguel had sought him out to transact his business.

Ordinarily the women of Pedro de Silva's house did not take supper with the men when there were male guests outside the family. But that night they were celebrating Francisca's mother's birthday, and Miguel had been invited to stay on.

Francisca remembered how her father, taking her hand, had introduced them. "May I present my daughter?" And Francisca, rising from a deep curtsey, had looking into fathomless blue eyes, tinged with a faint mocking smile.

"I did not know New Spain produced such beauties," he had said, his gaze lingering for a moment on her breasts, half-bared above her tightly laced bodice.

In that one fleeting moment she had felt as though he had brushed his lips on the bare, mounded flesh, and she went hot with embarrassment.

All through the meal, served on silver plates by the light of perfumed candles, Francisca had sensed Miguel's glances, and once when she dared raise her eyes, he shot her a look of such bold, masculine desire, her knees trembled. Men had looked with lust at her before, in church, as she passed from the coach to her door, even on rare occasions in her father's house. But never had she felt the slightest interest or experienced the smallest tremor of excitement. But now, at each stolen glance, she could feel the warmth rise to her cheeks. She hated that blush but had no more control over it than she did over the beat of her heart. She worried lest her sister, her mother, or, worst of all, her father might detect her inner agitation and either tease or scold her for it.

But her father had been too busy plying Miguel with questions concerning the news from Old Spain. Gossip involving members of King Philip's court was of little interest to Francisca, and she listened with only half an ear. It was only when her father inquired politely about Miguel's wife, who had remained in Seville, that Francisca was brought to attention.

So Miguel was married. She might have guessed that such a handsome, prepossessing man from one of Spain's leading families would not—or could not—remain a bachelor. He had a wife in Seville. Francisca did not know whether to be disappointed or nettled. Of course, it was customary for men of noble blood—married or not—to make conquests and take mistresses, but Don Miguel must have realized that the closely guarded daughters of an eminent citizen like Pedro de Silva were beyond his reach.

Francisca, now sitting behind the latticed window, watching the last of the procession come into the square, recollected the rest of that evening in vivid detail.

Don Miguel had talked about his voyage from Cádiz. He told of leaving port as part of a flota of thirty galleons and how fierce storms and an attack by pirates near the Bahamas had reduced their number to twenty. In recounting the story, he seemed to have forgotten about her and did not look at her for the rest of the meal.

Francisca had wondered then if she had imagined Miguel's bold stare. Or had his glances merely been those of a man who took casual note of any pretty woman who came into view?

Later that night she learned differently.

She was getting into bed when she noticed that her little lapdog, Pepé, who usually slept at her feet, was missing. Reasoning that he must have slipped unnoticed through the door when her maid had retired, she threw on a robe and went out to look for him. Moving along the gallery, she began her descent of the inner stairway that led to the dining room, where she was sure Pepé could be found nosing among fallen table scraps.

The stairs were dimly lit by a flickering oil lamp set on the landing, so she was startled when a shadow detached itself from the wall two steps below.

It was Miguel. Stripped of his velvet surcoat, he wore a white silk shirt and black doublet and hose, which outlined the strong contour of his legs. In the dim light he looked taller, his shoulders broader, the planes of his handsome face somehow more arrogant and haughty.

"I see you are also sleepless," Miguel said.

"That is not my trouble at all," she said, controlling her voice but not the hammering of her heart or the sudden weak feeling in her knees. How could a man she did not even know unnerve her so? He was probably no better than a common wencher for all his aristocratic airs.

"What is it, then?" he asked.

"My dog has run off," she said, feeling a little foolish, wondering why she bothered to explain.

"Perhaps I can be of some help?"

She raised her chin. "Thank you, but I wouldn't put you to the trouble."

"It will be my pleasure." His eyes so dark, almost black in the dim light, held a strange magnetic glitter as they rested on the strip of flesh exposed by the gap in her robe. She drew it tighter about her, her hand fluttering protectively to her throat.

"Do I frighten you?" he whispered.

"Of course not. Why should you? Please—if you will let me pass?"

But he was not a man to be easily discouraged or lightly dismissed.

"You are a beautiful woman, Doña Francisca de Silva y Roche."

"You repeat yourself."

"And I intend to do it again and again."

There was an air of animal virility about him that frightened yet captivated her. The nobles and hidalgos she had met in her father's house seemed soft and effeminate by comparison. She should have known by the very fact that Miguel captained his own ship—unlike other noble sons, who considered work of any kind beneath them—he was a man apart. True, he was dressed in velvet and silk and wore gold rings jeweled with fine-cut stones. But his strong, broad-fingered hands also bore calluses, the marks of lanyards and hawsers. He did not seem the least ashamed of these rough signs of his trade, as the cavaliers with their white, well-tended hands might be. Though he shared the hidalgo arrogance, the air of rightful command, and the eye that could strip and assess a woman, Francisca sensed he was different. And the difference disturbed her.

"I mean to have you," he said, looking up at her, his voice husky with desire.

Shocked, her knees trembling, she stared into his eyes for a long moment. "How dare you?" she began, fighting to control the tremor in her voice. "How dare you presume on my father's hospitality?"

He took the two steps that separated them. His breath was hot on her cheek, but he did not touch her.

Suddenly, insanely, she wanted him to. She wanted him to touch her, to take her in his arms. She longed to be kissed by that strong, mobile mouth, to know how it felt to have his lips on hers.

His face now was completely in shadow. The warmth of his nearness frightened yet excited her.

"I sense something in you that would not object to a small lesson in love," he said softly, his voice drawing her like a magnet. "Am I right?"

Before she could answer, he grasped her face in both hands, his mouth coming down hard on her parted lips. The breath left her lungs, and the cry of protest that began as a thought died on her captive tongue. So this was kissing, this coming together of lips on lips. She had never imagined such a sweet sensation, this light-headed giddiness as if she had drunk too much red Andalusian wine. It was all new to her. Her hand had been kissed by one or two forward gallants, but they had never touched her lips. Yet instinct told her that no other man could arouse such feelings of need, no other man would be able to conquer her senses so totally.

His arms went around her, pulling her closer, crushing her breasts against his hard-muscled chest. She felt the length of his booted legs through her silk robe, the sinewed muscles burning her skin. The fire spread as one hand parted her robe and found her naked breast, and the other pressed her buttocks into his burgeoning desire. She wanted him to go on kissing her, touching her in places he ought not to touch her, feeding the hot fire in her loins.

His mouth traveled down from her lips to her throat, where a wild pulse beat. He rested there, a small groan escaping his lips. Francisca's arms went around him, holding him, suddenly afraid that he might stop, yet afraid, too, that he wouldn't. Where this passionate kissing would end, she dared not think. She did not want to think. Only the moment mattered.

"Francisca." Her name on his tongue seemed to take on a sensuality it had never had before.

He raised his head, looking down at her with shadowed

eyes. There was no mockery in them now, only a tender smile that pierced her heart.

"Come with me," he whispered, placing his arm around her waist.

And she would have gone anywhere, done anything, had not reality suddenly shattered her trance. A clatter of wood-shod feet, and the shout of the night porter. "Who goes there?"

Miguel quickly stepped back into the shadows of a doorway a moment before the porter appeared at the foot of the stairs.

"Ahhh—'tis you, little mistress. I thought I heard a man's voice."

Drawing her robe together, she took a deep breath. "There . . . there is no one but me," she said. To be found in Miguel's embrace would have meant dishonor not only for her but for her family as well. The virginal Francisca kissing a stranger! She would be branded whore, the kind of stigma that could only be erased by a duel between her father and Miguel, and internment for herself in a convent.

"Pepé has run off, and I am looking for him," Francisca told the porter. She had forgotten all about the dog. It seemed hours, years, a lifetime, since she had put on her robe and gone through the door of her bedchamber in search of poor Pepé.

"You should have called your maid—or me. We would have been happy to serve you."

"It was of little import. But if you find him, I will be grateful. Good night." She started up the stairs.

She heard Miguel behind her whisper her name, but she did not turn. If he tries to stop me, she remembered thinking, what should I do? Scream? Let him have his will of me?

But he made no move to follow her, and when she had closed and bolted the door, she leaned her trembling body against it, feeling a vague sense of loss.

* * *

And now he was riding past her. Miguel in all his jeweled and feathered finery, sitting upon his horse with the easy grace and arrogance he was born to. Francisca tore her eyes from his receding figure and raised them to the platform where the officials of the Inquisition and the heretics had already been seated. The clergy occupied cushioned chairs; the criminals sat on the tiered benches, those accused of lesser misdeeds on the bottom rungs, those guilty of more serious crimes at the top.

Francisca could not look for very long at these wretched souls, their white faces under the miters etched in pain, some slumping forward, their bodies broken by torture.

The voice of the archbishop preaching the initial sermon reached Francisca only faintly. But she heard enough to make her shudder, for she had listened to similar sermons many times before, and today it seemed as though he were speaking directly to her. So many sins. To doubt or disbelieve a single article of faith, to question the wisdom of the clergy, to confess falsely, no matter how trivial the invented transgression, to have read or even leafed through a forbidden book in the Index, were all sins she was guilty of. And last night she would have willingly gone to the bed of a married man and added adultery to her wickedness. But there was more that weighed on her soul, much more and much worse.

The sermon ended in a thundering promise of hellfire and brimstone to backsliders. And then the secretary of the Inquisition rose to administer the oath of faith. His words were answered by a great roar from the crowd in one shouting tongue, promising to defend the Holy Office and its agents and to denounce all heretics.

Francisca, glancing at Leonor, saw that she had gone very white.

"Are you not feeling well, sister?" Francisca took her cold, limp hand. "Perhaps you'd best lie down."

"Oh, no," she whispered. "I mustn't. The servants here will take note and say I have something on my conscience because I have made an excuse to retire. Perhaps a glass of water . . ."

"Cousin Beatriz will get it for you."

"Oh, Francisca," Leonor went on, "I did not know it would be so terrible. The man there with the iron gag in his mouth. He will surely choke to death. Is he a . . ?"

"A blasphemer. The yoke is to silence him."

But more harrowing scenes were yet to come.

The prosecuting attorney began to read the sentences imposed upon the prisoners. A half-starved Indian slave, his bony arms protruding like sticks from his sanbenito, was the first. A blasphemer also, he had cried out under the lash of his master that he would rather be a monkey than a Christian. And so he was sentenced to fifty more lashes for his indiscretion. Two bigamists were condemned to lifelong service as galley slaves, a sentence of short duration since an unfortunate condemned to the stinking hold of a ship, and chained night and day to its oars, rarely lasted more than two years.

The sun was now at its zenith, beating mercilessly down on the square. But the crowd, sweating in the unseasonable heat, still stood mesmerized by horror and fear underscored with murmuring excitement. Francisca would have liked nothing better than to retreat into the comparative coolness and quiet of the house. But she, like Leonor, dared not arouse suspicion by leaving her post. Under her heavy brocaded dress rivulets of perspiration ran down her back and between her breasts. Her forehead, beaded in sweat, was only momentarily cooled by her fluttering fan.

The ordeal went on.

There were one hundred and nine sentences to be read. Fourteen prescribed death. These were the Judaizers, the Christian converts who pretended to be honest churchgoers while adhering to their Hebraic heritage. Black-robed friars exhorted the unrepentant to confess and embrace Holy Mother Church in these final hours before it was too late for their souls to enter Paradise.

"How could they be so stubborn?" Leonor said, her voice faint with fear.

"You mustn't think of it. Think of something else."

The unfortunate Judaizers (termed *marranos*, or swine, in Spain) were mounted on mules. One of them, Francisca had been told, was Anica de Carvajal, a woman of seventy whose brother Luis had been martyred at the stake in the *auto de fe* of 1596. According to custom, the condemned would be carried through the streets on mules so that the populace could spit on them, reviling them with curses on their way to the *quemadero*, the burning ground.

Francisca, watching them, felt a terror that constricted her heart in a tight, painful vise. A silent scream rose in her throat. *There but for the Grace of God go I*, her mind repeated again and again in dreadful cadence. It could have been her, ignominiously astride a mule, her face and body pelted with excrement, her humiliation reaching the depths of despair.

For Francisca, like the other members of her family, was a Jew.

Chapter II

"I wish we did not have to go as angels again," Leonor, wearing a tentlike white gown, was being fitted by Beatriz with a pair of gilded wings. "I would much rather be a Greek goddess or a princess. But Papá says no."

"It *is* unfair," Francisca agreed.

"Just because Papá pays for the Virgin's float shouldn't oblige us to be part of the decorations. Don't you agree, Beatriz?"

"I don't mind." Beatriz very rarely found fault.

The girls were discussing the upcoming *mascarada*, a gala parade, in this instance celebrating the Feast of Saint Francis Borgia.

Mascaradas were frequent in Mexico City. Any occasion of major or minor importance—births, baptisms, marriages, holy days, the safe arrival of the annual fleet from Europe—served as an excuse for the organization of a lavishly staged pageant. The rich welcomed these diversions to break the dull monotony of colonial life. The poor looked forward to them as a palliative to relieve the harshness of thankless, unending toil and the social indifference of the upper classes. In the *mascarada*, however, all classes, all ethnic groups, Negros, Indians, gypsies, mestizos, and pure-blooded Spaniards, participated, joining in the pomp and splendor, and the fun-loving gaiety.

"Well," Leonor sighed, "I suppose it's better to accompany the Virgin of Guadalupe and be part of the parade than to stay home and watch from the window."

Beatriz, having finished her task of sewing on the golden wings, held up a mirror. Leonor twisted and turned to see the reflection of her back in the dressing table glass. "How do I look, Francisca?"

"Very angelic."

"Must you sound so sour? You've been like that for days now. What is it?"

"Nothing. Nothing at all. I'm simply bored."

It had been three weeks since Francisca had last seen Miguel. He, along with the de Silvas and other notables of the city, had been invited to the viceroy's banquet given on the evening after the *auto*. She had been seated with her family at the long, lavishly appointed table, separated from Miguel by a dozen other people. They had exchanged glances, Miguel's steady blue gaze burning into her eyes with a look that brought the blood rushing to her cheeks.

Leonor, noting the high flush, had inquired, "Sister, have you a fever?"

Francisca fluttered her fan, annoyed with Miguel, annoyed at herself. "I'm perfectly well," she had answered with asperity. "I'm simply hot. The air is so close."

"I am uncomfortable, too. Perhaps Mamá will let us go into the garden. The meal is almost over."

Later, as Francisca and Leonor strolled under the leafy trees, they heard guitar music and the rhythmic clap of castanets coming from the house.

"Oh!" Leonor exclaimed in delight. "The gypsy dancers! Papá said the viceroy would have them. Let us go in and watch."

"Not just yet," Francisca replied. "You run along. I'll join you presently."

Francisca seated herself on a stone bench, folding her fan, tucking it into her narrow waist, sashed in bright crimson satin. The fragrance of night-blooming jasmine wafted across the garden on a fitful breeze. She breathed deeply of the exotic perfume, thinking of Miguel. She wondered if he had remained to watch the gypsy dancers or if he had gone on to more amusing entertainment. To some woman, perhaps, who waited for him. Some . . .

"Doña Francisca!"

Startled, she stiffened. He was at her back. But she did not—or could not—turn her head.

"Doña Francisca!" His voice was low and urgent.

She heard his footsteps on the grass. And then he was looking down at her, the torches that lined the garden path throwing his face into angled shadows.

"May I sit?" he asked politely, his eyes taking in the bared, creamy shoulders and half-visible cleft between her breasts.

She clenched her fists in the folds of her voluminous skirts to gain control of her racing heart. "Do as you wish," she said in a surprisingly indifferent voice. "I was leaving in any case."

She started to rise, but he put a restraining hand on her bare shoulder, a touch that felt like a brand. "Please, don't rush off on my account. I was hoping to have a few words with you."

"What could we possibly say to one another?"

"The other night—"

"I'd rather not talk about it." Nor did she want to think of that meeting on the dark stairs, his arms around her, his burning lips on her mouth, the melting weakness in her knees.

"Very well, we can speak of other things."

"I cannot. My parents—"

"They will hardly miss you. Why run off? Surely you don't find me that frightening?"

"Of course not." But she did. She did not trust Don Miguel. She did not trust him because he had the power (and knew it) to excite and fill her with these new, disturbing longings.

"May I?" he asked again.

"If you insist." She pulled in her skirts, and he seated himself beside her. His magnetic closeness made her breathless with a mixture of fear and heightened awareness.

"I have been trying to puzzle something out," he said, breaking a long silence.

"What is that?" It still amazed her, even now when she thought of it, how calm she had sounded despite her racing heart and trembling nerves.

"I cannot understand why thoughts of you should bedevil me so," Miguel went on. "They do, you know. I ask myself, is it because she is beautiful? But I have known beautiful women before. Because she is unattainable? But I have met the unattainable before. Perhaps, I tell myself, it is because this woman is Francisca, an irresistible creature who has captured my heart."

She pulled out her fan, snapped it open, and fluttered it with a vigor that shook her side curls. "You flatter me, Don Miguel."

"Do I?" And when she did not answer, he repeated, "Do I?"

She turned to face him. His eyes held hers, and in his drowning gaze she saw tenderness and desire. And the promise of passion. Her pulse quickened. Passion. Was it real? Something more than the words of a love song? Yes, his eyes seemed to say, yes, yes.

The fan dropped from her fingers, suddenly gone boneless. She wanted to turn away but couldn't. The soft, perfumed night, his eyes . . .

As if in a dream, she felt him move closer, felt his warm wine breath on her cheek, felt his heavy hand on her knee. She closed her eyes, felt his lips on hers . . .

"Francisca! Francisca!" It was Leonor. "Where are you? Papá says it's time to go home."

Francisca, her heart pounding, rose quickly on unsteady

feet. She did not speak to Miguel, did not look at him. But she heard his soft ''Adios'' as it followed her like the whisper of the jasmine-scented breeze into the house.

The next morning Miguel and her father had set out for Taxco to conclude their business. Pedro had mentioned nothing about Miguel's future plans or whether he would be returning to Mexico City.

Leonor was still talking about the *mascarada*.

''Rosa is to be a handmaiden to Amadis of Gaul on her father's float.'' Rosa Rodriguez, daughter of a prosperous wine merchant, was Leonor's dearest friend. ''But she says her father is complaining that the expenses of *mascaradas* are becoming unreasonable.''

''Rosa shouldn't repeat everything she hears, true as it may be.''

Rosa's father was not the only complainant. The wealthier merchants who were called upon to underwrite the cost of the *mascarada* often balked. But Don Pedro de Silva, unlike his contemporaries, gladly made generous donations to these public spectacles.

He was rich, he would say. He could afford it. But in reality his paramount motive was to remain in the good graces of the local authorities, both clerical and lay, in order to preserve the façade of an old Christian, a devout Spanish Catholic.

The façade had been carefully put in place by his grandfather, Isaac ben Samseca. In 1492 when King Ferdinand and Queen Isabella expelled those Jews who would not acquiesce to baptism, Isaac, a wealthy merchant, instead of submitting to conversion, had fled Spain. Taking with him his family and a greater portion of his wealth in gold, he had settled in Venice. But he had missed Spain, where his family had lived for centuries. Spain was in his blood. Seeking a way to return, he had paid to have documents (including one called *limpieza de sangre*, purity of blood) forged, records that attested to his impeccable lineage as a Christian. Instead of going back to Madrid, where he might be known, he came to Seville, giving out that he was a rich landowner from León who had retired to the city for his remaining years. Meanwhile, he went on quietly adding to his wealth, engaging in overseas trade with Turkey, Persia, Morocco, and Italy.

After the conquest of New Spain, he bought from the king, sight unseen, silver mines near Taxco. These mines were one of the reasons his grandson, Pedro de Silva, had come to New Spain. The other, more compelling, one was the Inquisition. Wily old Isaac had never converted. He had managed to practice in secret the tenets of the Hebraic religion, celebrating in particular the seder in commemoration of Moses' Exodus from Egypt, and the High Holy Days. His children and their children, however, had been baptized. Not to do so would have brought down the anathema of the church, which ruled the daily lives of the Spaniards with an iron hand, demanding blind obedience. But the de Silvas, marrying within their faith, had managed to keep their beliefs, transforming the wrathful Jehovah of the Old Testament into a loving and compassionate God. Their spiritual satisfaction, however fulfilling, was tempered by the knowledge that to be discovered as Jews would be fatal.

Pedro had thought the Inquisition would be more benign in the New World. It didn't take him or his wife long to discover that distance had not diminished that institution's zeal.

Francisca had often wished that her father would give up a religion so despised by everyone. But the *auto de fe* had changed her mind. The suffering of those poor souls sacrificed on a fiery altar to satisfy a jealous God seemed to her pagan. Wasn't it her father who once said that hellfire, purgatory, the devil, and witches were inventions of the human mind? But of course, it was a statement never to be repeated. To do so would be blasphemy. And Francisca had seen what happened to blasphemers.

"I'm not going to the *mascarada*," Francisca said abruptly. "I will tell Papá when he comes home that I feel ill. I refuse to be paraded through the streets in that ugly costume again.''

Beatriz laughed, but Leonor was indignant. "Francisca! If you don't, I won't either.''

"Yes you will. You just said you'd rather ride on the float than stay at home watching. I don't mind being left behind. I'll read a book. Perhaps I will reread Cervantes's *Don Quixote*. That always amuses me.''

"You and your books! Mamá says you will spoil your eyes and get wrinkles in your forehead reading so much, and I believe her. Who will want to marry you then?''

"Perhaps I shan't get married.''

"What? Become a nun?''

"Heaven forbid!''

"There is no other choice, sister.''

"I know of a third choice. Mistress. Mistress to an illustrious and dashing lover.''

Leonor laughed. "Now you are truly making fun. But I don't think Papá would find it humorous.''

"No,'' Francisca said slowly. "I don't think he would.''

Don Pedro returned from Taxco two days before the *mascarada*. Francisca was wondering how she could ask after Miguel without seeming more than casually interested when her father answered her unspoken question.

"Don Miguel did not accompany me on my return to Mexico City,'' he told the family.

A servant was removing his muddy boots as he sat sprawled in a chair. He was a short man of stocky build with wide shoulders and dark, graying hair. His bearded face bore the marks of his journey, a sunburned nose and reddened, fatigued eyes.

"He thought it best to go on to Veracruz and see to his ship.'' Pedro's boots and stirrup hose removed, a basin of warm water with soothing herbs was brought. "Don Miguel is an odd man for a hidalgo,'' he went on, inching his feet into the water. "Enterprising, shrewd in his business dealings, not afraid of a little work. He's also a devout Catholic, I might add. He went to mass whenever we stopped at a village.''

"Devout Catholic, my sainted grandmother!" Aunt Juliana interposed scornfully. A widow, built like an *olla*, a jug, she had a small head set on a rounded body with short legs. Given to gossip and gluttony, dangerously outspoken in her dislike for Papists, she shunted between the homes of her two daughters and that of the de Silvas.

"I hear that he games and beds women like any caballero,'' she continued. "His name was mentioned just yesterday in the marketplace. They say La Flor is his mistress.''

"Juliana!" Francisca's mother admonished. "Guard your tongue! This is not a subject for young girls' ears.''

Francisca, whose heart had plummeted at the mention of La Flor, struggled to find her voice. "But . . . Mamá, everyone knows of La Flor.''

The courtesan's notoriety had spread from the humblest abode to the pulpits of parish churches, where the priests had railed against her. Songs and verses had been written extolling her dark, seductive eyes and her golden limbs. Gossip claimed that she had conquistador blood running in her Aztec veins, that she traveled in a velvet-cushioned coach, curtained in scarlet silk and pulled by four matching white geldings. Men had bestowed priceless jewels, houses, and slaves upon her. It was also rumored that more than one duel had been fought because of her, and such was her feminine charm that a man once under her spell could never forget her.

And this woman, this Delilah, had become Miguel's mistress.

Had he held and kissed La Flor the way he had held and kissed her? Had he whispered in her ear, put his lips to the palpitating pulse in her throat? Had his hand . . . ?

"All the same," Mariana was saying, "I would rather not have that loose woman's name mentioned in our house. As for del Castillo, I suppose we've seen the last of him.''

"Unless he makes a return trip, which might be years away," Don Pedro said.

Years away. Perhaps never. Then why should I fret? Francisca asked herself. He has gone out of La Flor's life as he has gone out of mine.

Francisca's father made no objection when she expressed a wish to be left out of the *mascarada*. He assumed, like Leonor and her mother, that she would remain at home watching from the window. But Francisca had secretly decided to participate. She had always envied the mestizo and gypsy girls who formed their own section of the parade, whirling their multicolored skirts as they danced and sang. Their carefree laughter would reach her as she sat stiffly, dressed in lusterless angel garb on her father's float, a prey to dull convention.

But Miguel's kiss had brought out a restlessness, a piquant curiosity she had only vaguely experienced before. At his touch she had felt her heart pounding with excitement, the hot blood coursing through her veins, had known—if even briefly—what it was like to be alive. *Really* alive. Now, thinking of those moments on the dark stair, the smoldering rebellion deep within her sparked to flame. From the day she was born, her future had been mapped out for her. She would go from her father's care to her husband's, settling into sober maturity, still abiding by set rules, her freedom to move about strictly curtailed. She had never openly questioned the path she must take, had never defied propriety.

Yet why shouldn't she enjoy—at least for one night—the excitement and gaiety of a fiesta?

The day before the *mascarada*, Francisca stole into her father's library and extracted the key for the back garden gate from its hiding place in a volume of Catholic writings. The garden gate built into the wall that surrounded the de Silva house was unknown except to the *converso* friends of the family. Even the servants were ignorant of its existence. This entrance had been provided not only as an escape route, but for the protection of the few trusted guests who secretly came to the house to celebrate Jewish holidays. It was the only way Francisca could leave without being seen by the doorman, Manuel, who diligently guarded his post.

Muffled in a black cloak, her hair and part of her face covered with a scarf, Francisca stood hesitantly in the shadow of the shrubbery that hid the secret gate from the street. She had never left her house unaccompanied, and then very rarely on foot. Her passage through the city had been mostly by sedan or carriage. And now suddenly she was struck with a timid uncertainty.

But she couldn't turn back. If she didn't walk away now, she would never muster the courage to do so again. What is there to fear? she asked herself. She had known the streets of the Spanish quarter since childhood. She could easily find her way. And dressed as a servant girl, who would notice her? Chiding herself for cowardice, she stepped boldly out.

Hurrying along La Moneda, she traversed the square, passing the viceroy's house crowned by its clock tower, and the Orozco house, where she had watched the *auto*. At the far end she turned into the Merchants' Gateway. Here, crowding the dusty street, stood shop after shop, a bustling community of stone carvers, locksmiths, clog makers, chandlers, sword makers, pastry cooks, and chair makers. The ringing anvil of the blacksmith vied with the rasping saws of the carpenters; the cries of the grocers hawking melons and maize strove above the singsong voices of the weavers extolling their cloth.

Suddenly there was a shout, "Make way! Make way!" Negros in scarlet livery were bearing a sedan, its crimson, gold-embroidered curtains half-parted to reveal the face of a haughty Catalonian beauty. A group of laughing youths dressed in white, frilled shirts and black doublets followed on horseback.

Francisca, who had viewed this scene many times from the same sort of sedan that had passed a moment earlier, now saw it all with new eyes. It was exciting and wonderfully adventurous to stroll the street without her mother or Aunt Juliana dogging her footsteps. She could linger where she pleased, pausing at the silk seller or at the hatter's or stopping to inspect the latest import of Flemish lace, running the fine work through her fingers.

Turning a corner, Francisca arrived at the costumer's, a hole-in-the-wall nook crowded with clamoring last-minute buyers. The harassed merchant was shouting that it was too late to make up a new outfit; people would have to take what he had.

Francisca's eye was caught by a white gown banded in red satin that hung from a peg behind the counter. She elbowed her way forward.

"I'll have that costume," she said, pointing.

The red-faced, perspiring shopkeeper shook his head. "No, no, that is spoken for."

"Whatever has been offered, my mistress will double," Francisca said, staying within her role of servant.

The man look dubiously at Francisca's poor, shabby cloak. Francisca jingled her bag of coins.

"Very well, then. Four ducats."

"Four ducats it is. I shall want a mask. Not that one. It's too ugly." It was a gray mask representing some monstrous ogre with gnashing teeth and bulging eyes.

"Tell your mistress the grotesque is fashionable. However, if you feel it won't suit her, then there are only the plain crimson ones left."

Francisca, with her purchases hidden under her cloak, had a bad moment as she slipped through the garden gate. Leonor and Beatriz were at the far end of the garden playing with little Pepé under a sapodilla tree. The girls didn't see her since she was screened by a row of tall, flowering bushes. But the dog caught her scent and came bounding toward her, barking joyfully.

"Pepé!" Leonor called. "Pepé, come here at once!"

The dog went on barking while Francisca tried to silently shoo it away.

"Beatriz," Leonor said in an exasperated tone. "Go fetch him."

Beatriz came after the dog and scooped it up within a few inches of Francisca's feet. "Naughty, Pepé," she scolded, carrying it toward the house.

Francisca waited a few minutes, then, scurrying across the garden, stole up to her room.

Chapter III

After the family and the servants, who had been given permission to attend the *mascarada*, had left, Francisca got into her finery. She was delighted to find that her costume fit better than she had expected. The tight bodice hugged the tender curve of her breasts and snugly embraced her slender waist. Yards of skirt dropping into ruffled tiers fell to above her ankles, revealing two inches of white stockings thrust into black satin slippers. The fall-away shoulders came down to sleeves that flared in red-banded flounces at the elbow. A flower for her hair, her crimson mask tied in place, and she was ready.

Once outside, she threaded her way through already crowded streets and paused in the shadows of an arched doorway to wait for the parade.

Presently she heard the shrill piping of flutes, the flourish of trumpets, and the beat of drums which announced the approaching pageant. Her heart began to leap with excitement as she stood on tiptoe to catch a glimpse of the leading figures.

And there they were! A group of Indians wearing simple white loincloths, their brown, half-naked bodies daubed with clay paint and their hair stuck with feathers, swarmed through the narrow street. Shouting and whooping wildly, they brandished clubs, frightening the small children, who clung to their mothers' skirts.

The Indians were followed by a company of infantrymen in full uniform marching six abreast to the stirring strains of martial music. With standards billowing and brightly colored plumes fluttering from the crests of their helmets, squad after squad stepped smartly along.

After them came another contingent of natives, these representing the Aztec, Toltec, and Chichuneca royalty of conquest days. In full costume on floats or on foot, they presented an awesome spectacle. Each monarch bore a crown of turquoises surmounted by golden green plumes of the quetzal bird. Their *tilmas*, fastened at the shoulder by a knot, were embroidered with esoteric symbols, while their brown ankles and arms were adorned with precious jeweled bracelets.

Next came a group of some twenty-five or thirty citizens dressed in a variety of lavish, bizarre, or comical costumes. Francisca laughed with the rest of the crowd at Don Quixote with his broken lance, and the fat figures of Sancho Panza and plump Dulcinea riding beside him on decrepit mules. There were revelers in animal costume: cougars, coyotes, and two humped camels that bumped along next to Turks in tarbooshes and Romans in togas.

When a band of gypsies, dancing, singing, and strumming guitars, appeared, Francisca moved forward to join them.

No one questioned her or seemed to think it odd that she had stepped from the shadows to become a member of the gypsy band. Perhaps it was because she blended in so smoothly with the others, her body taking up the rhythm of tambourine and guitar without missing a beat. Gliding and twirling, her skirts flying above her trim ankles, she took her place between a guitarist and a stamping Romany. Francisca had learned the gypsy dances by watching the entertainers her father sometimes hired at special dinners to divert his guests. Afterward she and Leonor would amuse themselves in the privacy of Francisca's bedroom by imitating the provocative hip-swaying and heel-clicking motions of the dark-skinned performers.

Now, caught up in the ebullience of holiday revelers, she felt an exhilarating, magical lightness, a giddy sense of freedom she had not known from her practice steps at home. This, the hand clapping and catcalls, the shouts and head tossing, was far different. How wonderful it felt to be liberated from the starched gowns and heavy brocades she had been condemned to since early girlhood, how marvelous to fling herself about in a cool, corsetless gypsy dress! She felt tireless, as if her feet had wings. Closing her eyes, she let the throbbing guitars and the voices singing ballads of love and seduction, songs of haughty women and scorned *enamorados*, engulf her senses. The music became louder, the dance wilder and wilder. Francisca lifted her arms, swaying and twirling, moving hips and shoulders sensuously as if she had been born a daughter of Romany and knew no other life.

Then she stumbled over an uneven cobblestone, and the mask slipped from her face. She was fumbling with the knotted ribbons when the parade halted for a few minutes. It was then that she noticed a horseman sitting in the archway of an open door that led to the patio of a magnificent residence. He was dressed in the costume of a conquistador of old, his silver mail polished to a mirrored shine. A sword swung at his side, a halberd lay across the high saddle, and a burnished steel shield protected his left flank. His head and face were covered with helmet and visor, so that Francisca could not see his features. It seemed to her that he was staring at her, a blank, faceless gaze that made her turn uneasily away.

Twilight had fallen when the *mascarada* began to move again. Looking back, she noted that the conquistador had joined a troop of mounted men in the section behind the gypsies. Apparently he had been a latecomer like herself, waiting to cut in to the procession. Many of the paraders now carried lighted torches, and in the distance the shouts of merrymakers and the explosive pop of firecrackers could be heard. The *mascarada* was winding down. Francisca didn't want it to end. She felt as though she could go on singing and dancing until dawn. But she knew that after nightfall the *mascarada* deteriorated into drunken rowdiness. Already there were whistles and coarse remarks directed at her, and one reeling figure dressed as a court buffoon tried to grab her. She eluded him, only to have her gown snatched by an Apollo who reeked of cheap wine. She was trying to fight him off when a horseman galloped through the throng. Knocking her accoster aside with the butt of his lance, he scooped Francisca up and, swinging her across his saddle, rode off.

An astonished Francisca, grateful for her rescue, thought that once they had cleared the crowd, she would be released. But the horseman, instead of bringing his mount to a halt, clattered on. Craning her neck upward from her awkward position, Francisca saw that her benefactor was the conquistador she had noted earlier, his face still hidden behind helmet and guard.

"Could you put me down?" she shouted, raising her voice above the hollow beat of hooves and the jingle of harness. "Please?"

There was no answer, no indication that the man had heard. The horse picked up speed. Soon they were riding in darkness with only the gleam of an occasional torch, glinting off the conquistador's mail, to pierce the gloom. The streets led one into another, the dusty, darkened alleyways fragrant with night dew and flowering trees disappearing from view as the flying hooves thudded on. The distant torches and the far-away sound of the festive crowd disappeared. A fitful half moon veiled by wispy gray clouds gave a feeble, ghostly light. Francisca, half lying, half sitting, pressed into the saddle's hard wooden pommel on one side and the man's steely armor on the other, felt a stitch of pain in her side. Where were they going? She could only guess why this man refused to let her go, and for the first time since she had ventured out of her house, she felt a shiver of cold fear work itself along her bare arms.

She was this conquistador's captive, and they were galloping into the wind, traveling deeper and deeper into the night.
There was no one to rescue her now. It would be hours before
her family returned from the dinner they had been invited to
at the close of the *mascarada*. Perhaps, her mother had said,
they would stay the night. In any case, Francisca had asked
not to be disturbed until morning. She would not be missed.

"Where are you taking me?" she shouted once more.

The silence of her armor-clad captor terrified her. Was
there a living, breathing man of flesh and blood behind the
breastplate and chain mail? Or had she been abducted by the
ghost of Hernán Cortés himself? She was not superstitious,
yet tales of the great conqueror haunting the streets of the old
Aztec capital upon which Mexico City had been built still
circulated freely.

Finally, after what seemed hours, Francisca was aware
that they were passing through a gate into a patio. There was
the sound of muffled voices and the flare of blinding torchlight. She was unceremoniously handed down to waiting
hands before her captor dismounted. She opened her mouth
to speak, only to be lifted and slung over a mailed shoulder.
They mounted a staircase of tessellated tile, a broad, ar-
mored back and greaved legs carrying her up and up. A door
was opened to candlelight throwing elongated shadows on a
high, whitewashed ceiling.

The moment she was set on her feet, the animal instinct
to escape precipitated panic. As she whirled to flee, a gaunt-
leted hand gripped her arm. For a few moments she was
held in a bruising grasp, her body brought forcibly against
cold steel. Then her arm was dropped. Her captor brushed
past her. The door was booted shut, a resounding slam of
timber against timber. Francisca faced her abductor, her
breath coming in little gasps, her heart pulsing in her ears.

He looked taller, more ominous, more menacing, than he
had in the saddle. His polished breastplate glittered with
dancing light. He did not remove his helmet or visor, but
stood for a moment silently contemplating Francisca.

Suppressing a shudder, she drew herself up. "Sir, I would have you release me. This is outrageous! I am Francisca de Silva y Roche; my father—"

"I know who you are," the conquistador interrupted.

He lifted the helmet and the visor, to reveal a mocking smile above a tawny beard.

Francisca, shocked into speechlessness, could only stare.

"I'm sorry if I hurt your arm," Don Miguel said.

Her eyes fastened on his face; she absently rubbed the black and blue imprints he had left upon her white flesh. "I . . . thought . . . My father said you had gone to Veracruz."

"What—and miss a *mascarada*? Especially when you are so charmingly costumed for it." His eyes made a leisurely assessment, skimming over her bare, creamy shoulders and pausing for a long moment on the round swell of her breasts. "I had no idea your father would grant you such a liberty."

"He doesn't know," she said hastily, and was instantly sorry.

"I guessed as much."

He strode to a small table and placed his helmet upon it. Then he began to divest himself of his armor, the mail and the breastplate clanking as he deposited them on a chair.

The room was large, the windows curtained in figured red damask, the floor covered with scattered Turkish rugs and animal pelts. Blue figured tiles faced the fireplace in a Moorish motif repeated under the timbered ceiling. A large bed stood in one corner, its canopy draped in gold-tasseled hangings.

"The house belongs to a friend who was kind enough to let me use it," Miguel said. "Will you sit and have a glass of wine?" He indicated a cushioned chair.

"Thank you, but I think I should be going home."

"There's no hurry. The night is young."

He moved to a long, low sideboard and poured dark red wine from a carafe into two glasses.

"Let us drink to better acquaintance," he said, handing her a glass.

She took it, dismayed at the slight trembling of her hand. This was the second time in her life she found herself alone with a man not closely related to her. The same man. But what harm could a glass of wine do? He was polite and had made no remarks that could be construed as suggestive. Yet . . .

"Why have you brought me here?"

"So that we could be together without prying eyes watching us."

"No good can come of this meeting."

"But you are mistaken. More than good—joy. I fell in love with you the moment I set eyes on you. I could not get you out of my mind: so beautiful, skin like cream, and a mouth made for kissing. Ever since that night on the stairs, there has been nothing in my thoughts but your sweet, lovely face."

It was the extravagant flattery of the accomplished seducer. Francisca could understand why women found Miguel Velasquez del Castillo irresistible. In the glow of candlelight the proud, handsome head, the sculptured nose, the thin, almost cruel, mouth above the barbered beard, was that of a man who was accustomed to overcoming obstacles, a strong, virile man who took by strength what others tried to take by guile. His white, ruffled shirt, opened to the buckled belt at his waist, revealed a golden crucifix glinting on a muscled chest. His broad shoulders spoke of leashed power, a vitality reflected in the blue fire of his gaze. He could have easily ridden with Cortés as conqueror of the New World, although the conquest was now over a century old.

"My dear Francisca, you look at me as if you doubt every word I said. It's God's truth, but halfway to Veracruz I turned back, not because of the *mascarada* but because of you."

She set the glass down. "I cannot drink your wine. You are mad. Or arrogant. Or both. I am not La Flor or your other lady loves. I am Francisca—"

"Exactly. That is what I'm trying to tell you. There is no woman in the world who can compare to you. None."

He took a few steps toward her and, lifting her hand, put his lips to it. She stood stiffly, unyielding to his touch.

"Surely I am not repellent? Come, give me an hour. Let me make you happy."

She snatched her hand away and, sidestepping him, made a dash for the door. Laughingly, with graceful ease, he caught her fleeing figure, turning, crushing her against his chest. Again the sinewy hardness of his body came as a shock, and an involuntary shudder of pleasurable fear set her nerves to tingling.

"If you will . . . please . . . I beg of you . . ." The words of entreaty came haltingly.

He bent his head and touched her lips, smiling at the quiver that trembled on the soft curves of her half-open mouth. "You care for me, I can tell. I knew it when I first kissed you. You want me as much as I want you. Confess it."

Confess it? Sudden anger swept through her, banishing her momentary weakness. Did he think she could be won that easily? "How dare you presume?" She wrenched herself free, and raising her hand, she struck him with the full force of her outrage.

An angry flush rose to his sun-bronzed cheeks, and his eyes darkened into a look that constricted her heart.

"I shall do that again unless you release me," Francisca threatened.

His midnight-blue gaze raked her heaving breasts. Before she could speak again, he pulled her into his arms. She tried to free herself, beating furiously at his shoulders with knotted fists, but his arms, like bands of steel, held her fast. As he lowered his face, she jerked her head away. He brought it back, cupping the back of her skull, his mouth grinding into hers. No gentle kiss this, but a hard, demanding one that left her lips swollen.

"Don't ever try to lift a hand to me again," he said, drawing away.

"I hate you!" she exclaimed, tears of rage beading her thick lashes. "You're a beast, a savage!"

His heavy scowl vanished suddenly, and he laughed at her impotent anger. "Am I then?" He lifted her heavy, dark hair and kissed the tender curve of her slender throat. "Don't struggle, my dove," he murmured, his lips burning her skin. "You will see how pleasurable it can be."

"No!" But even as she protested, he was kissing her throat, her shoulders, raining hot kisses on her face, his lips searing a path of fire to her cleavage. Without raising his head, he blindly found the half-shouldered sleeves with his hand and pushed one, then the other down her arms, exposing her white, pink-tipped breasts.

"You mustn't!" she exclaimed. But her voice had lost its vehemence. And as he nuzzled a breast, licking at the nipple, a fluidity like honeyed wine entered her veins, melting her bones. Soon she found herself leaning against him, gasping when his pursed lips caught the other rosy point, sucking, drawing gently, nibbling with his teeth. Exquisite sensations radiated out from the stiff peaks, bringing a fevered flush to her skin.

And now he was kissing her mouth again, forcing it open, raiding the inner sweetness, his hands pulling her gown to her hips, tugging at the strings of her undergarment. Cold air prickled her skin as he stripped the last of her clothing, letting it fall in a heap at her ankles. Then, stooping, he lifted her in his arms and carried her to the high, canopied bed.

The drop from his arms to the straw-filled mattress brought her to her senses. What was she allowing him to do to her, this arrogant hidalgo who boasted of his skill in making women happy? She watched in growing trepidation as he shed his lace-fronted shirt and tossed it aside. His golden muscles rippled in the candlelight as he removed his hose and doublet. He was naked, narrow hips tapering to well-formed legs. But, oh, his manhood—turgid and swollen—so frightening!

Francisca slid to the far side of the bed and leaped to her feet. Dodging Miguel, she made for the door and had her hand on the ornately carved knob when he captured her.

"This game has grown tiresome." He held her fast, her naked back pressed against his chest.

"Then let me go."

"When I'm so close to the prize?"

He turned her. She brought her hands up, clawing his face, her nails scoring his right cheek.

With a curse, he dragged her to the bed, pulling at her arm so that it nearly left the socket. Throwing her on it, he flung himself over her, pinning her to the rustling mattress. A hard knee separated her flanks. Her hips rose in sharp, painful protest as he entered her, his manhood plunging like a sharp-edged sword into her very being. A strangled cry burst from her lips as he moved inside her, his fullness rasping at her tender flesh.

When he had finished, he held her while she sobbed. "Francisca, don't cry, my love, don't cry. I am at fault, I admit. I swear by the Holy Trinity, by God and Mother Mary, I had not meant to take you against your will. But when I'm struck in that manner, it brings out the devil in me. Hush— don't cry. I give you leave to do what you want, to punish me in any way you see fit."

He leaned backward and drew a short knife from under the mattress. "Here, love," he said, putting it in her hand. "If you think I deserve death, I present myself." He twisted his torso so that his chest, with the dangling crucifix, hung a few inches from her face.

Lying on the pillows, she looked into his eyes and saw contrition there, a concern she knew in her heart was not feigned.

"I can't," she whispered.

He took the knife from her hands, and she heard it clatter as he dropped it to the floor. Then he gathered her in his arms, caressing her hair, his fingers gently brushing the tears away. When he kissed her softly, she found herself responding, a whispering pressure of her lips upon his. He spoke her name kissing her eyelids, her still wet cheeks, his hands outlining her shoulders, returning tentatively to her breasts, stroking and coaxing to upright stiffness the ruched crests.

Slowly, as his hands moved tenderly over her sensitive skin, touching, kneading, stroking, her desire returned.

Sensitive to her mood, he got bolder. As he lowered his head, his mouth brushed her stomach, inching down to her thighs, kissing the inner flesh, making them fall open. She gave a little start when his seeking hand parted the dark patch of curly hair on her mound, his fingers slipping inside. With practiced rhythm he titillated the button she had no idea existed until now, fluttering it, exciting her with a sudden wild, passionate longing. Oh, he must stop, he had to stop, she would lose her mind if he didn't stop. She would die if he did. She could feel the wetness, the moist heat between her legs, and she moaned with shock and delight. Now—now! her mind screamed.

He rose above her, thrusting into her with a fullness that seemed to fill the very essence of her soul. She grasped his corded muscles as he moved, fitting her hips into his, breathing in unison with his own hard breaths until at last an unbearable series of shudders shot through her in a dazzle of exploding light.

She lay under him, her hands tangled in his coarse red-gold hair, replete, curiously happy.

"We are one now," he whispered in her ear. "My Francisca."

"Yes," she said, her voice catching with happiness, giving him her heart, a gift bestowed in trust and innocence.

Chapter IV

Francisca arrived home before dawn, just as the cathedral bells were tolling the hour of four. The house was silent except for the loud snores of Manuel, the doorman, sleeping off the effects of his nightlong debauch at the *mascarada*. Replacing the gate key, she tiptoed up the staircase to her room on winged feet. Joy filled her heart. The feeling of Miguel's hot kisses still lingered on her lips; the passioned warmth of his caresses still wrapped her in a delicious cocoon. He had sworn he loved her, vowed he would let his ship rot in Veracruz before he left her.

Though Francisca's mind, the same cool, percipient intelligence that had pored over the books in her father's library, told her that elaborate declarations of love were a hidalgo's stock-in-trade, she wanted to believe Miguel. She wanted to believe that he loved her as she loved him, that he belonged to her as she belonged to him. That nothing could separate them, that somehow they would find a way to be together always.

She did not want to think of his wife or La Flor or the women he had known before. She did not want to know if he had used the same love words, swearing undying devotion to his mistresses. She had no wish to probe into his past life, to ask whether he had ever loved his wife and thought of her even as he held her, Francisca, in his arms. For her these women did not exist. She wanted to imagine that she was his first as he was hers.

Most of all she wanted to forget the abyss that lay between them. He was a Christian with ties to an inquisitor. She was a *converso*. If he discovered her true religion, it would be his duty as a devout Catholic to report her to the Holy Office. But he wouldn't, for she would never tell him.

When she climbed into bed, she lay awake for a long time, reliving the hours they had spent together, their laughter afterward as he brought her home through the dark, silent streets. They would meet again. It could be arranged, Miguel had assured her. He had a friend, Tomás, who owned a house on the Calle de Las Infantas. It was shut up now since Tomás had gone to Spain to fetch his parents and wife. Miguel had been given free use of the house, and it would serve him and Francisca well since it was thought to be empty. Could Francisca manage to get away for a few hours the next afternoon? She had agreed, had said yes with a last fevered kiss.

She was wondering now, as she lay on her tumbled bed, how she could elude the ever watchful eyes that guarded her name and honor when she thought of a plan.

"Aunt Juliana, I hope you haven't forgotten that I'm to have a Latin lesson today with Sister Inés."

Sister Inés was a Carmelite, the proud, educated daughter of a prominent Castilian family, who had chosen the veil instead of marriage. Francisca had met her a year earlier. Pedro, aware that the Inquisition was stepping up its activities, had felt that the family should improve its pious image. Among other things, mass was more punctiliously attended, alms given more freely, and a stained window donated to the Saint Dominic monastery. In addition, Pedro encouraged his daughters to take up charitable work for the nuns. In this way

Francisca, giving out loaves to the poor, had discovered Sister Inés's erudition and begged for Latin lessons.

Aunt Julia, about to pop a fig into her mouth, paused. "Today? Aren't your lessons every other Wednesday?"

"Yes. But Sister Inés asked me to come this week on Tuesday instead."

Francisca held her breath. Juliana hated those visits to the convent. The dank piety, the hushed voices, and the chaste, pale faces irritated and bored her.

"Perhaps your mother can accompany you," Juliana suggested.

"Mother, Leonor, and Beatriz go to the Jerome convent on Tuesday."

A lucky coincidence.

"Couldn't we miss this once?" Juliana's plump fingers chose another fig. "I was thinking of visiting the Benavidos."

Francisca pretended to think a few moments. "Why don't we do this?" she said, brightening as though the thought had just flashed across her mind. "You can escort me to the convent and leave me there. I will be perfectly safe—while you have your visit. Then afterward, say at six o'clock, you can fetch me."

"Hmmmm."

"On the way home perhaps we can stop at Carlos's," Francisca continued. "His second batch of *rosquillas* should be ready by then." The lightly fried doughnut was one of Juliana's favorites.

"Well . . . as you wish. But, Francisca, I don't know what good all that learning will do. A lady has no need of Latin."

"It amuses me. Shall we leave at four, then?"

Breathless with her hurried passage through the back streets, her heart pounding with excitement, she pulled the latch of Tomás's outer door and entered the courtyard.

"Francisca!"

She looked up. He was there, leaning over the gallery rail,

smiling, the midnight blue of his riding cape contrasting with his red-gold hair.

She ran to meet him as he came down the stairs, rushing into his arms, pressing against him, returning kiss for passionate kiss.

"Am I late?" she asked, pulling away, one hand on her heaving breast.

"Yes. But we shall make up for it."

"I have only two hours."

"They will be the happiest two hours of our lives."

He lifted her as she clung to him, her arms about his neck, as he carried her up.

"I couldn't sleep for thinking of today," he said as they entered a room where sunlight spilled across a polished floor.

"Nor I."

When he put her on her feet, he embraced her again, taking her lips in a deep, exploring kiss. She surged against him, the gold ornament he wore as a clasp pressing into her breasts, a small pain that was pleasure. Everything about Miguel was pleasure. He had spoken the truth. Never had anyone made her so happy.

Murmuring softly in her ear, he uttered words of erotic love that she only half understood as he removed the combs one by one from her hair. Catching a handful of the dark, perfumed torrent that had fallen about her shoulders, he brought it to his lips.

"Mine, Francisca, mine. You are all mine."

Could she deny it?

She undid her cloak. He took it and tossed it aside, then brought her into his arms again, kissing her slowly, lingeringly, tasting her lips, the sweetness of her mouth, the pure curve of her throat. His hand cupped a breast, and he drew his head back when he felt the taut nipple pressing against the silk fabric.

"Little minx. How quick you are to desire."

"As quick as you?" she asked flirtatiously, her hand timidly descending to the large bulge in his breeches.

He grasped her fingers and held them there for a few moments. "I was aroused long before you appeared. The thought of you alone . . ."

It was true. His good fortune in taking her to bed had amazed even him, no stranger to good fortune. Long after they had parted he still seemed to breathe her intoxicating perfume. He had been amazed at the beauty of her naked body, at the white, satinlike skin, the beautiful little breasts, the hips, the belly that had fit so like a glove into the angles and surfaces of his own body. The face, those haunting dark eyes, had followed him into sleep, had smiled at him in his dreams, had slowly filled with tears the moment before he woke.

And now she was kissing him back, her hands clutching his shoulders as if she could not bear to let him go. There had never been a woman whose lips had tasted sweeter, never one who had kept him so long from his ship and the business of his masculine life.

He led her to the bed and sat her down, tracing her upturned chin with a finger. Then, kneeling, he removed her high-cut brocade shoes. Reaching up under her skirts, he tugged at her garters, skillfully pulling her stockings free of her legs, leaving her small feet bare. He kissed them tenderly before helping her rise.

As he unhooked her gown, she watched his face, the small frown as his fingers momentarily fumbled over a stubborn eyelet, the growing impatience as he discarded one petticoat after another. She did not help him. She wanted to savor the delicious luxury of having this virile man, her lover, her loved one, undress her. Oh, but he was handsome, the strong cut of his bearded jaw, the straight nose, the thick, untamed hair, so unlike the perfumed locks of the city's cavaliers.

"You are truly beautiful," he murmured, surveying her naked body. The raw desire glittering in his narrowed eyes made her tremble. She remembered then how he had taken her by force, how easily his Spanish temper could be aroused. She still bore the bruises on her arms where he had held her pinned helpless to the mattress, and a thrill of fear chased up her spine. She lowered her eyes, no longer able to meet his fierce gaze.

"Miguel," she began, flustered, not knowing how to tell him she was suddenly afraid.

"You haven't changed your mind?" he asked, harshly, misinterpreting her hesitancy. "You're not sorry you came?"

His hands fell on her shoulders as he pulled her roughly to his chest. He circled her waist with bands of steel, his lips pouring a storm of hot kisses across her cheeks, her forehead, her mouth, searing kisses that left her breathless and dizzy.

"Say you're not sorry," he demanded, his mouth poised above hers. "Say it!"

"I'm not—"

But he was kissing her again, his insistent mouth parting her lips, sending wild tremors racing up her spine. Her fear faded, disappeared. She trembled now with desire and excitement, her hands guiding his down to her breasts, wanting to feel, again, the sensations he had aroused before.

He stood for a few moments, his hand cupping her breasts; then, with an impatient groan, he lifted her and placed her on the bed. Through lowered lashes she watched while he disrobed, her heart beating erratically in anticipation. Hurriedly unlacing his thigh-length boots, he kicked himself out of them. Next came stirrup hose, doublet, and shirt, torn off in haste and flung into a corner. The bed rustled and swayed as he knelt over her, a quiver running through his muscular arms before he lowered himself to burn her mouth with his kisses.

The rasp of his beard on her cheeks, on her throat, across her shoulders, inexorably moving down to the ripe mounds of her eager, upthrust breasts, tingled and tickled. But it was the touch of his hands, the firm stroking that traced the curve of her hips, lightly kneading, massaging her thighs, then parting them, as he tongued her nipples, that swiftly engulfed her in a whirlwind of dizzying sensations. Ecstasy, joy, pleasure, poor words to describe the exquisite fever that brought a husky laugh to her throat.

Hearing it, he grunted. She wanted to touch him, too, in places she could only guess would pleasure him, but the languor that gripped her limbs and held her in thrall was still too new. Oh, Miguel, she wanted to cry, tears burning behind her eyes, I do love you. But she was afraid to speak, afraid to break the spell.

He shifted his weight slightly and brought his hand up again between her thighs, finding the delicate little place, fluttering it with a finger until she felt as though she were riding a towering wave, exciting yet terrifying, a huge comber that threatened to crash and drown her.

She heard herself protesting weakly, whimpering, moaning under his weight, calling his name. He did not—or pretended not to—hear. Sliding down the length of her torso, his tongue entered the place where his fingers had been. Her body jumped with shock. But he held her fast, his tongue pointed as it licked in quick rhythm. Biting her lip to stifle the scream of pure, unbridled rapture, she arched her hips, digging her fingers into Miguel's muscled back. She could feel the approaching shore, the growing, swelling tide that now, *now*, finally burst inside her, sending her into a shattering void.

She was still shuddering in climax when he rose quickly and entered her, plunging deeply inside, moving back and forth, his breath hot on her cheek. They were one, body and soul, man and woman, Adam and Eve, who had eaten from the tree of knowledge and were unafraid.

Holding her, he felt her heart beat, a steady pulse beneath her lovely breasts. She was his. And yet he felt no triumph, no victory of conquest. Instead he wondered how this young, untried virgin, reared in gentility, could suddenly mean more to him than any woman he had ever known. Not even La Flor, skilled by upbringing in the art of pleasing a man, could arouse in him such insatiable desire. But there was something else here, something he could not define.

Was it love? He thought not. Love was an emotion conceived by the bards, by the guitar strummers who sang sickly songs of pining hearts and disappointed lovers. He knew nothing of love and did not believe in it.

His marriage had been an arranged one when he was seventeen. His wife, Doña Ana de Tovar y Molina, niece of Count-Duke Olivares, royal favorite and grandee of Spain, had been considered a good catch. She was eight years older than Miguel, a cold beauty who later proved barren. She had disliked Miguel even before the wedding and loathed him after he had deflowered her. From that first night forward she made every pretext to keep herself from his bed. He had not missed her presence there. Nor did he mourn the marriage into which he had been cozened. Doña Ana had come with an ample dowry, a large sum that had enabled Miguel to buy his beloved *Espíritu Santo*. On rare occasions when he saw her, he treated her with the respect that was her due. A polite exchange, a chill kiss on the turned-away cheek, was the sum of the connubial intimacy they shared. She repelled him with her excess piety. He felt sure that she would be happier in a nunnery. Still, it was a marriage he felt duty-bound to honor, and it had never occurred to him until Francisca that it could be otherwise.

She stirred in his arms. "We have so little time, Miguel."

"Don't think of time, sweet," he said, caressing her hair. "We have this moment, and that is all that matters."

She sighed, nestling closer. "What's to become of us?"

"I know not."

"We have dishonored your wife."

"Shhh." He placed his finger on her soft, rosy lips. "There is no dishonor where you are concerned. Let's not speak of it."

This was an aberration, this wild affair, this torrential lovemaking, he decided. He would tarry a week, perhaps two, then he would make for Veracruz.

"I can't think of life without you," Francisca said, the glow of happiness lighting her dark eyes.

That eager, happy look gave him a slight twinge, one that he studiously ignored. "You know that my business is with the sea. I would give my last drop of blood to remain here always, but I cannot."

Francisca digested this with a little sigh. Of course he could not stay. What was she thinking of?

"Part of me will go with you, Miguel."

He pressed her hand, his arm drawing her closer. "Hush. Let us not think of parting yet. There is tomorrow. You will come tomorrow?"

"Oh, yes, yes! I will find a way."

For two weeks Francisca met Miguel every afternoon at the house on the Calle de Las Infantas. The owner, Tomás (she never learned his surname), apparently traded in vanilla, for there were sacks of it stored under the gallery, and the fragrance of the beans permeated their room. Years later a mere whiff of the mellow scent would bring back those bittersweet hours, and she would be there again with the sun slanting through the iron grillwork of the high window, its beams glancing off the wooden carving of a young Christ hanging from his cross on the opposite wall.

She and Miguel would come together in an explosion of frantic kisses as though they had been separated for months instead of hours. They would fall on the bed in a frenzy of passion, their naked limbs entwining, mouths and hands grappling, exploring, their bodies rocking to the eternal, searing rhythm that took them into an ecstatic realm of their own.

Afterward they would doze, then wake. Francisca, nestling protectively in Miguel's strong arms, would question him about his voyages, fascinated by tales of the strange lands he had visited, the white beaches of Africa, the tropical sugarcane fields of Jamaica, the rocky shores of lower California. He did not like to talk about his childhood, and she never asked about his marriage. The questions Miguel put to her, Francisca answered guardedly, the soulful eyes of the bearded young Christ on his teakwood cross reminding her that she held a secret Miguel must never guess, must never know.

Except for that tiny worry nibbling at the back of her mind, she lived for those hours spent with Miguel, jeweled minutes, each one replete with happiness. She did not wonder again what would become of them; she did not want to think of the future. They were sinners, but she did not care.

Francisca explained her daily trips to the Carmelite convent by saying that she was now helping Sister Inés with the embroidery and lacework of an altar cloth promised to the archbishop, Fray Garcia Guerra. It was imperative, she told her mother, that it be done by Easter. Aunt Juliana, who disliked embroidery and lace making almost as much as Latin, escorted her niece to the convent each afternoon. At six she would return and bring Francisca home. She never went inside to talk to Sister Inés, never showed the slightest interest in examining the altar cloth.

Her mother or Leonor would sometimes inquire about her work at the convent, though Beatriz seemed to accept her tale with the passivity that was her nature. Francisca hated to lie, but she had no choice. She lived in fear that her mother would stop at the convent and mention the altar cloth to Sister Inés. Her absence there discovered, Francisca would be questioned, and finally the truth would come out. Her father, inexperienced as he was in the use of arms, would be forced to challenge Miguel, whose reputation as the best swordsman in Seville had followed him to New Spain. Miguel would have no choice but to fight. Blood would be spilled. Whatever the outcome, she herself would be banished to a convent, for no man (*converso* or otherwise) would want a woman who had given her maidenhead outside the bond of marriage.

Francisca realized it had to end. They couldn't go on trysting, spinning out their days with no thought except their own joy. Luck had been with them; God's thunderbolt aimed against the breakers of His commandments had been withheld. But it had to come. Yet she could not bring herself to speak of parting.

One evening, when Francisca was sitting in her room dreaming before her mirror, Beatriz came to tell her that her father wished to speak to her.

"Tell him I'll be down in a little while," Francisca said.

"He wants you to come at once."

A tight cord suddenly wound itself around Francisca's heart. There could only be one reason for this imperative summons. Her father had found out about her trysts with Miguel.

He was waiting in the library. If sweets were Juliana's weakness, books were his. About one third of his collection was of a religious nature, such writings as those of Santa Teresa of Avila, *Saint John of the Cross* (where the key lay hidden), and the Book of Hours, the latter considered indispensable to any Christian household. But he also possessed novels, popular works by Cervantes, Quevedo, and Céspedes, and the philosophical coda of Maimonides. The latter, a proscribed book and dangerous to own, he kept hidden behind the religious ones.

"Ah, there you are, Francisca. Come in, come in! Please close the door behind you." Pedro was standing with his back to the tiled fireplace. His face, crosshatched with fine wrinkles, held a sober expression.

"Sit down, daughter. What I have to say to you is of utmost importance."

Francisca, her mouth dry, her knees quivering, sat slowly down on a carved, hard-back chair.

He studied her for a few moments. As always, he was dressed conservatively in the fashion that was popular some ten years earlier, wearing a blue velvet doublet, a silver-trimmed jerkin, and breeches that were tied below his knees with garters. His face, framed in the *golilla*, a wide, standing collar of lawn edged in lace, gave his features a grave dignity.

"I have been thinking seriously about you and your future." He clasped his hands behind his back for what seemed an overlong interim of silence.

Francisca swallowed. Her future. Had he already decided that she should take the veil?

"In a few months you will be eighteen," Pedro went on. "Your mother and I agree it's time you were married."

Francisca drew a long breath. He didn't know. She was safe. Miguel was safe. There would be no disgrace, no duel, no stain on the de Silva honor.

"We have given the matter much thought. It has always been our wish that you marry within our faith, but no proper suitor has presented himself. Now, however, there is one." He paused. "Are you listening, Francisca?"

"Yes, Papá." She was, but inattentively. Her mind was again taken up with Miguel. They must be more careful. She must change her routine, skip a day, find an excuse other than her obligation to Sister Inés. Perhaps she and Miguel ought to meet in a different place. There was no assurance that someone, some afternoon, would not recognize her as she crossed the Plaza Mayor.

"He is not a complete stranger to you," her father was saying. "He has had more than one meal with us. In fact, he presided over our New Year services. Can you guess of whom I'm speaking?"

"No, Papá."

"Don Ruy de Diaz."

Francisca looked blankly up at her father. "What of Don Ruy, Papá?"

He made an impatient sound with his tongue. "Just as I supposed. You haven't heard a word. Wool-gathering instead of paying heed to a matter which affects all of us. I was right. It's high time you settled into becoming a wife and mother."

"Time?" Now Pedro had her full attention. "Why should it be time? I know that most girls are married by their seventeenth birthday. But you once promised you would not rush me.''

"That was when you were a little girl. Your marriage seemed such a long way off. But now we must face reality. Taking all things into consideration, I find that Don Ruy would make you the kind of husband both your mother and I approve of.''

"Don Ruy?'' Her voice quavered in disbelief. "But he's an *old* man, Papá. At least twice my age. And I don't love him. Oh, I can't . . . I can't!''

"Francisca . . .'' He paused, a flicker of distress in his eyes. But when he spoke again, both eye and voice were stern. "Let me tell you that love does not enter into arranging a marriage. Love may come later, often does, as witness your mother and me, but if we were to be guided by romantic love in seeing to our daughters' welfare, we would be in deep trouble. Marriage is for life, and you must be practical about it.''

"But he's *old*!'' she repeated distastefully.

"Hush. You are too immature to realize what an older man can do for you. He will cherish you, be father, brother, and husband to you. He will care for you—and Don Ruy, I might add, has the wherewithal to do so. You will never lack for comfort, for servants, pretty clothes, and jewels. And he will be faithful. What younger man can promise the same?''

"He has offered, then?''

"He has indeed. He is quite smitten with you.''

"I have a considerable dowry. Perhaps he was smitten with that.''

"The dowry is of little importance to Don Ruy. He is a man of means.''

"But, Papá,'' she said, reasonably, "do you remember you arranged for Beatriz to marry Julio Busmonte, and she refused? You did not force *her*.''

"She was a fool to refuse Julio. Instead she wanted Don Alfredo de Contreros, a wastrel. I did not forbid it, if you remember, I simply said I would withhold her dowry. But we are not here to talk of Beatriz. It is you I am concerned about.''

Francisca twisted her hands in her lap. "Oh, Father, I cannot. Please, please . . ." Tears sprang to her eyes. Marry Ruy, bed with him, when her heart ached for Miguel? She couldn't. She wouldn't. "Don't make me do this, I beg of you, Papá!"

Pedro chewed his lip, a sign, Francisca knew, of his exasperation.

"Control yourself, daughter. You sound as though you loathe Don Ruy, a man, I might add, you hardly know. Or is it because you have taken a fancy to some young, good-for-nothing caballero?''

"God forbid!" she said emphatically, dismayed at the red that rushed to her cheeks. Although Miguel was not a caballero, one of those profligate rich sons who hung about the taverns and gambling establishments, he was much younger than Don Ruy, and she had taken more than a fancy to him. Pedro had come too close to the truth.

"Then be sensible. I have always considered you to be different than most women, who think only with their emotions. I'm sure after you have considered this proposal, you will find it quite acceptable if not desirable.''

"I *am* sensible. Feeling the way I do, I don't see how I can make Don Ruy a good wife.''

"Nonsense. I think if you got to know Don Ruy better, you would like him. He is a very intelligent and learned man. He carries in his mind Hebrew prayers that have been forgotten since the Expulsion. A fine, pious man, a childless widower, he is also kind and thoughtful. You have only to allow yourself to view him without prejudice and you will see that I speak the truth.''

"And if I still refuse?''

The jaw under his short, gray beard hardened. "Remember, you are my daughter and I am your father. I don't choose to compel you. But if I must—for your own good—then I will.''

"Papá . . ." she began, a pleading note in her voice.

"It is useless to argue, Francisca. I may have indulged you when you were a child, but I can no longer do so. This is too grave a matter."

But I love Miguel, she wanted to cry. *If I can't have him, then I don't want anyone else.*

"My child," Pedro said, his voice and expression relenting, "do not look at me as though I am about to beat or torture you. I am not a hard father. You know that. I love you as I do myself. Come . . ." He bent forward and placed a finger under her chin. "Give us a smile."

She tried, but all she could muster was a weak grimace.

"That is a little better." He stopped and placed a kiss on her cheek. "A year from now you will thank me for this. Now go along and get ready for supper."

She walked up the broad staircase to her room, not weeping as she had thought she might, but spine straight, her lovely jaw set. She would not marry Ruy. At the moment she did not know how she could dissuade her father, but dissuade him she must.

Chapter V

The next day at siesta time Francisca stole down the stairs. Using the garden gate, she let herself out on the deserted street. Previously she had never left the house during the midday hours. It was too risky since Leonor, unable to nap or rest, would sometimes come to Francisca's room, bringing with her a bit of embroidery and a need to gossip.

But today Francisca felt she could not wait until four o'clock. She had to see Miguel. She had spent a tumultuous night, turning and tossing, her mind churning as sleep continued to elude her troubled mind. The morning had been endless, her impatience all the more acute because she couldn't show it. What Miguel could do for her, she did not know. But she had to talk to him.

When she reached the house and climbed the stairs to the room, she found the door was locked. She knocked several times, but there was no answer. Thinking she heard a rustling behind the oak panel, she put her ear to it. Was that a whisper, a muted voice? For a few moments she wondered if Miguel was on the other side, between the legs of another woman, making violent love and ignoring her summons. But there was no other sound, only silence. He had not yet arrived. Her disappointment was so keen, she could have wept.

She was descending the stairs when the gate swung open and Miguel appeared. She lifted her skirts and tripped down the stairs, rushing to meet him.

"Francisca!"

She was so relieved, so happy to see him, she could not speak as he held her.

"What is it? Has something happened?"

She nodded mutely.

"Come upstairs."

Seated on the edge of the bed, with his arm protectively about her shoulder, she felt somewhat better.

"Now, tell me," Miguel coaxed. "What is so terrible?"

"Everything. Oh, Miguel, my father has arranged a marriage for me." She withdrew a lace-edged handkerchief from her sleeve and dabbed at her eyes. "I tried to argue, but he . . . he wouldn't listen."

Miguel drew in his breath. "For a moment I thought . . ."

"Thought what?" She lifted her head, her brown eyes questioning.

His lips quirked in a smile. "That you were with child. It would not be an impossibility."

"Would it make you unhappy?"

"*Unhappy?* Zounds, no! I should be delighted. I have no children, you know."

"But it would be a bastard."

"I would have it legitimized."

Then he does love me, she thought, and the next instant shuddered inwardly. To have a bastard, even Miguel's, especially Miguel's, would banish her from home and family forever.

"Nevertheless, Francisca," he went on, "apparently that is not why you came. You say your father has arranged a marriage. Is he serious?"

"Very. He means to marry me to the widower Don Ruy de Diaz."

"The name is unfamiliar."

"Don Ruy has recently come to live in Mexico City. He

is from León, where he owns an *encomienda*, a huge one with thousands of Indians who herd cattle and grow hemp for his benefit.''

"He is rich, then. And what other qualities does this wealthy grower of hemp possess that make your father think this is a good match?''

Before she realized it, she answered truthfully. "He is of the same faith.''

There was a small silence during which she seemed to hear the grand inquisitor pronouncing sentence to the solemn beating of drums.

But all was not lost. Miguel was smiling. "I should hope so. Thanks to the zeal of the Holy Office, Spain and her colonies do not harbor heretics gladly. So, my dear, we are all of the same faith.''

"That is true," Francisca said in a small voice. She could never tell him. Never.

"Be honest with me, Francisca; do you find this would-be suitor of yours attractive?''

"Oh, Miguel, how can you ask such a thing?'' she cried in protest, noting the sudden suspicious look that had come into his eyes. "Even if he was the most handsome, dashing man on earth, I would not look at him twice.''

"Is he?'' he asked, grasping her hand in a steely grip, his sea-blue eyes gazing intently at her. "Is he the most handsome man on earth? And if so, would you look at him a third time?''

Seeking to nip his budding anger, she said lightly, "Why, you are jealous, Miguel.''

"Have I cause to be?''

"No.'' She tugged at his wrist, but he held on, though his grip had eased. "Don Ruy is old—older than Papá—old with bad teeth and sour breath. I cannot conceive of our nuptial bed, of having him—''

"I would kill him first. Don't think of it. I will not allow you to marry this—this Don Ruy.''

"But my father—''

"A curse on your father!"

Shocked, Francisca wrenched her hand away and crossed herself out of habit. A curse was anathema! It brought on pestilence, poverty, and death. "You must not say that! Ever! You must not curse my father. He may want to marry me to a man I do not love, but is that so unusual? He is only thinking of me. He loves me. Please, Miguel, take the curse back!"

"You superstitious little fool. All right then, I'll take the curse back. But you are not going to marry Don Ruy."

He got up from the bed and went to the cupboard where he kept a jug of wine. Pouring a glass, he stood for a long time frowning down into it before he drank.

Francisca had seen the frown and felt a growing uneasiness. Perhaps he was planning to do away with Don Ruy. How? Challenge him to combat? But for a duel, one must have a reason, and Miguel had never met Ruy, much less been insulted by him. He could hire an assassin, but that did not seem to be Miguel's way. Poison? A woman's weapon.

Then there was always the instrument of the Holy Office. One had only to whisper into a familiar's ear that Don Ruy de Diaz had blasphemed or that he had been seen in the company of a witch or that there was some cloud on his ancestry. They would take him away, and under torture he would reveal that he was a Jew, he would name names and . . .

Francisca, unable to think further, closed her eyes. "You mustn't . . ." she began hesitantly, breaking the silence, "you mustn't blame Don Ruy."

"No more than I would blame any lecher who lusts after a young girl."

"Oh, Miguel, if it weren't Don Ruy, my father would find another man for me to marry. He says I'm of age, it's time I took on a husband and children."

He drained the glass, then with a sudden angry movement, flung it against the opposite wall, where it shattered with a loud crash. "Then perhaps," he said with deadly vehemence, "you ought to do as your father wishes and marry Don Ruy."

She gave him a despairing look, meeting the dark glitter in his eyes. His wrath had been fed by her defense, no matter how feeble, of Don Ruy and her father. He had every right to be angry. Perhaps he thought that she didn't love him, and her opposition to the marriage was all for show.

She turned her face from his gaze so that he could not see the tears that welled up in her eyes.

"Well," he said in a cold voice. "Is that your wish also?"

She tried to speak but was afraid her voice would betray her.

He rose, towering over her. "Answer me, Francisca!"

She shook her head, then despite her resolve, burst into sobs.

He knelt quickly beside her and, removing her hands from her streaming face, kissed them. This sudden transformation from anger to gentleness made her weep all the harder. Still kneeling, he cradled her in his arms. "Don't cry, my darling. There is nothing to cry about. Do you think I really meant it?"

"Yes," she whispered in a muffled voice.

He lifted her chin and, smoothing back her hair, kissed her forehead, then her warm, moist lips.

"I have been thinking of a plan," he said. "Now, listen carefully. My ship sails for the Philippines in ten days. Two weeks at the most. I want you to go away with me."

She stared at him, not quite comprehending. It was as if he had asked her to step off the edge of the earth.

He took her hands, holding them tightly in his. "I can't bear to leave you. And if you love me . . . You do love me?"

She threw her arms about his waist and leaned up to kiss him. "My darling, there is no need to ask. You know that I do."

"Then come with me. You may not find the comforts of home aboard ship, but we will have each other. We will be happy, I promise you, Francisca. Will you come?"

She thought for a few moments, her fingers twisting the tassels of her shawl. "Are the Philippines a long way off?"

"Across a wide ocean called the Pacific. But then, you have probably seen them on your father's globe."

"Yes, but the islands seemed fairly close."

"It is a voyage of two, three, sometimes four months, depending on the weather."

"Than what? I mean after the Philippines."

"I'll trade my cargo of silver and mercury for brocades, silks, pearls, marbles, and porcelains, and we'll return with that rich load around the Horn to Veracruz."

"If I go with you, Miguel, I cannot come back to Mexico City."

"Why not?"

"I will be your mistress, Miguel. My family would shut the door in my face."

He shifted, releasing her, sitting down on the bed beside her. "Would it hurt that much? If you love me, nothing else should matter."

"But it does. Have you no family yourself? Have you no father, no mother, no sister you miss, or you would mourn if you never saw them again?"

"No," he said, biting down on the word. "There is no fondness between my older brother and myself. As for my father, he is a cruel and heartless man. He killed my mother, murdered her in cold blood."

Francisca's eyes widened in horror. "Surely punishment was meted out to him."

"Punishment?" He gave a short, barklike laugh. "He was congratulated, clapped on the back, told he did well to defend his honor. You see, he accused my mother of having an affair with her confessor."

"A priest?"

"Yes, poor devil. My father claimed he caught Fray Esteban Sanchez and my mother together in her bed. But it was a lie. Francisca, my mother was a good Christian, a pious woman whose only sin was her devotion to the church. But she had money that could only go to my father on her death. He invented that falsehood to get his hands on it. He killed her because of that. I would not mourn him should he drop dead at my feet. As for my wife—she is a stranger to me.''

Francisca sat beside him in silence, thinking of her own parents, who loved each other with a tenderness born of sharing a life together fraught with danger. They had raised their daughters with strictness tempered with affection. If she never saw them again, she would grieve, she would grieve deeply.

''You haven't given me an answer,'' Miguel said, drawing her close. ''Or do I take your silence for assent?''

''I want to go with you, Miguel. I want to with all my heart. But you must give me time to think. It's so sudden. I don't know what to say.''

Had she once chafed under the restrictions her father had set down, wanting to be free? But that had been a childish wish, her venture into the gaiety of the *mascarada* an escapade, nothing more. Now she had been asked to exile herself from New Spain, leave the house she had always known, never see mother, father, sister, again. And what of the secret she kept locked within her, her belief in God, Jehovah, the one God she had sworn never to abandon?

''What must you think about?'' Miguel asked.

''My family. My home.''

''But you are no longer a child. You are a grown woman.''

There was so much she could not explain to him. ''Please, I beg of you, give me at least a few days.''

''Tomorrow? The day after?'' He smiled at the uncertain look in her eyes. ''All right then, Thursday. You will never regret your decision, I promise you.''

His lips touched hers, a light, teasing kiss that evoked a soft sigh from Francisca. ''I will never stop wanting you, my darling.''

He grasped her more firmly, his mouth, warm with the taste of wine, rocking back and forth on her lips until they opened, giving him admittance. Hungrily he explored the honeyed mouth, his hand traveling down to cup a breast where the taut crest stood erect against her silken bodice.

Bending his head, he kissed the side of her neck, his lips moving to her ear. "Let us love one another, Francisca."

"I can't—not now. I must return. Aunt Juliana will be looking for me. Oh, please . . . Miguel . . . Miguel . . ." His hand had climbed down her bodice, caressing the naked flesh, his fingers closing around the firm mound, thumbing the straining peak. A languid warmth stole through her veins. Her mind, trying to separate itself from the sensual web Miguel was weaving, told her she must stop him, that she must leave.

Before she could speak again, he had slipped her gown and chemise from her shoulders and was covering her smooth ivory skin with impassioned kisses. Bold, hungry, wild kisses that made her forget caution. She trembled under the onslaught, her heart pounding, excited, aroused. Her hands came up in one last futile gesture of protest. But when his insatiable mouth began to savage the ruched crests of her breasts, she went limp in his arms.

He eased her onto the bed. Kneeling above her, he quickly unbuttoned his breeches, then shoved her velvet skirts upward, his hand sliding along her thigh. He smiled to feel the moistness between her legs, proof that she wanted him as he wanted her. Gathering her in his arms, fitting the soft curves of her body into his, he thrust into the hot sheath, waiting a moment, watching for the ecstatic round O of her mouth to urge him on. She gasped, the "Oh!" forming, as he had anticipated, on her lips. Pressing his cheek into hers, he began again, gyrating upward, then down, again and again and again. In her sweet agony her nails raked his back, the silken shirt tearing under them. Then, closing her eyes, she gave herself over to wanton abandonment, winging to new heights, loving this man who had taught her the meaning of joy.

Francisca arrived home to find her mother hurrying from the kitchen through the garden to the storeroom, carrying covered baskets. In them were the foods that would be used that night in the Passover feast. Of necessity the preparation had to be done during the servants' siesta, and the meal itself held in secret, late at night, after the servants had gone to bed.

"Where have you been?" her mother asked.

"I went to the weaver's down the street to get some embroidery thread." The lie seemed to burn Francisca's tongue with guilt, a guilt compounded by the fact that she had completely forgotten this was Passover eve.

"You picked a fine time. Well, hurry then, and give me a hand."

The de Silvas, like other Judaizers, had no traditional Jewish calendar, but approximated the few holidays they observed according to dim, half-forgotten memories. Nevertheless, for all their incorrect and fragmentary knowledge, they offered worship with as much dedication as their brethren in other lands.

The guests were greeted with warmth as they entered silently through the special gate. They were a small group: the Quesadas, Don Ruy, Aunt Juliana, the Orozcos, the Benavidos, and the Rodriguez family. As they arrived, Don Pedro escorted them to the storeroom he called, on these occasions, *shul*. There a trestle table covered with a white linen cloth had been laid with platters of bitter herbs and unleavened bread. Francisca, seated at Don Ruy's right, glanced covertly at him before her father started to speak. Don Ruy was as old as she remembered, a man with yellowed skin and pouched eyes. His dress, however, could not be faulted. Unlike her father, he dressed in the height of fashion. His coat of rich velvet was made to fit his sloping shoulders without a wrinkle, and his snowy white falling-hand collar was trimmed with exquisite lace. Gracing the forefinger of his left hand was a gold ring set with a ruby as large as a pigeon egg. She did not realize she was staring at it until Don Ruy said, "It's a beautiful stone, don't you think?" His voice was low and gentle. "It is said the ring once belonged to the Emperor Cuauhtémoc."

At the head of the table Don Pedro rapped for attention. "Shall we begin?" He looked around, then cleared his throat before he spoke.

"This holy observation commemorates the time long ago when God took the children of Israel out of their bondage in Egypt and brought them across the desert to the promised land."

Ignorant of the Haggadah service, an integral part of Passover which had been lost to the exiles, Don Pedro went on to give the Judaizers' version of the Exodus. When he was through, Don Ruy recited from the Psalms.

> "When I look at the heavens, the
>   work of Thy fingers,
> The moon and the stars which
>   Thou has established:
> What is man that Thou art mindful
>   of him?
> Oh, Lord, our Lord
>   how majestic is Thy name on all
>   the earth!"

Francisca had never heard these biblical verses before, and she listened raptly, finding in them a beauty and solace that made her forget for a brief time that her religion and her race were despised.

After the meal was cleared away, the guests lingered at the table, sipping Málaga wine and conversing.

Don Ruy turned to Francisca. "Your father tells me that you are being instructed in Latin."

Francisca's heart skipped several beats. Fearful that Ruy would catechize her and discover her lie, she quickly said, "I'm afraid I am a poor student. After all these weeks, my feeble intellect has retained but a few words."

"It takes time, time and patience." He smiled, a smile

that lit up his face with a gentle sweetness that momentarily diminished his homely appearance.

Francisca decided that she could like Don Ruy as a friend, but she could not picture herself in his arms. Perhaps if she had never met Miguel, she might consider this match. Perhaps not. She didn't know. But since Miguel had come into her life, every man she looked at was somehow diminished.

Now she must choose between Miguel and Don Ruy.

Married to Don Ruy, she would still be part of the family, could still share in the warmth of holiday celebrations, all the more precious because they were held in intimate secrecy. She would not be far from the home she had known all her life, the crenelated towers that were a landmark on the Calle del Reloj. Don Ruy would care for her, as her father said. Life would be constricted and dull, but it would be free of subterfuge and pretense. On the other hand, if she went off with Miguel, she would be living with a man she feared to trust with her innermost soul. Could she continue to love him knowing that she must always take care not to give herself away?

The question remained like a stone on her heart all that restless night. In the morning her mother took the girls to mass and Communion at the Great Cathedral, making sure they were seen by Fray Rafael Cortés, an agent of the Inquisition. The de Silvas thought it politic to attend mass (especially after celebrating one of their own holidays) where their presence would be noted. So much of their lives was governed by the necessity to allay suspicion that the genuflecting and kneeling and tasting of the wafer had become automatic.

After the service they walked out into the bright sunlight, standing before the cathedral's wide wooden doors waiting for their carriage.

"Look!" Leonor exclaimed, pointing to a passing coach and four. A familiar-looking horseman rode beside it. "Isn't that Papá's acquaintance, Don Miguel?"

He was dressed in chestnut-brown velvet, and on his head he wore a shallow-crowned hat with a sweeping golden plume. The coach's occupant, a woman, leaned out to laugh up at Miguel as they came abreast of the church. Her bone-white face was powdered with ceruse and painted with lip dye and rouge. Her satin gown was a startling red, cut low to expose all but the nipples of full, ripe breasts. Francisca knew from the stories that had made the rounds of the city that this was the courtesan La Flor.

Francisca felt as though a sword had run her through. She was amazed to find herself still standing, her face expressionless, her eyes following the disappearing coach. Neither its occupant nor the horseman had seen them. She fought the urge to run after Miguel, shouting, upbraiding and cursing him like a *pulquero* who has been cheated by a customer. She had been duped by Miguel, taken in by his caresses, the thin, hungry, sometimes cruel, sometimes tender mouth. From his impassioned words she had assumed that she was now the only woman in his life. Though they had never spoken of La Flor, she had thought the affair was over. Apparently not. The idea that he may have gone from her bed to La Flor's sickened her.

Oh, God, why had she been so gullible? She had warned herself in the beginning that Miguel was a gallant who would use any ploy to seduce a woman. But she hadn't relied on her own good sense. She had naively swallowed his protestations of undying affection. She had believed him. She had loved him, and more painful yet, still did.

"Francisca," her mother said gently, taking her by the elbow, "the carriage is waiting."

Like a puppet pulled by invisible strings, she walked out to the carriage, stepping up, settling herself next to her sister.

"Why doesn't Don Miguel come to the house anymore?" Leonor asked.

"I suppose," her mother answered, "because his business with your father is finished."

No, Francisca wanted to cry, *it's because he can't face Papá after having seduced his daughter.* He has made a fool of me, she thought. Did he really mean that I should run away with him? Could he have asked La Flor to accompany him, and when she refused, tried to persuade me? He needed a woman to warm his bed across that wide ocean, a woman to relieve the monotony of a long voyage; any presentable doxy would have done.

Suppose she had decided to go, and when they reached their destination in the Philippines, he abandoned her there. Men like Miguel Velasquez del Castillo tired quickly of their mistresses. He would cast her adrift in the pestilent city of Manila, which her father had once described as a haven for criminals, soldiers of fortune, sleight-of-hand artists, the hopeless and insane. She would be alone there without a protector, sinking into God alone knew what abject depths.

"Francisca, you are very quiet," her mother observed.

"I'm sorry, but I have a headache."

And a heartache. She would not go to their rendezvous. Let him fret and fume, wait for her in that room on the Calle de Las Infantas. Let him pace the floor, gnash his teeth, hurl wineglasses and crockery at the walls. She did not care. The thought that she had contemplated becoming his paramour appalled her.

"Go upstairs and lie down," her mother instructed as they drew up to the door. "You look pale as death. I will have Beatriz bring you cloths soaked in vinegar."

The cloths helped her head, but not her heart. From under the acerbic coolness of moist linen, tears oozed and spilled. She could cry now. The shades were drawn and the door closed; she had the privacy she had yearned for since the moment she had seen Miguel and La Flor. But after the first trickle of tears, anger replaced self-pity.

If I were a man, she thought vehemently, I would take a dagger to him and bring him to his knees. I would cut his heart out. She thought of all the ways she might seek revenge, how she might humiliate and humble him. But when she finally dozed off, it was to dream of Miguel holding her and tenderly kissing her closed lids.

Thursday, the day on which she was supposed to meet

Miguel with her decision, was a torment. Her determination not to keep their rendezvous, to never see him again, had to be bolstered, as the hours passed, by the memory of La Flor's painted mouth wide in laughter, her half-naked breasts offered for view to a bending Miguel. Even now they might be entwined, naked limbs tangled with naked limbs as they heaved and panted together.

She hated him. She would not go.

Late afternoon found her pacing the garden, up and back along the flagged walk. The blossoms of lemon and orange trees imported from Spain gave off a sweet fragrance, their fallen fruit rotting in the grass underneath. She passed and repassed the statue of Saint Agnes, greened by time, watching her with sightless eyes. She almost wished she could become a statue, too, a thing of stone immune to pain. She pressed her hands to her flushed face. This will pass, she kept repeating silently. A year from now I will have forgotten Miguel.

But she knew she never would.

An hour passed, and still she walked. Suddenly she heard a thud behind her and a rustling in the hedges that bordered the wall. Before she could turn to look, a hand was clapped over her mouth, her struggling body held in a viselike grip. She fought, trying to bite, to kick, to scream. Her eyes bulged, her lungs screamed for air, her heart seemed near to bursting with terror, as the trees and sky revolved in a sickening mist. And then a merciful blackness descended.

Chapter VI

She drifted up from darkness to the clip-clop sounds of horses' hooves and the creaking jolt of a carriage. Startled, she opened her eyes. "Where am I?" she asked weakly.

Her head was raised, a flask put to her lips. "Drink this. Dutch schnapps. It will clear the cobwebs."

She gulped at the fiery liquid, coughing and sputtering as it burned down her throat. When she tried to move, she was restrained by strong hands.

"Be still, Francisca." Miguel gazed down at her with brooding eyes. "No harm will come to you unless you bring it on yourself."

She was lying across his lap, her head resting on a velvet-clad arm. The interior of the coach was richly appointed with gold knobs, teakwood paneling, and red silk curtains at the windows. For a moment it crossed her mind that the conveyance might be La Flor's.

"What have you done?" she asked hoarsely. "Where are you taking me?"

"It is I who should be asking the questions, not you." He stared so long and hard at her, a dull flush rose to her hairline. She tried to summon indignation, but her struggle in the garden had drained her strength.

"We had a rendezvous today," Miguel went on coldly, "or had you forgotten?" He was hatless, a bit of green leaf tangled in his bright tawny hair.

She stared at the leaf, the chalky smudge on his right shoulder. "It was you who climbed over the wall, wasn't it?" The schnapps fanning out in her chest revived her. "You took me by force," she accused.

"There was no other way. Why weren't you at the house today, as promised?" The velvet-clad arm beneath her head stiffened. "I am not a man to be kept waiting like a simpering petitioner. Well?"

She met his dark, angry eyes coolly. "I'm surprised you haven't guessed. The answer is quite simple. La Flor."

"*Who?* Don't speak in riddles. What has La Flor to do with us?"

Francisca eased herself to a higher position. "She was your mistress. Do you admit that much?"

"Gossip."

Scorn twisted Francisca's lips. "Always the gallant, aren't you? A gentleman does not reveal the names of his loves. Spare me. If you wish me to speak frankly, then have the courtesy to do the same."

"Damn your courtesy! So what if La Flor was my mistress. You didn't think I lived the life of a monk, did you?"

"Not *was*. Confess it now: La Flor still is your paramour."

"By God, you try my patience!"

When she attempted to swing herself free of his lap, he caught her shoulders, his fingers digging painfully into her flesh. Then abruptly he let go. She moved then, shifting to the plush covered seat next to Miguel, gathering her skirts, trying to put as much distance between them as possible.

"You speak of patience," she said tartly, noting through a gap in the curtain that dusk had fallen. "Since yesterday my patience has also grown thin. I saw you and La Flor as my mother, sister, and I were coming out of the Great Cathedral. She was in a coach—this one perhaps?—and you were riding beside her, talking, laughing, smiling together like lovers who had never parted. Don't deny it, Miguel.''

"What a vixen you have become. You are not only a vixen, but an unreasonably jealous one as well. I am not in the habit of explaining myself, especially to a woman."

"Then I shall be obliged to think the worst."

"Think what you will and be damned."

"It is you who will be damned, not me," she retorted.

Francisca met his angry glare with one of her own, lifting her chin in defiance, one corner of her mind wondering at herself. Was it the schnapps that gave her the courage to face down this man whose black temper could frighten her, or was it that his arrogance, never more apparent than now, had tested the limit of her patience? Whatever it was, she would not be bullied.

Several moments passed in hostile silence. Then suddenly Miguel threw back his head and laughed. "I see where I might have met my match. Very well, then, my appearance with La Flor had nothing to do with her charms. Our association was over the moment I met you, you ungrateful wench. I was begging the use of her coach so that we—*we*, you and I—could leave the city without arousing suspicion. And if you don't believe me, I shall tumble you out alongside the road and let the coyotes feast on you."

She said nothing, her face blank, doubt mirrored in the depths of her eyes.

"Is it to be the road, then?" he asked, a sudden harsh impatience edging his voice. Holding her with one hand, he leaned over and jerked the paneled door open. A rush of cool wind fanned across Francisca. She caught a glimpse of dark trees and thick, shadowy vegetation rushing by.

"You can't mean it!" she cried as he hoisted her up in his arms. "Miguel—don't!"

He slammed the door shut. "Will this convince you?"

He put his mouth to hers. She twisted away so that his kiss fell on her cheek. He held it there, his lips warm on her skin. She felt the beat of his heart, the slight tremor of forced control that ran along his arms. His touch was something she had never been able to bargain for even in anger. And now as his mouth moved to her own and bore down, she felt again a rush of blood to her head, a delicious sense of surrender. Doubt, mistrust, jealousy, fled as his passionate kisses covered her face. She brought her hands up, tangling them in his red-gold hair, leaning into him as his probing kiss deepened.

"Now," he said at long last, lifting his head from her bruised mouth. "Do you believe me? Do you believe that I love only you?"

"Yes," she whispered breathlessly.

"Then we shall leave in the morning for Veracruz."

"In the morning? But my family—they will be ill with anxiety."

"Would you have me go back with you, hat in hand, to ask for their permission?"

"Miguel—you must give me more time. Perhaps you should sail for the Philippines without me, and when you return—"

"You'll give me your answer? No. I won't be fobbed off with your protestations for more time."

"But I must think of a way I can leave with the least hurt to them."

"You can think of it at your leisure—while you are with me."

She sat bolt upright. "You can't hold me against my will."

"Can I not?"

"I shall hate you for this."

"On the contrary, you will thank me."

"You are a fool if you think—"

He put his hand over her mouth. "I have no wish to debate the matter. It is settled."

When she tried to bite his hand, he cuffed her. It was a light blow, but she felt the restrained savagery behind it and for a moment felt a thrill of fear. She knew all too well how quickly he could erupt in violence. Perhaps she didn't love

him? No, she did love him. But she wasn't ready to leave her
world behind. Why couldn't he wait?

They had arrived at their destination. It was too dark to
see clearly, but Francisca sensed at once that he hadn't taken
her to the house on the Calle de Las Infantas. Tall trees
towered over them, their branches swaying and clacking in
the wind as he helped her from the coach.

"Where are we?" she asked.

He did not answer. Instead he cupped her elbow with a
strong hand and led her toward an open door. Outlined
against the lamplight streaming from the house was a tall
man in linen pantaloons with a red kerchief at his throat. A
short dagger and a snaphance firearm were thrust into the
wide scarlet sash that belted his stout midriff.

"Ah, booty," he said, going over Francisca's figure with
avid eyes.

"Mind your manners, Gaspar," Miguel warned, raising
his arm in a threatening gesture. "You are speaking to a lady
of gentle birth. I will have your throat cut in a trice if I hear
anything but words of respect from you."

The smirk instantly disappeared from the man's face.
Miguel, still gripping Francisca's elbow, directed her into an
oak-beamed room where a fire leaped in a stone fireplace. A
man with the curled shoulder-length hair and the furbelowed
waistcoat of a French dandy sat eating at a trestle table. He
inclined his head as Miguel, with a reluctant Francisca, went
through. For one wild moment Francisca thought of appeal-
ing to the diner but could think of nothing to say. That she
had been brought here was proof enough that the two men
were known to Miguel and, if not overly friendly, subser-
vient.

They ascended a short flight of stairs. Opening a heavy
wooden door at the top, Miguel ushered Francisca into a
small bedchamber, then slammed the door shut with a backward kick. The room, like the one below, had few furnishings: a wide testered bed, a chest of drawers, and a commode.

"You must forgive me if these quarters are not up to the

de Silva standards," Miguel said acidly, releasing his hold on Francisca. "But since we will be here for only a short time, it doesn't matter."

Removing his cloak, he tossed it on the bed. Then, going to the chest, he opened the carved lid and brought out a flagon of wine.

Francisca, her heart beating rapidly, drew herself up. "It *does* matter. If you mean to intimidate me by an abduction, you are wrong. I am not your chattel, nor your obedient servant like the ones downstairs."

He laughed. "What a fine little speech."

"And if you think I will allow you to make love to me, you are again mistaken."

"Now that you mention it . . . ." He paused, his eyes going slowly over her. "Perhaps it is not such a bad idea." He set the flagon down. "Will you undress or shall I do it for you?"

Color stained her cheeks. "You are not to touch me, do you hear?"

He laughed again.

How she hated that laugh! She was cornered and he knew it; he was savoring her surrender beforehand.

Slowly, with an assured, measured casualness, he drew close, his hand resting on the sheathed dagger he wore slung in his sash.

She knew then—looking into his narrowed eyes—why he had a reputation for being ruthless and cruel, how the blood of the conquistadors which ran in his veins could be so easily aroused. She had challenged him. But this was not a duel on the field of honor. She had not meant to be his adversary. Why was he being so perverse?

"Miguel, if we could talk about this amicably—"

"There is nothing to discuss. Will you undress?"

"No," she said stubbornly, lifting her chin, her hand splayed across her breasts as if to protect them. "I shall not do as you ask."

He flung her hand aside and, drawing his dagger, placed

the point at the collar of her gown. "Do you prefer that I cut it from you?"

"No!" she exclaimed, horrified, for even the rich valued their clothing, the satins and silks so hard to come by.

He stood gazing at her, the angry look slowly fading from his eyes. "You fool." He replaced the dagger. "Did you think I would force you?"

She took a step back, still defiant. "How could you treat me in such a manner?"

"I could ask the same of you. You promise to meet me, and then, because you see me talking to another woman, you come to God knows what conclusion without giving me a chance to speak for myself. And now you still rush to conclusions without hearing me out. I warned you once before that I come easy to bad temper."

"And what of me? I am not as quick to take offense as you, perhaps. But I have feelings, too."

A tic pulsed in his cheek. "It seems we are both in error," he muttered. Turning from her, he walked back to the table, lifted the wine flagon, and drank from it. After a long silence—still with his back to her—he said, "It grieves me that we must quarrel."

"Oh, Miguel," she said softly, "it is not of my choosing, either."

He turned and held out his arms. She went quickly into his embrace, laying her head on his chest. He pressed his lips to her hair. "Kiss me, then, and say I'm forgiven."

She looked up at him, her thick lashes suddenly moist with tears.

"You were never more beautiful," he whispered.

She touched his cheek with a tentative finger, then as his mouth moved to her temple, and then to the small pulse that beat in her throat, she circled his neck with one arm, bringing his lips to her mouth.

With her head on his shoulder, he led her to the bed.

He was deliberate, slow, infinitely patient, undressing her with skilled, unfaltering hands, the old Miguel, the one she knew, bringing her gradually to sensual hunger again. I do love him, she thought, her body responding in joy to his touch, her soul flying out to meet his impassioned words of love. "Miguel!" she heard herself exclaim, calling to him, a cry that was lost in the fever of their mutual excitement. Again and again he brought her to the brink, and then when she felt she could not endure the sweet torture another moment, his shuddering body sent her spinning into a rapturous, convulsive climax.

Afterward he held her again, idly stroking her hair.

"Are you hungry?" he asked, breaking a long, euphoric silence.

"Yes."

Suddenly she thought of home. If she were there now, her family would be sitting down to their evening meal. Papá, at the head of the table, would intone a small prayer before the servants came in with the food. There would be chatter and laughter and the gleam of candlelight on china. In the courtyard just beyond the dining room, José, the footman, would take up his guitar, and the soft strumming of a familiar tune would make them pause a moment in their conversation.

The picture in her mind filled her with a sudden, inexplicable longing. She couldn't understand why she should think of home with this queer pain under her heart when she was in the arms of her lover. But she did. Perhaps it was because she would be urged in another moment to leave it, to go away forever.

"Of what are you thinking, sweet?" Miguel withdrew his hand from her tangled hair and turned her face so that he could look into her eyes.

"Of home," she answered truthfully. "Miguel, my parents—by now they should have missed me. They will have raised a hue and cry. People will be searching for me, the servants, friends, neighbors, the constabulary."

"Their discomfort will be temporary. In four days I will have a friend deliver a note saying that you have gone away with me. By that time we should have sailed for the Philippines.''

"As your mistress. Can you imagine what terrible pain it will cause my father and mother? They will feel dishonored, shamed. They will not be able to hold up their heads in public. I beg of you to return me while we can make up some plausible excuse for my absence.''

"Return you? And what of the hurt it would cause me? If you love me, you would not consider such a possibility.''

He got out of bed and drew on his breeches. The sight of his naked torso, burned to a golden bronze by tropical suns, reminded her only too eloquently that minutes before, she had lain against him, felt the moving corded muscles of shoulders and back in gripping hands that wanted to hold on forever.

She loved him, but she loved her parents, too. Why did God give her such hard choices?

"I must leave you for a short while, Francisca. I go now to barter for another horse to replace a lame one." He shrugged into his shirt, fastening the neck band. "In the morning we travel to Veracruz. I would prefer not to carry you aboard ship over my shoulder like a sack of meal. It's up to you."

Carelessly slinging his coat across his back, he turned and left the room.

Chapter VII

Supper was brought by an angular-cheeked Indian woman with black obsidian eyes. Her look as she set the tray down on the chest was one of scorn. Already, Francisca thought, I'm considered Miguel's doxy. His kept whore. Even this *indio* feels it unnecessary to show respect. And how can I expect anything but disdain, sly looks, and ribald asides from the men downstairs, the one with the ribbons and furbelows and the one with the neckerchief of a seaman?

She ate little of the meal, picking at the roasted rabbit and yams, nibbling at the coarse-grained bread. Her mind played with the thought of escape. She wondered if Miguel had taken the two men downstairs with him. If so, as near as she could guess, she and the Indian woman were alone in the house. She had no idea how far out of the city they were, but if she could manage to get free, she felt sure she could find her way back.

Did she really want to run? Never, she thought, had a woman a more compelling, passionate captor. If she fled, would he come after her? Or would he feel a second pursuit was not worth the effort? It was useless to ask, "How much does he love me?" Love could not be measured. He wanted her; of that she was certain. But was wanting the same as love? And what of the women he had known before? Had he wanted them in the same way, too? When she was with him, when she lay replete in his arms, her head nestled on his chest, listening to the strong beat of his heart, she did not doubt his love. It was only when he was away that she began to question, to speculate.

The door behind her opened, and thinking it was the Indian woman come to fetch the tray, Francisca said, "I've finished."

However, when she turned, she saw that it wasn't the Indian woman, but the dandy from belowstairs.

"Permit me," he said, removing his plumed hat and giving her a low, sweeping bow, "but I fear our host did not introduce us." He wore an obvious wig of shoulder length, elaborately-curled hair that was a shade darker than his waxed mustache and pointed beard. The wig and the lace-fringed petticoat breeches added to his dandified appearance.

"I am called Don Carlos here in New Spain."

Francisca nodded politely, wondering what he wanted, why he had come. There was something about his manner, something faintly sly about his smile, that she did not like, that made her uneasy.

"And *your* name?" he inquired with the same smile.

Francisca hesitated. "Your pardon, but I wish to remain anonymous."

"As you wish. But a lovely lady like yourself does not need a name. *La Belle Señora* will do. May I sit?" He indicated the one other chair in the room.

"Is there need for it? I am not receiving company. Furthermore, if there is any communication you wish to make with me, I must ask you to do it through Don Miguel."

He looked her up and down. "So you are still playing the proper lady, eh?" he sneered, discarding his polite manner.

"I don't know what you mean," she answered stiffly.

He tossed his hat on the empty chair. Then he unbuckled the velvet baldric which held his sword, carefully placing them on the window ledge. "A pity Don Miguel had to leave.

But then, he was never very good about sharing his women; that is, not until he was done with them. Perhaps that is why he left, eh? Is he done with you?''

Francisca rose to her feet. ''I must ask you to go. At once!''

''Go, before I have given you a chance to see what a skilled lover I can be? Come, let us have a tumble. You will not regret it.''

''Get out!''

''Perhaps you wish to hear the ring of my money.'' He withdrew a pouch from inside his coat and extracted several gold coins, tossing them on the table.

Francisca scooped up the minted gold and flung it in his face. Then, with all the dignity she could muster, she walked past him to the door.

Quick as a cat, he slid between her and the wooden panel. ''Don't run away, *ma cherie*. I was destined to possess you. And if you require a little urging, so be it.''

He clamped hard fingers on her wrist, swinging her away from the door, catching her other arm as she flailed out at him. He was strong, stronger than she had supposed from his effeminate garb, and her writhing body, held tightly against his chest, felt as though it had been caught in a steel trap. He freed her wrist and, with his hand, brought her face around, bringing his mouth down in a sour-tasting kiss.

Her hand caught at his wig, and she gave it a hard jerk. He let go with an oath. And in that moment, as he struggled between vanity and lust, she rushed to the door again.

Lust won. He reached her in two strides, yanking at the back of her gown, ripping it. As she tottered back, his arm hooked around her throat and he dragged her, half choking, to the bed. Forcing her down upon it, he straddled her, pinioning her arms above her head. She went rigid, panting and gasping, her breasts heaving. Then, gathering strength, she brought her knees up, catching him in the groin. He raised his arm to strike her just as the door slammed open, crashing against the wall.

Don Carlos turned his head, an oath dying on his lips. The

next instant he was lifted from Francisca and thrown bodily across the room.

"Get on your feet, turd, and tell me how you wish to die." Miguel's face was livid, his nostrils pinched with anger.

Don Carlos eased himself up, using the wall as a prop. "I swear, Don Miguel, she invited me in. No sooner had you gone but—"

"Bare hands, dagger, or sword? Be quick or I shall run you through, skewer you like a weasel."

Don Carlos slid along the wall and, when he reached the window, grabbed his sword.

"That's better," Miguel challenged. "Fight like a man."

Don Carlos, wetting his lips, slowly unsheathed his weapon. Then, before Miguel could remove his own sword, Carlos lunged at him, catching his collar on the tip, tearing it from his neck.

"Son of a whore!" the dandy cried, his voice shrill with bravado. "Come ahead and kill me, you swine!"

If he had thought to enrage Miguel, he was wrong. Miguel was too cool a swordsman to be taunted into reckless play. He stood his ground, poised, his steady gaze following Carlos as he danced on his toes, feinting, drawing back, moving around Miguel in a slow circle. Suddenly Miguel thrust. There was a clash of steel on steel. The men sprang apart, both wary, both seeking an opening. Carlos lunged, aiming for Miguel's heart, only to meet Miguel's weapon crossed protectively against his chest. Carlos withdrew, another lunge, another withdrawal. Their heavy panting mingled with the ring of steel and the creak of floorboards as their booted feet stamped and pivoted.

Francisca, watching on her knees from the bed, held her hands tightly clasped at her breast. This was not for show, not a game, but a mortal battle. If Don Carlos won . . . But she would not let herself think of that.

Then suddenly Carlos's slashing sword caught Miguel's, knocking it from his hand. It clattered to the floor, but instead of returning it to Miguel, as any honorable opponent would have done, Carlos came at Miguel, meaning to finish him off. Miguel, stepping sideways and back, withdrew his dagger. Now the fight was uneven, for Carlos had the length of the sword to keep Miguel at bay. The dandy was grinning now, sure of his victory, when suddenly Miguel, ducking under Carlos's sword arm, plunged the dagger into Carlos's chest.

He went down with a look of astonishment on his face, blood bubbling from his mouth. A few moments later he was dead.

Miguel turned to Francisca. "Did he harm you?"

"No, no. Oh, Miguel"—her voice trembled—"if you hadn't come . . ."

"Let's not think of it, sweet." He knelt and pulled the dagger from Carlos, wiping it on the fallen man's petticoat breeches.

Still kneeling, he crossed himself. "I suppose I should commend his soul to God. But this one will go to the devil. I don't enjoy killing a man, but in truth, him I could kill twice over. Renegade Frenchman. No one will miss him."

Miguel rose and went to the door. When he opened it, Gaspar was waiting outside. "Listening at keyholes again, eh? Take this offal and get rid of it. Bury it or throw it to the vultures."

After Gaspar had dragged the corpse from the room, Miguel came and sat beside Francisca, taking her in his arms. "I hadn't meant this to happen. I had been gone but a few miles when I realized I shouldn't trust Carlos. He was seeking passage on my ship to Cuba, a stranger to me. I couldn't be too sure of Gaspar, who is one of my crewmen, either. I should have realized he would be poor protection for you. It was all my fault. Will you ever be able to forgive me?"

She nodded mutely, nestling close in his arms, trying to warm her chilled, still-trembling body.

He helped her into bed, bringing the covers up, tucking them in. "Go to sleep, dove. I will stay here and watch over you."

* * *

Miguel, leaning on an elbow, looked down at her as she slept. How beautiful she was! Her dusky lashes rested above the soft curve of her cheeks in twin arcs that hid the dark, luminous eyes he found so enchanting. She lay on her back, one white, rounded arm flung above her head across a cloud of black hair. The coverlet had slipped to reveal a milk-white shoulder and the firm globe of a breast. The nipple was now quiescent. He resisted the urge to take it in his mouth and feel it harden against his tongue. He wanted to gather her up, hold her, fit the curves of her hips into his loins, feel the hot warmth of her eager anticipation, the way she joined him in the rising crescendo of their lovemaking, hear the little cries she made as he drove her to greater and greater heights.

But he let her sleep on, poor, tired little dove. He had been awake for hours, thinking, and toward dawn had come to a decision. He loved her. Yes, she had done something he had never thought possible: she had given him a belief in love. He could not bear to be parted from her, yet he understood how proud she was, that to be at his side as his mistress would embarrass and shame her. No, she was too well-bred for that. Though not of the nobility, she was the product of a long line of old Christians who traced their family tree to the time before the Moors. Women of good family were known to be taken by the king as mistresses, but Miguel doubted someone like Francisca would even consent to that dubious honor.

She stirred, muttering his name. He kissed her gently, and she opened her eyes. For a few moments there was bafflement in their brown depths, then she recognized him and smiled, an irresolute smile not quite sure of itself.

"I did not hear you come to bed," she said. "Have I slept that soundly?"

"Yes. Would you like to break your fast? The *indio* makes a passable fried cake."

"I should go home, Miguel."

"We will talk of that later," he said firmly, but with a smile. "Fried cakes, then?"

"Very well. But first, is it possible for me to have a bath?"

"A bath?" He looked at her in surprise. One took a bath only on grand occasions. "I suppose I could arrange it."

While Francisca lay in bed, a keg was brought up, and later, much later, the Indian woman toiled in with buckets of hot water. She dumped them into the keg, and when Francisca indicated in sign language she wished a towel and soap, the stolid woman's visage seemed to brighten. Some ancestral Mayan memory must have stirred in her brain, for she seemed to understand the rite of cleanliness better than her Spanish conquerors did.

Francisca, her heavy black hair pinned to the top of her head, was splashing about when Miguel came into the room again.

"You mustn't!" Francisca shouted, turning bright red. Sleeping with a man stark naked was one thing, but to have him see her naked in her bath was another. "Go away!" she ordered.

Smiling, he sauntered over to the bed and sat down, watching her. "I can't decide whether you are more beautiful in a keg of water or between my legs."

"Why must you be so crude?"

He laughed, not the sinister laugh of the night before, but a laugh of mirth and enjoyment. "It's rather late to speak of crudeness, is it not?"

She turned her back on him, ignoring him, hoping he would soon become bored and leave. To her chagrin, he remained. But she went on with her bath, pretending to be alone, though she was conscious of his eyes upon her. She had finished soaping and rinsing, the water had grown tepid, then cold, and yet he stayed on. Finally, shivering, she got shakily to her feet.

"Ah, Susanna rises from the pool," he paraphrased from the old biblical tale. He rose and, coming across the room, lifted her streaming body from the keg. "Let me be your servant."

He toweled her briskly, moving down her breasts, across her back, down her thorax and abdomen. Francisca's skin tingled, her cheeks taking on a pink glow. Kneeling, he drew the towel between her thighs, his movements slower now, teasing. A slow heat rose from Francisca's loins. "I must get dressed," she heard herself murmur.

To her surprise—and disappointment—he let her go. But when she reached the bed, where her clothes lay, he came up from behind and whirled her around.

"You are much too tempting." He crushed her to his hard chest, burying his face in her neck. "You smell of jasmine, of the Garden of Eden."

The ivory buttons of his coat dug into her flesh, and Francisca, taking an involuntary step back, threw Miguel off balance, and they both fell on the bed, half on it, their legs dangling on the floor. Laughing, Miguel undid his breeches and, rising over her, spread her flanks. He watched her face as he moved within her, the velvety moistness enclosing his sheath, saw the little frown between her eyes, saw the dew of rapture appear on her forehead. "Do you love me?" he whispered, clasping her tighter, wrapping himself around her as her legs came up to embrace him. "Are we one now as truly as man and wife?"

"Yes, yes," she breathed. "Oh, yes! Yes!"

"Then marry me," she thought she heard him say.

They sat at a small table that had been brought in, drinking almond water and eating fried cakes.

"I have given our situation much thought through the night, Francisca. I did not speak in jest a while ago when I said, 'Marry me.' "

Then it hadn't been her imagination. "But how can I when you already have a wife?"

"One that I haven't seen for five years. Listen, Francisca,

we have no children; I can claim the marriage was never consummated, and have it annulled.''

"Your wife—her family would never permit it.''

"I will return her dowry. In addition, I will make a generous settlement on her. She will be happy to be rid of me; then she can go into her convent and be the nun she has always wanted to be.''

"But . . . you are certain she will make no objection?''

"As certain as I am sitting here. I love you, Francisca. I want you to be my wife. Your family will not refuse my suit.''

"I'm not sure. . . .'' she said hesitantly.

"What reason could they possibly have for witholding their blessing?''

You are not of our faith, she wanted to say. But her parents could not give that as their reason without revealing their true identity. Would they allow her to marry Miguel because not to do so might bring a hornet's nest down about their heads? And what if she did become Miguel's wife? She must then live out her life with that secret buried inside her. Her family, of necessity, would keep their distance, be cool to her, always afraid that at some weak moment she might, by design or accident, betray them.

"The annulment might take a year,'' Miguel said. "But I can wait if you will, my darling.''

Many things could happen in a year, she thought. But she knew by now how single-minded Miguel could be. He was a man who not only thrived on challenge, but one who invariably attained the goals he set for himself. He would get his annulment.

"First I must negotiate a formal betrothal with your father,'' Miguel was saying, "and seal it by signing a marriage contract.''

Dear Lord, Francisca thought, he *is* serious.

"We will be wed in the Great Cathedral,'' Miguel continued, smiling happily at Francisca. "The archbishop himself will officiate. It will be the talk of Mexico City; people will fight to get invitations. Of course, you realize that the pomp and circumstances mean little to me. I had all of that before. But you should not be denied. A woman's wedding day is important. Don't you agree?''

"Oh, yes, my love. Very much so. And you would do all this for *me*?''

"For you. But you haven't said if it's agreeable, if you accept my proposal.''

Her eyes filled with tears. "Oh, Miguel, you do me an honor. I hadn't thought . . .'' She wiped a tear away. "With all my heart I accept.''

The notables of the city would attend, the viceroy, the Marquis of Medina las Torres, and the Count of Calderon, the old Jesuit, who himself was a *converso*.

She would be Doña Francisca de Silva del Castillo y Roche, living a lie for the rest of her life.

"Miguel . . .'' She looked across the table, her eyes searching, half pleading. "How much do you love me?''

"You silly goose,'' he answered, reaching out and taking her chin in his hand. "I'm delivering body and soul into your hands, and you ask such a question.''

"Would you feel you were marrying beneath yourself? My family are not connected to the nobility—and I myself was born in New Spain, which makes me a Creole.''

"I always thought it unjust for pure-blooded Spaniards to be called Creole because they saw the first light of day in Mexico City instead of Madrid or Seville.''

Francisca got up and moved to the window and stood looking out upon a small orchard of mango trees. A blue-feathered bird sat on one branch, pecking at the greenish-yellow fruit. She suddenly wished she were that bird with nothing on her mind but to sit on a branch eating sweet mangos.

"Francisca, what is it?''

She turned. "I don't know if I can marry you. I want to— I love you—but I don't know—''

"For God's sake!'' He rose to his feet, an angry flush on

his face. "I have done everything but cut my heart open! Everything! And you stand there and tell me you don't know!"

He came to her in two strides and, grasping her by the shoulders, held her, looking into her face, scanning it with hard, icy eyes. "There is someone else. There must be. You are in love with someone else."

"No! I swear it!"

"Perhaps you have decided to marry Don Ruy after all."

"No!"

"Then there is someone else." He shook her until her hair fell wildly about her shoulders. "Who? Who is it so I can kill him, and you—you ungrateful wench—into the bargain? *Who?*"

"There is no one."

"Swear by the holy cross." He withdrew the crucifix he wore about his neck. "Swear!" He grasped her wrist cruelly.

"I cannot!" She glared back at him, stung by the pain of his iron hold, angry at his groundless jealousy. "The cross would mean nothing!" she spat at him. "I am a *converso*, a Jew!"

There was a stunned silence. "My God." His hands fell to his sides. "But your family . . ."

"Also. We are all Jews." She was suddenly terrified of the look of incredulity on his face, terrified because in the heat of argument she had given them all away.

"A Jewess. A member of the hated tribe of Christ killers."

"Don't say that! It's not true!"

Stunned, he didn't hear her. His entire upbringing, his mother's teachings, his years as a student with the Dominicans, pledged to wipe out the scourge of heresy, his daily prayers, had instilled in him a scorn for this despised race. And he had to fall in love with one of them. He should have guessed. She did not wear a crucifix; her insistence on the bath; her refusal to eat pork at a meal they once shared—all signs that she observed the religious practices of a Jew. It was as though an abyss had opened before him. His Francisca . . .

Chapter VIII

The story Francisca told her parents was that she had been abducted by four masked men. Their purpose, she said, was to hold her for ransom, but by talking through the night, she had persuaded them to let her go. In return she had promised that there would be no reprisals, no search or arrest.

"You were not harmed?" her mother asked for the third time.

They were sitting in the *sala* on cushioned benches that ran along one wall. Don Pedro was smoking a cigarette, the smoke rising from it to mingle with the vapors of the votive candle kept lit day and night for show in front of the Madonna figure placed in a corner niche.

"No, Mamá. They did not harm me. I was treated with the greatest courtesy. They seemed to be gentlemen."

"Gentlemen?" Doña Mariana asked in disbelief.

She's getting old, Francisca thought with surprise. Her black hair has streaks of gray, and there are lines in her sweet face I have never seen before. Have I done that to her, aged her in less than twenty-four hours? And what of Leonor, who Papá says has taken to her bed to calm an attack of hysteria?

"They appeared to be gentlemen by their dress and speech, Mamá."

"I don't believe that gentlemen would do such things."

Don Pedro shook his head. "Mariana, my dear, you your-self have seen these young bloods. Sons of hidalgos who have gone through their patrimony, hanging about the square, dressed in their finery on their way to a cock- or bullfight or staggering home from a tavern. They are always short of money, always in debt. It's no secret that many of them turn to vice."

"Then we must go after them," Mariana said.

"No Mamá. I promised." Francisca was tired, bone-weary with a fatigue that was more than physical. Yet exhaustion had not numbed the pain in her heart. She wished that her parents were done with this interview. She wished that she did not have to sit there composed, as if nothing of much import had happened. Pretending that she had spent the night cajoling a few "gentlemen" to release her took an effort that seemed beyond her strength. But she did not want to think how ill her parents would be if she told them that her Christian lover had abducted her, that she had come close to rape and had seen a man killed, or that the assault had left her less distressed than Miguel's rejection. (Rejection? she thought. What a pitiable way to describe a world that had crashed about her feet.) She longed to creep into some dark hole where she could nurse her mortal wound, yet she must go on answering question after question, piling one falsehood upon the other.

"Francisca is right," Don Pedro was saying. "But it is more than her promise we must consider. Thus far we have confined the news of Francisca's disappearance to servants and close friends. Thank God, Juliana is in Tacuba visiting her daughter, and knows nothing. The less people know, the better. To inform the constabulary would only publish this unfortunate incident to the entire city. Tongues will wag, and Francisca's reputation will be ruined."

"Well, I suppose that is true," Mariana reluctantly agreed. "Go, child, get some rest. I will send Beatriz to you."

Francisca ascended the stairs feeling as though she were

mounting a ladder to her own hanging. Now that she was away from the searching gaze of her parents, bitter tears pressed behind her eyes. But she would not let them come. To someone standing below watching, her carriage had the same grace: the straight shoulders, the lifted chin. Not even under the torture of hot pincers would she ever reveal what had happened, that she had had a lover who now despised her because she would not kneel to the same God as he. From the very start she had realized that Miguel must never know, yet in the innermost reaches of her heart she had hoped that their love would leap this barrier. She had somehow dreamed that if and when the time came for her to tell him, being a Jewess would not matter.

She had been a fool to dream and hope. She should have listened more closely to her rational mind, which told her that a member of the nobility had an obligation to uphold the church. Miguel's devoutness was ingrained in him from birth. False tales of Hebraic rites of sacrifice and bloodletting were an interwoven part of his upbringing. He could no more cast them off than he could shed his skin.

But the terrible thing was that she had done more than damage herself by confessing her identity in a moment of heat. She had incriminated her family. And for that she would never forgive herself.

"Francisca . . . !"

It was Leonor, wrapped in a head-to-foot white rebozo, standing in the door of her room.

"Why, Leonor!" Francisca went to her. "Mamá said you were ill. You are shivering. It's cool here on the gallery. You ought to be in bed."

Leonor, her dark eyes enormous in an ashy face, grasped Francisca's arm. "Were you taken by the Holy Office? Were you? Papá says no. He says that they would have arrested us all. He says—"

"Come inside, Leonor." Francisca led her sister back into the bedchamber. "Your hands are like ice. Get into bed."

Francisca pulled the coverlet over her sister, tucking her in, spreading another blanket across her feet.

"What did they do to you, Francisca?" Leonor's mouth trembled as she spoke. "Did they torture you?"

"No, little pigeon." She sat down beside her sister. "I was abducted."

She told Leonor much the same story she had told her parents.

"You are certain?" Leonor asked anxiously. "You are not making it up for my benefit? I should die if . . . I couldn't . . ." Tears appeared in her frightened eyes.

"It's God's truth. I am not lying. I was not harmed. The men who abducted me merely wanted money. Put your fears to rest. We are all safe, I promise you."

But were they? Miguel, as a Christian of conscience, was duty-bound to inform the Holy Office that the de Silvas were *conversos*. What was more, he himself could be brought to trial for failing to disclose the damning fact that Francisca and her family followed the Jewish religion. Would Miguel, a man who had broken bread with Don Pedro, who had been willing to set his wife aside to marry his daughter, betray them? She did not think that fear for his own skin would move Miguel to such an act. She knew without having to be told that he feared nothing or no one. But would he feel impelled by his strong belief in the righteousness of orthodox Catholicism to give the de Silvas away? He might be doing so now, even as she sat here reassuring a trembling Leonor. At this moment he could be meeting with a familiar in the flat-roofed building of the Holy Inquisition, speaking in low, confidential tones. . . .

But no. He couldn't knowingly send her and her dear ones down the path that would lead to death at the stake. He had loved her, and though that love had changed, the memory of what they had meant to each other should be enough to seal his lips.

"You are sure we are safe?" Leonor asked.

"Very sure."

Was she? I will never be sure, she told herself. And that is what I must live with hour by hour, day by day, year after year.

The nights were the worst. The constables acting in the name of the Inquisition or its agents, the familiars, usually came after dark, often in the wee hours of the morning, when least expected. Francisca would lie awake listening for the peremptory pounding on the door, the loud voices demanding entrance, the sound of heavy boots on the stair. Sometimes roused from a doze by the creaking of a board or the scurrying of a rat under the eaves, she would sit up, her heart in her throat, thinking they were already there, going from room to room searching each of them out. Staring into the blackness, she imagined the summoned servants, cowed and huddled in a corner while their master and mistress and she, Beatriz, and Leonor were pushed and prodded down the staircase and taken away.

Francisca lived this scene over and over as she went about her daily routine. She drank her morning chocolate, ate her noon and evening meals, chatted with Aunt Juliana, took walks in the garden, read or played her guitar, her ear cocked, her nerves stretched, waiting for that knock on the door. To her family, to her friends, she presented a tranquil face. She smiled, she laughed and gossiped. Looking at her, no one would guess that behind the high-held chin, the poised demeanor and charming smile, a terrible uneasiness gnawed.

Soon, however, Francisca had something else to worry about.

Mornings when she awoke, the smell of hot chocolate at her bedside turned her stomach sour. Food taken before noon made her ill. When a week went by without the onset of her monthly flux, she knew by the swelling of her breasts, the slight thickening of her waist, that she was with child.

What was she to do? She had heard tales of an Indian woman who dispensed a potion that would rid a woman of an unwanted pregnancy. But the idea repelled her. She could not do that to Miguel's child. On the other hand, this was one secret she could not hide. In time, very shortly perhaps, the servants would notice the absence of her monthly cloths to be laundered; they would put their heads together and wonder. Though they might not speak of it to her parents, one day her growing girth would give her away. She would be sent to a convent, an order that was rigid in protecting its inmates from the outside world. There she would give birth to the infant, only to have it taken from her and placed with a family whose name would not be revealed to her. She would never see it again.

Or she could marry Don Ruy.

It was an agonizing choice to make.

One afternoon she was sitting in the library with a book on her lap, not reading but gazing blankly into space. Her father sat busily writing in his ledger at a small desk near the window. They had not spoken for some time, and Francisca had almost forgotten his presence. She was daydreaming. In her mind she was traveling the high seas with Miguel, standing arm in arm at a ship's rail watching a brilliant sunset. She had never been to sea, had never seen a larger body of water than Lake Texcoco outside the city proper, but in her imagination they seemed the same. Miguel was pointing out the shore and the thatched Indian huts lining it. In her reverie his arm went around her waist and she leaned her head on his shoulder. He pulled her closer, bending to kiss her hair, then her lips. "Are you happy?" he asked.

But the picture faded, and she saw the book-lined shelves and the dark oaken beams of the library ceiling, and heard the rumble of wheels along the street outside. She wasn't aboard the *Espíritu Santo*, but in her father's house. The other was fantasy, this was real. She was pregnant with the child who would never see, never know its father.

Her chest heaved with a deep sigh.

"Francisca."

Her father's voice gave her a start. He was looking at her with tender compassion. "What is it, Papá?"

"My child, you seem so downcast."

"No, Papá, it's just—just a little boredom."

He got up from his chair and came to her, patting her head as he often did when she was small. "I know you well enough to guess that it is more than boredom. Is it because of Don Ruy?"

"Partly." It was not entirely a lie. She had been thinking a great deal about Don Ruy these past few days.

"I cannot bear to see you so sad. You need not marry him if that is your wish."

"Papá, I don't know. I admit I was set against him when you first proposed our marriage, but since I have come to know him . . ." She broke off, seeking the right words. For now she saw with a sudden clarity there was no other way for her to keep Miguel's child without branding it bastard except to marry Ruy. Yet she had to make her change of mind seem plausible.

"He is a kind, a good man," she went on slowly, as if giving it thought. "And there is no one in our circle who is eligible, except Luis Méjor."

"Luis Méjor is poor as a *lépero*. He lives in a house with a dirt floor and barely makes enough at his peddling to keep himself in tortillas. No. As good and faithful a Jew as he is, he is not a husband for you."

"I must admit that next to Luis, Don Ruy seems a prince."

"You are not saying this just to please me?"

"No, Papá. Let me think on it a day or two."

At the end of two days Francisca came to her father in the library, where he sat in his favorite chair reading a book.

"Papá, I have arrived at a decision." She sat down on a low stool at his feet. "I would welcome Don Ruy as a husband."

"You are certain?" he questioned. "Good, then. I think you are wise."

Pedro did not ask Francisca if she loved Don Ruy or even if she *could* love him. Her father had said from the very beginning that love had little to do with marriage. She could see that now. Love is a hoax, Francisca thought bitterly, illusory, a will-o'-the-wisp that can be blown away at the first puff of an adverse wind. Perhaps it was best that I did tell Miguel the truth, even though it was a great risk. If he had discovered it later, say after the child was born, then his hate for me would be all the harder to bear.

One afternoon, ten days after the conversation with her father and two weeks before the wedding, Francisca was awakened from her siesta by the sound of voices. Don Pedro, Mariana, Leonor, and Beatriz had gone to Tezcuco to visit acquaintances, and (with the exception of the servants) she was alone in the house with Aunt Juliana. As far as she could make out, Juliana was talking to a man, for she could hear Juliana's high, rather treble voice and the low tenor of a man's.

Francisca, mildly puzzled, turned over on her pillow and was settling into a doze when she thought she heard her name spoken in anger by Juliana. She sat up, curious now as to who Juliana's visitor might be. Throwing a wrapper about her shoulders, she tiptoed barefoot to the door, opened it a crack, and peeked out. They were in the patio, under the gallery.

"Of course, I have no intention of discussing this meeting," Aunt Juliana said, "and I trust you will do the same."

The man murmured some words Francisca could not make out.

She stole to the railing and leaned over, but all she could see of the man was a brown velvet-clad shoulder and arm. For one heart-stopping moment she thought it might be Miguel. She tried to get a closer look, bending forward at a perilous angle, and in so doing, dislodged a hanging flowerpot, which went crashing into the patio below.

Francisca immediately sprang back, ashamed to be caught eavesdropping.

"Is that you, Francisca?" Aunt Juliana called.

A guilty flush spread over Francisca's features. "Yes,

Auntie," she answered, coming forward. "I was looking for Pepé."

"I haven't seen him." Juliana stood, hands on hips, ostensibly waiting for Francisca to return to her room.

Francisca, left with no alternative, went back inside, shutting the door.

A little miffed and still curious, Francisca cornered Juliana after supper that evening. "Who was your visitor?" she asked point-blank.

"My, my, you are meddlesome."

"No more than you. Who was he? A lover?"

Juliana laughed. "At my age? You flatter me. If you must know, busybody, I was arranging to buy a wedding gift. It is to be a surprise, and you will *not* get what it is out of me."

"For a few moments I thought it might be . . ." She broke off, reluctant to name Miguel.

"Who? You thought it might be who?"

"Never mind."

Foolish to think of Miguel, she told herself, miles and miles away by now.

Francisca would have been content with a simple wedding. But Don Pedro was a rich man, and his standing in the community demanded a ceremony with all the extravagant trappings, followed by a lavish feast. The real marriage, the Hebraic one, would be held in their storeroom, the *shul*. That marriage rite, half improvisation, half dimly recalled liturgy, would take place under the prescribed canopy the next day.

Francisca had seen Don Ruy only once between the time she had agreed to marry him and the wedding date. Their meeting, taking place at the signing of the contract, had been a brief one. They had exchanged only a few polite words, but Ruy's sweet smile and his gentle manner reassured her that married life with him, though uneventful, would not be unpleasant. She could trust him. She could be herself without fear or subterfuge. They would live quietly; she would run

the household and its many servants, he would sit in the
library and work on his ledger or go out to oversee his various
enterprises, just as her father had done. She would be a good
companion, would bear his future children and try to make
him happy.

She would put Miguel from her mind, forget the room on
the Calle de Las Infantas with the late afternoon sun angling
through the curtains, forget the passionate kisses and wild
caresses and the sea-blue eyes that had probed her soul. And
if dreams of a phantom lover sometimes haunted her at night,
they, too, in time would vanish.

But on her wedding day, as she sat before her mirror while
Beatriz dressed her hair, she thought of Miguel again. She
closed her eyes and imagined that it was him she was about to
wed, Miguel who would be waiting for her at the cathedral.

Beatriz, running a comb through Francisca's newly washed
hair, chattered on, her words making little impression on a
Francisca lost in memory.

"I've heard that court ladies are wearing a curled fringe
over the forehead," Beatriz was saying. "It would suit you,
Francisca."

"Mmm."

Beatriz picked up a pair of scissors and held them for a
moment poised over Francisca's head.

Francisca's eyes caught the flash of steel in the mirror.
"What are you about to do?" she asked suddenly in alarm,
rudely awakened from her fantasy.

"Cut a few locks to make a fringe."

"You are not to cut a single strand," Francisca warned.

Miguel had loved her hair. He would undo the bun at the
back and let it fall in a rich cascade over her shoulders and
down her back. Or lying in bed, he would lift the rich ebony
mass, spreading it out to make a halo for her face on the
pillow. How many times had he kissed her hair, bunching it
in his fingers, burying his head in its fragrance, whispering
love words . . . ?

"Cousin, we must do something different for this special occasion," Beatriz pleaded, still with the scissors in her hand.

"Put those down. Who will know what my hair looks like since it will be covered with a caul and a lace veil?"

"The bridegroom will know."

The bridegroom. Not Miguel, but Don Ruy.

"Nevertheless," Francisca said, "no fringe."

Three hours later she came down the aisle of the Great Cathedral (the same aisle that Miguel had pictured for her) on the arm of her father to the full-throated chorus of "Te Deum." Her tightly fitting bodice was of ivory satin sewn with gold braid, embossed with pearls and emeralds and rubies that winked and glittered as she walked. The skirt—also of ivory brocade and also jeweled—spreading abruptly from Francisca's waist, was draped over a wire cage, falling to the floor in a circle as wide as her height. She moved slowly, her satin-slippered feet treading with measured grace, her back erect, her face serene under Belgium lace.

But the serenity cost her dearly. The dress was heavy; the ruby pendant (a bride gift refashioned from Ruy's ring) she wore on a gold chain dragged at her neck. The stays of her tight bodice cutting cruelly into her ribs, and the hundreds of lit candles, smoking and guttering along the walls, made breathing an effort. Beneath the waist-length cloud of veil she could feel sweat gathering on her brow. And yet her smile was fixed in place, as though her face was on view for all to see.

Don Ruy was waiting for her at the altar. Dressed in a jerkin embroidered with precious gems, satin breeches tied at the knees with fringed ribbons, and shoes buckled with silver roses, he presented a finer figure than Francisca had imagined. She tried to keep her thoughts on him during the ceremony as they knelt before the priest, and succeeded until after the ceremony, when they were seated in the carriage and he leaned over to kiss her. A dry, dutiful, passionless kiss.

She was married. Until she died she was married to this

man whose kiss she would always compare to another's and find wanting.

Except for those few moments in the carriage, Francisca did not allow herself to indulge in self-pity. There were other, more important things to think of. She must face a hurdle that she could not avoid. After the Hebraic ceremony, the marriage would be consummated. She was not a virgin. Don Ruy was an experienced man; he had been married before, and would know at once. Dare she try the old trick she had once heard Aunt Juliana gossiping about? A girl, a certain Spanish young woman who had recklessly lost her maidenhead, had fooled her bridegroom by surreptitiously cutting her finger and staining the sheet with telltale blood. Francisca felt that deception was something Don Ruy did not deserve. But how could she be honest with him? If he knew that someone else had been to the well before him, he would rightly assume that the child she bore was not his. And it was for the child she had married him.

As it turned out, Francisca was spared the need to hide the truth.

By the time Don Ruy—having overimbibed in ritual wine—reached the connubial bed, he was very drunk. Francisca helped him undress, trying not to feel repelled by his thin, bowed legs and the concave chest sprouted with gray hairs. Clothed, his appearance had been somewhat deceptive, for Francisca discovered that he used padding for the calves of his legs and for his chest.

Again she caught herself comparing, remembering the well-shaped, muscular torso, thighs, and legs, the golden-fuzzed chest upon which she had rested her head. But I mustn't, she reminded herself. What does it matter if Ruy is not Adonis? I and my child will be safe with him—or as safe as possible—but with Miguel I would always walk a tightrope of uncertainty. In any case, there had been no choice. The moment Miguel had discovered her true identity, he had gone through the door with a few curt words and a piercing look that had cut to the bone like a knife.

"Francisca, *mi pequeña esposa*, my little wife, let me kiss you."

Ruy embraced her, his hot, rancid-smelling mouth aimed at her lips falling on her turned-away cheek.

"To bed, to bed," he sang thickly, tumbling on the mattress, bringing Francisca with him. She lay passively under him for some moments before she heard the first rising snore and realized he had fallen asleep.

The next morning he awoke long after Francisca was up and about. But she was there when he opened his eyes, greeting him with a smile, telling him she would fetch a pot of chocolate.

"No, my sweet, not chocolate. Water. A flask of cool water, please. My head feels like a thousand hammers are pounding it. And my thirst . . ."

"I'll only be a minute. Rest quietly."

When she returned with a jug of water, he was sitting up, bleary-eyed, his thin hair in peaked tufts. "I apologize, Francisca," he began. "It is not the way I planned our wedding night. I was remiss in my duties as husband. I promise—"

"Hsst! You were not remiss at all." She managed a blush, not difficult since she was disturbed by the lie she must tell.

"You mean . . . ?"

She nodded. "Yes, husband. I am truly a married woman now."

"Was I—did I—was I gentle?"

"I couldn't have asked for a more considerate husband."

His sigh echoed her own relief. She would wait a few weeks, then announce he was to become a father. He would be overjoyed. It would be like a miracle from heaven, since he had tried so many years to impregnate his first wife, with little success. He would accept the child as his own. They would make a life together; they would be happy.

The only shadow that hung over Francisca's picture of her future with Don Ruy was a fear they all shared, the fear of being discovered by the Inquisition. Only Francisca knew how much closer they were to that possibility now.

Chapter IX

Francisca's son was born in February of 1651. He was baptized as Jorge de Diaz y Silva. But in Don Pedro's secret register, kept behind a hidden panel in the library, he was inscribed as named Benjamin Ben Imar. He was not circumcised, according to Jewish law; to do so would have put him in jeopardy.

After a few weeks, when the infant's features began to take form, it became apparent that he would resemble his mother. He had the same dark hair, the same dark eyes. The nose, now almost lost in baby fat, gave promise of being as straight and well defined as Miguel's. Except for that one feature, there was nothing of her lover in him. To Francisca this was a blessing, for how would she explain tawny hair and blue eyes when she and Don Ruy had neither?

As Francisca predicted, Ruy was ecstatic. To be able to sire a son in his middle age was like receiving a gift from God.

"We shall have many," he said happily to Francisca. "Many sons, and daughters, too."

For his family he needed a new house. He and Francisca had been living on the Calle de las Olas in a slate-roofed mansion that he and his late wife had shared. But after the advent of Jorge, Ruy began to look about for larger, grander quarters. He had agents scour the city, while he himself interviewed prospective sellers. Finally he was offered a residence he thought suitable. Situated on the Calle del Aguila, it belonged to a representative of the Crown who had grown bored with colonial life and wished to return to the more interesting bustle and intrigue of King Philip's court.

Ruy thought the sum Don Diego asked was excessive (Ruy was a close bargainer), but the house was the equal of Don Pedro's in elegance, and Ruy felt Don Pedro's daughter deserved no less. It had been built from the dressed stones of a ruined Aztec temple, great blocks whose pagan carvings had been gouged and scraped out and replaced with figures of the saints. In the patio marbled columns speckled in gold and silver supported the gallery that ran around it. Imported from Spain at great cost were high feather beds with headboards that bore the royal insignia inlaid with gold leaf. There were Far Eastern rugs on the tile floors, silken covers on the ornately carved tables, and Michoacán featherwork and oil paintings on the walls.

Francisca was happy there, or as happy as she thought she could be. Her thoughts of Miguel, swinging between longing and anger, had not faded as she had hoped. They were never stronger than on the nights when Ruy turned to her in the high feather bed. Anxious to increase his family, he made love to her as often as he could, an exercise that Francisca endured with patience. Under his wet kisses and inexpert hands, she could not help but think of Miguel, of the passion with which he fired her, of hands and lips and manhood that had left her gasping and moaning with pleasure. She would wonder if he had found another woman (whore or virgin, but Catholic) to take on his voyage, and decided that he had. Miguel, though devout, was not a man to abstain from adultery or fornication, even if he did break the church's rules. Had he used her as he had La Flor? Or had he really loved her? He must have if he had offered her marriage, yet it was a love that was not strong enough to withstand the shock of having as its object a *converso*.

But he hadn't informed on her. That much she thanked him for. As the weeks and months, then a year, went by without the dreaded knock of a familiar at her door, the watchful tenseness went out of Francisca's eyes. She could relax, play with her growing son, preside over Don Ruy's table, gossip with sister, Beatriz, and Juliana, read her books, or play the guitar without a tense knot between her shoulder blades.

Then one morning in church attending mass with Leonor and Beatriz, she became aware of a man staring at her. He was sitting in a side pew, dressed in vest, *chupa*, and linen breeches—the garments of a workman. The face was disturbingly familiar, but she couldn't place it. When she rose to go at the end of the service, she threw him another glance. He smirked at her, a sly, knowing look that froze her blood.

It was Gaspar, the tall, burly seaman. The same one who had once referred to her as booty and had witnessed the duel and the death of Don Carlos, the dandy in French furbelows. Did his presence here mean that Miguel had returned to Mexico City? But she would have heard. The arrival of ships from overseas was an event made public with great fanfare. Miguel was known. Her father, who had done business with him in the past, would have mentioned his name.

It was on the Thursday following the day she had seen Gaspar in church that a servant came to her while she was playing with Jorge and said that a man at the kitchen door wished to see her. Like her mother, Francisca pitied the poor and followed Mariana's custom of having her cook distribute tortillas, maize cakes, and beans every Thursday morning to the indigent who came to the kitchen door. If there were any messages or offerings of thanks, they were left with the cook.

"What does he want?" Francisca asked.

"He says it is a private matter. He says he will not leave unless he can see you."

When Francisca entered the kitchen, Gaspar was standing respectfully to one side, hat in hand. The cook, busy at the cutting table slapping tortillas from hand to hand, threw him dubious glances.

"What is it you wish, my good man?" Francisca asked through lips that had gone dry at the sight of him.

"May we speak in the garden, señora?" His manner was servile, almost cringing. "Your husband has ordered some orange trees and says they must meet with your approval before I am to be paid."

She knew he was lying, but with the servants' eyes upon her, she had no choice but to sweep past the little crowd of supplicants at the door, who made way for her.

She led Gaspar to the grape arbor, thankful that Ruy was not at home. He would be gone for ten days, occupied with overseeing his affairs at his hacienda near Tula, where he owned several thousand acres on which he grazed cattle.

Turning on the graveled path to face Gaspar, she gave him a hard look. "Now, what brings you here?"

She thought for a few hopeful, yet fearful minutes he had come with a message from Miguel. But he hadn't.

"I have fallen on hard times," he said. "Don Miguel dismissed me before he sailed, and I had to find a berth on another ship, a scow, hardly bigger—"

"Please, state your business," she interrupted sharply.

"As I said, I've fallen on hard times. My last ship sank two days from Veracruz, and I lost all my belongings and the few pesos I had managed to save. When I saw you in church it came to me that you are a lady, as Don Miguel said, a very rich lady." He paused and licked his lips. "I was hoping you could part with a small purse—say, a thousand ducats? In gold."

The dog! She would have liked nothing better than to ask her doorman to throw him into the street. But she didn't dare. He knew too much. "That is not a paltry sum," she replied tartly.

"For a rich lady it is. Or would you rather your husband—Don Ruy de Diaz, isn't it?—know about your stay at a certain country house? Not to speak of poor Carlos, who is buried in the woods beyond.''

"And so you think you can extort money from me? My husband is fully aware of what happened in that house.''

"Is he, now? He can't be a very proud man, can he?''

"That is none of your concern.''

"I am willing to wager he knows nothing—unless I tell him. What will it be? The gold or a scandal? Eh?''

Had he called her bluff? Should she go on insisting Ruy knew everything? Suppose Gaspar wasn't taken in by such an allegation? Could she be sure that he would not approach Ruy? She thought it prudent not to take the chance. Perhaps there was another way to foil this blackguard. She would think of something. She must.

"I cannot give you ducats, either in gold or silver. My husband deals with the money. He pays the tradesmen and the servants. I have none.''

"But you have jewels. Give me what you can to equal a thousand ducats. I am not greedy. I don't ask for more than I deserve.''

"I cannot spare my jewels. They would be missed.''

Gaspar shrugged. "The money, then.'' He grinned at her, then wiped his mouth with the back of a dirty hand.

A sudden murderous hate choked her, and for a few moments she could not speak. She wanted to lash out at him, to claw the smirk from his ugly face. How dare this low, filthy scum come to her house and ask for money? But if she was angry, she was frightened, too. Gaspar, out of malice, might announce her indiscretion to the world if she did not pay for his silence.

She swallowed her rage. "Very well,'' she agreed coldly. "You must realize I am not able to get that many ducats at once. Tomorrow, perhaps. I don't want you to come here,'' she added hurriedly. "I will meet you tomorrow night, say twelve o'clock under the west causeway at the floodgates.''

"Such a distance, señora?''

"I prefer not to be seen.''

* * *

After her interview with Gaspar, Francisca went up to her room. Dismissing the nursemaid, she lifted her sleeping son from his trundle bed. Bracing his small head against her shoulder, she sat down on her favorite chair near the window. The child slept on, nestled against her breast. How comforting the warm little body feels, she thought, kissing the dark crown of his head. The little hands with their dimpled knuckles clutching her collar, how dear and sweet. He is my treasure and my salvation.

In moments of distress, as now, Francisca found a certain measure of calm came to her in just holding her son. She could not explain why. He was only two, too small to understand her problems should she speak of them. Yet his existence was not only a source of pride and joy, but her reason for being as well. Since his conception, everything she had done had been done for him.

And now his safety as well as hers was threatened. She did not know what Don Ruy would do if he should learn of her association with Miguel. But once he discovered her past liaison, then the paternity of the child would be questioned. Honor might force him to brand her beloved Jorge a bastard and banish her to her father's house. And would Don Pedro accept mother and son and the shame that went with their ignoble return? For all that they were secret Jews, her father and husband were still Spaniards, imbued with a machismo that demanded their women be pure and unsullied.

She could see no other way but to accede to Gaspar's demands.

Obtaining the thousand ducats would not be difficult. She could take it from the strongbox and tell Don Ruy she had given it to the Bethlehemites for the founding of a hospital or to the brothers who ran the Magdalen Asylum for the insane. Since she donated to charitable orders from time to time, he would accept her explanation, although he might cluck his tongue at such excessive generosity.

The question is, she asked herself, shifting Jorge to her

shoulder, will Gaspar be satisfied with the thousand? Most likely not. The promise to leave the city she would exact from him would probably mean nothing. How could she trust the word of an unscrupulous *lépero* such as Gaspar? He would return to the house, not once, but many times, slowly bleeding her of money and jewels, while she would find it harder and harder to explain their disappearance to Ruy.

Then what could she do? Hire an assassin to kill him? That would only exchange one blackmailer for another, shifting Gaspar's extortionate demands to the assassin's. If she was to be rid of Gaspar, then she must do it herself.

The thought was frightening. It would be murder, a man's blood spilled. How could she, who had turned away from the sight of the Frenchman's gaping wounds, who took care not to watch the final bloody moments of a bullfight or the butchering of a lamb, kill a man? That he deserved to die, that he himself would not hesitate to dispose of her, made only a slight impression on her troubled conscience.

Yet she could not allow this rapacious beast to endanger Jorge's good name, to ruin whatever happiness she had managed to give Ruy, or to cause a scandal her beloved parents did not deserve.

On the following night she waited until well after the cathedral bells tolled twelve and the servants were safely in bed before she quietly let herself out of the house. In the purse she had stuffed down her bosom were roughly five hundred ducats of gold, enough to keep Gaspar counting for what time she might need. Concealed up her sleeve was a well-honed kitchen knife. She was not sure what her approach would be, but she felt it would be wise—and safer—if she could trick Gaspar into surrendering his own weapon.

As she hurried along the moonlit streets, hugging to the shadowed walls, trying to avoid the lighted lanterns of the watch (curfew was at ten), she thanked God that Ruy was away. His presence in the house would have made her mission, if not impossible, difficult.

It was a long walk, and the barking of dogs as she passed

silent houses tightened her nerves. She imagined that unseen eyes were watching her from behind barred and shuttered windows. At any moment she expected a light to flare, a door to open, and the shout "Who goes there?" to echo down the street. But all remained quiet within, the good citizens of the city resting undisturbed in their slumber as her footsteps clacked noisily along the cobbles.

She could tell she was nearing her destination by the foul stench of the canal, and presently the outline of moored boats along its banks came into view. She followed the noisome waterway for another half mile before the causeway suddenly loomed up before her. A bulky shadow detached itself as Francisca approached. Her knees shook and her heart thudded, and for a few moments she struggled with the urge to turn and flee. But the sight of his ugly face as he moved into the light of a high-sailing moon, the sly, conspiratorial smile that suddenly broke out, reminded her of the murderous rage she had felt in the garden.

"You brought the money?" he asked.

"Yes. But—wait! I don't trust you. How do I know you won't be asking for more next week or next month?"

"I give you my word."

"That's not enough. As a token of good faith, I want you to pledge your dagger."

"My dagger? I've lived with it for nigh on thirty years. A man's dagger is his best friend. I'd sooner part with my arm."

"That might be, but look at it this way. I'm buying it for one thousand gold ducats."

He mulled that over for a moment, assessing her slender figure as if to decide how she could possibly harm him.

"All right, then." He removed the dagger from his baldric and threw it on the ground at her feet. Ignoring the insult, she kicked it behind her, not daring to stoop to pick it up. He was dangerous, twice her size and at least three times her weight. But anger and loathing rose above fear.

"Where's the money?" Gaspar demanded.

"I have it."

When she reached under her cloak, his eyes took on an avid gleam. The moment she had the purse in her hands, he grabbed it from her and greedily undid the drawstrings.

"It's all there," she said as his fingers dipped into the purse.

Moving behind him, she fumbled at her sleeve. The knife glinted as she brought it up. *Now!* she told herself, *now, one good stab between the shoulders!* Her hand wavered as a tiny doubt flickered across her mind.

In that moment of indecision, Gaspar, sensing something amiss, whirled about. Before Francisca could draw breath, the knife was wrested from her with a wrenching, agonizing twist of her wrist.

"Trick me, would you?" He captured the other wrist and held both with one hairy paw while the other thrust the knife point under her chin. "How'd you like some of the same?" he queried, his hot, fetid breath making her flinch. "Scared, are you?"

"No," she lied between gritted teeth. "You wouldn't dare kill me." She knew her bravery to be a thin veneer masking a trembling terror that threatened to overwhelm her. Yet to show the least sign of fear to this bully would give him an advantage she could not afford.

"My maid, who is my trusted confidante," she went on in a cold, carefully controlled voice, "knows that I went out to meet you. She knows your name and your purpose. If I should not return, my husband and my people will track you down and cut you to small pieces and feed you to the dogs."

He gave the knife a twist, pricking her skin. "It's all talk. If you took your maid into your confidence, you never would have come to meet me alone."

"She is keeping watch at home."

"A lie. All lies." The knife moved again, this time drawing blood. Gaspar laughed. "You might be right, señora. I have no wish for the hounds to be on my trail. I have a better idea."

He stuck the knife into the band at his waist and, still

holding on to her wrists, pulled her toward the shadows of the causeway.

"I always meant to have me a fine lady. And now is my time, eh? 'Twould be better to have a feather bed and silk sheets under us, but it can't be helped."

Her body went taut. It was one thing to be knifed, a clean death, and another to be used by this filthy animal.

"Don't be shy, señora." He jerked her up against him, his slobbering, odorous mouth crushing her lips. He smelled foul; his mouth on hers was a defilement! Her instinct was to fight, to struggle, to claw his face and beat at his head. Instead she suddenly went limp.

"Seems you're going to like it, eh?"

He let go of her hands and brought his ugly face to hers again. She did not stir, did not make the slightest sound of revulsion as his furry tongue pried her lips apart and invaded her mouth. Slowly, steathily, her right hand came up between them, her fingers curling around the knife handle. With a sudden, spasmodic movement, she dragged it free of Gaspar's belt. Before she could turn it on him, he leaped back out of reach.

He laughed, a loud donkey's bray. "I've caught a wild one in my trap. That will make your taming all the more enjoyable. Come, come." He motioned with his hand. "Come and get me."

He danced around her, hee-hawing as she turned, following his movements. He was playing cat and mouse, knowing that in the end he had only to lunge and, with a sideswipe of his huge, hamlike hand, render her senseless. Still she would not give up. Her mind kept leaping about, seeking a way to get at him. It was apparent she would not be able to get close enough to stab him. Then why not throw the knife, as she had seen the gallants on the square do at each other or at targets? The impetus behind the thrown weapon would not be as strong as she wished, but it might wound him enough for her to get away.

She advanced toward him with the knife held high. Laughing still, he stood his ground, facing her with his back to the canal.

"Come, come," he urged.

She drew her arm back and flung the knife. He dodged it, throwing his body sideways, taking a step back toward the edge of the canal. The step was fatal. It encountered empty air, and he went tumbling into the canal. At that moment the floodgates opened to release the canal's impounded water, as they did every morning. Francisca, rushing to the edge of the bank, saw a struggling Gaspar being swept away. Then he was lost to view beneath the swirling waters.

God had saved her from murder. Nevertheless, she prayed that Gaspar would drown and that she would never see that odious face or hear that dreadful laugh again.

Chapter X

In September of 1656 news reached Mexico City that the annual flotilla had arrived safely from Cádiz at the port of Veracruz. Among the ships was the *Espíritu Santo*.

"I expect the cargoes will reach the city on muleback within ten days," Don Pedro said.

It was Friday, and the Diazes were having their customary Sabbath eve meal with the de Silvas.

"And none too soon," Ruy said. "Oil and wine have become scarce, and what remains is dear."

"The same with mercury," Pedro put in. "Without the quicksilver we can't separate the dross from the silver at the mines. I shall be glad to see the first of those mules trotting over the causeways."

"They say the captains and agents are already beginning to arrive," Ruy commented.

"Indeed. And though the royal commission alone is empowered to sell mercury, I have a man, one of the galleon owners, who can obtain special treatment for me. At a price, of course. I have done business in the past with Don Miguel Velasquez del Castillo, a good trader and honest. I recommend him highly."

If Francisca had thought she could hear her former lover's

name again with equanimity, she was wrong. When the first tidings of the *Espíritu*'s arrival had been cried in the public square, she had experienced mixed feelings, the old dread underlaid with ghostly memories of joy and pain. But then she had reassured herself that nearly six years had passed since Miguel had sailed to the Philippines, that the *Espíritu* could have changed ownership, not once but several times, that Miguel could have obtained another ship, perhaps two, or remained in Spain engaging in the Mediterranean trade.

But he was here on these shores, perhaps in Mexico City at this moment.

While her father discoursed on royal commissions and the need of a good, honest agent to intervene for him, Francisca sat with an implacable face, her heart bounding in her chest like a hare on the run. Her hands trembled so she could not eat, her mind swinging wildly from one thought to the next. She wanted to shout a warning to her father that this man knew they were Jews, and that they must not trust him. And then, in the midst of her agitation, an inexplicable longing seized her, a need to see his face again, to hear his voice, to feel the touch of his hand.

But it was wrong! Wrong! How could she have such shameful feelings about a man who was their enemy?

"If you would like to meet Don Miguel, Ruy," her father was saying, "I plan to invite him to supper next Tuesday. I think you will find him a shrewd bargainer, but he won't cheat you. As I said, he is more honest than most."

Here in this house! Francisca thought, aghast. She looked at her son, who sat with blinking eyes and nodding head, trying to keep awake. Whatever happens, Francisca thought fiercely, Miguel must never know about Jorge.

"Papá," Francisca began, wetting her lips, "perhaps Ruy would prefer buying from the man with whom he has always done business."

Don Ruy stroked his sparse beard. "It's true, I would. In the past I have traded with Don José Perez, but I've been told that he died at sea a year ago. So I am in need of finding a replacement.''

Pedro said, ''Meet Don Miguel, then you can decide.''

When the de Diazes returned home that night, Francisca took Jorge directly up to his room. ''I'll put him to bed,'' she told Eléna, Jorge's nursemaid.

She removed Jorge's clothes, the boy falling asleep before she finished pulling his nightshirt over his head. Lifting him on her lap, she sat rocking her body to and fro as though in prayer. Jorge was big for five, and heavy. But she held him close as if he were still the infant who had given her comfort. Absently humming an old lullaby under her breath, she thought of the sin that had conceived him, even as she told herself that the boy was innocent. Only she was to blame. Her only excuse had been love, a reckless, passionate love.

She no longer loved Miguel. How could she? How could her love prevail against his hate?

She did not want to see him again. But it was not a question of merely avoiding him, something she could easily manage. She struggled with another dilemma. Ought she tell her husband and father that Miguel knew they were *conversos*? If Miguel had not informed upon them five years earlier, then perhaps he would keep silent now. Perhaps. Should she take the chance? She needn't reveal the extent of her past intimacy with Miguel. But whatever story she told, the Diazes and the Silvas might find it prudent to flee Mexico City, abandoning all their properties and going into hiding before finding refuge in another country. If they were lucky enough to get away.

All because of a slip of the tongue, words used in a sudden show of mindless temper. Oh, God, if she could only take them back!

Jorge stirred in her arms. ''What is it, Mamá?'' he asked sleepily.

''Nothing, my darling.''

She put him down on the bed, pulling a light blanket up under his chin. He fell asleep again almost instantly, a dark lock of his hair falling over his brow. She brushed it back and stooped to kiss him. She did not care about the houses and the mines, the plantations, the jewels and gold they might be forced to forfeit. But to lose Jorge . . .

No, she wouldn't think of it.

As she stooped to blow out the bedside candle, she heard the door creak behind her, a stealthy sound that sent an icy current along her arms.

"Who is it?" she whispered.

The door slowly opened, and Miguel came into the room.

"You?" Startled, she drew back, her hand going to her mouth.

"In the flesh."

She took a deep breath to steady herself. Miguel stood only a few feet from her, Miguel in black velvet and white linen, smelling of leather and horses and the sea.

"How did you get in?" she asked in a low, husky whisper. When he started to speak, she cut him off. "Don't answer. I recall how adept you are in clambering over garden walls."

"It pleases me that you haven't forgotten." He smiled.

That smile: the white, even teeth in a bronzed face, the eyes that looked dark, almost black, in the shadowed room, reminded her of other smiles, other rooms. . . .

She drew herself up. "Why are you here? Why have you come like a thief in the night?"

"Curiosity," he replied easily. "I heard that you had married Don Ruy after all. And that you had a son. I came to see if the child was mine."

"He is not. And if he were, what concern is that of yours?" she asked sharply. "He would be half-Jew, a child with tainted blood."

Miguel said nothing, but silently approached the bed. He stood for a long time looking down at the boy, his features expressionless. He was hatless, his shoulder-length red-gold hair glinting in the flickering lamplight. Francisca eyed him with rancor. Yes, he was handsome, as handsome as she remembered, the Latin profile so like a heathen god's, the proud head and the thin, sensuous mouth above the beard still the same. But she had not forgotten *who* he was or how he had cast her aside because of her faith.

"Now that you've seen him," she said with asperity, "I must ask you to leave."

"What did you name him?" he asked, ignoring her request.

"Jorge, Jorge Carlos."

"He favors you. But the chin—"

"My husband's. Are you relieved, Miguel, relieved that you haven't fathered a *marrano* bastard?"

He turned to face her, the smile gone, a hard, arrogant look in his eyes. The look angered her; he *was* relieved, damn his soul! He had come to make sure that he hadn't spawned a by-blow unworthy of the pure del Castillo blood.

"Is he your husband's? I want the truth, Francisca, or by God . . ."

"By God, what? How dare you come here, how dare you threaten me?" She tried to bring her temper under control, but the memory of the humiliating way in which he had dismissed her twisted her heart. Damn him! "You want the truth?" she spat at him. "All right, I'll give it you! I was carrying the boy when I married Don Ruy. There you have it. Now, go and inform your uncle, the Inquisitor, that you have a Jew for a son. Because according to Hebraic law, the mother determines her child's race. Go on! Go on!" she taunted, beside herself with anger.

It was an anger that had grown, accumulating through the years, an anger building up out of sorrow and pain, out of sleepless nights and silent tears, an anger so large she had not guessed at it until now. He had come back, not with regret, but with curiosity. *Curiosity!*

"Lower your voice!" he commanded, a cold glitter in his eyes. "Or would you prefer waking the household?"

She swallowed, clenching her fists at her sides. "This is my home. You have no right to be here."

"Haven't I?" His voice had resorted to its usual cool tone,

but beneath his words she caught the resonance of an anger to match her own. "Where can we go where we won't be heard?"

"I have nothing more to say."

He gripped her arm with fingers of steel and pulled her close. "You forget that I'm not one to be ordered about."

He was hurting her, bruising her skin, and she sensed the anger simmering under the deceptively calm surface. She could tell by his rapid breath, the slight tremor of his muscled arm, that he was keeping himself in check, that he could break her in two if he wished.

"Let me go or I'll scream."

"I think not. Scream and you will not live to regret it."

She was suddenly afraid of him, afraid of what he might do. How far would anger goad him? Enough to kill her, the impure mother of his son? Kill her and abduct Jorge, passing him off as the offspring of a union with a Christian mistress. Or would he harm Jorge? No. Not that. He had always wanted a son. But not hers.

"There must be a place in this large house where we can remain undisturbed." His fingers took a fresh purchase on her arm.

"You're hurting me."

He let go. "I'm not a bully. But so help me . . ."

The menace in his voice sent another finger of fear up her spine. "There . . ." She wet her lips. "There is a room below, used for sewing and weaving."

"Let us find it, then." He propelled her toward the door.

"I must speak to my husband. He will wonder why I haven't come to bed."

They went out onto the gallery. "Wait here," she said in a low voice.

He grasped her skirt as she started away. "If you do not return in a few minutes," he whispered, "I will follow you."

When she entered the bedchamber, she found Ruy already asleep, lying on his back, soft snores issuing from his half-open mouth. She stood for a few moments, her hands at her breast, listening to her heavy heartbeats. She must get rid of Miguel as soon as she could. She could never explain his presence here in the house. Oh, why did he have to come?

When she returned to the gallery, she thought for a moment that he had gone. But no. He detached himself from the shadows and took her arm once more. She led him down the stairs to the dining room, where she lighted a candle from the oil lamp kept burning there.

The weaving room was across the patio and through a dark passage. As Francisca opened the door, they were assailed by the astringent odor of new leather and fermenting indigo. This was the room where hired artisans skilled in leather-work, needlework, dyeing, and weaving produced the household's clothing. In one corner was a pile of cotton, still to be seeded, and beside it a bale of tanned hides.

Francisca put the candle down on a chest next to a loom, the flickering light throwing crouching shadows across the whitewashed ceiling. When she turned, Miguel was closing the door behind him.

"What is it you have to say?" Francisca asked coldly, though her heart was beating in a loud, erratic way.

He came across the room, his hand resting lightly on his sword hilt. He halted a foot from where she stood, his narrowed, probing eyes going over her, pausing at her waist, lingering at her breasts.

"Motherhood seems to have agreed with you," he said, breaking a tense silence. "Tell me, do you love him?"

"My husband? Yes. Very much," she lied. "He is kind, he is faithful and generous to a fault."

"And he beds you well?"

"It is no concern of yours. However, if you insist on knowing, the answer is yes. I could not ask for a more ardent lover, passionate beyond anything I could expect."

Francisca saw a muscle twitch in his cheek. Good, she thought. No Spanish male likes to hear of a rival who pleasures his paramour—past or present—as well or better than he.

"I think you lie, my beautiful Francisca." The silky voice was more menacing than if he had shouted at her.

He moved closer, his eyes burning with a strange glitter.

"You . . ." She swallowed, steadying the tremor in her voice as she went on, "You cannot abide the truth when—"

"Enough!" He reached out, inserting his hand in her bodice, and pulled her roughly against his hard chest. He stared down at her, eyes narrowed, the way he had stared over the length of his sword at the luckless Don Carlos. She felt a tingle of fear at the back of her neck.

Then he brought his mouth down, savaging hers, a punishing kiss, not caring if it hurt. Her balled fists struggled up, beating at his arms and back, sliding futilely down as his tongue and teeth pried her lips open. Her hand touched his sword hilt and came up again, grasping it.

Aware of her intent, he pushed her away, so violently, she fell back against the chest. He unbelted his sword and, throwing it in a corner, advanced on her again, bringing her upright.

"You have a way of forcing my hand," he said grimly, swiftly unlooping the small buttons at the front of her gown.

"No, Miguel. No!" She tried to wrench herself free, but he steadied her by grasping a shoulder. Flushed, angry, trembling, she could think of nothing to say except, "You—will get me with child again!"

"You did not seem to care before." He pushed her protesting hands away. "Would you rather I tore the clothes from your body? You have no choice, Francisca. Submit."

"Never!"

"Such drama."

Pinioning her wrists with one strong hand, he undressed her with the other, his supple fingers skillfully maneuvering buttons, hooks, and loops. When she stood shivering, naked, and quiescent, he began to unbutton his doublet. Francisca, freed of his hold, bolted for the door. He caught her and flung her upon the heap of cotton, falling over her, covering her with his weight.

"Don't do this," she whispered, "I beg of you."

He buried his head in her throat, pressing her into soft, yielding cotton bolls beneath. For a long time he held her thus, the gilded buttons of his doublet digging into her naked flesh. Then he started to kiss her, softly this time, his lips a feather touch upon her cheeks, her mouth, the side of her neck. Lifting himself slightly, he brought his mouth down to a breast, taking the tender nipple in his mouth, his tongue swirling about it.

She caught her breath as she felt the crest harden. It had been years since her breasts had been so erotically caressed. Ruy's clumsy kneading had always left her cold. But this . . .

"You mustn't," she said weakly, bringing up her hands to push his head away. But they faltered as Miguel took the other nipple in his mouth, sucking with warm lips, his thumb gently manipulating the rosy peak he had just left. Her hands tangled in his hair as the old familiar, half-forgotten languor began to take possession of her body.

"Francisca, must I not?"

She did not answer, did not move as he finished stripping himself of doublet and breeches.

Then he was over her again, caressing, kissing, spreading her unresisting flanks. When he entered her, pressing deep inside, filling her as she hadn't been filled in six long years, she moaned, her senses expanding, reeling, taking wing. She surged against him, raising her hips, moving with him, linking her hands across the rippling muscles of his back, as if to draw him closer. He dug his chin into her shoulder, whispering words she could not catch. But words were meaningless in the torrent of sensations that tore through her. Her veins ran with molten lava, her bones melting in the heat; she would die of it, die happily. Miguel's thrusting grew wilder and wilder until, pulled into a revolving vortex, they were both suddenly thrown into blinding light.

For a long time nothing could be heard but their heavy breathing as Miguel's damp, perspiring body lay over hers. He was her lover, her love. Nothing, not even Miguel himself, had changed that. But it was a lost love, a hopeless one. Tears crowded her eyes and slipped from her closed lids before she was able to stop them. She must not weep. Above all she must not let Miguel know that he had triumphed again over her soul as well as her body.

"Please go now," she said when she could find her voice.

He rolled from her, raising himself on an elbow, trying to read her face in the dim light.

"You cannot mean that my lovemaking meant nothing to you."

"When it is over, what is left? The hottest of fires leaves nothing but ashes at the end."

He rose and silently got into his clothes. At the door he turned and gave her a hard, cold look. "I shall not trouble you again. If I need a bitch in heat, there are plenty for the taking."

Then he was gone.

Don Pedro was hard put to understand why Miguel del Castillo had refused his invitation to supper.

"He claims he has lost his influence with the royal commission and cannot help me," a puzzled Don Pedro told Ruy and Francisca. "And is too busy to take an evening off for a visit. A feeble excuse at best."

It was Friday night again. The family had spent a half hour in their secret place of worship, lighting the Sabbath candles and reciting a simple prayer. This time they had been led by Jorge, who had memorized the Eighteenth Psalm of David, "I love Thee, oh Lord, my strength . . ." while the family had followed his words, beaming at him with pride. Now they were at supper.

"Have you in some way insulted del Castillo?" Don Ruy asked.

Francisca sat with downcast eyes, tracing the pattern of the damask cloth with her spoon. She was still struggling with the need to warn the men that Miguel knew their true identity. She had been on the verge of confession more than once, but somehow had not been able to find the right words.

"I cannot think how I might have offended him," Don Pedro said. "Whatever it was, it could not have been too serious. He has given me the name of a merchant who might be instrumental in getting me a larger allotment of quicksilver than the Crown currently allows."

"The Crown." Don Ruy shook his head. "They are stifling trade with their monopolies, decrees, and senseless ordinances forbidding us to trade directly with England or France. If we could conduct business with foreigners, it would be to the advantage of the king in the long run. As it is, contraband trade flourishes to the detriment of honest folk."

Don Pedro sighed. "True. But it is not for us to question. We have not done badly despite the restrictions. And I, for one, am willing to let well enough alone."

Always, Francisca thought bitterly, we take the cautious approach, tiptoeing through life, afraid to antagonize the authorities in the slightest matter, fearful of calling attention to ourselves. But what else could they do? To challenge the Crown was treason, punishable by banishment, imprisonment, or a sentence to the galleys. For a Jew to do so was certain death.

"I have no reason to quarrel with things as they are, either," Don Ruy said with a smile. "A lovely wife, a son, one of the finest houses in Mexico City. What more could a man ask?"

What more? Francisca thought. Freedom to practice our own religion. Safety. The secure knowledge that they could not be harmed for what they thought. Tonight, Francisca promised herself, after we have gone to bed, I will tell Ruy.

But when they got home, Ruy said he wasn't tired enough to retire. "I'll sit with a book for an hour or two. Why don't you go up to bed?" he suggested. "I won't be too late."

Francisca fell asleep waiting for him, and when she woke some time later, he was already in bed beside her deep in slumber. She was resettling her pillow when a loud pounding on the door below echoed through the silent house.

Francisca's heart leaped into her throat. Who would come at this hour? Dear God!

More pounding, footsteps, voices. The hairs on the back of her neck stiffened.

A fusillade of ominous rat-a-tats again, a voice crying, "Open up in there! I say, open up in the name of God."

Terror shot through Francisca's veins. That which she had dreaded for so long had come about. She bounded out of bed and threw a cape about her shoulders. Ruy, sitting up, said, "What is it?"

Francisca did not answer, but lit a candle from the coals on the hearth and went out on the gallery. Leaning over the rail, she saw the doorman holding a lamp while Diego, the footman, drew the heavy bolt. The door swung open with a crash. A tall man, the constable, followed by four hooded figures in the livery of familiars with the frightening green cross of the Holy Office sewn on it, entered. One remained guarding the door while the three others stationed themselves upon the stairs.

"Where is Don Ruy de Diaz? Let him come forth at once!"

"He is not here," Francisca answered loudly, descending the staircase, flicking a look of disdain at the familiars. Petty volunteers, the lowliest officers of the Inquisition, they carried out their duties with nasty tyranny. "He is gone to Acapulco."

"Then search the house!"

As the familiars turned to obey orders, Don Ruy, fully dressed, appeared.

"There is no need for that," he said quietly. "I am here. What is your pleasure?"

"It is not for you to ask. Come with us."

"No!" Francisca cried, clinging to Ruy. "I won't let them take you!"

"My dear, the Lord, God, will protect me. Be brave."

She watched as he was escorted through the outer door, a

man who had never harmed a soul, squaring his thin shoulders against whatever would come.

The worst had happened. Miguel in his anger had finally betrayed them to the Inquisition. But it was she, Francisca, who was entirely to blame.

Chapter XI

One of the most terrifying aspects of the Inquisition was its secrecy. Once a prisoner had been taken, it was as if he (or she) had vanished from the face of the earth.

Those on the outside would have no communication with the accused; no letters, no messages, not so much as a whispered word would reach them from the charged who had disappeared behind the *Casa de la Inquisición* walls. Rumor would run rampant, but whether based on fact or fiction was impossible to ascertain. Family and friends lived in daily fear, for who knew what the imprisoned might say or who might be implicated under the relentless questioning—or torture—of jailers?

A tearful Francisca belatedly confessed her relationship with Miguel to her father. She had expected anger from him, a sweeping command to take her bastard and never show her face again. But Don Pedro was too crushed by events, too stunned by Ruy's arrest to do more than shake his head sadly. "Folly, my child, such folly. And see where it has brought us?"

He had become an old man overnight. The sight of his lined face, the hollowed eyes, trembling hands and voice, was a punishment far worse than his anger could have been.

Mariana wept silently, a sound that wrung Francisca's heart. It was Leonor who went into wild hysteria, screaming and laughing and tearing her hair.

"You must try to get hold of yourself, please, Leonor," Francisca begged.

She had gone up to her bedchamber with a jug of honeyed wine into which she had mixed a powder, hoping to put Leonor to sleep. But the moment Francisca stepped through the door, her sister, her hair streaming in wild disorder, began dashing about the room, flinging pillows, jars of ointment, and hairbrushes at Francisca.

"Sister, sister—you will harm yourself," Francisca pleaded, dodging the flying objects.

"Don't come near me!" Leonor screamed. "I won't go to jail. I won't! I'm a good Christian." She crossed herself swiftly, then went down on her knees. "See how I pray to the Holy Mother Mary. I am not a Jew, I swear it."

She put her head in her hands and began to sob. Francisca went and knelt beside her, gently taking the girl in her arms.

"It's going to be all right. All right," Francisca crooned.

"How?" Leonor lifted a tearstained face. "How can that be so?"

"Don Ruy will say nothing. They will ask him a few questions, then let him go."

"You know it isn't true. He will never meet his accusers. They will torture him. . . . Oh, Francisca, I couldn't bear it if—"

"Shhh!"

Mariana tried to persuade Don Pedro that the only recourse open to them now was to flee. (Juliana and Beatriz had departed posthaste the moment of Ruy's arrest for Juliana's daughter's house in Tacuba.) The family could slip out through the secret gate in the middle of the night with just the clothes on their backs, make their way to the port of Veracruz, and take ship for another country.

"And just how can we escape without being detected?"

Pedro asked. "A man or a pair of men, yes, but three women and a child? It is a ten-day journey, six if one does not tarry. And once we get to the port, what then? All ships sail to the Indies or Spain. The Crown has banned direct voyages to foreign ports. They would catch us like fish in a net."

"Then let us go into the interior," Mariana said. "To León or Taxco—or even into the jungle. They would never find us there."

"You don't know what you are saying, wife. If the Chichimec savages did not finish us off, the mosquitoes and wild animals would. Aside from that, we cannot desert Ruy. Believe me, Mariana, if there was some way I could spirit you womenfolk away, I would."

"Then we are doomed."

"Have you no faith in the Lord? He will see us through this ordeal."

Francisca wanted to tell her father that if God could see them through the ordeal of the Inquisition, then surely He could look after them as they tried to make their escape. Perhaps her father would consider such statements impious. She had caused enough misfortune. Best to hold her tongue. Yet she knew that if it were left to her, they would not remain in Mexico City.

What puzzled Francisca was why Miguel had chosen to report Ruy to the Holy Office, and not her or another member of the de Silva family. Was it because he was jealous of Ruy? Or was it an impersonal choice, a feeling that any one of them, once in custody, would break down and implicate the others?

The news of Don Ruy's arrest traveled quickly, leaving terror in its wake. A shout of "Plague!" in the streets could not have made the de Silva and de Diaz neighbors bolt their doors and windows with greater alacrity. Friends and business associates who had dined at Ruy's table now shunned the family, turning away to avoid meeting should they chance on them in the square or at church. When Don Pedro greeted his Christian friends, the de Bustos, at a city function, they looked through him as if he did not exist. They had heard his son-in-law was a *converso*, and however Catholic Don Pedro still pretended to be, it followed that he was tainted, too.

The Orozcos left Mexico City, vanished, no one knew where. Had they been arrested, too, or had they fled to the vast hinterland of New Spain? The Benavidos put a brave—some said brazen—face on it and went about their business as though nothing had happened. But they took care not to be seen in the company of the prisoner's family.

Don Pedro again reiterated to a distraught Mariana that it was futile to flee. To quiet her—and Leonor, who daily went into screaming and laughing fits—he contrived hiding places within the house. By hollowing out niches in the thick walls behind the paneling in each of the bedrooms, he managed to provide a temporary feeling of security. Now if the midnight knock came upon their door, they could conceal themselves.

Two weeks went by. Francisca moved into her parents' house, leaving empty the luxurious dwelling Ruy had so proudly bought for her. Three days after she had gone, agents of the Holy Office took possession of the de Diaz house, claiming it as property of the Inquisition. In addition, they confiscated Ruy's numerous holdings, his ranches and the shops he owned in the square, his horses, carriages, clothes, and what money they could find. Each candlestick, chest, rug, and peso appropriated was duly inscribed in an inventory that would be part of the judicial proceedings. Everything done by the Inquisition—arrest, trial, execution—was done according to prescribed ecclesiastical law, written down, and noted. Only the final punishment was made public.

Not knowing if Ruy was ill, broken by torture, or dead, a worried, guilt-ridden Francisca succeeded in bribing a guard to carry a message to her husband. "All is not lost," it read. "Believe in God and be brave." She was never told if Ruy ever received those encouraging words or if she had paid the bribe in vain.

Three weeks, almost to the day, the dreaded hollow pounding, the voice crying, "Open up!" came to the de Silva door again. The moment she heard it, Francisca, who had not had a restful night's sleep since Ruy's arrest, gathered Jorge in her arms and hid behind the paneling in her bedchamber.

Cowering in the narrow space, she held tightly to Jorge, who seemed to know instinctively that he wasn't to utter a sound. She could hear men's voices calling one to another, the slamming of doors, the stamping of boots on the stairs.

The door of Francisca's bedchamber crashed open. "Have a look under the beds!"

She heard the tearing of cloth and could visualize a familiar slashing the bed curtains, the portieres, the wall hangings. Lids were opened and slammed shut.

It was stifling in that small hole. Francisca tried to breathe shallowly, saving whatever air there was for Jorge. Sweat ran down her forehead and between her breasts, a cramp had formed in her right hip, but she dared not move.

"They're somewhere. By all that is holy, I'll find the pigs!" The voice was on the other side of the panel, inches away. Francisca's heart was beating like a drum, the loud thump-thump throbbing in her ears. Surely they must hear it? Any moment the panel would be torn open and she and Jorge exposed.

More footsteps and another voice, a gruff one like the croak of a frog. "They have fled. There are no servants, only an old crone in the kitchen who is stone-deaf."

"We shall have to dispatch a rider to Veracruz," another voice said, "and send the alarm to all the villages round about should they have gone by another route."

Francisca heard the door leading to the street below close. After that she waited a long while before she ventured out.

Wiping Jorge's brow with the hem of her skirt, she told him over and over, "You were the best of boys. A little man."

He put his small arms around her neck. "Will they hurt us, Mamá?"

Always the same question, and the answer, of necessity, always false.

"No, *hijo mío*. I will not let anyone harm you."

Leonor had again gone into a state of shock, this time a silent one. As the family gathered in the shuttered dining room the next morning to break their fast, she sat staring into space with vacant eyes. No coaxing, no tender words, could bring her out of her trance. She did not (or did not want to) recognize anyone.

"They believe we are gone," Don Pedro said. "And we must not do anything that would persuade them otherwise. No lights, no fires, no stirring beyond the inner confines of the house. We have enough food to last several weeks, a month, perhaps two, if we eat sparingly."

"And then?" Mariana asked. Already she seemed to have grown thinner, folds of once rosy flesh creased in sallow dewlaps under her chin.

"Why, then," Don Pedro said, "they may have forgotten about us."

"And if they haven't forgotten?"

He leaned over and patted her hand. "We must put our trust in God, Mariana."

Francisca would have liked a more concrete, less nebulous answer. She only wished that her faith was as strong as her father's.

"Papá," she said. "We are already under siege, prisoners of the Holy Office whether we wish it or not."

"Being a prisoner in our own home is a far cry from being thrust into a jail cell. Let us hope that God in His infinite mercy will spare us from such a calamity. But if this is not God's wish and we are apprehended, we must face our enemies with fortitude and admit nothing."

The following day while they were in the shuttered dining room eating a simple noon meal, the outer door was bombarded once more with the blows of a demanding fist. There were a few moments of startled silence, each questioning the other with a look, for the agents of the Holy Inquisition had not come in daylight before. Then Francisca scrambled to her feet and, pulling a bewildered, frightened Jorge by the hand, made for the stairs. Mariana, with Leonor in tow, was right behind her; Don Pedro, breathing hard, brought up the rear.

As she hurried up the stairs, Francisca's face burned with an indignation that momentarily replaced her fear. To run like rabbits at a knock on the door, the proud de Silvas reduced to scurrying, hunted animals. God, if she had a sword, she would unbar the door and slash at the first to enter. It was a wild fantasy, and she knew it. She couldn't fight back. They would not only kill her outright, but slaughter the others as well.

From down below came the sound of a battering ram. Francisca reached her hiding place just as the door crashed open. A few moments later the heavy-booted familiars were boiling up the staircase. Again she heard the slamming of doors, voices calling one to another.

Then suddenly Leonor, from behind the protective paneling in her bedchamber, began to scream.

In a matter of minutes, the others were dragged from their cubbyholes and brought down to the patio.

They were roughly handled, their arms tied securely behind them. Leonor fainted and had to be carried from the house. Mariana wept; Pedro, trying to console her, was dealt a blow across the mouth that sent him reeling. Jorge, the only one left unshackled, flew to his mother's side, only to be torn away.

"You can't!" Francisca screamed, struggling to free herself. "Turn me loose! Jorge! What are you going to do with my child?"

"Never fear," said the one with the frog's voice, his small, bloodshot eyes raking Francisca, "he will be given to a good Catholic family. In time he will forget he was ever a pig of a Jew."

As the familiars started to lead their prisoners away, Francisca balked, trying once more to reach her son. For her pains she was rewarded by a slash of the whip across her back. She had one last view of his tearstained face as he was hoisted into the arms of a mounted familiar.

"Mamá!"

It was a cry for help, a baffled wail, a desperate plea to his mother not to forsake him. She had promised that no harm would come to him, promised she would protect him. And now they had taken him from her, to do God alone knew what. More than anything that happened, this cruel separation was the hardest to bear.

She had never hated Miguel as much as she hated him at that moment.

They placed Francisca in solitary confinement. The cell was small, cold, and damp. The only light came from a high slitted window and a crude oil lamp, a feeble wick afloat on a saucer of rancid oil. A slop jar in one corner exuded a foul odor. In another corner a heap of dirty straw stirred with the movements of what she suspected were rats. There was a stool, a rough table, and a dirty tick mattress that Francisca soon found was infested with fleas.

When she asked after her father, mother, and sister, she was answered with a shrug. A meal was brought to her the first night, thin, greasy gruel with chunks of pork swimming about in it. Pork was forbidden under Hebraic law, and she would not touch it. But when she realized that this was a test, that her jailers, well aware of the Jewish dietary laws, had purposely given her this dish, she consumed it.

Afterward she had second thoughts. She must decide how she would answer the inquisitors when they began their questioning. Should she admit she was a Jewess, but one who was anxious to renounce her faith and embrace the church? By doing so, some fortunate souls were able to escape the stake, receiving minor punishment. In these cases the accused were required to wear penitential garments, the sanbenitos, and to renounce their own faith in favor of Catholicism.

Or should she deny ever having been a follower of Judaism? It would be a useless lie, since Don Ruy must have confessed enough to implicate them all. She did not blame her husband. Stronger men than he had been broken by the relentless questioning or brought to cringing confession by fear of the torture chamber. She herself did not know how steadfast she could be if she were hung from the ceiling by weights, said to be one of the preferred methods for breaking a heretic since it did not draw blood.

Francisca had no wish to be a martyr. On the other hand, she was determined to try her best not to crawl or beg for mercy. For her mother and her poor sister she would ask clemency, but not for herself. Yet despite the resolution to be courageous and stand up to her accusers, she was terrified. Fear was like a winding sheet, wrapping itself with cold, clammy fingers about her body, and chilling her heart. That first terrible night in the flickering darkness she went on her knees and silently prayed for strength.

Soon Francisca lost count of time. She had no idea whether it was day or night, morning or noon. She could have been in prison a day or a week. When the light in the dish went out, she banged her fists upon the door and cried out for another. Darkness, total Stygian blackness, was the enemy of hope, and she fought it with every ounce of her faith, fought it with thoughts of her family, who were suffering because of her, fought it with thoughts of Jorge and how she must outwit the inquisitors so she could be reunited with him.

In the past her jailer appeared at the door at regular intervals bearing food. Sometimes he removed the slop jar and brought her an empty one, sometimes he did not. Francisca's request for a light, like her request for news of her family, was met with silence. The warder was a shrunken man with a limp and, Francisca believed, without a tongue. She was beginning to think he was deaf as well as mute when, after a short spell, he materialized with another crude oil lamp. Emboldened by this charitable act, Francisca asked for pen and ink. To her surprise, these were also brought. She set about writing notes to her mother and father, not knowing until later that these missives were delivered directly to the inquisitors in the hope that they would further incriminate the de Silvas.

In her letters to her parents she begged for their forgiveness. "Tell them nothing," she advised. "They have only arrested you on suspicion. It is me they are after."

Francisca was not entirely sure this was true. But it was the only thing she could think of that might lift their spirits.

It was not knowing what was happening to them, what had happened to Ruy, where they had taken Leonor or Jorge, that was her constant torment. The unrelieved dimness, her inability to keep clean, the stench, she could somehow bear, but to be held in ignorance as to the welfare of her loved ones sent her to pacing the littered floor. She tried to pray again, but now the only prayer she could remember was one of David's psalms, "My God, my God, why has Thou forsaken me?"

Yet why should God listen to her particular plea? Why single her out of the hordes of sufferers, those innocents afflicted with the loathsome diseases, the maimed, the weak and defenseless, the widows and orphans? Why should she put the blame on God? It was a human mind, not God, who had designed the Inquisition; it was she, Francisca, who had loved Miguel and, in a moment of unbridled anger, had betrayed her family's secret.

If only she could make amends. If only she could somehow extricate them from this horrible situation. But how? Escape, even for herself, was impossible. The cell in which her jailers had put her was like a sealed tomb. The window was too high and narrow; the timbered door was without a grating and bolted from the outside. She had already gone over the floor and walls, inch by inch, trying to find a place

where a plank might have been pried loose, a hole gouged
out. How that would help her, she did not exactly know. To
tunnel her way out of the prison with only a lamb bone or
the pins in her hair as tools would take years. But it was
better than pacing the floor and wringing her hands.

She was examining the door for the third time when she
discovered a peephole in the rotting wood about six inches
above her head. Apparently it had been made by someone
taller than herself. But by standing on the stool and putting
her eye to the splintered hole, she could see the corridor
beyond. In terms of escape, the hole did not mean much, but
to Francisca it was like the opening of a window on the
world. Now when she heard footsteps, she could run to her
peephole and look out to see who was passing by.

The first afternoon she saw her mother, flanked by a familiar on either side, being led along the corridor, she wanted
to cry out. Were they taking her to the audience hall or to the
torture chamber? Mariana looked ill, her face a sickly yellow, her walk slow, like that of an old, old woman. To stand
there and watch her pass so close and not be able to give her
a few words of comfort, to touch or embrace her, was agony
for Francisca. She clung to the door, her neck twisting, her
eye straining, until the three figures disappeared from view.

She kept to her post, hoping that her mother would pass
again. While she waited, there suddenly arose the same aw-
ful, bloodcurdling screams, the cries for mercy, that she had
heard before. "God pity me! Pity me! Have mercy!" It
sounded like a woman's voice. Francisca was sure now that
her mother had been brought to the torture chamber. The
thought of her sweet, gentle mother tied to knotted ropes that
were twisted tighter and tighter on her body sickened and
enraged her.

She began to strike the door with her fists. "Beasts!
Beasts!" Tears streamed down her face, her hair tumbled to
her shoulders, her fists turned bloody, and yet she went on
pounding. Other prisoners took up the cry, and soon the

corridor echoed with shouts, thumps, bangings, and whackings. Suddenly a shout could be heard above the tumult.

"Be still! Quiet! Or I'll have the hides off your backs." The sound of a cracking whip echoing along the corridor brought Francisca's eye to the peephole. She saw a powerfully built man disappear into one of the cells, and a moment later she heard the agonizing cries of some poor soul paying for his fleeting outrage under the lash. When the warden reappeared, Francisca was horrified to realize that it was Gaspar. So he hadn't drowned! What was he doing here, a servant of the Holy Office, a man as godless as any brown-skinned pagan? She watched, mesmerized with fear, listening to the stinging crack of the whip and the bleating screams of the punished as Gaspar went from cell to cell.

When she knew she would be next, she got down from the stool. Smoothing her hair, she twisted it into a knot on her neck and stood in the center of the cell, waiting.

It took him a few moments, squinting in the gloom, before he recognized her.

"So it is you, señora!" His face broke into a grin. "What a surprise! I was planning to pay you a little visit, and now you are here. What luck. What have you done? Blaspheme? Slept with your neighbor's husband? Or are you a Judaizer?"

When she did not answer, he came toward her, slapping the butt of the whip in his hand. "Or could it be attempted murder?"

He had left the door open, and Francisca, dodging his bulk, made a dive for it. The whip snaked out and caught her around the waist before she could get a foot over the threshold. He laughed, his donkey's laugh, yanking at the whip, pulling and dragging her back so violently, she lost her balance and fell at his feet. He brayed again. Then, while she lay panting, he stepped to the door and slammed it shut.

"Now we shall have the fun we missed at the canal. Remember?"

She untangled herself from the whip, scrambling to her feet, looking about wildly.

"You're caught, my little pigeon," he said, advancing slowly, reaching out to her. "No tricks to play here, eh?"

She dodged behind the table as if that flimsy, rickety piece of furniture could protect her. He was right. She had no weapon, not even an eating bowl she could fling at him. There was nowhere to run, no one to help her. She could scream and scream until her throat went raw, but in this hell, what was one more scream?

"I shall tell the judges," she challenged. "They will not like it if I were harmed before they had a chance to question me."

"Easy enough to say that you tried to escape. You did, just this last moment. I can do with you as I please."

He moved closer to the table, savoring her trembling fear, licking his lips in anticipation. She picked up the crude oil lamp and threw it at him with all her strength. His arm went up, an oath breaking from his lips as burning oil splattered over his face and hair. Then, diving forward, he dragged Francisca across the table, bringing it with her in a shambles of sundered wood.

The lamp's wick, by freakish happenstance, floating in a tiny puddle of oil, had not gone out but gutted and wavered on the floor, giving enough light for Francisca to see Gaspar's features contorted with rage. He held her, face-to-face, for a few moments, then turning her, threw her against the wall. Her forehead hitting it sent wave shocks of pain rebounding in her skull. Stunned, she clutched at the grimy plaster, her nails digging hard to prevent her from falling again.

"Bitch, bitch," he muttered.

She heard the crack of the whip, and the next moment it was singing through air, striking her back, a razor-sharp agony that made her cry out. Again and again the whip slashed at her, ripping through her gown, laying the tender flesh bare, raising a bloody wetness along her naked skin. Pain engulfed her, a red mist, a scarlet lake in which she felt herself drowning, fighting for breath, clinging to a fast-ebbing consciousness.

Then suddenly the wick went out, plunging the room into darkness. Gaspar swore, cursing Francisca, lashing out at her again in the blackness. But she had slid along the wall out of reach. She could hear him stumbling about, uttering a string of maledictions, groping, searching for her. A crash and clatter brought a fresh flood of curses as he fell over the rubble of the upended table.

Her hand to her mouth, not daring to draw breath, Francisca waited for the sound of his movements. She heard his heavy breathing slowly ebb. Then silence. Had he been knocked senseless by his fall? On tiptoe, taking care not to make a sound, she inched toward the door. She was within reach of it when, with a sudden wild cry, Gaspar caught her skirts.

Flinging her to the floor, he fell over her, his suffocating weight grinding her face into the dirty straw. He straddled her, turning her over, chuckling, wheezing at her futile, weak struggles. She felt him fumbling at his breeches, his hardness bucking at her stomach. Then he was rucking up her skirts and petticoats over her thighs.

She tried to scream, but all that came out was a muffled groan. *God help me, help me!* her mind begged.

Then suddenly a burst of light angled across the cell as the door was flung open. Gaspar, blinking, turned. A black-clad figure strode into the room. Before Gaspar could get his dazed wits about him, he was lifted from Francisca. Without uttering a word, the intruder plunged a knife into Gaspar's heart. Falling, he toppled over Francisca's legs.

The black-clad figure kicked him free, then helped Francisca to her feet. Though her rescuer's face remained in shadow, she saw by his habit that he was a Dominican friar.

"Did the jackal harm you?"

For a long moment Francisca could not speak. That voice . . . !

"I should have killed him long ago," the friar said, moving to the door.

Francisca stood on weak and trembling legs, her hand at

her mouth. Could it be? Or had she sunk into some kind of feverish dream. "Miguel?"

He turned on the threshold, his face in full light. No dream. It was Miguel.

Chapter XII

"Jailer!" Miguel called from the doorway.

The little man with the bowed legs came running. "I want this cadaver removed."

"But, Friar, where am I to put him?"

"It matters not. Throw him on a dung heap, for all I care. He has paid for a heinous crime, attempted rape under God's roof."

"Aye." The little man peered past Miguel, his eyes squinching up. "I'll need help. He's a big one."

"Get it, then, and be quick. And while you're about it, fetch me a candle, a basin of clean—*clean*—water, and a cloth."

Francisca, feeling weak, had seated herself on the stool and was distractedly fumbling with her fallen hair, trying to twist it into a knot at the nape of her neck. Stunned, in pain, she still groped for comprehension. It was all so confusing: Miguel's sudden appearance, and in a Dominican's habit. What did it mean?

"Did that dog harm you?" Miguel had turned from the door. The question was an echo of a similar one he had asked long ago.

"Only with the whip. Miguel . . ." The name felt odd on

her tongue. He had his back to the light. She could barely make out his features. "Miguel, how came you here?"

"In a moment I shall tell you. Ah, here is our candle and water. Jailer, I am present on secret orders from the archbishop. Should you speak of this episode, you will answer to him. Do you heed me?"

The bowlegged man and his assistant, a tall, heavily bearded warder, nodded mutely, then each taking one of Gaspar's legs, dragged him from the cell.

Miguel, setting the candle on the floor, knelt behind Francisca and silently began to wash the wounds on her back. His touch sent a shiver through her, but apparently mistaking her reaction for pain, he said nothing. His hands wiping the blood from her lashed back seemed impersonal, like those of a physician or Sister of Charity. The murmurs of sympathy she might have expected were not voiced. He had rescued her from rape, killed a man for her, and was now ministering to her wounds, yet he seemed strangely remote.

"The habit," Francisca asked, breaking the silence. "Have you taken vows?"

"A disguise. It was the only way I could get inside the Flat House. The so-called secret orders from the archbishop were for the jailers' benefit—a lie to buy their silence."

He touched a welt that hurt worse than the others, and she gave an involuntary gasp.

"Am I too rough?" he asked, a warm question without warmth.

"No, oh, no."

She wondered about his apparent coolness. But there were more troubling questions. Why, for a man who had connections in high places, was it necessary for him to wear a disguise in order to gain admittance to the prison? Why was he here?

Then, as if in answer to her unspoken question, he said, "Francisca, I am going to find a way to bring you out. At present I have no plan, but I will think of one."

"Take me out? Oh, Miguel, is it true?" Francisca's mind

spun. She could hardly believe her ears. He had come to free her. She never dreamed that Miguel, who had been the cause of her imprisonment, would be the instrument of her release. Why was he doing this? If he hated her as a Jew, why should he want to interfere with the trial and judgment of the Inquisition? Was he a spy?

"I don't understand," she went on, perplexed. "The last time we met you were repelled because I was a Judaizer. I haven't changed."

He got to his feet and looked down at her. "No. I suppose you haven't. We won't discuss it now. I must hurry, Francisca. If I linger too long, they will suspect something. Where is the boy?"

"I don't know. They took Jorge from me and said they would give him to a Christian family."

"Which family?"

"I don't know," she repeated, her hand kneading her skirts, the agonizing memory of her parting with Jorge suddenly washing over her. She saw and heard it all again: the fear in Mariana's eyes, the hooded familiars on the stairs, the constable's implacable face, her sister's mad laughter, her father's pleas, and her child's anguished cries.

"Oh, Miguel." She looked blindly up at him, immersed in that terrible vision as if she could still smell the stale, sweaty odor of her captors. "I promised to protect him, and I failed. The look on his face when the familiar pulled him from me—" Her voice broke, and for a few moments she could not speak past the constriction in her throat. "I shall never forget it. He wept, Miguel. He's only five. He didn't understand. He cried, and it was all my fault."

If Francisca expected Miguel to reassure her, to say that she was blameless, she was wrong.

"You have no idea where they took him? No clue as to whom he was given?"

"None. They tell me nothing here."

"I *must* find him. I was hoping that you would know. I

have friends in the city—but to question openly is dangerous. Still, I will have to run that risk. Somehow I'll manage it.''

"My freedom will mean little unless I have Jorge." Francisca clasped her fingers tightly. When he remained silent. she continued.

"Miguel, much has happened. My husband was the first to be imprisoned.'' She paused, then went on in a rush. "I was at my parents' house when the bailiffs came after us. Leonor broke under the strain and went mad. She was carried from the house, to where I do not know. My father and mother . . .'' She bit her lip. "I saw my poor mother pass in the corridor; I heard her cries from the torture chamber. Better . . .'' She swallowed, trying to gain control, and failed. Oh, Miguel, she wanted to sob, why did you do it? What made you inform on people who never did you harm?

"Francisca—I cannot tarry.''

"Wait—you say you will free me. I am grateful, but I cannot leave without my mother and father and my husband.''

"Your husband is dead.''

Francisca stared into Miguel's eyes, her own wide with shock.

"He died under torture.''

"He . . . died. . . . You are certain? God help us! Such a fine, decent man.''

Miguel's jaw stiffened, a hot blue light flared up in his eyes, then faded, leaving them empty of expression, but she was too distraught to notice. She had not loved Ruy, but he had been more than kind. He had been solicitous and caring, even as her father had been. She had only to express a desire for some trinket, a rug, a necklace, or a book, and it was hers. When she was pregnant he had urged her to remain in bed of a morning, dismissing her maid, waiting on her, with his own hands bringing a tray with her breakfast of chocolate and comfits, cosseting her, a woman who was carrying another man's child.

"To the last he refused to recant," Miguel was saying, his voice empty of emotion.

"He was steadfast? God bless him! I thought under duress he might implicate us further."

"My informant tells me that he tried to protect you."

She pressed her hand to her mouth. Tears stung her eyes, clung to her lashes. Poor, poor Ruy. To die in horrible pain with his lips sealed. "He was not a strong man physically," she said in a muffled voice. "But no weakling when it came to courage."

Miguel gave her a sharp look. "You have my condolences. You must have loved him very much."

"He was a hard man to dislike." She wiped her tears with the back of her hand. Now was not the time to go into the niceties of like and love. So much tragedy, so many things to weep bitter tears for.

"And what of my mother?" she asked, her throat raw with grief. "Please God, she isn't dead, too."

"I know nothing of your mother. But I will try to find out what has happened to her. Your father also."

"I cannot leave this place without them."

"I will see what can be done, Francisca. I go now. When I have found Jorge I will be back with a plan. I'm sure you realize how important it is to say nothing of this visit."

"Yes . . . and Miguel—"

"Francisca, there isn't time to talk. One last word of advice. If the inquisitors question you, perhaps it would be best to admit you have erred, that—"

"No! Never!" she interrupted in a choking voice. "Admit and have Ruy's death on my conscience? Never!"

Again she wanted to ask why he had come, but he was at the door, impatient to leave. "What day is this?" she asked.

"Tuesday." And the door closed behind him.

Tuesday, she thought dazedly. I must keep an account of time, a mark, a tally of some kind. She took a pin from her hair and scratched a slash upon the wall. How many of these would she have to make before his return?

She sat down on the stool, clasping her knees. It was difficult for her to believe that Miguel had been here in this dismal, dank dungeon, Miguel in the flesh come to rescue her. It all seemed so unreal. Perhaps it was because he had acted like a stranger. The Dominican garb, the cool, impersonal voice. Except for cleansing her wounds, he made no effort to touch her. Not one intimate word had been spoken. Her tears for Ruy had only elicited an impersonal "My condolences." There had been no apologies for his former behavior, no explanations, nothing said that referred to the past and what they had once been to each other. She had not realized until now how much she had wanted him to take her in his arms, how she had longed to lay her cheek against his strong chest, to hear him whisper soothing words.

If only he had said, "I'm sorry, I still love you." But he hadn't. She must take comfort from his promise that as soon as he found Jorge, he would make plans to rescue her and her family. Why he should make such a dangerous effort, she did not know. It puzzled her. If he had informed on Ruy, putting them all in jeopardy, then why had he suddenly decided to save them from the Inquisition, which he, and all nobles like himself, had sworn to uphold? Second thoughts? An uneasy conscience? Some faint remnant of love. Whatever his reasons, she prayed God that he would succeed.

Yet behind her reasoned self-assurance a thought kept nagging like the dull ache of a sore tooth. The abyss that separated her from Miguel remained unbridged. He was still a devout Catholic, she a secret Jew.

A week went by. The tiny slashes on the cell wall marking each morning grew from seven to fourteen. And still no sign of Miguel. Francisca, impatient for his return, took to pacing her cell. Back and forth, ten steps to one dirt-blackened wall, ten to another. What was taking so long? She tried to learn from her jailer what was happening to her parents, but the little, bowlegged man turned mute on her again.

Then one morning, after her jailer had delivered her breakfast of tortillas and water, two familiars entered her cell.

"Come with us."

The commanding voice, the sight of the sacklike livery sewn with the Inquisition's hated green crosses, put a cold finger on her spine.

"Where are you taking me?" Francisca asked in a firm voice that gave no hint of the sudden lurching beat of her heart.

"The judges wish to question you."

Francisca threw a ragged shawl about her shoulders to cover her torn gown. Then, head erect, she went out between the two familiars, marching down the corridor with one on either side. They walked in silence, past closed doors behind which voices groaned or sobbed, then up a short flight of stairs.

She was ushered into a large room lit by torches and gray daylight streaming in from a high, barred window. Two judges dressed in dark, loose garments and wearing brimless, high-crowned hats sat with a scribe at a table placed on a dais. In front of them was a brass casting of Christ on the cross. Another man, beak-nosed with small, piercing eyes, sat a little distance from the table under one of the four posted arches that supported the ceiling. There was something about him that seemed vaguely familiar to Francisca, but she could not remember where she had seen his face.

Except for the table and the chairs on which her interrogators were seated, there were no furniture, no rugs on the cold tile floor, and only a large crucifix for decoration on the walls. It was a bare, chilly, intimidating place.

Francisca was led to the center of the room, where she remained standing, facing the table.

One of the judges spoke to the man seated under the arch. "Señor Lopez, you may proceed."

When Señor Lopez rose, Francisco recognized him as the inquisitorial prosecuting attorney who had carried the gold-tasseled banner in the *auto de fe*. Tall, thin, with a chalklike

face, his appearance here turned Francisca's hands to ice.
She remembered his thundering denunciation as he read the
verdicts imposed on the condemned heretics. Pictures of their
pitiable, suffering faces rose before her. Had they foreshad-
owed her own doom?

Señor Lopez approached her with a large crucifix in his
hand. "Swear by God, our Good Lord, Jesus, and the Holy
Ghost that you will tell the truth else God strike you dead
and remand your soul to hell for all eternity."

Francisca, clenching her fists at her side, forcing herself
not to betray any of the terror she felt, swore in a loud, clear
voice, telling herself that *her* God would forgive any lies she
might say under duress.

"Please state your name, age, birthdate, whether married
or not."

Francisca answered truthfully. The scribe's pen scratched
across the parchment.

"Please name the members of your family, husband, children, mother, father, sisters and brothers, and so on."

Again the scribe took note. The Inquisition already had
this information. How much more they knew or were able to
wring from Ruy, she could not guess. Miguel, of course, had
known nothing but that the de Silvas were Judaizers.

The prosecuting attorney, took a step closer to Francisca.
His eyes had a feverish gleam, the hunter stalking the hunted.

"Are you a *converso*?"

The key question, point-blank. She would have liked to
admit it, shout yes! proudly. But she remembered her father's
admonition. Admit nothing.

"I am a de Silva. I come from old Christian stock. My
father was born in Toledo, my mother in Seville. On both
sides they are descended from Spanish Catholics without a
trace of Moorish or Jewish blood."

The judges, bearded men, one with a high forehead and
pinched nostrils, the other with sagging jowls and pock-
marked skin, fixed twin gazes on Francisca.

"Do you know why you have been imprisoned?" the prosecutor asked.

"I can only surmise that someone, jealous of our position and wanting our property, has falsely testified against us."

The judge with the pockmarked face motioned to the prosecutor, who went back to his chair. The judge said: "Let me remind you that it is not customary for the Holy Office to arrest anyone without ample cause. Your presence here signifies that there is an accumulation of incriminating evidence against you."

He paused. Francisca's legs ached. Her face felt like a frozen mask. Yet she dared not show any sign of weakness, any hint of fear. To do so would be to concede guilt.

"You are admonished to unburden your conscience," the judge with the pockmarked face went on, "and disclose the truth by making full confession. By doing so, you will earn the mercy of the Holy Office. If you do not confess, know that justice will be done."

Francisca straightened her shoulders and answered in a clear, carrying voice. "How should I confess when I have committed nothing against the Holy Church either in words or deeds?"

The prosecutor took up the interrogation again. "You are the wife of Don Ruy de Diaz?'

"I am."

"He is an admitted Judaizer and tells us that you and he practiced rites according to the law of Moses."

They were trying to trap her. They were unaware that she knew of Ruy's death, that he had acknowledged his Judaic faith but had protested that his wife and her family were innocent.

"Under torture," Francisca said, "a man will say anything. Don Ruy knew—knows," she hastily corrected, "that we were entirely ignorant of his heretic beliefs."

The prosecutor tried another tactic. "You have an aunt, Juliana Torres?"

"She is my father's sister."

"And she, like Don Ruy, is a Judaizer?"

"I have always found her to be a devout Christian."

"Don Ruy informs us otherwise."

"Then he is speaking again under duress."

"Where is Juliana Torres to be found?"

Juliana, together with Beatriz, she hoped, had remained in hiding in Tacuba. Or perhaps they had sought a safer refuge in a village nearby.

"She is now living in León," Francisca lied without hesitation. Let them travel the breadth of Mexico searching for her on a wild-goose chase.

"Señora, what is Beatriz Reyes to you?"

"A second cousin on my mother's side."

"She has also been accused as a Judaizer."

"By whom?"

Señor Lopez threw her a scathing look. "That we cannot say. Please answer." The expression on his bloodless-lipped face made no attempt to disguise his hostility. "Do you know her as a Judaizer?"

Again Francisca replied in the negative.

"Where is she living now?"

"I do not know."

The judges and Señor Lopez conferred in low voices. Francisca waited, debating whether it would be politic to ask after her father and mother. Would they tell her the truth? Most likely not. In all probability they would say that both Mariana and Pedro had confessed, implicating her. This was the way of the Inquisition: divide and conquer.

Señor Lopez said, "For now we remand you to your cell. We advise you to think about your situation. Full confession and the mercy of the court, or holding back and just punishment. I caution you, there is no escape from these alternatives."

Francisca spent the next week again pacing her cell, hurrying to the peephole each time she heard a footstep in the corridor. Once she saw her mother, the flesh hanging from her in ugly folds, her eyes sunk in their sockets, shuffling like an aged crone between two familiars. A sob caught in Francisca's throat. The torture chamber again? She waited at the door, her heart beating violently. But she heard no sound, no cries, and a short time later she observed her mother being escorted back to her cell.

It was agony not being able to speak to her mother, agony not knowing how much she had revealed. And what of her father? Was he going through the same suffering, the same torture?

Francisca could not understand why Miguel had failed to reappear. What was taking so long? Had he been unable to locate Jorge? She told herself that the boy may have been sent to another city, perhaps a hacienda some distance from Mexico City. Even so, three weeks had passed. And time was not on the de Silvas' side. If their incarceration continued much longer, her mother would not survive. And God alone knew what had happened to her father. Perhaps, like Ruy, he was already dead.

Another week went by, and still no sign of Miguel. Francisca cautioned herself not to lose hope. Miguel had important connections in the city, his uncle was the grand inquisitor of Seville, he had friends in high places. If anyone could arrange an escape—or perhaps, pardon—he could.

She was called again to the audience chamber. The same two judges, the same Señor Lopez, and the same scribe were waiting for her.

"I remind you that you are still under oath," the prosecuting attorney warned her.

Francisca had been told by the familiars who escorted her that Señor Lopez was noted for his particular zeal in bringing Judaizers to justice. Not one heretic under his jurisdiction had ever escaped punishment.

He rose now and addressed her. "Doña Francisca de Diaz, if you wish to be represented, this court will appoint an attorney."

"May I ask if it's possible to have a lawyer of my own choosing?"

"Only if you select one among those connected with the Holy Office."

As she guessed. They would appoint a defense lawyer who would attempt to pry an admission from her that she was a secret Jew, advising her that for the safety of her eternal soul, it would be best to tell the truth.

"Then I must refuse," Francisca said.

Señor Lopez inclined his head toward the scribe to make certain this statement was recorded. Then, turning to Francisca again and fixing her with burning eyes, he asked, "Do your mother, father, and sister observe the Mosaic laws?"

"No. They observe the faith of Jesus Christ."

"How do you know they observe the faith of Jesus Christ?"

"Because they attend mass regularly and pray to Jesus Christ and our Mother Mary."

There was a long pause. Señor Lopez strode to the table where the two judges sat and picked up a key.

"Do you recognize this?"

"It is a key," Francisca said coolly, though her heart sank at the sight of it.

"I have been informed that this is a key to a secret gate in the garden by which friends and relatives came to rites held in the storeroom of your parents' house."

Who had told him? Ruy? But Ruy had died without giving his interrogators the information they sought. Leonor in a maniacal rage? But it didn't seem possible that these diligent servants of the Holy Office would give credence to a madwoman's ravings. Had it been her mother under torture?

"I know of no such key," Francisca said, stubborn in her determination not to cooperate by acknowledging in the slightest way anything they called "evidence."

"The key was kept in a hollowed-out book, *Saint John of the Cross*. Does that shake your memory?"

"I know of no such key," Francisca repeated.

"I am also told," Señor Lopez went on relentlessly, "that the Orozcos, the Benavidos, and the Rodriguezes attended your secret meetings."

Someone had implicated their friends. More and more she believed it must have been her mother. Poor Mariana.

After a long, chilling silence, the judge with the pock-marked face spoke up in a voice that had all the ironclad authority of the Grand Inquisition of Spain behind it. "If you confess, the court will be merciful."

"I have nothing to confess," she said quietly, the lies she had told sitting lightly on her conscience. She had no allegiance to these men, no allegiance to their faith. It was false and deserved false answers. "What I have said is the truth."

The next day she was again escorted to the audience chamber. She stood as tall as her height would allow, hoping that her air of dignified innocence had not diminished, though cold, sick fear had settled like a permanent ball in her stomach. She knew she had lost weight by the way her gown hung on her. Despite the lack of facilities, she had tried to keep clean by using her drinking water to wash. She had no mirror; nevertheless, she had sought to maintain a tidy appearance, combing her hair with her fingers and pinning it in a knot at the back of her slender neck. For all that, she felt haggard and exhausted. Only her faith in God and her hope for Miguel's return stayed the darkness that sometimes threatened to overwhelm her.

Señor Lopez held a sheaf of papers in his hand. "Again I call on you, Francisca de Diaz y Roche, to reveal to this court what you know."

"I have told you all, señor."

"Then you leave us no alternative. The inquisitorial board has voted unanimously to remand you to the secular arm, which will subject you to torture. We pray that if you die or be maimed in the said torture or if there ensues an effusion of blood or mutilation of flesh or limb, the burden will be upon you and not us."

Francisca was then ignominiously stripped, her gown and petticoats removed by rough hands. To protest, to struggle, would only rob her of her last shred of dignity. She stood rigid, pretending she was a conquered warrior of noble blood who was being divested of sword and dagger. Dressed in a sanbenito, flanked by the familiars, and led by the two judges, the scribe, and the prosecutor, she moved down the corridor to the torture chamber.

Not a muscle in her face betrayed anything but stony fortitude. Pride forbade her to show her feelings. But she was afraid, terrified not so much of the pain as of what she might do when put to the test. She tried to prepare herself by reciting a silent prayer, begging God to give her strength. But when the procession reached its destination, Francisca gasped in horror.

Her mother, her dear, sweet mother, dressed in the cloth of shame, was stretched and tied to the torture frame.

Francisca, breaking loose from the familiars, went down on her knees at her mother's side. "What have they done to you, Mamá?"

Her mother's blue lips forced a faint smile. "They have not broken my will, daughter," she whispered hoarsely. "I have told them again and again that I am a believer of Jesus Christ."

A familiar dragged Francisca to her feet. So it wasn't her mother who had told them about the key, its hiding place, the secret gate, and the services held in the storeroom. Who, then? Her father? But Pedro was the least likely of them all to cooperate with the inquisitors.

And yet, Francisca thought, looking about the gray, high-domed room, the hooded familiars standing by their instruments, the water basins, the contents of which would be poured down a victim's throat, simulating drowning, the pulleys and weights used to drag at some poor wretch hanging from the ceiling, and the fire on the hearth with which to burn feet—how can anyone withstand this?

A man dressed in clerical garb entered the room. Another

inquisitor, Francisca thought. He stood over Mariana, making the sign of the cross. "Doña Mariana, I again admonish you to tell the truth."

Mariana turned her head aside. The inquisitor gave a sign, and the hooded familiars on either side of Mariana twisted the sticks attached to the ropes that bound her body.

"Have mercy," Mariana begged, moaning pitifully. "Oh, God in Heaven, have mercy. I have told you everything I know."

The inquisitor inclined his head, and the ropes were twisted tighter. Francisca's mother groaned, then screamed.

Francisca went to her knees. This is my torture, she thought. This is why they have brought me here. To see my mother put to the rack. I can bear anything—the knotted cord, the weights, the burning brand, the water cure—but not this.

The inquisitor spoke for the third time and gave the order for another excruciating twist of the ropes. Mariana's scream was heartrending. Her eyes bulged, and thin streams of blood began to ooze from the places where her skin had been broken.

"Leave her be!" Francisca shouted. "In God's name, leave her be! I will tell you all you want to know."

She got to her feet, pale and shaking. "Release my mother. I will not say a word until you have released her."

Mariana was untied and helped, half fainting, from the rack. When Francisca tried to go to her, she was restrained. Unable to walk, Mariana was carried from the room. Francisca herself was led back to the audience chamber.

"Yes, I am a Judaizer," she said. "My mother, father, and sisters are also Judaizers." It was an admission she had been preparing to make should worst come to worst. Since the Holy Office was already convinced of this fact, she felt she had given little, if anything, away. But she did refuse to implicate the others: Aunt Juliana, Beatriz, the friends who had broken Passover bread at the de Silva table.

"As God is my witness," Francisca said, "these people

are devout Christians who know nothing of our own practices.''

Señor Lopez fixed her with a knifelike stare. ''If you continue to withhold information, then we must resort to stronger inducement. Tomorrow you and your mother will return to the torture chamber. I give you until an hour after cockcrow to think about it.''

Back in her cell, Francisca sat with clasped hands. What was she to do? Should she confess all, then later repudiate her confession, saying that she had told lies under compulsion? Was it possible to outguess, outfox, the prosecutor and the judges?

She got up and began to pace wall to wall, the oil dish's wick throwing her shadow on the ceiling. The warder brought her dinner, pork swimming in lard, a meal they knew she would not eat, since she no longer had to pretend she was a Christian. It was their way of taunting her. She rapped on the door and, when the little, bowlegged man returned, asked him to take her food away.

She felt alone, more alone than she had ever felt before. For the first time she had faced the possibility that Miguel would not return. Had something happened to him? An accident, discovery? In her mind she went over their last conversation, recalling how he had looked, what he had said. The one thing that seemed to strike her now was Miguel's repeated questions about Jorge.

Had he come to her dressed as a Dominican friar, saying it was a disguise, to lull suspicion? Francisca had seen how clever the Holy Office could be, how they had used the trick to divide her family, saying that one had informed on the other. Was Miguel a spy? Had they induced him to wring information from her? Or had he come on his own initiative?

She could not see Miguel as an informer. He would never consent to be anyone's lackey, paid or unpaid. No, he had visited Francisca for personal reasons. She supposed that he must have felt it unwise to approach the Holy Office and ask point-blank where Jorge had been sent. In doing so, he might have aroused suspicion that the boy was his, a fact that he would have to conceal. But if Francisca told him of Jorge's whereabouts, then Miguel could spirit the child away without anyone being the wiser as to his true parentage.

The more Francisca thought about this possibility, the more it seemed likely. She recalled Miguel's coolness, his voice, his look. He had made no loverlike moves, no embrace, no kiss. His feeling of distaste for her had not changed. But he wanted his son; he had no heirs, and would raise the boy as a Christian. And if his mother and her family died at the stake, all the better.

She had been a fool to hope, to believe that Miguel had meant to return and free her and her parents from the dungeons of the *Casa*. And now there was nothing but pain and death to look forward to. Francisca had fought hard to retain her courage during these trying weeks, but now she sat on the low stool, her face in her hands, while the scalding tears ran down her face, weeping partly from anger and frustration and partly from grief, convinced that she and her family were ill-fated and that she would never see Jorge again.

Chapter XIII

For a reason known only to her inquisitors, Francisca was not taken to the torture chamber the next morning. Her slop jar was emptied; the warder, mum as usual when questioned, brought her bread soaked in water to break her fast. Francisca tried to guess why the judges had delayed her session in the torture chamber. Had they deliberately decided to let her wait, assuming that uncertainty would weaken her will?

A few hours later the jailer opened her door and roughly shoved a woman inside. "Here is another Judaizer to keep you company," he said.

It was Aunt Juliana.

Francisca stood stunned for a long moment. Then she ran to her aunt, embracing her, holding her tightly, weeping for joy. Juliana had lost none of her plumpness; her cheeks were still round as apples, her color high. It was so good to see a member of the family who was whole and in good health, and not broken by the rack or pale with fear.

Francisca smoothed Juliana's white lace collar and hugged her again. "Oh, Auntie, how wonderful you look, and you smell so *clean*! It distresses me to see you here. But you will forgive me if I say, never was a friendly face more welcome."

"Poor child." Juliana looked around the cell, her nostrils pinched, her gaze taking in the odorous straw, the dirty mattress, and the slop jar. "It's a wonder you are not ill."

"I am as well as can be expected. But, Auntie," she warned, lowering her voice to barely above a whisper before she went on, "we must be careful lest the jailer has his ear to the door. I suspect they have put you in with me thinking to overhear our conversation."

"The idol-worshipping lackeys! I will be careful, blessed child. But you live, and that is what is important."

"Yes, I live. But, Auntie, Ruy—Ruy is dead. He—he died a martyr's death under torture."

For a moment Juliana was struck dumb. She clasped her hands over her heart. "Ayee! God help us all! What a terrible loss! Such a good, pious man! Dead! Killed by dogs! And who was there to wash his corpse, to cut his nails and hair, to wrap him in a shroud and place a gold coin on his brow? No one but the accursed inquisitors, who have most likely buried him like a pagan. Nevertheless, God will surely take him into Paradise. Have you prayed for him, Francisca?"

"Yes, Auntie. That is not all. They took Jorge from me, tore him from my arms, saying they would give him to a Christian family. Jorge, so little . . . he . . ." Her voice caught on a sob. "He didn't understand."

"My dear niece, my dear niece," Juliana murmured, patting Francisca's hand. She lowered her weight on the stool, and Francisca seated herself on the floor at her aunt's knees, putting her head in her lap as she often had done when a little girl.

Juliana touched Francisca's cheek. "You have been badly used. Have they also tortured you?"

"Only my mind. I sorrow for Ruy and Jorge. But Ruy is out if it, and Jorge, I hope, is receiving kindness, even though it be Christian kindness. But, Juliana, they forced me to witness Mamá on the rack. Auntie . . ." Her voice broke again, and she could not go on.

Juliana kissed her niece, smoothing back her hair. "There, there," she crooned.

Francisca, swallowing her tears, went on. "She was so brave, so brave. They—they twisted the rope, but she would admit nothing. . . . It was I who gave way. I could not bear to hear her cries of pain."

"And . . . ?"

"I told them that Papá, Mamá, Leonor, and I were Judaizers. That was all. I informed on no one else. I said not a word about you and Beatriz having gone to Tacuba."

"But we weren't at Tacuba. Beatriz and I had moved to Seguro and were hiding in the house of a former Indian servant, a woman my daughter trusted implicitly."

"Who gave you away? The 'trusted' servant, perhaps?"

"Not Catalina. She hates the Office. They sent her husband to the galleys for spitting at a priest."

"Then Beatriz is also in prison."

"No. Beatriz managed to escape. When she heard the knock on the door, she guessed what was coming and climbed through a back window. She is young, you know, quick and fleet, and she ran into the fields. The constable was unable to catch her."

"Then who informed on you?"

She shook her head. "I truly don't know."

Francisca drew a long breath. "I'm glad Beatriz got away. I wish her well. If only we had taken flight, too. But it's useless to lament over what should have been done. It's now I am concerned with. They have promised to take me and Mamá to the torture chamber again. For myself, I do not fear the rack as much as I fear what will happen if I must watch them torment Mamá."

"You must pray for God to give you strength, my child. His mercy is eternal for us and all of Israel." She kissed the top of Francisca's head.

Francisca hugged her knees. "I had much hope until yesterday. A man, a friend from the past, visited me dressed as a friar, and promised to return to help me, as well as Mamá and Papá, escape."

Juliana's mouth fell open. "Well, why did you not say so before? Who is this friend?"

"Miguel del Castillo." She hesitated a moment and, thinking a confession meant little now, added with a tinge of irony, "The father of my child."

"Ah," Juliana said, letting out her breath. "Your lover. Though you have never named him, I guessed as much."

"You knew Jorge was not Ruy's son?" Francisca asked, astonished.

"Not for certain. Just a feeling in my bones. Jorge had nothing of Ruy in looks or manner. When did Don Miguel come to see you?"

"Three, perhaps four weeks ago. Now I realize that he made an empty promise. He came because he thought I knew where they had taken Jorge." Francisca's mouth hardened, and her voice was bitter. "Auntie, I'm sure it was he who informed on us. In a rash moment I let slip that we were Jews. He once swore he loved me—but it was a lie. He has never loved me." Francisca paused, her mind suddenly looking back to the day he had asked her to marry him, and how a few words had changed him from lover to enemy. A tear appeared on her lashes and slowly rolled down her cheek.

Juliana said nothing, but rose and began to walk the tiny cell, clasping and unclasping her hands. Finally she stopped and looked down at Francisca, brooding over her for a few moments.

"Do you still love this Don Miguel?"

"How can I love a man that has betrayed us all?"

"You have answered my question with another question. I want the truth. Do you still love him?"

Francisca turned her eyes away from her aunt's sharp gaze. "I don't know. There was a time when I did with all my heart. But now . . . How can I answer after all that has happened?"

"I want the truth, Francisca. Do you still love him?"

Francisca lowered her head and, in a voice so low, Juliana had to bend to hear it, said, "In my heart I suppose I have never stopped loving him."

"Then I have something to confess."

"You?" Francisca looked up sharply. "About Miguel?"

"He came to the house one afternoon, shortly before your wedding. The others were out. You were having your siesta. I spoke to him—"

"Wait! I remember! I overheard only one meaningless phrase. I saw his arm—russet velvet. Later you said you were having a conversation with a merchant about a wedding gift. But it wasn't a merchant, it was Miguel, wasn't it?"

"Yes. It was Miguel. He wanted to see your father. I told him that Don Pedro was out. He said it was a matter of urgent importance. 'Surely,' I told him, 'if you have wine to sell, the matter is not that urgent.' 'You don't understand,' he replied, 'I have come here to ask Don Pedro for his daughter's hand in marriage.' "

"He said *what*?" Francisca rose to her feet slowly. "He came . . ."

"To ask for your hand in marriage. He said he loved you, that there had been a quarrel, but he hoped to make amends. I asked him if you and he had been lovers, but he refused to answer my question. He repeated that he wished to have you as wife."

Francisca stared at her in disbelief. "Why was I never told?"

"I did what I thought was best. How could you marry a Christian, a relative of a hated inquisitor? Your life wouldn't be worth a grain of salt."

"I told you he already knew."

"In the first flush of love, perhaps it didn't matter. But later—"

"No! Can't you see he didn't care? Oh, God, if I had only known. What did you tell him?"

"I told him that you were very much in love with Don Ruy, that whatever had been between you and him had been a flirtation on your part, nothing more. That you yourself had told me that Don Ruy meant more to you than any man you had ever known.''

"Oh, God, God! And you sent him away?''

"Francisca, I did what I thought was for your own good.''

The urge to rage at Juliana, to upbraid her for having been stupid, blundering, and meddlesome, came and went. What was important now, more important than scolding Juliana, was that Miguel had loved her. He had had second thoughts. He had decided, whatever she was, Judaizer or Moslem or pagan, he loved her and had wanted her to be his wife. And Juliana had sent him away, thinking Francisca had used him as a man used a maid before he settles down to marriage with someone else. Was it any wonder that Miguel had been cool to her when he had come to her cell? He had seen her shock and dismay at the news of Ruy's death, heard her praise Ruy as kind and decent. Miguel had believed that she loved Ruy. Yet he had been willing to risk all to save her. And her family.

"Something must have happened to him," Francisca said, worried now, certain that Miguel had met with some mishap. "He may have been discovered and arrested.''

"It's possible. No one is immune, especially if suspected of trying to help a prisoner escape.''

"There may have been others, men he hired to assist him, and among them an informer.''

"People are afraid," Aunt Juliana said. "If they make confession to their priest and even hint that they suspect a Judaizer, they are urged to report it to the Holy Office or face damnation. Fear is what gives the Inquisition its power.''

Juliana was escorted to the audience chamber the next morning. What would happen to her there, Francisca could only guess. In all probability the same questions would be put to her aunt, and Juliana, surely defiant, would proudly admit she was a Judaizer while refusing to name others. She was not returned to the cell, and though Francisca continued to expect her, she was never to see Juliana again.

In the meanwhile Francisca waited, hope renewed that somehow Miguel would overcome what obstacles had delayed him and return. He couldn't be dead. She would not allow herself to think of it. Nor could he have left New Spain without her. He loved her. He had told Aunt Juliana that he wanted to marry her. She kept that thought close to her heart, warming herself by it through the long, dismal hours, pacing or sitting, or on the lumpy mattress when sleep would not come.

Daily she expected the familiars to arrive and fetch her to the torture chamber. She wondered about her mother. Every step in the corridor would bring her quickly to the peephole, her eye straining to see. But Mariana's broken figure shuffling between her guards never materialized. What had they done to her? Had she perished from the pain of bruised flesh and broken bones? Pictures of her mother's suffering as she lay stretched upon the rack threatened to drive her mad with rage and frustrated helplessness. Only the thought that soon, soon Miguel would release them steadied her, calmed the urge to scream and throw her food at her jailer.

Then one night, as she lay listening to the scurry of rats, the cell door cautiously opened. Her heart leaped and bounded as she saw a Dominican monk enter, candle in hand, the hood of his habit pulled low.

"Miguel!"

He put his finger to his lips, then silently beckoned. Francisca snatched up her shawl and followed. The corridor was strangely silent. No wardens or familiars were in sight. Sleeping? Francisca wondered. Or had they been bribed to make themselves scarce?

The figure ahead moved swiftly, turning a corner, taking a staircase down to a lower level, into the bowels of the *Casa de la Inquisición*, housing those already condemned. Here the dampness was more acute, the walls sweating with moisture, the plaster peeling in strips. In the silence the drip-drip of water could be heard, then as they passed a grilled door, a rustle of straw, muffled sobbing, and a soft cry of "Mercy!"

They came to the end of the corridor and paused before a large oaken door. The Dominican unlocked it with a key from one of many on a large brass ring. They entered a room, a narrow cell that stank of its former occupants. When the figure Francisca had thought was Miguel's closed and barred the door, she had her first inkling that something might be wrong. This Dominican was not tall enough; the shoulders, even in the habit, were too slender. Another trap?

"Who are you?" she asked in a whisper as the friar placed the candle on a keg.

The hood was thrown back.

"Beatriz!" Francisca's astonishment gave way to joy. She rushed forward and embraced her mother's cousin, so delighted she hardly noticed the way Beatriz stiffened at her touch. "Oh, Beatriz, I cannot tell you how happy I am to see you. How did you find the habit? How did you manage to gain admittance? Did Miguel send you? And the keys, how . . . ?" She was aware that she was babbling, but it was from sheer relief. No trap. Nothing to fear. It was Beatriz.

Francisca went on in a calmer tone. "You must tell me all, once we are shut of this terrible place. You are here, praised be the Lord. Mamá is in a bad way. I have heard nothing of Papá. And Juliana—"

"Wait!" Beatriz cautioned. "There is something I must ask before we proceed. The Benavidos—do you know where they may have gone?"

"No. You know as well as I that they left without telling anyone their destination. Is it important?"

"Yes. They never wrote or tried to communicate with you? And what about the Rodriguez family? The Orozcos?"

"I don't know. Why do you ask?"

"I have my reasons, which you will learn presently. One more thing. Did your father ever succeed in converting Fray Luis Morales?"

"Why, he was already a Judaizer. But, Beatriz, I don't understand any of this. Shouldn't we be hurrying on? You have the keys—thank the Lord for that, a miracle, as Aunt

Juliana would say—and if we don't make haste, it may be too late."

"It will matter little," Beatriz said with a downward twist of her mouth. "You are not going far, cousin."

"Beatriz," she chided. "You are jesting, and this is no time for—"

"I am not jesting. I speak in sober truth."

"But Beatriz—"

"You thought I had come to rescue you," she interrupted again, venom in her voice. "You were wrong. You are still a prisoner, and will be until sentence is passed. And for my pleasure, your punishment will be the stake."

Francisca had a moment of blackness, when the dim room grew even dimmer, and her heart pounded crazily in her ears. With force of will she stayed the threatening darkness and brought Beatriz's face into focus again.

"So . . ." Francisca took a deep breath, amazed that she could speak at all. "You are with *them*." This was a blow, a disaster she had never in her wildest imagination foreseen. She had been betrayed, and by one of her own. Beatriz's questions about the Benavidos, the Rodriguezes, should have warned her. But she had walked into the trap as trustingly as any babe.

"Yes," Beatriz said, "I am one of them."

"But when, how? What brought you to such a pass? Torture? It must have been."

"Why are you so sure that I have chosen to be on the side of the Holy Inquisition because of torture? You are wrong. I renounced Judaism long ago. Any fool could see that clinging to a despised religion could bring nothing but scorn, imprisonment, and eventually the *quemadero*."

"And you gave us away. All of us—Ruy, Mamá, Papá, Leonor, Juliana, myself, Jorge, and our friends? Why?"

"You would never understand, Francisca. You who were the great lady, waited upon hand and foot since infancy, catered to and coddled, given an extravagant dowry and a splendid wedding. While I was always a mestizo, a half-caste, the poor relation, treated like a servant. Don't you think I was humiliated? 'Fetch me a glass of water, Beatriz,' " she mocked, her face, always plain, but ugly now, twisted with hate. " 'My shawl, Beatriz; hold my fan, Beatriz; be a good girl and run to the fishmonger, Beatriz; I have a rip in my skirt—could you mend it?' "

Francisca gazed at her in astonishment. "You resented us; all these years you resented the very errands or little services I myself would have performed gladly? We thought that by making yourself useful, you would not feel beholden." They were to blame, the entire de Silva family, Francisca thought; they were to blame for not guessing at the canker of envy growing year by year in Beatriz's breast. "I see where we were wrong. If only you had said something."

"You would have called me ungrateful, reminding me that you had taken me into your home out of the kindness of your hearts. Kindness. I spit on your charity!"

Confounded, Francisca said, "But if you felt this way, why wait until now to betray us?"

"Do you remember Don Alfredo de Contreros?"

"Of course I do." What had Don Alfredo to do with all this? "He was the profligate hidalgo who would marry you only if Papá gave you a large dowry."

"I loved him," Beatriz said, snatching Francisca's arm, holding it in a bruising grip. "Do you know what I am saying? I loved him, and I didn't care about his weakness for wine and women, about his wanting me for my dowry. I did not even care if, by marrying him, I would have become a lady. I wanted him, and your father dismissed him out of hand."

"Beatriz," Francisca said in a reasonable voice, plucking her cousin's hand from her arm, "once he had his hands on the silver ducats that came with you, he would have made himself scarce. He was not to be trusted."

"If I had him in my bed, he would have never left."

"Can't you see where Papá was only trying to protect you?"

"No. It was meanness. Your papá saw no reason to give a lowly mestizo a generous dowry. I hated him then, I hate him now! All of you!" She paused to wipe the spittle from her lips. "Do you recall when I was dressing your hair before your wedding to Ruy? I held the scissors in my hand, wanting to cut a fringe. You did not know how close I came to plunging it into your back."

Francisca suppressed a shudder. The girl was as mad as Leonor, but in a different way. When Francisca thought of the times she had entrusted Jorge to her care, the nights her cousin had slept within call, she could not believe how blind they had been, how they had lived under the delusion that Beatriz was one of the family.

"I thought about giving you away so often," Beatriz went on. "Then I met up with Don Alfredo by chance three months ago. He said he still wished to marry me, but unfortunately, could not afford to marry a penniless girl since his debts had mounted even higher. When I approached your father and begged him on my knees to give me this boon and he refused, I went directly to the Inquisition."

Francisca felt a sick knot form in the pit of her stomach. "So you told the Holy Office everything, where to find the key, about the gate, about the storeroom. You gave our friends away. And just now you tried to wring the last bit of information from me."

"Yes."

And all the time, Francisca reflected in stricken wonderment, I believed that it was an angry Miguel who had informed on us, and that further details had been extorted from Papá or Mamá on the rack.

"You have become a true Catholic, then?" Francisca asked.

"I have embraced it wholeheartedly. Every morning I go to mass and stay to recite the Lord's Prayer and the Hail Mary. I believe that Jesus Christ was our Savior, not some Messiah that might appear in the millennium."

"Beatriz, you are a hypocrite. I think that you have converted not only out of malice but as the easiest way to save your skin.''

"Whatever reason I have for my conversion, I would advise you to do the same. That way," she added maliciously, "you will be garroted before the scorching flames reach your flesh."

"At least I won't be a toady," Francisca said scornfully. "You say we treated you like a servant. And how do you think you are being treated now? Like a lackey, a slavering paid informer, a—"

"Hold your tongue, bitch!" Beatriz, her dark skin dusky with rage, swung at Francisca's head, missed, and swung again, catching her this time with a stunning blow. Francisca fell back. Beatriz hit her again, and Francisca's head struck the wall. Before she could recover, wiry hands grasped her around the throat, blocking her windpipe, squeezing the breath from her lungs. Francisca made a desperate effort to struggle free, heaving and twisting, bringing her hands up, trying to dislodge Beatriz's stranglehold. But weakened by fasting and poor fare, her fingers lacked the strength to do more than pluck ineffectually at Beatriz's ironlike grip. It was like drowning, fighting for air, her chest heaving, her eyes starting, her tongue lolling. Was she to die this way? No, no! her heart, beating hollowly, cried. No! But there was a ringing in her ears, a growing blackness . . .

Then suddenly Beatriz let go. Francisca fell to her knees, her head swimming, her gaping mouth taking in great gulps of air. Dimly she heard a pounding on the door.

Beatriz unslid the bolt and opened it. A hooded familiar entered, carrying a packet under his arm. He hesitated a few moments, taking in the scene.

"What are you doing?"

"This Judaizer had the effrontery to attack me," Beatriz claimed in a put-upon voice.

Francisca, barely able to talk, said, "She tried to kill me."

The familiar threw back his hood.

"Don Miguel!" Beatriz gasped. "I had thought—"

"You had thought me dead. Trickster, traitor!" A knife flashed in his hand.

Chapter XIV

"Don't kill her!" Francisca cried, stumbling to her feet. "You will have her blood on your hands!"

Miguel, his face crimson with rage, shook Beatriz, bunching the front of her white robe as he held the knife poised at her throat. "Would you have her run from here and sound the cry?" he demanded harshly. "She has already given us away."

Miguel must have relaxed his hold, for the next moment Beatriz, with a sudden jerking movement, snatched the knife from Miguel, raising it.

Miguel caught her arm in its downward plunge, knocking it aside, and then dealt her a blow on the side of the head. She went down to her knees, then crumpled to the floor.

Miguel retrieved the knife, standing over her.

"Don't!" Francisca pleaded.

"It's a mistake to let her live. She would have sent you and your family to the stake and laughed while she watched you burn."

He picked up the packet. "Get into these, a familiar's livery. Quickly, quickly! We haven't time."

She heard rather than saw the descending knife—a faint thud as it plunged into Beatriz's body—and out of habit, her

Catholicism ingrained side by side with her Judaism, she crossed herself. She got out of her ragged dress and petticoats, shuddering as the chill air hit her bare skin. Quickly donning the plain familiar's uniform, she leaned against the wall to pull on the hose, trying not to look at Beatriz.

"Hurry!" Miguel urged as she pulled on the flat shoes. He took the ring of keys and the candle from the table where Beatriz had set them down earlier. "Ready?"

He locked the door behind them. "Luckily, there are few guards at this hour. But if we should meet one, don't speak. Mutter an answer to a question if you must, but nothing else. Pull down your hood."

The corridor was empty, but when they ascended the stairs, they found their way barred by a pair of familiars.

"Who goes?"

"Pedro and Luis," Miguel said, picking two common names. "Stand aside, if you will."

The taller one of the pair looked at his companion. "Is not Pedro home sick with a fever?" He turned back to Miguel. "Let me see your face."

"Are you challenging me?" Miguel said angrily, stepping up to the familiar's level while Francisca shrank back against the wall.

Before the familiar could answer, Miguel grabbed each of the inquisition agents, knocking their heads together with a crushing impact, stilling the outcry on their lips and rendering them both unconscious. He threw the keys to Francisca.

"Run ahead and find an empty cell."

Stepping over the fallen bodies, she sped along the passageway until she came to a door with an iron-grilled window. After fumbling with several keys, she found the right one and unlocked it. Miguel, now behind her, dragged the two familiars inside. "If you can't bear to look," he said, unsheathing his knife, "turn away."

"Miguel—"

"I must. I don't know how long they will remain in a

stupor, but once regaining their senses, they will have the entire Office in pursuit.''

A minute later they were hurrying along the corridor.

''My mother,'' Francisca said. ''I believe she is at this end.''

''Which cell?''

''I know not. This perhaps.''

Miguel fitted the key in the lock, and the door creaked open. ''Empty.''

They found her in the next. She was lying on a pile of filthy straw, her eyes closed. Francisca, her heart thumping with fear and anxiety, ran to her, kneeling, taking the cold, limp hands in her own. ''Mother?''

The sunken eyes opened, starting at the sight of a familiar bending over her. But when Francisca pushed the hood back, a ghostly smile flitted across her face.

''Francisca, my darling, am I already in Paradise?''

''No, Mamá, we have come to rescue you. To take you away from this place.''

''Away?'' she asked, baffled, rising on an elbow, looking past Francisca to the familiar in the shadows.

''It's all right. It's Don Miguel del Castillo. He is here to help us. Can you stand up?''

Francisca, with Miguel's help, tried to raise her, but she sagged between them. ''I cannot,'' Mariana groaned. ''I'm in great pain. My legs—I think they are broken.''

''We will carry you.''

''No, no, put me down, I beg of you. Put me down. I am not long for this world. Let me die in peace.''

''No! You are not to speak in that manner! I will not hear of it!''

''Daughter, we do not choose our time of death, but leave it to the good Lord, who in His wisdom knows best. Go now, save yourself. I would only be a hindrance and most likely die on the way.''

Francisca's eyes filled with tears. ''I can't.''

Miguel said, "She is right, Francisca. You—we—will fail if we linger."

"A moment," Francisca begged, trying to wipe away the tears now flowing fast with her sleeve. A moment—and so much to say, Francisca thought. A lifetime would not be enough. How, in this brief, hurried parting, can I possibly thank my gentle mother for the thousand and one little acts of love she has performed on my behalf? My childish tears, the little bumps and bruises cared for so tenderly. My heart breaks to leave her like this. I can't.

"Francisca . . ." Miguel waited impatiently in the shadows near the door.

"Mamá," Francisca's voice was choked with sobs. "You go with me in spirit. May God bless and keep you." Still kneeling, she recited all she knew of the prayer for the dying. When she had finished, she kissed the wasted face, where the light was already receding. Then, grasping Miguel's outstretched hand, she got to her feet and reluctantly followed him into the corridor.

They had only taken a few steps when voices at the far end halted them.

"The keys!" Miguel demanded.

He unlocked the cell door on his right, and he and Francisca slipped inside.

The cell had a prisoner, a man in tattered rags with lank hair, his faded, crazed eyes glinting in the flickering light of crude oil lamp. Seeing two familiars suddenly appear, he began to wail. "Ow! Ow! Don't take me there again! I have told all!"

Miguel muffled his cries with his hand. Francisca could hear footsteps now. When they paused on the other side of the door, she broke out in a cold sweat, her heart hammering against her ribs.

"The old man is shouting again. Do you think we ought to have a look?"

"What for? He has already told the court all they need to know. Besides, he is as mad as a dog chasing its own tail."

"I say we should go in."

"If you insist."

A key rattled in the lock. Francisca moved closer to Miguel. They were done for. Unless Miguel could overpower the familiars who in another moment would be facing them, they would have lost their bid for freedom. How he could battle with the two and still keep the demented prisoner in check, she did not know.

"I should have killed this one, too," Miguel whispered.

The key scraped again. "*Madre mía!* The key does not fit. It is the wrong one."

"Let us go, then. The idiot will keep." They moved away.

In the meanwhile, the ragged prisoner had fainted, whether out of fear or from loss of breath, Miguel did not stop to ask. The knife was already in his hand when Francisca pulled at his arm. "For the love of God, spare him, an old man out of his mind."

"It's a mistake, but I haven't time to argue. Come."

He and Francisca quickly edged through the door.

"My father," Francisca whispered.

"Which cell?"

"I don't know."

They opened several doors, without success. "We can't delay any longer," Miguel said. "We shall have to let it go."

"But—"

Distant voices echoed along the corridor.

"Come along, quickly!" Miguel whispered.

Up they crept, up and down another corridor, then they were out in the open, crossing a patio, entering the kitchen, already abustle with cooks and servitors. With lowered heads they threaded their way past rows of hanging pots and pans and strings of garlic. No one took notice of them. A man with a load of charcoal entered from a service door, leaving it half-open. Miguel and Francisca slipped through.

It was still dark with no hint of dawn when they stepped into the empty street. They walked rapidly northward past boarded-up shops, past the glow of a baker's oven as he prepared the first loaves for the day, stepping over a pair of drunks who lay head to head in the gutter.

They hurried along in silence. Francisca longed to tell Miguel that she never knew he had come to her father's house to ask for her hand, that Juliana had lied when she had told him that she was in love with Ruy and had used Miguel, flirting with him. She wanted to tell him that she forgave him for taking her against her will in the weaving room, that she had loved him through all the years of their separation. She wanted to say that even when she had thought he had betrayed her, she still loved him. But he gave her no chance to speak. He strode along, setting a fast pace, his face set in stone. Francisca, breathing hard, her throat still burning from the imprint of Beatriz's strangling hands, her heart mourning for her poor mother and wondering about the fate of her father, was beginning to lag when Miguel stopped at the door of a small adobe house.

"Here," he said.

They went inside. A pine torch and the fire on the hearth revealed four men in the clothing of muleteers sitting around a rough-hewn table. Francisca, blinking in the light, looked about for Jorge. But the only other person in the room was a woman, a plump, dark-skinned mestizo. She stood at the hearth, stirring a pot that hung over the fire on a hook. From the back of the house came barnyard sounds: clucking hens, a crowing cock, and the bray of a mule.

A stockily built man with graying hair and ruddy cheeks sprang to his feet. "Don Miguel, safe, thanks be to God."

"Yes. Is all in readiness?"

"All, señor. The mules with their burdens wait in the yard beyond. We were having a bite to break our fast, but if you say time is precious, we'll do without."

"I don't know how soon they'll be raising the hue and cry, but I think a few more minutes will do no harm. Francisca." He turned to her. "This is Don Alvaro, my second-in-command aboard the *Espíritu Santo*. Doña Francisca de Diaz y Roche."

Don Alvaro bowed from the waist.

"And these three men have agreed to take us to Veracruz with them. Martin, Carlos, and Esteban."

They lumbered to their feet, two sunburned and wind-bitten mestizos and one dark, curly-headed mulatto.

"Pardon our humble dwelling," apologized Martin, a lean, muscular man. "But would you care to join us in a bowl of *atole*?"

"Thank you, but I am not hungry." She hadn't eaten this past twenty-four hours, but food was the furthest thought from her mind. Where was Jorge? she wondered, looking around. There were a dozen other questions on her tongue. But everything had happened so fast. There had been no time for explanations, for talk. And here there was no place where they could have a private conversation. The house consisted of the single room in which they now stood, a brick-floored *sala* which served as kitchen, bedroom, and reception room. Along one wall were benches, presumably used as beds at night.

Miguel said, "Francisca, we must change our clothing again. We will travel as muleteers on the road to Veracruz. The constable and his minions are sure to be looking for us dressed in our customary garb."

"I have the clothing here for you," Martin said, going to a chest, opening it, bringing out various items. "I will put up a curtain; and the lady may dress behind it."

Before she disappeared behind the curtain, Francisca whispered, "Miguel, I must speak to you. Jorge . . ."

"I was hoping to break it to you gently, under more favorable circumstances."

Francisca could feel the blood drain from her face. Dead? After all that she had borne, Ruy dead, her mother dying, and God alone knew what had happened to her father and Juliana—and now Jorge. What was the point of her flight if all was lost? Everything, everyone gone.

Miguel, reading her distress, said, "Jorge lives; of that I'm sure. I had him . . ." He looked past Francisca, momentarily forgetting her presence, his blue eyes bitter with some memory Francisca could not guess at. "I tell you, I had him! But they snatched him from me, damn their savage hearts!"

"Who?" Francisca cried, bewildered. "Who snatched him? Miguel, answer me; who?"

His eyes came back to her. "It's a long story. I will tell you all of it, but for now, we must hurry."

Francisca got into a pair of long cotton trousers, a homespun shirt, and a short, not very clean hide vest. Over these she drew a serape. A pair of rope sandals had been provided as footgear. They were much too big. Looking at her slender ankles, the soft, pinkish-white toes, she suddenly thought of the Francisca who had worn slippers of softest doeskin buckled in silver and who had never trodden with bare feet except on carpets of fur or finest wool. Were that girl and the one now dressed in humble clothing the same person? It did not seem possible.

When she emerged from behind the curtain, the men had already gone out to see to the mules. Miguel, also dressed as a muleteer, handed her a broad-brimmed palm leaf hat.

"Don't take it off," he advised. "It will hide your hair and face. Let us go."

"Wait! Is there no chance . . . ? It is so hard to leave Jorge behind."

"Do you think it is easy for me?" he asked bitterly.

With the mules jogging at a steady click-click of small hooves, and the bells attached to their bridles jingling musically, they proceeded over the causeway, now beginning to show signs of traffic. They passed peasants bringing baskets of produce in from the outlying farms and a boy in tattered pantaloons urging his flock of gabbling geese along. A horseman clattered by on a lathered mount, scattering geese and peasants, ignoring the curses that followed him.

The sky grew pale, then flushed with red and gold as the sun rose, glinting off the snowcapped peaks of Ixtacihuatl and

Popocatepetl. It promised to be the kind of morning that made hearts hopeful of good things to come, and indeed, some of the men broke into cheerful song. And for a brief spell Francisca shared their mood, thinking that all was not lost, that her mother would by some miracle live, that Pedro and Juliana would be released, that Leonor would regain her sanity, and that she would be reunited with Jorge. If such happy wonders could come to pass, she thought, then her only wish would be that Miguel would love her again as he had once six long years ago.

She was thinking of him when Miguel fell into step beside her.

"How are you bearing up?" he asked of Francisca.

"Well enough."

He was no more a muleteer than she was. The way he carried himself, head and shoulders above the other men, his easy step, his confident air, gave lie to his menial dress. Whatever he wore would seem like velvet and silk. The frayed palm leaf straw hat sitting cockily on his tawny head could have been plumed beaver, the kerchief tied at his neck, fine lace at his throat.

"When we reach the outskirts, you can ride," Miguel said.

"Wouldn't that seem strange? A muleteer riding one of his own beasts of burden? I can walk."

"For how long in your present state? No one coming out of the *Casa* is in condition to make an eighty-league walk. It is not necessary for you to do penance. None of this was your fault. If your parents had brought you up to be a good Catholic—"

She turned to him, flushed and resentful. "I *chose* to be a Jew. Will you never understand that?"

He gave her a sharp look, then turned away. They walked on in silence, Francisca's anger gradually ebbing. She regretted her outburst. He had done so much for her. She couldn't expect him to change. Perhaps someday, but not now.

"Let us not have angry words between us," Francisca said, swallowing her pride. "Please tell me about Jorge."

Miguel flicked his whip at the mule ahead, who seemed inclined to break out of line. "Jorge." He paused, a frown creasing his brow. "You cannot know how difficult it is for me to speak of it even now."

"Please," she urged. "Don't be angry with me."

"Francisca, you mistake my reluctance for anger. It's simply a painful subject." He jerked at the mule's bridle. "Where to start? At the beginning, I suppose." He took a deep breath. "When I left you, I had no choice but to consult my friend Tomás, who has connections with certain members of the Inquisition in Mexico City. Bless Tomás. He asked me no questions, but in a day or two, acting discreetly, he found out that Jorge had been given into the care of a certain Antonio Flores and his wife."

"Flores? I don't know them."

"He is a saddle maker, no longer young. Both he and his wife are devout. One daughter is a nun; their youngest is studying for the priesthood in Spain. Unfortunately, Flores and his spouse, together with Jorge, left for Zacatecas, a mining city to the north, where their son-in-law had established himself as a carpenter. Hindsight shows me how foolhardy it was to make the journey with only one companion, Alvaro."

"Poor child," Francisca said, thinking of Jorge's face wet with tears. "What a wrench it must have been to be taken even further from his home."

"I thought of that, too. Luckily, we met no misadventure on the way and made it in good time. Dressed as a Dominican friar, it was a simple matter to convince the Floreses by waving a forged document that I had the authority to bring Jorge back to Mexico City."

"Was he well?" Francisca asked anxiously.

"Well and thriving."

"Did he ask after me?"

"When I said I had come to take him to you—I did not tell him you were in prison—yes, he did."

"And then?"

"We were preparing to make our return when we were delayed by a series of storms that flooded the rivers and churned the paths—there are no decent roads over those mountains—to mud. The waiting, the loss of time, irritated me, but on the other hand, it gave me a chance to get acquainted with my son." He paused and smiled, not so much at Francisca, but at some memory that amused him. "He is so bright and clever. So quick. I thought it would be beyond his understanding if I were to announce myself as his father at once, so I told him I was closely related to you. And after we had been together five, six days, do you know what he said?"

Miguel's voice had softened, and he looked at Francisca with that proud smile again. "He said, 'You are like a papá to me.' "

Francisca laughed, a laugh close to a sob. "He is a very loving child."

"And manly. Even at five, already manly. We tarried a week. I got to know Jorge well. I had always wanted to sire a son, but I had never known, never anticipated, the feelings of a father. Francisca, when I sat him on a horse, a princeling could not have had a more regal bearing."

Francisca, her voice bursting with pride, said, "He is good at everything he tries. We had bought him a pony, just before—" And she stopped, suddenly remembering. What was the use of this exchange when the beloved object of their conversation was lost to her? "But you haven't told me what happened."

"Alvaro and I, with Jorge in front of me on the saddle, started out as soon as the weather had cleared. We were a day out of Zacatecas when we were ambushed by a band of Chichimecs."

"Ambushed? Dear Lord! I had thought the Chichimecs had been subdued."

"Not so. Other tribes have been tamed, given villages, land, promised immunity, many persuaded to work in the mines. But the northern branch of the Chichimecs has proved elusive and troublesome. One moment we were trotting along, descending the trail into a wooded canyon, the next we were surrounded by savages, their faces painted in hideous rainbow colors, their bows drawn. Alvaro and I pulled out our guns, and if it weren't for the boy, I would have commenced shooting, killing as many of the heathens as I could. But something, an instinct, made me order Alvaro to hold his fire. It was strange, but the Indians sat their horses, waiting for their chief to give the signal to attack. And he didn't give it.

"He motioned to us to dismount. Jorge was very quiet; he did not seem afraid. I murmured a few words of encouragement to him as we swung from the saddle. And he stood beside me, tall and brave. So brave. The chief also dismounted and, to my amazement, began to speak to us in broken Spanish. The gist of his speech was that he wanted Jorge."

"*Wanted* Jorge?"

"Yes. All the while I argued with him, I was looking around for some way out of our dilemma. There were fifteen of them, effectively surrounding us, boxing us in. They are good bowmen, Francisca, never missing a target even at twenty feet. I had very little choice except to talk my way out. I told him that the boy was my only son.

" 'You lie,' " the chief accused. 'Christians who wear black and white *vestido* and cross not allowed to have sons.' I was still wearing my Dominican habit, and nothing I said would persuade him that I was anything but a friar pledged to celibacy. Finally, losing patience, he said he would kill us all. I knew he meant it. Francisca, I would have died for Jorge, but I was not willing for him to die, too."

"They took him," Francisca said dully. "Why should they want him, a white child?"

"I don't know. Perhaps this savage had no son of his own.

Perhaps he had had one that died. My heated queries were answered with a shrug, a pretense that he did not understand. The motion of his hand on the bow pointed toward Jorge decided me that it was futile to argue any further.

"When they had gone, Alvaro and I went back to Zacatecas. We managed to raise a band of a dozen men. We went from village to village, searching house to house, but never found the cursed Indians who had taken Jorge. I would have gone on looking, but I was aware of your danger, Francisca. That you might be put to the rope and rack was a possibility. . . . Well, I *had* to come back. Do you see why?"

"I do. But I wish it weren't so. Can we do nothing?"

"The Holy Office in all likelihood is on our trail now. They will guess that our destination is Veracruz, and their agents will be questioning travelers and innkeepers on the road. The one thing in our favor is that they do not know who I am. Beatriz was the only one who could tell them."

"Yes, of course. But how came you to Beatriz?"

"When I returned to Mexico City, Tomás told me that the Inquisition was looking for your aunt Juliana and cousin Beatriz. A little bribe here and there, and I found out where they had gone. I was too late for Juliana, but Beatriz had come back to Mexico City and was supposedly hiding in the home of some people named de Sosa. I say 'supposedly' because Beatriz, as we both know now, was a spy of the Holy Office. Like a fool, I never suspected. I told her of my plan to rescue you and your family. That night I was attacked on the street by two masked men. I managed to dispatch them both but did not connect my assassins with Beatriz until later."

"So she came to the Flat House dressed as a Dominican thinking you had already died?"

"Exactly. Fortunately, the de Sosas, who are inclined to be less than sympathetic with the Inquisition and who claim they can smell an informant a mile away, had doubts about Beatriz. When they told me they had discovered the habit of a Dominican monk under her bed, I guessed what she was up to. I changed my disguise and, by good luck, arrived in time. Now you see why I had to kill her?''

Francisca, tired and footsore, had not protested when Miguel lifted her onto the back of a mule. She rode, fighting sleep, her lids heavy, her head lolling forward, then jolting upright when the mule stepped into a hole or stumbled over a tree root. They were climbing a mountain on a tortuous path that snaked upward around rocky outcroppings, skirting deep, river-threaded canyons, the surefooted mules, their bells tinkling, plodding along to the urgent cries of *"Mula, mula, echa, mula!"*

Miguel walked beside her. It had been some time since he had spoken. Thus far there had been no speech between them that could be construed as tender or amatory, nothing said that hinted at the passion they had once known. Yet Francisca felt his vital presence. At intervals he would grasp the mule's bridle, his sleeve brushing her knee, and she would feel the blood suddenly quickening through her exhausted body. Every step reinforced her certainty that her feelings for Miguel had not changed. But how did he feel about her? Perhaps Juliana's words had killed any love he might have felt. Yet he had risked his life to save her. Why? Not his conscience, for it was Beatriz who had betrayed the family. The challenge? Some grudge he had developed against the Inquisition since she had last seen him?

Thinking back, she could see now that she had angered him when she refused to answer his direct question as to whether she loved Ruy. Naturally he had assumed she did. And his assault in the weaving room—had it been made out of anger and lust or was there some remnant of love still lingering in his heart?

They reached Puebla at sundown. A good-sized city of ten thousand inhabitants, it was seated in a low, pleasant valley, overlooked by a snowcapped mountain. Here, in addition to stopping for the night, the muleteers would pick up five more mules carrying cloth that the Pueblans claimed rivaled that of Segovia in Spain.

They put up at the Posada del Alba, an inn near the main market frequented by muleteers. It was a two-story building of rough-hewn logs built around a courtyard, where the mules were corraled for the night. The del Alba was a noisy place, the common room's floor littered with the refuse of past meals, the straw bedding dirty, the air reeking with the smell of dung, over which hung clouds of flies. Because a fair was being held the next day, the inn was crowded, and Francisca and Miguel had to share a bed with two others in the sleeping loft.

For Francisca it was a miserable night. Her neck and back stiff from the day's jolting, she slept in her clothes, wedged between Miguel, who fell asleep the moment he stretched out, and one of the muleteers, whose unwashed body stank and who mumbled and cursed between loud fits of snoring.

The next morning it was still dark when the muleteers descended to the patio below to load their mules for the next lap of their journey. Francisca was picking the straw from her clothes by the light of a fitful candle set in a sconce next to the window when the sound of unusually loud voices above the braying and cursing drew her attention to the patio below. Torchlight illuminated muleteers swinging panniers across the backs of restive mules, tightening buckles and riatas. In the center, ringed by this bustle, were three men dressed in dusty black robes arguing voluably with the innkeeper. When one, the tallest, turned his face so that the full light of a torch fell upon it, Francisca's hand flew to her mouth.

It was the hawk-nosed prosecuting attorney, Señor Lopez. The Inquisition had caught up with them.

Chapter XV

Miguel came bounding up the ladder, carrying a length of rope looped over his arm.

"Francisca—"

"I know," she said weakly, her heart pounding with the same cold, sweating terror she had lived with these past few months. "I've seen."

"They have questioned the muleteers and are asking to search the place. Do you think they would recognize you?"

"The tall man with the hawk nose is Señor Lopez, the prosecuting attorney."

"He must want you badly to join a constable and familiar in their search."

"They say he never loses a prisoner." She pressed her chill, damp hands together. "Can you trust the muleteers?"

"I wish I could be sure. They have been paid well to hold their tongues until we safely reach Veracruz, but with the agents of the Holy Office interrogating them, they may have second thoughts."

"Then we must leave at once," she said, struggling against panic. "Is there another way out except through the patio?"

"There doesn't seem to be."

"None? You are sure? God in heaven!" Again wild fear

leaped and bounded with the rapping of her heart. She should have known that escape was only an illusion. She would be caught like a rat in a trap. Dragged back to prison, the dark, stinking cell, the stark audience room, the torture chamber with its instruments of pain and terror—all to be faced and endured again. And at the end a horrible death. She wanted to scream, "I can't! I can't!" And for one blind moment she thought of begging Miguel to take her in his arms, to soothe, to kiss, and tell her he would never allow them to have her.

But she couldn't. He would think her weak, childish, and rightly so. She remembered Ruy and her mother, her father, and her son. She owed it to them to face what she must with courage, even if that courage was half sham.

When she spoke again, it was in a steadier voice. "You are armed; perhaps you could—" she hesitated—it was still hard for her to use the word *kill* "—do away with them."

"I cannot, much as I would like to," he said. "Nor can Alvaro, who was unrecognized and remained below. Too many witnesses, and Lopez and his men would immediately be replaced by others. Puebla swarms with clergy. No, we must elude them."

Outside there was an imperceptible paling of the sky. Taking the candle from its wall holder, Miguel prowled the room, inspecting the ceiling.

"Ah . . . the trap door!" Miguel pointed. "There is no ladder, but if I place you on my shoulders, do you think you could open it?"

"Yes! We must hurry!"

They could hear steps, a loud voice in the common room below, asking, "Is there anyone in the sleeping loft?" And then a muffled reply.

Miguel lifted Francisca, hoisting her to his shoulders, holding her by the ankles. Swaying uncertainly, her nervous toes curling and uncurling, she groped with sweating hands for a way to open the trap door. It must have a catch or a bolt, but where, oh, God, where?

At the foot of the ladder the loud voice that Francisca

recognized as belonging to Señor Lopez proclaimed, "Then we shall see for ourselves."

Under her, Miguel, fixed as a rock, whispered, "Feel to the right."

A sudden wave of dizziness overcame her, and for a moment she thought she would fall.

Miguel took a firmer grasp of her legs. "Steady, steady!"

Recovered, she went on with her search, perspiration streaking her forehead, her hands sticky with cobwebs. Suddenly she touched a latch. She pried at it, then pried at it again. It refused to give.

From down below, voices were still in conversation. Señor Lopez said, "I have my duty to perform; that must come first. We have two dastardly criminals. One a female, a Judaizing heretic, the other a murderer. A prisoner who saw them says they were dressed as familiars. He could have been wrong—he is not quite right in the head. On the other hand, there might be some truth to his ravings. A tall man, he said, with a copper-colored beard. You say you haven't seen one by that description? But three men in the yard claim that one of the muleteers had such a beard. And he has vanished? I must search every nook and cranny, landlord. Then I shall accept your kind offer to have a glass of wine."

The landlord said, "But surely you can take a moment?"

"Later," the attorney stubbornly replied.

Desperate now, tearing at the bolt with bloodied fingers, Francisca finally got it free. Lifting the door, she felt the cool rush of air and glimpsed a handful of glimmering stars. She grasped the edges at the opening. Miguel gave her a shove, and up she went, using elbows to lever herself onto the roof. Once out, she quickly fastened the door open by means of a long rod that hooked into an iron ring. Then she lay flat on her stomach, reaching down. Miguel threw the rope to her.

"You can't hold my weight," Miguel whispered. "Is there something you can tie this to?"

"Yes." With fingers straining for steadiness, she looped

and knotted one end of the rope to the iron ring. The other end dangled far short of where Miguel stood.

They could hear the landlord plainly now. "There is no one up there, and if there were, the only way out is down this ladder. Rest easy, and share some wine with me. It is newly arrived from Seville."

Señor Lopez again demurred. "Thank you, no. I shall rest easy only when I have seen for myself."

Miguel leaped at the rope, caught it, and began to pull himself up. Francisca's heart jolted in her mouth as she noticed the rope beginning to fray where it rubbed against the opening. Not now, she thought fiercely, as if thought alone could keep the rope from breaking. For God's sake, *not now!*

Straining, she reached down and caught Miguel's sleeve, then his wrist. A moment later he was beside her. The rope was quickly hauled up, the trap door shut.

"You can see for yourself." The landlord's voice came to them on the other side of the trap door. "Empty."

Francisca, leaning against Miguel, felt as though she had been snatched from the fire once more. Her legs still shook; her forehead, damp with effort and anxiety, rested against the rough wool of Miguel's serape. The respite was brief, she knew, but it did not keep her from wishing that this feeling of safety, of being cared for, could go on. There was a slight movement above her, as if Miguel's lips were brushing her hair. Was he kissing her?

She looked up, but though he had put his arm about her shoulders to steady her, his eyes bore a distant look as if he were concentrating on listening. From the common room came the sound of murmuring voices again. The enemy, satisfied, had descended the ladder to partake of the landlord's wine.

The muleteers would not tarry. They must be on their way at first light, covering as much of the road as they could before sundown. To travel at dusk or later was to court disaster, for their route was beset with thieves, hidden in the brush or in ditches, ready to ambush, to rob and kill.

"What are we to do?" Francisca whispered.

The sky was growing lighter. Afraid they would be seen, Miguel suggested they take refuge at the roof's edge behind the wooden parapet that bordered the flat roof. They crouched there, listening to shouts of *"Vamos! Vamos!"* the signal to start the mule train on its way.

"We can't go directly to Veracruz," Miguel said in a low voice. "They will have people posted at every inn. I realized it the minute the Inquisition's agents dismounted and started questioning all around. I thought of Tampico to the north. Once there, we could find a small boat to take us down the coast to Veracruz."

"Then we shall be in Veracruz in any case."

"Only briefly. By the time we reach it, they may have given up the chase."

Alvaro was not too sure Miguel's plan was practical. "Tampico is hundreds of miles out of the way. Once we leave the main road, there will be little more than mule paths up the Sierra Madre Oriental, and when we descend, we shall have the jungle to contend with. Needless to say, our route leads in many places through hostile Indian country. It's too dangerous."

Miguel disagreed. "I still think the risk is less than walking into a trap the Inquisition has set for us. They now have a partial description of me, a full one of Doña Francisca. We can get horses from the landlord, a good fellow. He understood immediately that I wanted his silence when I pressed several gold pieces in his hand. I think I can trust him. We are armed; we are both excellent shots."

Alvaro tugged at his beard. "If it were just the two of us, I'd say why not? But with a woman—with all due respect, Doña Francisca—I have grave doubts."

"Francisca," Miguel said, turning to her, "do you ride?"

City born and bred, carried in litters or by carriage, Francisca's only experience with horses had been when, as a child, her father would lift her into the saddle, holding her before him as they rode.

"If I can sit a mule," she said haughtily, "I can ride a horse."

Both men laughed.

Miguel shaved his beard and mustache. It pained him to do so, but since the inquisitors were looking for a man with a copper-colored beard in a country where most males were dark-bearded, he felt he had no choice. The face that looked back at him in the courtyard well was younger, the thin, finely molded mouth sensuous and self-mocking, the naked jaw hard. It was the face of a man who has set himself upon a dangerous course, not minding, but welcoming the danger, yet finding it hard to understand the reasons that had propelled him to risk all for a woman who did not love him.

The search for Jorge, he never questioned. His son, though a bastard, was his heir, the blood running in the child's veins his. He would return to Zacatecas once he got Francisca safely away and look for and find him if it took the rest of his life.

As for Francisca, it was torture being with her day after day, seeing her sad and downcast, knowing that she was mourning not only for Jorge—that he could understand—but for her dead husband as well. Don Ruy. What had she ever seen in the old goat? Not a word had she spoken about their own past, the long afternoons when they had made love with such wild, sweet passion, sharing an intimacy that had given them both such happiness. He had made the mistake, a momentary one out of shock, in turning his back on her, but perhaps she would have married Ruy in any case. Nor was there any altering the fact that she was a Jewess. Still, she was the mother of his child, and he could not desert her when to do so would mean her certain death.

Before they set out, he asked her to cut her hair.

"You can't always hide it," he said. She had worn it pinned tight to her skull, tucked under the hat. "An accident, a high wind taking your hat, the pins and combs coming undone, and your disguise will mean nothing."

"I can't cut my hair, Miguel." There had been a time when he had loved its rippling sheen, when he had spread it out on the pillow, run his hands through it, buried his head in the thick, tumbling silkiness, made her promise she would never cut a lock. And now he wanted it shorn!

"Stubborn woman! Do you think for a moment I welcomed the loss of my beard?" he asked, resisting the urge to give her a clout.

"I shall be very careful, Miguel," she said doggedly. "I will sleep with a head covering, never take it off."

Shrugging, he let her have her way.

An hour later they rode out under the arched gate mounted on fresh, well-fed horses, the men on geldings, Francisca on a mare. Miguel had also bought a fourth horse to carry provisions, blankets, mosquito nets, cooking utensils, two extra long-barreled pistols, and ammunition. Francisca, who found her horse a little too frisky for her taste, was dressed like her companions, in clothes they hoped would not attract attention: shirts with wide collars loosely bound by neckerchiefs, vests, short jackets, knee breeches with long leggings, and on their heads, low-crowned, wide-brimmed hats. With Miguel in the lead, they headed north to Tulancingo, some seventy miles distant, taking a trail used by *tamemes*, Indian porters who had been the sole beasts of burden before the Spaniards introduced the mule, horse, and wheel to New Spain, lowly carriers who still plied their trade.

"We'll spend the first night at Montaña Hermosa, a hacienda owned by an uncle of mine, Don Luis Valdez," Miguel said. "I haven't seen him since I was a boy, but like a good Spaniard, I'm sure he will greet me as though our parting had only been yesterday."

"Can you trust him?" Francisca asked.

"The brother-in-law of an inquisitor? Hardly. But he doesn't have to know anything except that I, my second-in-command, and my cabin boy are traveling to Tampico on business. If I remember, he is a very garrulous fellow, and his interest in us will only be one of minimal courtesy. I'm willing to wager he will talk mostly about himself.''

Miguel was right.

Don Luis, a puffy-faced man with a large stomach that overhung his silk sash, regaled them at the supper table with a long-winded story as to how he had managed to acquire an additional ten thousand acres a month earlier. Already the holder of over a hundred thousand acres, he had done well in New Spain, and was bent on doing better.

"Cattle," he said, "that's the thing. I know that many prefer eating mutton, but mark my words, the populace will soon develop a taste for beef. There's a great deal of money in cattle. Not only the beef, but the hides as well. My boy, you ought to give up the sea and join me here at Montaña Hermosa. I could use a man of your intelligence and ability.''

"Thank you, Uncle. But I must decline. I have the sea in my blood.''

"Nonsense.''

Guests were infrequent at La Montaña Hermosa, and Don Luis, taking advantage of his captive audience, went on and on about heifers and prize bulls, and what should be bred with what, until well past midnight. When they were finally shown to their rooms, Francisca was so tired and stiff she could scarcely walk.

"I have some liniment that will help you,'' Miguel told her.

"I think a good night's sleep is all that I need.''

"A good night's sleep alone won't cure your sore back and stiff legs. I know what it is to be in the saddle all day when one is not accustomed to it. A rubdown will loosen those muscles. And I suppose you will want a hot bath, too, although it will take some doing to get the bath. Seamen, young or old, don't bathe. But I'll manage.''

They had been given rooms on the ground floor under the arched gallery that ran the oblonged shape of the house. All the rooms faced a huge patio, planted in imported and native shrubs, vines, and trees. A hedged stone walk circled a marble fountain, whose splashing waters made a musical sound.

Francisca, as cabin boy and ostensibly Miguel's servant, would sleep on a small cot at the foot of her master's bed. It was not an arrangement she looked forward to. But the cot, with its clean linen and warm blankets, looked far more inviting than anything she had slept in for a long time.

Mountain nights are cold, and a leaping fire had been built in the small stone fireplace. Francisca sat on the cot, staring at it, waiting for Miguel, yawning and blinking to keep her heavy eyelids open. She had eaten too much rich food—chicken mole and beef with hot peppers—and had drunk too much Madeira. But after two months of prison fare and the Puebla inn's coarse food, everything at Montāna had tasted too delicious to resist.

She dozed off, then wakened with a start, thinking she heard a step outside. She had no idea how long she had napped. Deciding that Miguel's uncle had detained him with more talk, Francisca began to undress for bed. She had proceeded as far as removing her shirt and vest when she fell asleep again, slumping sideways on the cot.

She awoke to find a smiling Miguel bending over her. "Your face is dirty," he said.

Her hand went to her cheek. "Where?"

"Your chin. A bit of pepper sauce."

She felt her chin. "There's nothing." When she went to raise herself, her lower back felt as if it had been speared with a red-hot iron. The groan escaped her lips before she could stifle it.

"Now, you see what I mean? Worse, isn't it?" He arranged the pillows behind her. "And the legs no better, I'll warrant."

He was interrupted by a knock on the door. "Ah—here is the maid with the water buckets and bath."

Francisca scrambled under the cot's blankets, covering her head, taking care to hide her giveaway hair. Servants were notorious gossips, and to be seen by the maid without her disguise would set tongues wagging. Embarrassing questions would be asked, suspicion aroused, a condition to be avoided at all costs.

"*Gracias,*" she heard Miguel say as he shut the door on the departing maid.

The water felt heavenly. Steaming hot, smelling of rain, and fragrant with lavender. On a chair close at hand lay a clean linen towel and a bar of scented soap. Pure luxury. She lay back, closing her eyes, forgetting Miguel, who had gone to sit on a stool near the fire.

The crackle of a settling log sending sparks upward roused her. She sat up and began to vigorously soap her legs, her arms, her torso, rinsing herself with palmfuls of water. Then, unpinning her tightly coiled hair, she dipped her head forward, immersing it, bringing it up, shampooing vigorously, washing out the prison stench, wishing she could wash out the cruel memories and the feeling of loss along with it.

Flicking back her wet hair, she noticed that Miguel had shifted his position and was watching her with a pensive, brooding look in his eyes. Pity? Perhaps that was all he felt for her.

"Of what are you thinking?" she asked abruptly.

"Jorge," came the answer. "My son."

"He is my son, too," she said with asperity. "Why do you always refer to him as *your* son? Don't you think I had anything to do with bringing him into this world?"

He threw her an enigmatic look. "Have you had enough of your bath?" he asked, apparently not wishing to pursue the subject.

"Yes," she answered shortly. "Please, turn your back."

Her modesty reminded him of his wife's, whose nakedness he had never seen in all his years of marriage. Francisca's attitude seemed ridiculous. Did she think he had forgotten the abandon with which she had responded to his embrace, her gasps of pleasure when he caressed her round little breasts with hands and lips? Her present coldness angered him.

"Turn your back," as if he were some sort of lackey. Damn her. For one black moment he fought the urge to throw the bottle of liniment at her and stalk from the room.

But he restrained himself. If she did not have the proper rubdown, she would be stiff as untanned leather, unable to sit the saddle for more than a few hours at a time. And they had some hard riding ahead, a journey that must be made as quickly as possible. He couldn't allow the *Espíritu Santo* to sit idly at anchor for too long.

"I'm ready," she said.

She was lying on the bed, facedown, wrapped toe to chin in a sheet.

"God's teeth!" he exclaimed. "How am I supposed to massage you through *that*? Enough of your prudery!" He took hold of the sheet, unwinding, tumbling her about, and at the last, ripping it from her body.

Gasping, she snatched a pillow and slammed it into his face. "How dare you!" she cried, angry at him, dimly aware that her anger had been building up over the days because of his coolness. She might as well have been his cabin boy or a younger relative. He hadn't kissed her once and, except for brotherly concern, hadn't shown a sign of real affection. "How dare you! Take your cursed liniment and get out!"

He tore the pillow from her, tossing it aside. She elbowed herself up, eyes flaming. He pushed her down, slamming her head against the mattress as she tried to rise again.

"Be still, damn you! If you're going to behave like a spoiled child, then you'll be treated as one." He straddled her, sweeping her flailing arms aside, flipping her over on her stomach. When she continued to struggle, he smacked her across the buttocks, a stinging slap that brought a small scream to her lips.

"Be quiet! Do you want the household to think I'm a sodomite, making love to my cabin boy? I said, be quiet!" he repeated through gritted teeth. "You are going to be rubbed down whether you like it or not."

He reached for the liniment. Francisca slid upward from

between his knees like a hare slipping a noose, rolling toward the far side of the bed. Leaping to her feet, she raced across the room. He caught her by her flying hair, jerking her back. She felt as though her scalp were being lifted from her head, the pain slicing down to her eyes, her face, and neck. Recovering her breath, she opened her mouth to scream. He choked it off with a heavy hand.

"And where do you think you can go? Out there? Into the arms of the inquisitor's brother-in-law? You fool!" He shook her until tears came to her eyes.

"Let—me—go."

He paused, breathing hard, as if he had run a mile. He held her by the shoulders, gazing defiantly into her eyes, now liquid with unshed tears. Her hair—the hair she had fought to keep—was in wild disarray, tumbling over her shoulders and chest, one naked breast peeping out, the white, full globe rosy in the firelight, rising and falling with agitation. For all she had been through, she was still beautiful, the most beautiful woman he had ever known.

He felt her tremble in his grasp, a shiver that tightened his loins like an aphrodisiac. He did not care if she had gone from his bed to another's, if she had preferred to marry an old man; he wanted her.

"Francisca." He caught her parted lips before she could speak, drawing her close, one arm around her slim waist, the other resting across her shoulders.

She had meant to resist, but the moment his mouth claimed hers, anger ebbed and vanished. It was a long kiss, a fusion that weakened her knees and sent a melting warmth through her veins. She knew now why she had longed for this, a purely sensual feeling where the mind did not have to think or to feel pain. She had forgotten how tender he could be, this man of steel whose glance could shatter another's courage, a man who could fight savagely, plunging a dagger into his enemy without a second thought.

His breath was warm in her ear. "Why are you so perverse?" he whispered. "Why do you fight me?"

"You are wrong. I think it is you who are perverse. I think—"

But he was kissing her again, her mouth, her cheeks, her chin, her eyes, her breast, kissing her greedily with mounting passion. The last of her anger drained away. She closed her eyes against the erotic onslaught, a languorous desire bringing heat to her cheeks. She felt light-headed, a delicious floating intoxication that roused a giddy laugh in the back of her throat.

He pulled back in surprise. "Do I hear right? A laugh? I have not heard you laugh in years, but if my kisses are amusing—"

"Oh, Miguel!" She flung her arms about him, bringing his head down, meeting his seeking mouth with a force of her own. They stood for a long time clasped in each other's arms, mouth to mouth, as if they could never have enough of kissing.

Then he was leading her to the bed. Lifting her, holding her in his arms, his sea-blue eyes locked with her melting gaze for a timeless moment before he placed her among the rumpled bedclothes where only a few minutes earlier she had fought him. When he came to her naked, her arms reached up for him, pulling him down. They were kissing again, his hands finding her breasts, the sweet, slender curve of her waist, the flat belly, the sleek thighs. Murmuring words of desire, he stroked her pearly skin, kissing the coral nipples that hardened under his flicking tongue, pressing his lips to the pulse that beat in her blue-veined throat.

The years fell away. They were lovers again, passionate, wild, insatiable, shameless, demanding more and more. Francisca's pelvis rose to meet his penetration and pounding thrusts, her hips twisted, riding with him, a savage, ecstatic joy gripping her as they both clung and strove to the final shuddering release.

"I love you!" she gasped. "Oh, God. I do love you."

He held her against his muscled chest, where his heart still thudded to the heavy beat of her own. "It has been, will always be, the same for me. It seems, my darling, that we are doomed to love forever.''

She felt rather than saw his smile, and wished for a brief moment that he had not used the word "doomed" before she fell asleep in his arms.

Chapter XVI

Francisca opened her eyes to find Miguel smiling at her.

"My arm's gone to sleep," he said in mock complaint, thinking that he would have given his entire fortune and the *Espíritu Santo* thrown in if once during the bleak years that had separated them, he could have had reason to say the same.

She shifted her head to the pillow, freeing her long, dark fall of hair from behind her neck with a graceful movement of white, rounded arms.

He rose on an elbow and, with a tender hand, spread the silken mass in a fan over the pillow, framing the face that glowed up at him with a shining incandescence.

"Still stiff?" he asked.

"A little," she replied, tentatively moving her neck from side to side. She had been too ecstatically happy to take more than passing note of her aching muscles. But now she felt the soreness in her thighs, her calves, and backside, and the dull pain that had settled at the top of her spine.

"Negligent of me to forget, was it not? I wonder why. Mmmm?"

Laughter bubbled up in her throat. He bent and kissed her forehead, her lips, pausing there, clinging to her mouth.

"Enough!" he said abruptly, tearing himself away, "or I shall forget again. Now, where did I put that liniment?"

It had an acid sting to it. But, oh, how wonderful it felt, the sure, strong hands moving over her back, kneading the sore flesh and tired muscles.

"Did I hear you right?" Miguel asked, rubbing more liniment on her legs. "You *do* love me. It wasn't something you said in the heat of passion?"

"It was—Ouch! Not so hard, Miguel—the truth."

"And your husband?"

"Ruy was good to me, Miguel. But I never loved him. Aunt Juliana lied to you. She wanted me to marry Ruy because he was of the same faith. I never knew she had sent you away. All I could think of was how you had walked out of that room with only a few cold words."

"I was a fool, Francisca. I realized it the minute I closed the door that day. But for pride, I would have admitted it at once. But I couldn't, not then. Not until a week later, when I realized that life without you would be hollow, without purpose, and I went looking for your father."

"If I'd only known. I thought you didn't love me, that you had informed on us."

She heard the abrupt intake of his breath as his hands ceased their movements. He flipped her over roughly, an angry flush staining his face. "How could you think so little of me? Call me a thief, a liar, a brigand, even an ass. But never an informer."

"Miguel," she chided gently, touching his cheek, "you are not the only one who can make a mistake."

Slowly the flush faded from his face as he contemplated the loving smile that lit her soft brown eyes.

Placated almost against his will, he lifted her, gathering her in his arms, holding her close, rocking her. "Francisca, Francisca, how cleverly you disarm me."

They made love again, a joyful coming together laced with laughter and wild kisses. Yet their passion carried with it an undercurrent of desperate need, as though this were the first and last time they would be locked in this most intimate act.

Afterward, lying side by side, they talked in low voices, interrupting each other in their eagerness to explain away past misunderstandings, amused to find that each had thought the other cold.

Miguel mapped out their future. Escape to Spain. There he would get his wife's consent for an annulment, then on to Rome, where he would gain an audience with the pope to hasten the procedure. Once married, they would find a place to live, in Genoa, perhaps, or Amsterdam, a seaport in a country that did not persecute people of another religious faith. When all had been settled, Miguel would return to Zacatecas to search for Jorge.

Snuggling close on that chilly, windy morning with the rising sun staining the mountain peaks beyond their window in flushed pinks and bright gold, the future seemed bright and hopeful, the years ahead full of promise.

After two days at Montaña Hermosa, they prepared to resume their journey. The horses they had obtained in Puebla were traded for ones bred for the higher altitudes, heavy-coated animals, somewhat smaller than their previous mounts, but surefooted, accustomed to the narrow, winding paths they would encounter.

"You must not overtire them," Don Luis warned. "There will be no inns or hostelries along the way where you can obtain fresh horses. Also I advise a guide. There is a young man on my estate, Pico, an Indian, native to the mountains, who would serve you well. You are properly armed?"

"All three of us with guns and daggers, and enough powder to carry us through an attack or two."

"Good." Don Luis observed his nephew quizzically. "It is none of my affair, but is it absolutely necessary for you to go to Tampico?"

"Yes, Uncle. A man there owes me a great deal of money."

"Ah," Don Luis acknowledged. "There is a saying, 'To collect a debt, one would travel the road to Hades.'"

They climbed all of the first morning, urging the horses up through the trees to sheer, dizzying heights, where the wind whipped at their flimsy straw hats and poked icy fingers down the necks of their serapes. The guide was in the lead, followed by Miguel, then Francisca, while the rear was brought up by Alvaro, who led the horse carrying their supplies.

Occasionally they would pass a dwelling literally carved out of the stony escarpment, a crude log hut abutted by a tiny spur of land planted in corn and hot peppers. Once, jogging down to a ravine, they rode through a village, a cluster of log huts with thatched roofs. Barking dogs ran alongside, nipping at the horses' heels, yellow-fanged, rangy animals who cringed at a flick of their whips. Indian women, some with sleepy, sloe-eyed babies in their arms, came out waving for them to stop, thinking they were peddlers. Riders seldom arrived from the outer world, Pico explained in his broken Spanish. But when they did, the most sought after commodity was salt, bought in dribbles, for the price of salt was dear to these people.

They camped that night in a grove of pines on the banks of a rock-tumbled stream. It was bitterly cold. The fire they built under the lee of a boulder heated their faces and hands, while their backsides remained chilled. They ate tortillas and frijoles, washing them down with strong coffee. Alvaro, producing a guitar, entertained them with Andalusian songs, his weather-beaten features relaxing into nostalgia in the orange glow of the fire. Pico sat a little apart with an expressionless face, gazing into the flames, his high cheekbones making planes of shadow on his dark-skinned face.

Francisca made no protest when Miguel indicated they would share the same blankets. The girl who had once recoiled at the thought of what others would say if she became Miguel's mistress had found that such things hardly mattered. She had been through too much to fret about convention now. Love was too precious to hide or postpone.

Snuggled close, they warmed each other with slow, burning kisses. Miguel, aroused, tried to restrain himself out of delicacy, for the other two men had bedded down only a few feet from them. But Francisca's soft breasts pressed against him, her hands caressing the thigh he had slung over her delectably rounded hip, was too much. With a low moan he tugged at her trousers, while she, suppressing a giggle, unfastened his. His fingers found a breast under her shirt, teasing at the nipple until it hardened in his palm. He kissed her lips again, edging his knee between her thighs, rubbing it slowly, sensually against the inner tenderness. Francisca's hand pressed against his chest, moved to his face, the back of his head, her fingers losing themselves in the crisp red-gold hair. Still on his side, without turning her, Miguel entered the warm moistness with a gliding thrust that brought heat to her face, a pulse beating in her throat. Together they moved, in slow, erotic rhythm, their hearts thudding against each other, a rising excitement gripping both, their need a passionate hunger as they strove to catch the golden ring, and then in one glorious, indescribable moment, they had it in their hands, a triumph that sent them clinging together as they plummeted through space.

The horses were kept at a walk, Miguel husbanding their endurance for the long, difficult journey ahead. The terrain through which they passed was magnificent: peak after peak wearing misty crowns, long rocky slopes, wooded gorges, valleys far below that looked toylike from the heights, rain falling in slanting sheets across a deep barranca, the sun catching the top of a roaring cataract in an arched rainbow. Miguel and Francisca were to look back on those days in the mountains and their nights of love under the stars that hung like flickering lamps over their heads, the pine-scented air, and the feeling of otherworldliness as the happiest they were to know in a long while.

On the fourth night their guide and his horse vanished,

silently melting into the darkness while they slept. Why he had gone, where he went, they were never to know. Alvaro, who had been through this section of New Spain years earlier, had only a hazy memory of the way. For the rest they must trust to instinct and to Miguel's ability to read the stars.

In the late afternoon of the fifth day as they crossed a high, dry mesa, they encountered masses of flies and gnats, attacking both man and beast with a vindictiveness that drew blood. It was useless to try and sweep them away. They only returned a fraction of a moment later, fastening themselves on their faces and hands and every inch of exposed flesh.

"Are you getting tired?" Miguel asked, riding beside Francisca as the road widened.

"No," she lied, her parched lips parting in a cracked smile.

He reached over and squeezed her hand. "I love you, my darling."

His smile was drink to her. The blue eyes, so startling in his bronzed face, so full of love, banished discomfort. Miguel loved her. Thirst and weariness were forgotten. At that moment she felt as though she could travel on across an endless desert forever simply on the strength of that tender smile.

Late that day they had passed two riders who warned them of bandits in the neighborhood. When their little company camped that night, they did not light a fire, but ate their food cold: maize cakes and chili peppers that bit the tongue. The men took turns standing guard. Francisca, shivering under her blanket, was glad when Miguel was relieved by Alvaro. As she nestled close to him, his kisses returned the warmth to her limbs.

When he began to undo her trousers, she raised herself on an elbow.

"Miguel—perhaps we should be more restrained. I've been thinking, Alvaro . . ."

When she arched her back in resistance, his arm circled her waist, wrapping her tight, his mouth capturing hers in a hungry, searing kiss. Yielding, boneless, she felt love and desire ripple through her on waves of joy. He kissed the curve of her neck, turning her over, straddling her. His hand pulled the serape over her head, then went to the buttons of her shirt.

"Miguel . . ." Her voice trailed off as he bared a breast, bringing his lips to the full roundness, his tongue teasing the little nipple.

Naked in his arms, binding herself to him, she rose and fell with his strong, relentless pounding, her body melded to his, her hands clinging to the corded muscles of his back. Each wove an enchantment for the other. The cold mountain mist became a diaphanous veil; the hard ground upon which they lay became a soft bed with silken sheets and down pillows. He brought her to the brink, then retreated, brought her there once more and, the instant before release, pulled away again. Moaning, she tore at his hair, striving for the golden moment, grinding her hips into his pelvis until, with a powerful last thrust, he brought both of them out of their striving into the shattering light.

They were descending now, the horses stepping carefully down the rock-strewn trail, their hooves sending pebbles flying and bounding into the deep ravine thousands of feet below. The path twisted, bending around an outcropping of rock on which a lone tree had managed to take root, growing outward above the blue void below. On the far side of the sharp turn, coming toward them, was a line of *tamemes*, native porters, toiling up the precipitous trail, bent double under their packs. They carried charcoal, from where to where, Francisca's party could not guess. As the three of them drew aside, hugging the rocky wall, the *tamemes* passed silently, single file, without lifting their stoic Indian faces.

Toward late afternoon the trail flattened out, leading through a copse of trees. To the right on a cleared space stood a ruin, a tiered pyramid with steps leading to its flat top. Niches were carved in its sides, at close, even intervals on each layer, giving the impression of a many-roomed, many-

storied mansion with open doors. Each niche was crowned
by a stone image of a plumed serpent, a snarling jaguar, or
a taloned eagle. Weeds grew waist-high about it, seedlings
sprouting on the stone steps and in the fissures of the walls.

An eerie, ghostly air hung over it, a haunting silence that
made Francisca shiver in the hot sun, and Alvaro cross himself.

"Pagans," Alvaro said with disdain. "They would have
killed each other off if the Spanish hadn't come to save them
from their bloody rites."

"So we killed them to save them," Miguel said, irony
tinging his voice.

"You know very well that many of their own kind fought
with Cortés to overthrow their bloody priests."

"To their ultimate dismay, perhaps?"

"You speak oddly for the grandson of a conquistador."

"The truth is never odd, friend. Perhaps toward the end
of his life my grandfather might have thought the same. *Quién
sabe?*"

A mile from the ruin they observed a settlement nestled
in a shallow valley below the trail. They drew up and sat
looking down on the tiled roofs of four or five Spanish houses
and the thatched roofs of perhaps a dozen native ones. In the
tiny square around which the Spanish houses had been built,
a flock of vultures were feeding, while high overhead, two
more were wheeling.

"Something's amiss," Miguel said. "Let us go down."

No one came out to greet him. A mongrel barked half-
heartedly from an open doorway. And then they saw it, fly-
covered corpses pierced with arrows or with bashed-in heads
strewn about the dusty lanes, slumped in doorways, and
hanging from windows. A terrible stench of rotting flesh
permeated the air.

They trotted slowly down the street, covering their noses
with their kerchiefs. At their approach, cruelly beaked vultures cawed, rising with a flap of black wings.

They drew up in the shadow of a small, rustic church. Miguel dismounted. "Stay here; I'll only be a minute or two."

They watched as he entered a house, going from it to a second and third.

"A massacre," he said on returning, his face grim, "and recent from the looks of it."

Alvaro, shifting in the saddle, crossed himself again. "God have mercy on their souls." He looked around, his gaze lingering for a few moments on the trees beyond the houses. "Those savages could not have gone far. Pagan butchers! A curse on them!" His narrowed eyes scanned the carnage-littered street. "This place smells of evil, evil not yet finished. We should not linger, Miguel."

"I agree. Our friends here deserve a decent Christian burial, but there are too many. It would take days, a week. However, the least we can do is pray for their souls. A small—"

His words were abruptly halted by an arrow whining past his shoulder, embedding itself in the church wall, its tail quivering.

With one easy, graceful movement, Miguel swung into the saddle. And then he was leading them down the street at a furious gallop. Naked brown men erupted from behind walls and trees and, with bloodcurdling yells, sent a rain of missiles after them.

Francisca leaned low, hugging the mare's neck, her heart pounding with fear. She heard the sound of shots, and a moment later her hat flew from her head. God! Close, too close! Afraid that Miguel or Alvaro might have been hit, she raised her head for a quick look. All right. Miguel in front, Alvaro behind, shooting over his shoulder at their pursuers.

Up they went, clouds of dust rising under flying hooves, the tireless horses streaking along the ascending trail. From behind, the attackers whooped and shrieked, and mingled with these unearthly howls, Francisca could discern the sound of horses in pursuit. An arrow whizzed by her ear, and a second. Wheeling, Francisca followed Miguel as they thundered through the trees, branches slapping her humped back, tree trunks and moss-covered rocks flashing by at a dizzying speed.

Then they were out in the open, racing across the cleared

space where they had paused earlier, heading toward the ruined pyramid. Suddenly Francisca heard the twang of an arrow that had found its mark. She cried out as her horse faltered, stumbled, and went to its knees.

Miguel, still in the lead, whirled about, galloped back, and leaning over, grasped Francisca's outstretched arm, pulling her up to his saddle. The shouts behind them quickened, echoing with a note of triumph. But Miguel, exhibiting the kind of horsemanship that had won him accolades on the riding fields of Seville, pranced his horse about, and they were off, driving hard through the tall grass toward the pyramid.

When they reached its base, Miguel dismounted, shouting, "Up to the first platform."

They led their lathered horses—Francisca helping Alvaro with the pack horse—up the shallow, broken steps to the wide stone ledge.

"This will do," Miguel said.

"But we are so exposed," Francisca protested, momentarily expecting a murderous barrage of arrows and shot.

"If my guess is right, they won't dare come within shooting range," Miguel said. "They're superstitious; they're afraid of this place. Look."

Below them at a safe distance the Indians had gathered, a huddle of scantily clad little brown men, chattering among themselves and pointing. They were soon joined by another, larger band brandishing long guns.

"They must have captured the horses and guns from the Spanish," Miguel said, "Though only a renegade could have taught them how to use a wheel lock."

"Who are they?" Francisca asked.

"Pames, most likely," Alvaro answered. "Although I'm not sure."

The Indians hunkered down, prepared for a siege. Despite Miguel's assurances that they would not attack, Francisca felt uneasy and was relieved to see the sun sink into the west. Presently bonfires appeared, flames leaping high, throwing the figures of the Indians in sharp relief. They were cooking

their evening meal. Smoke sifting upward brought the smell
of burning cedar wood and roasting meat.

The ledge was cold and uncomfortable. The horses
stamped impatiently. Francisca mourned the loss of her little
mare, who had served her so well and faithfully. The wet
flanks of the three remaining ones had been rubbed down,
and now they wanted to be fed and watered. Miguel instructed Alvaro to empty the canteens into the tin bowls they
carried for their own use and give the water to the horses.
After that the beasts were offered the last of the maize cakes
and tortillas, which they sniffed at and finally ate.

Francisca's stomach rumbled, but more disconcerting was
her parched throat. She thought of the bubbling mountain
streams they had passed, the bounty of those icy waters that
were now out of reach. When Alvaro took a small orange
from his pocket and peeled it with his dagger, her mouth
ached to taste it. He handed it to her.

"Yours," he said. "It will help."

She insisted on dividing it into three portions, but the men
refused. Never in her entire life had an orange, wizened and
full of pips though it was, tasted so sweet.

How long the three of them—and the horses—could last
when even now hunger and thirst sat like the crouching, tooth-
baring stone images on either side and above them, she dared
not ask.

Alvaro, as if sharing her thoughts, said, "They'll outwait
us. The Indians are very patient."

"We could shoot our way through," Miguel said. "At
risk that one of us—or more—wouldn't make it. But I have
a better idea. We'll cut up our serapes and use the pieces to
muffle the horses' hooves. We can only pray they don't nicker
and give us away."

They divided the pack horse's burden among the other two
mounts, discarding blankets, utensils, and precious sacks of
provisions in order to lighten their loads. Descending stealth-
ily in the darkness, a cautious Francisca held her breath as
she led her horse down the wide stairs. The Indians, with the

exception of a sentinel who stood on guard a little distance away from the others, had stretched themselves out around the fire. The night was overcast, black as pitch, a situation that proved to be a mixed blessing. They could not be seen by the sentry, on the other hand, they must feel their way, each descending step a matter of touch and guesswork. If a horse should stumble or balk or neigh, then the pyramid would be surrounded, still from afar, but effectively enough to cut off any attempt at escape.

Francisca hung tightly to the bridle, whispering encouragement to her nervous mount, feeling its weight against her shoulder, testing the edge of each stair with her toe.

Finally they were on level ground. A wordless Miguel led them through the grass away from the fire and into the trees. Here they paused.

"Is there no other road except the one we took earlier?" Miguel asked Alvaro.

"None that I know of for certain."

Walking the horses down the mountain in the dark, where the next abrupt bend or a misstep would send them plunging into nothingness, took iron nerves. In addition, Francisca found her shoulders and neck muscles tensing, expecting at any moment to hear a chorus of wild cries and the thunder of hooves behind her, a signal that their flight had been discovered.

They walked until the gray, pearly light of dawn showed that they had reached a mesa. With the horses' hooves still muffled, they mounted and, kicking the animals into a canter, crossed the flatland. They rode for another two hours through a forest and out into the open again, pausing at last on the banks of a swift-running river.

It was only then that Francisca felt she could draw a safe breath.

Chapter XVII

The last leg of their journey was made through swampy low-lands, where the torrid heat and clinging humidity sapped their strength and tested their will.

It rained every day, at times a brief shower, clearing by midday, at other times a steady drenching downpour that continued through the night. They rode wet to the skin under dense, dripping foliage, plodding along muddy paths that sucked at the horses' ankles. Often the trail became obscure, and the men would bring out their daggers, slashing at the rank vegetation, the ropelike parasitic vines and contorted branches that sought for a ray of sunlight under the over-hanging green gloom. Twice they lost their way and had to retrace their steps through the sweating jungle.

Francisca, fighting crawling centipedes and huge, hairy spiders, rivers of biting ants and clouds of voracious blow-flies, soon lost her fear of an Indian attack. She could not imagine any human, red or white, living in this torrid, torpid climate where one trod the ground carefully in fear of poi-sonous snakes and lizards.

The abandonment at the pyramid of their blankets, cook-ing utensils, mosquito netting, and most of their food was a serious one. They were forced to subsist on whatever wild fruits they could find. At night, avoiding the soaked ground and crawling wildlife, they slept on nests of leaves they built in the forks of trees.

Miguel worried about the horses. As they were bred for the thin, clear mountain air, he was afraid they might sicken or founder before they reached their destination. Every night he rubbed them down and saw that they got clean water. Forage was another matter. Accustomed to corn and meadow oats, they would only nibble at the leaves and grasses brought to them. They grew lean-ribbed, their heads drooping, their chests heaving with the effort to breathe as they shambled heroically on. One evening as the weary trio prepared for sleep, Francisca's gelding lay down and died. In the morning they found Alvaro's mount had also perished.

With the men on foot and Francisca riding Miguel's horse, they finally reached Tampico three weeks after they had left Puebla.

The town, hardly bigger than a village, was built on marshy land cleared from the jungle. Situated on the banks of the Pánuco River six miles inland from the sea, it consisted of a cluster of wooden and adobe houses, overlooked by a church and a fortress. The heat and rain here were no less omnipresent than they had been in the steaming forest. A hurricane had battered the town only a week earlier and uprooted trees, shattered thatched roofs, and piles of debris still lay scattered about.

They spent the night as paying guests of a Don Alonso Benitez, the owner of a salt mine in the interior. He listened with an air of scarcely concealed dubiety to Miguel's story of being waylaid by Indians and having lost all but the gold he carried in his belt. Nevertheless, Don Alonso obtained passage for them on a small fishing boat that would take them down the coast to Veracruz.

The owner of the boat, Pablo, was a sinister-appearing mestizo with close-cropped, frizzy hair and a deep, ugly scar across his left cheek. When Miguel caught him looking at Francisca with hungry eyes (though she was still dressed as a boy), he threatened to cut his throat. At night Miguel and Alvaro took turns on watch. When they slept, they kept their guns between their knees. Francisca did not move unless she was within eyesight of Miguel or Alvaro, an awkward situation when it came to attending to bodily functions. In addition, the boat was small and stank of fish, and the water they drank was putrid. Still, Francisca felt luck had been with them. They were alive, and while she had suffered from a slight attack of dysentery in the jungle, none of them had taken seriously ill.

Sailing south, they hugged the coastline, passing white beaches and river mouths and, now and then, a clutch of Indian huts nestled against the backdrop of the jungle. They put in once or twice for fresh water, Pablo bartering with the natives for coconuts and shrimp. Miguel, afraid he might coax the Indians to join him in an assault, kept Pablo under surveillance. It was not a restful voyage, and nothing could have been more welcome to them than the sight of the island of San Juan de Ulua and the harbor fortress that guarded the port city of Veracruz.

Alvaro had a friend, Hernando, a wine agent, who lived in an adobe house not far from the squat little church Cortés had built at the time of the conquest. Miguel also knew and trusted Hernando, but not enough to tell him they were fleeing from the Inquisition. His story was a half-truth. They were wanted, Miguel said, for engaging in the illicit silver trade and withholding the king's fifth.

Miguel shaved off his beard, which had grown during their journey, and went out to the harbor to ready his ship for sailing. While he was gone, Francisca, attended by a half-caste maid, took her longed-for bath. Seated on a backless stool close by, Hernando's wife, a fat, heavy-jowled woman with a gap-toothed smile, watched her.

"You are his mistress?" Hernando's wife, Dolcina, asked, her black eyes bright with curiosity.

Francisca blushed. She couldn't say she was married. Miguel's friends and acquaintances knew he had a spouse in

Seville. And it would have been laughable to say that she was traveling with him as a friend. Young women did not accompany men who were not close relatives unless they shared their beds. On the mountain, in the jungle, in Tampico, where she had been dressed in male clothing, it hadn't mattered. But now, in the settled, civilized world of Veracruz, she experienced a sudden sense of the old shame. She had not been brought up to be a mistress.

"Of course, one could hardly blame you," Dolcina went on when Francisca did not answer. "Don Miguel is such a handsome man."

"He is more than handsome," Francisca said defensively. "He is courageous, a strong man with a noble heart."

And suddenly in her mind's eye she saw him risking everything as he led her through corridors of the Flat House; she saw his eyes filled with tender passion, and the smile that had come to mean the world to her.

No. She was not ashamed.

"I am his love," she added, lifting her chin. "And proud to be."

Miguel thought it best that Francisca remain in seclusion until they were ready to sail. He instructed Dolcina to have a seamstress come to the house and make up several gowns for Francisca. She was delighted. Her boy's outfit had been given to a ragpicker, to whom it justly belonged, and the dress Doña Dolcina had lent her was much too big.

The seamstress and her assistants were nimble-fingered enough to have the first ensemble ready in a few days: a pale blue silk with a square-cut neckline, a delicate lace collar, and full white sleeves tight at the wrist. Next, with great risk to their eyes, the seamstresses strained over tiny stitches, producing underclothing, petticoats and shifts of gossamer-thin cotton.

They had nearly finished a second gown, a nut-brown ensemble with a billowing skirt inset with panels of ivory satin, when Miguel burst into the house, calling for Francisca.

"The inquisitor's agents are looking for us," he said. "I thought they would have been gone by now, but I was wrong. They know who I am and have already searched the ship. I fear they might be able to trace us here. I don't wish to put Hernando at risk, so we must leave without delay."

"I shall have to pack at once."

"Throw what you can into a case. I give you ten minutes, not more," Miguel warned.

It was noon when they reached the ship. Anchored under the guns of the fort, held fast to the palisade by large iron rings, the *Espíritu* rocked on the incoming tide. A square-rigged four-masted galleon with a towering poop and forecastle, and carrying eight muzzle-loading cannons between decks, it was scheduled to leave with the flota on June 6. But Miguel could not wait. He knew it was risky to brave the pirate-infested waters of the Caribbean without the protection of Spanish men-of-war, yet with the Inquisition breathing down their necks, he felt he had no choice.

And in fact, they had no sooner boarded than a lookout reported that a longboat flying the green and white flag of the Inquisition was headed their way. Leaving instructions that the agents of the Holy Office were to be told that he was in Mexico City and that they were ignorant of the existence of a Francisca de Silva de Diaz y Roche, he whisked Francisca down below to the cargo hold.

It was a dark, musty hole, smelling of bilge and alive with the squeal and patter of rats. Space was cramped because of the crates of silver, sacks of cochineal, and dyewoods Miguel was taking back to Spain, and very little air sifted down to them from the closed hatches. They stood together, Miguel's arm protectively circling Francisca's waist, a grim half smile on his face.

"If only I could lop their heads off and throw their corpses to the fishes," Miguel said. "It's not my way to hide, skulking in a dark corner."

Francisca realized how hard it was for Miguel to refrain from facing his enemy openly. Yet if at any time he had thrown caution to the winds, had recklessly slashed at their pursuers, he would have been quickly overpowered, and both she and Miguel would have either been captured or killed.

He knew it. He was more than strong and virile, he was too clever to let the rash, cavalier need to prove himself overcome his intelligence.

And she loved him all the more for it.

Miguel tightened his hold on Francisca at the sound of footsteps on the deck directly above them.

"Señor Lopez . . ." they heard Alvaro say.

So he was here, inches away, the prosecuting attorney, the indefatigable stalking hound of the Inquisition.

"You have been here before," Alvaro went on. "I cannot allow you to inspect the hold again without written permission from the governor."

"In matters concerning the Holy Office, the governor's regulations do not obtain."

"But you are not of the regular clergy," Alvaro argued. "You merely represent the secular."

Miguel drew Francisca away from the ladder to a narrow space between a stack of crates and kegs. "Don't breathe," he cautioned.

"But where are you going?" she asked anxiously as he moved away.

"Shhh!"

He disappeared, and presently she heard the squeal of a rat. Peeking around the edge of her hiding place, she could barely make out Miguel's figure clambering over bulging sacks. He was bareheaded, his hat in his hands. God Almighty. He was catching rats!

"Are you splitting hairs, señor?" Lopez's voice demanded. "Or perhaps you have something to hide?"

"Not at all."

"Then I suggest you open the hatch. And have someone fetch a brand so we can see."

The moment the hatch was lifted, Miguel sent the rats scurrying up the ladder. Francisca heard a stifled "Ayeee!"

and then Alvaro saying, "You see, señor, as I told you the first time, only cargo and rats."

Later they had a good laugh, sitting in the captain's cabin over glasses of good red wine while Alvaro, with tears in his eyes, described the hasty departure of the Inquisitor's servitors.

That night they weighed anchor and, without the usual priests' blessings and the booming of guns, slipped through the channel and out to sea. Soon they were under full sail, running before the wind, hoping to put distance between themselves and Veracruz before morning. Francisca, standing at the rail under the mainmast, watched the sailors as they clambered down from the rigging, securing ropes and tightening winches. A brisk wind teased her hair and flapped the skirts about her legs. She breathed deeply, inhaling the invigorating salt air. Oh, it felt so good to be free of the pestilential heat, free from having to run and to hide. And for a short while, as she stood there lifting her face to the breeze, like a parched desert sojourner will lift his face to the rain, she felt a dizzy thrill of relief. They had evaded the bloodhounds, made mock of the Inquisition. The prison and chase were behind them. At last they were on their way to a new, and better, life.

The captain's cabin was small and plainly furnished with a bed, a chest of drawers, a table, its top inlaid with oyster shells, and an unvarnished desk. The only extravagant fixture was a large coffer with a domed lid, its gilded lock plates fashioned in the shape of dolphins. This, along with the other pieces, had been nailed down to avoid shifting with the rock and pitch of the ship.

Supper that evening, served in the officers' mess, was a gala affair, a banquet of roast fowl, fish *picante*, leg of mutton, and spiced yams, washed down with quantities of wine. They ate off of pewter plates, using silver spoons and knives, and drinking from mugs of thick pottery.

Seated at the square table was Miguel, with Francisca, resplendent in the nut-brown velvet, at his right. Alvaro sat at his left. In their places on either side were the surgeon, Pedro Aguilar, a swarthy little man with tobacco-stained chin whiskers, the boatswain, a sun-dried veteran of some two dozen voyages, and the master gunner, Rodrigo Andrade, who spoke little, laughed easily, and got very drunk halfway through supper.

Francisca herself felt rather giddy by the time she and Miguel retired to his cabin.

"Well, at least they did not speak or look at me as if I were a whore," Francisca said, the wine having loosened her tongue. "What they were thinking is another matter."

Miguel unbuckled his sword and threw it aside. "I don't like such talk. And I forbid it. When you say such things, you demean not only yourself but me."

"Oh, Miguel!" She gave him a sweet, tipsy smile, leaning toward him.

"And I don't particularly like it when you drink more wine than you can carry."

"You're scolding me. And I'm not so sure I like *that*. I'm not a child, you know."

His eyes went over her, taking in the white curve of breasts that pushed themselves up from her low-cut neckline.

"No, I don't suppose you are." He gave her a sudden impish grin, the kind of boyish smile that always melted her heart.

"Miguel . . ."

He drew her into his arms. "My darling, drink and eat as much as you like. God knows, you deserve to enjoy yourself."

For the first time since leaving the hacienda, they had a private place of their own. Still feeling the wine, she pushed herself free from Miguel's arms and began undressing for him. Flirting and coquetting with her eyes and a seductive smile, she slowly undid the looped buttons of her bodice.

Shrugging out of it, she tossed it carelessly over one creamy white shoulder, her provocative gaze never leaving his face.

When he made a move forward, she pushed him into a chair. "Please, sit," she ordered. "I'm not quite ready. You may observe if you like, but no more."

Extracting a cigar from the oyster shell case at his elbow, he lit it from the wick of an oil lamp. Then he leaned back, puffing as he watched.

"That's better," Francisca acknowledged. Unfastening her voluminous skirt, she pushed it with coy delicacy over her hips, using the tips of her fingers. Stepping out of it, she scooped up the velvet folds and tossed it to Miguel, who sat with it draped about his knees, hardly seeming to notice, so absorbed was he in Francisca's performance. What a woman! Every day he learned something new about her.

The petticoats came next, the fine lace-trimmed cotton garments the seamstresses in Veracruz had labored over, one following the other, falling in a white froth at her feet. She kicked them aside with exaggerated nonchalance. Then, sitting on the bed, she removed her slippers. With a slight pucker of concentration on her pink mouth, she rolled the stockings from her shapely legs.

She stood up in her silk shift and, lifting her arms, stretched, the silk outlining the nipples of her breasts, the slender curve of her hips.

She saw Miguel's eyes narrowing through a cloud of smoke, and laughed, a teasing laugh.

"Not yet," she cautioned.

With a swiftness that startled her, he ground out his cigar, brushed aside the encumbering skirt, and reached for her, pulling her down to his lap, crushing her in his arms, catching her surprised mouth in a hungry, possessive kiss.

"Tempt me, will you?" he growled, his hot breath scalding her cheek.

His hand snaked down between them, gathering the hem of her shift, pushing it upward, his fingers returning to slip between her thighs.

"But Miguel, I haven't finished. I . . ." But already a pleasant sensation was stealing through her veins.

Stroking, caressing, his fingers crept upward until one found the place and entered, titillating the warm wetness. Francisca swallowed as a growing tension seized her loins, an ache, a longing, a desire that flooded her senses.

"Don't," she whispered, even as her arms linked about his neck and she pressed her breasts into the silver medallion he wore about his neck. "Don't."

He bent his head and nipped at a flushed pink earlobe while he continued the intimate, unbearable stroking. *Don't! Stop!* She was losing her mind, her sanity, all rational thought vanishing in a frenzy of sensual pleasure. Her skin became moist with the fever of rising passion. Suddenly she gasped as the final heady rush of relief shuddered through her.

Miguel separated her legs, curling them about his back. Releasing his turgid erection, he lifted her slightly, then brought her down slowly so that his hard member slid into her sheath. Then, with a rocking motion, he thrust again and again, his fullness probing deep within her, the sweet agony returning fourfold. She held him, bobbing to his rhythm, her cheek pressed to his, his heartbeat under hands laid lovingly on his chest. Together they rode, sharing their ecstasy, two bodies, two souls, merging in one joy and rapture.

Afterward, satiated, their desire banked, they sat, exchanging tender kisses, until Francisca, with a deep sigh, rested her head on Miguel's shoulder.

"To think," she said, "that at long last we have a decent bed and didn't use it."

"Ah, but the night is young," he murmured, his hand gently pushing the tumbled hair from her moist brow. "And think of how many more before us."

Chapter XVIII

If all went well and fair weather held, they would reach Havana in fifteen days. With billowing sails, the flag of Spain flying from the mainmast, Miguel's pennant with the del Castillo coat of arms fluttering atop the mizzenmast, they cut their way through the azure waters of the Golfo de Campeche.

Even in calm weather the crew was kept busy. Miguel, believing that card play and dicing among the men led to squabbles, if not bloodshed, had instructed the boatswain to see that each man had his duty. The helmsmen took shifts, working two and two together, the carpenter saw to repairs, the cook to meals, the surgeon to the sick. Every morning the decks were scrubbed down and the pumps worked, for even in flat seas, water washed in from the scuppers and gun ports, or leaked in through the seams.

"A wooden vessel is never entirely dry," Alvaro told Francisca. "Belowdecks is the worst. Dark, dingy, with the reek of bilge. And airless, especially in bad weather, when the gun ports are closed. Once the rain or seas drip down from the upper decks, one learns to go to sleep wet and get up wet. The *Espíritu* is better than most, for Don Miguel sees to it that each man has a blanket. But I've been on many a voyage when all I had for bedding was the jacket I worked in."

It was the first time Alvaro had spoken of his past. From his accent Francisca had already guessed that he was not of the elite class. Now she wondered how he had risen from the lowly position of a seaman who slept below decks to Miguel's second-in-command.

"You have known Don Miguel long?" she asked, not wanting to inquire directly, but hoping that a tactful question would elicit some sort of explanation. To her disappointment, his answer was courteous, short, and hardly informative.

"A very long time," he said.

Later, when Francisca, her curiosity piqued, asked Miguel, he explained, "Alvaro's a tight-lipped fellow even with me, his closest friend. He has mentioned Cádiz as his birthplace, and that he never knew his father. Apparently he was apprenticed to a cooper at a very early age, a man who beat him regularly. I have the feeling that he killed him before he ran off to sea, for he never disembarks when we anchor at Cádiz, although the deed, if done, must have occurred some twenty-five years ago."

"And he shipped on with you?"

"Not directly. After knocking about a bit, he came to me ten years ago. He was an ordinary seaman until one day he saved me from the knife of a would-be mutineer. I grasped his intelligence at once. And over the years he has become my right hand. As I told you earlier, I would trust him with my life."

If Miguel's life could be trusted to Alvaro, Francisca had her doubts about some of the crew. Though she never ventured to the forecastle, where the men slept and ate, she could watch them at their work. They seemed a motley lot in their salt-encrusted, patched clothing, heavily bearded, their faces cracked with sea wind and sun. Miguel had told her that only the most hardy could survive a life at sea. What with fever, scurvy, cramps, and catarrh, not to speak of the dangers in working aloft in storms, it took luck, a stout heart, and a strong body to carry them from one voyage to another. Miguel had heard that scurvy could be combated with fresh vegetables and oranges, but these were hard to provide on a voyage that might last two months or more.

"It's true," Miguel said, "that many are recruited from the gutters of Seville and would as soon cut a man's throat over a tot of wine as blink. Discipline is the only way to keep them in line."

She was an inadvertent witness one evening to Miguel's "discipline." A seaman had stolen some biscuits from the cook's galley and, as punishment, was stripped to the waist, tied to the mainmast, and flogged. When Francisca later admonished Miguel for what she thought was too severe a penalty for the purloining of a few pieces of bread, he told her that the stealing of food aboard ship was a serious affair.

"We can only carry so much in the way of provision, a good part subject to spoilage. To steal from a limited supply that must last for long periods of time is more than a misdemeanor, it is a crime."

Once they entered the Gulf of Mexico, Francisca noticed that some of the men had armed themselves with cutlasses, short, curved, razor-sharp swords they wore tucked in their belts. Alvaro reported that there were murmurings among several of the men that they should have never ventured beyond Veracruz without the flota to protect them.

"They all knew the chances they were taking before we sailed," Miguel said in disgust. "Why else did they think I offered them extra wages? What a pack of old women."

Alvaro shrugged. "There are always the few who seem able to stir up the rest."

"Find them," Miguel ordered. "I'll have no cowardly talk. A touch of the lash might cure them."

Nevertheless, as they neared the island of Negritis to take on fresh water, Francisca could feel the tension aboard ship reflected in the frowns that both Alvaro and Miguel now wore.

"Miguel," she said one evening after they had retired to their cabin, "I think I should learn how to use a pistol or a musket, perhaps a sword."

"What?" He was astounded. "A woman has no business with a weapon."

"There might come a time when I must defend myself," she pointed out reasonably.

"With me beside you? I cannot see it."

"All the same, it would amuse me, if nothing else," she coaxed, smiling. "I'll make a wager with you. If I cannot handle a sword within a week reasonably well, then I will forfeit . . ." Forfeit what? She had nothing but the jewelry Miguel had managed to buy for her in the short time they were in Veracruz: a ruby ring and a gold neck piece. "My ruby ring."

He grinned. "Put that way, why not? As for my bet, what say, a thousand pieces of eight?"

Francisca had always been agile, an excellent dancer, light on her feet, well coordinated, and graceful in motion. Her skirts hampered her a bit, but Miguel said he had seen enough of her in pantaloons; he would give her a handicap.

They practiced with blunted sword points on the aft deck, to the entertainment of the sailors. It was all done in fun with a great deal of merriment, and by the third day Francisca was well on her way to winning her wager.

One afternoon Francisca was sitting in the shadow of the cabin, feeling very housewifely as she mended a pair of Miguel's hose. Alvaro, who had come up to retrieve a chart, paused to sit beside her while he waited to consult with Miguel.

"He's gone down to look in on a crewman who is with the surgeon. They feel several of his toes might be gangrenous." The man's foot had been crushed by an iron chock that had fallen on it.

"God help him," Alvaro murmured.

After a small silence Francisca said, "Do you think the other officers mind very much my being on board?"

"Good heavens, why should they?"

"Well, as I understand it, they are forbidden to bring their own wives or . . . women."

"It's up to Don Miguel to set down the rules. He is not only owner, but master and captain as well. As for you, Doña Francisca, you represent a triumph over the Inquisition for Don Miguel."

"A triumph? I don't quite understand."

"Did he not tell you? A favorite quartermaster of his was arrested in Seville by the Holy Office, accused of being a Protestant, and burned at the stake."

"No, he never told me," Francisca said slowly, a sudden suspicion creeping into her mind. Why hadn't he? Why had he kept the incident a secret? "So he obtained his revenge by saving me?"

"Oh, you mustn't misunderstand, señora. I have no doubt his love for you is sincere. But it did give him a great deal of pleasure to know he had thwarted the inquisitors."

They did not speak for a few minutes. Francisca went on plying her needle. A puff of wind billowed the top sails, snapping at the canvas and ruffling her skirts. The ship's cat sat on an overturned butt nearby, licking her paws.

"Tell me," Francisca said, "*was* the quartermaster a Protestant?"

"No. Don Miguel will have no one but Catholics aboard." And then, realizing his mistake, Alvaro blushed a deep red. "Excepting you, señora."

"Of course." She gave him a forgiving smile. Then, because he seemed vulnerable at this point, she asked him another question. "Have you ever met the Doña Ana, Miguel's wife?"

"I have not had that pleasure. But I have been given to understand that she is pious to a fault, and virtue in excess is not always pleasing to a man."

He was playing the diplomat. How else could he describe a wife to a mistress?

"Is she beautiful?" Francisca probed.

"I am told she is very beautiful, indeed."

Francisca felt as if a dagger had been thrust into her heart, inflicting a sickening wound. She tried to minimize the pain by telling herself that no matter how beautiful Doña Ana was, how Catholic, it was she, Francisca, Miguel loved.

They sighted Negritis on the eighth day. It was a small, wooded island that rose out of the sea like a green crown of leaves circled by white, sandy beaches. Negritis was uninhabited and as yet unused by the marauders who roamed these seas in their pinnaces and shallow-drafted barques.

Within a mile of shore the *Espíritu* hove to and dropped anchor. Two longboats carrying empty kegs were launched, their rowers heading for a tiny inlet at the mouth of a river. Fresh water, always a problem on a voyage, was their quest. Though they were little more than a week out of Veracruz, their water had already turned brackish, breeding slimy little creatures that made it offensive to drink. Francisca had noted that very few of the men had made use of the spigoted barrel that was kept at the door of the cook house.

"They prefer their ration of wine," Miguel told her. "And I won't let them have more lest we have a problem with drunkenness. They'll get thirsty enough when the fresh meat and fruit gives out to salt fish and dried beef."

"Will we be living on salt fish and dried beef, too?"

"Not entirely." He smiled at her. "Would you mind?"

"No,' she said, linking her arm in his. "I could exist on love alone."

"What a romantic you are, my sweet Doña Francisca. I have half a mind to instruct the steward to serve you an empty plate tonight to see if you mean it."

"Of course I do," she laughed up at him.

* * *

It was the morning of the tenth day. Francisca had been awake since before dawn, her stomach feeling the roll of the ship. Something she ate? She couldn't understand it. This was the first time she had experienced any seasickness. The weather was calm enough. Why now? Unless . . . Could she be with child again?

She felt her breasts. They seemed normal enough. She could not remember when she had had her last flux. Sometime on their flight through the mountains, perhaps. That was more than a month ago. Perhaps she was pregnant. If so, she did not know whether she should welcome her condition or not. It would mean another bastard. She hated the word, but there was no escaping it. She was not married, and her offspring had no legitimacy, though Miguel would be happy to have further proof of his virility.

He *was* happy. "When?" he asked, beaming.

They were still abed, the faint voices of the men at six-o'clock prayer reaching them from the lower deck.

"If my calculations are correct," Francisca said, "next January."

"I shall hope for another boy. If he is born in Rome, it will be a great thing to have him baptized there."

Francisca said nothing for a moment or two. "And what if I should say I don't approve of baptism, that I don't want him or Jorge—God bless and keep him—brought up as a Christian?"

"Be reasonable. I am not saying *you* must convert, but my sons—"

"They are *my* sons, too!"

"They shall not be Hebrews, not with del Castillo blood in their veins."

She sat up, eyes blazing. "So! You haven't changed. You are the same. The 'del Castillo blood!' as if mine were tainted." Her voice trembled with rage. "All is well as long as I remain compliant and docile in your bed, but if I dare—"

"Oh, for God's sake!" He tossed the covers aside and got to his feet, staring down at her, his face flushed with anger.

"You compliant? You've never been compliant when it comes to that damned religion of yours."

"So my religion is damned and not yours! Why did you ever come to the Flat House to release me? Don't answer!" Her own fury was so great, she had to pause and swallow spittle. Yet dimly, under all that anger, reason tried to intrude, reason that told her how foolish it was to quarrel about such a matter. But she was too far gone now and could not stop. "I'll tell you why you rescued me. Because you had a grudge against the Inquisition. You wanted revenge for destroying your shipmate, didn't you? Admit it!"

His lips tightened into a white line of exasperation. "And because of a grudge you think I risked my life?"

"Yes. It would be like you. You went into it as if you were pacing a dueling field."

"And what if I did?" He jerked on his pantaloons. "I saved your damned neck, didn't I?"

Where had love gone? The honeyed words, the sweet promises? They were hurling words at each other they might both regret. But she wasn't going to submit with a humble apology. Just as she was beginning to think his feelings had altered and that he had accepted her as she had accepted him, he had revealed himself as the same, obdurate, doctrinaire. He still felt that as a Jew of less than noble birth, she was beneath him. What arrogance!

"You wanted a woman," she threw at him. "You accomplished two things with one act. You evened the score with the Inquisition, and you got a mistress into the bargain."

"You mean I got a shrew. A screaming fishwife!" He buttoned his coat as he strode to the door. "I wish to God I had let you rot in that cell!"

She did not see him all that day. His chair at mealtimes remained empty. If the other officers missed him, they gave no sign, and she was too proud to ask what duty kept Miguel away from the table. He did not appear at bedtime. Where he slept, if he slept at all, Francisca did not know.

The next few days were the same. Miguel continued to be

absent, sending no word or explanation. Once or twice she espied him on the poop deck talking to one of the helmsmen, but that was the closest he came. She missed him. She missed his banter, the long, gossipy talks they had of an evening; she missed his wild, passionate lovemaking, missed sleeping with his arms wrapped about her. Without him the cabin seemed deserted, the bed a cold and lonely place.

She could almost forgive him for his assumption that their children were his to dispose of and bring up as he liked. No woman, whether peasant or *condesa*, would question a husband's decision. That was the way of the world. But she had hoped for some tempering of his prejudice, some compromise they both could reach. Now she knew how implacable, how iron-willed he was. Yet she loved him, and regretted bitterly that she must tell him she had been mistaken in thinking she was pregnant.

She was sitting on a chair in the cabin with these thoughts going round in her head when his shadow loomed in the open doorway. She turned, prepared to smile at him, to make some light remark, when he said, "Well, Princess, have you sulked long enough?" in a tone that put the onus of their quarrel upon her.

Francisca searched his face and found no warmth or sign of reconciliation. "I thought it was you who were sulking," she said in a cold voice. His air of self-righteousness so close to contempt angered her. And to think only a moment earlier she was ready to say she was sorry. "Or did you think to punish me by your absence?"

He contemplated her with a chill, impassive look in his blue eyes. "If I wished to punish you, I would have used a more telling method."

"Oh, I see," she acknowledged tartly. "Perhaps bread and water? Or the lash administered by the tyrant himself?"

"Francisca, I warn you . . . !" He took a step forward, his face dangerously dark. She was wondering, with a mixture of fear and strange excitement, what he intended to do when a cry from the crow's nest rang out.

"Ship to the starboard!"

Miguel hesitated, and when the cry was echoed from the bow, he whirled about and, with one stride, was out on deck.

"What colors does she fly?" he called.

"A green turtle on a white background. Her pennant is the red jack!" came the distant shout.

"Damnation!" Miguel cursed. Then, raising his voice, he shouted, "Boatswain! Furl the spritsail! Rodrigo! Where in God's name . . . ! Rodrigo, prepare for battle! Run out your cannon for point-blank range!"

Miguel rushed back into the cabin, flipped open the lid of the coffer, and began arming himself with pistol, cutlass, and sword.

"What is it? Who are they?" Francisca asked, one hand at the base of her throat. "What is their flag?"

"Pirates of Tortuga! The red pennant means surrender or no quarter."

Alvaro and the other officers rushed in and quickly took up arms from the chest.

Alvaro said, "Pity we can't outrun them."

"Damn their hides, no," Miguel cursed. "The Spanish build their ships too clumsily for the chase. We shall have to face and outgun them. See that the carpenter's gang downs the bulkheads and that each man gets a musket."

He turned to Francisca. "Lock yourself in. Under no circumstances are you to come out on deck."

"But—"

"Francisca, do as I say!"

He left, slamming the door after him. Francisca moved to the open porthole. Careful not to be seen by Miguel, who stood with Alvaro at the rail, she strained her ears to hear.

"Mother Mary!" Miguel exclaimed, peering through his glass. "There are ten of them as I count. An entire fleet. A brigantine, five barques—and yes, coming up behind are three pinnaces. Here, have a look."

Alvaro took the glass. "One flies the French colors. It may be Jean Blanchard's buccaneer fleet."

"To hell with him. He'll soon get a taste of our shot."

"They'll make for our bow, where none of our guns can reach them," Alvaro said. "I'd say send a dozen of our best muskets there to keep them from jamming the rudder and boarding."

"A dozen! I should have two dozen. Can't be helped. For all their grumbling, what we have are stouthearted enough. Go down, Alvaro, and have the men string their hammocks in the netting to shield them from enemy fire. I'll have a word with the helmsmen."

And then they were gone. Francisca heard the sound of running feet, shouts, and the clank of iron. Suddenly she felt the lurch of the ship as she heeled.

Unable to bear the tension, she stole out on deck. Ten minutes later the *Espíritu* sent its first blast echoing across the water. She saw a puff of smoke and a distant fountain of spray as the ball fell short of the brigantine leading the pack. Slowly the buccaneer ship drew closer, its cannon barking, the pirate crew lining the rail plainly visible now. Raising muskets, they began to fire, the *Espíritu* answering, her guns flashing in rapid succession, their recoil rocking the decks. The noise became deafening. The booming of the cannon and the sputter of muskets mingled with shouts and curses and the cries of the wounded. Francisca saw two crewmen slumped at their posts and one man with a bloodied leg being lifted and carried down to the surgeon's quarters.

Miguel stood on the quarterdeck, his eye to the glass, speaking calmly to Alvaro, who from time to time shouted an order to Rodrigo.

Presently a pall of yellow smoke eclipsed the enemy ships. Then, as it drifted skyward, Francisca saw that the brigantine's mizzenmast had taken a ball and hung crookedly from its rigging. Coming up close in a wide circle were the barques and pinnaces like jackals, biding their time, waiting for the kill. The brigantine's master, seemingly unperturbed by his wrecked mast, swung slowly, making for the *Espíritu*'s bow. Miguel barked an order, and a dozen musketeers ran through the waist of the ship to the forecastle. Taking up their positions, they set their guns to blazing, the shout of the chief marksman rising above the clamor. "Keep it steady. Load! Fire!" The brigantine boldly replied with a thunderous cannonade from a stern-chase swivel gun.

Francisca felt the impact of the volley moments before the cry of "Pumps!" went up. The Spanish vessel had been hit midship, but still she held steady, her guns spitting shot. The hoarse yell of "Fire!" jerked Francisca's head around. Orange flames leaped up from a coil of spare rigging dangerously close to where the kegs of powder had been placed. Powder was deliberately kept at a distance from the guns to avoid just such an incident. Once the flames reached it, the powder would explode, blowing the ship out of the water. A seaman was trying to slap the fire out with his coat when, overcome with heat and smoke, he fell back. Miguel leaped down the ladder, racing toward the flames, grabbing a bucket of water as he ran, flinging it at the fire. Then two crewmen lifted one of the tubs of water kept handy between the guns for the purpose of dousing any chance spark and hurriedly brought it forward, dashing its contents at the leaping flames. The last glowing shreds of the burning rope were quickly stamped out.

In the meanwhile, the brigantine at the head of the pirate fleet was closing the gap between them. Miguel, resuming his post, caught sight of Francisca and angrily waved her inside. She replied by crouching out of gunshot against the rail. But she wouldn't retreat to the cabin, where she could see nothing, wondering what was happening, not knowing from moment to moment how the battle was going.

Suddenly the *Espíritu* shuddered, jolted by a series of deafening cannon shots. Francisca cautiously raised her head and peeked over the rail. The barques had come within firing range and were hitting the Spanish merchantman with round after round of devastating fire. The foremast went with a thunderous crack; sails were shot through and left hanging in tatters. In return, the *Espíritu*'s guns had disabled one barque, tearing away its single mast. Another barque apparently had been hit below the waterline, for it could be seen listing, and then a few minutes later it sank. But the pirate's brigantine, still flying the red pennant, clung to its position—a ship's length off the bow—with the tenacity of a bulldog.

Francisca's hands had turned clammy with cold sweat. She did not fear for herself as much as for Miguel, who to her seemed unnecessarily exposed. He had positioned himself on the quarterdeck and was firing a musket as fast as he could reload it. His hat had been shot off, and his red-gold hair gleamed through the smoke. She wanted to shout, "Protect yourself, please, for my sake!" But he would not have heard, and if he had, would not have listened.

The wounded and dead lay where they had fallen, as the men were too busy to carry them away. The surgeon, apparently, had his hands full belowdeck. Francisca, feeling more and more helpless as she watched the battle rage, now saw where she could be useful. Moving quickly into the cabin, she pulled the bedding away and tore the sheets into strips, using teeth and hands in a frenzy of haste. Grabbing a bottle of brandy, she ran out and quickly descended the short ladder to the deck.

The smoke was thicker here, almost blinding, its acrid fumes choking her lungs and bringing tears to her eyes. The groans and pitiful cries of the men, the sight of gaping wounds and the odor of blood, sickened her. Standing there, one hand still on the ladder, she fought the urge to flee the inferno of fire and smoke, a hell where the noise of the bombardment mingled with an unholy heat and the stink of death.

But her hesitation lasted only a few moments. Squaring her shoulders, she stepped down into the chaotic madness, going from one wounded man to the next, forcing herself to kneel, trying to bind up torn flesh, the legs and arms, heads and torsos, that had been ripped through by enemy fire. The brandy bottle was soon emptied. She ran to the water keg and filled a leather bucket. It was shot from her hands before she could carry it a few feet. Back she went, filling a nearby jug, too absorbed by her task to feel fear.

Men clutched at her skirts, begging for a drink. The hoarse cry of "Water!" followed her as she stepped over the dead, their glazed eyes staring up at her in seeming reproach. Aware that her feet were getting wet, she looked down and saw to her horror that her slippers were sodden with blood. Perspiration ran in rivulets down her grime-streaked face, gathering under her arms and between her breasts, soaking her bodice. The strips torn from the sheet had long since gone, and she began to rip up her petticoats. She was bandaging a seaman's head when a chorus of shouts made her look up.

Above them, bow to stern, loomed the mast of the brigantine, her rigging swarming with pirates armed with grappling hooks.

"Look to yourselves!" came the cry. "They're going to board!"

The pirates came in a rush, leaping from the rigging to the decks of the *Espíritu*. Those on the pinnaces and barques scrambled up the sides as agile as monkeys, brandishing cutlasses and poleaxes. They were a terrifying sight, and the greatly reduced company of Spaniards was no match for them. Yet they fought bravely with anything that came to hand: cutlasses, knives, muskets, pistols, and linstocks. The melee of plunging arms, dodging feet, and twisting bodies was accompanied by screaming oaths and shrieks of pain. Through the din and the crush of men fighting hand to hand, Francisca, by hugging the rail, managed to make her way up to the quarterdeck.

There Alvaro and Miguel stood shoulder to shoulder engaging a pair of bearded ruffians in a duel to the death. Flattened against a bulkhead, Francisca watched, her heart leaping in her throat, her gaze never leaving Miguel, as if will alone could protect him. His face glistening with sweat, his eyes blazing with savage hatred and contempt, he fought with contained skill. Lashing out, dodging and ducking, then lashing out again. The pirate, tall as Miguel, with black, curling hair and a hawk nose, smiled as he parried Miguel's thrusts, calling him a soft Spanish dandy. Miguel held his tongue, saving his strength for the business at hand. A flick of white light and he scored a point, slashing the pirate's shoulders, drawing blood. The pirate leaned forward, bringing his weapon down, aiming for the heart, but Miguel deflected the blade. Still they fought on, steel ringing on steel. Frightened as she was, her knees shaking in terror, Francisca nevertheless felt a thrill of pride run through her veins. There was no one like Miguel; there would never be.

Then suddenly Alvaro whirled about, clutching his chest. A knife had been thrown from the rigging, striking him through the heart. He went down without a murmur. The brigand who had been fighting him kicked his body aside and turned his attention to Miguel. Now Miguel was dueling two adversaries.

It isn't fair! Francisca wanted to scream. She edged around and picked up Alvaro's bloodied sword. Before she realized what she was doing, she had engaged the second brigand. The attack by a woman caught him off guard, and Francisca, taking advantage of his momentary surprise, rammed the sword through him with all her strength. He fell at her feet, his body jerking convulsively, then going still. As she pulled the sword from him, it passed through her shocked mind that she had actually killed a man and hadn't shrunk from it.

But she didn't have time to ponder or wonder. A short, lean corsair had bounded up the ladder and was now seeking to wrest the weapon from her. But she wouldn't allow it. Cutting at him, crossing steel with steel, she brought into play every trick Miguel had taught her. Suddenly her attacker drew back, feinted, then with a jab and twist of his wrist, cut her overskirt from her. He laughed, showing gap-toothed gums. Angry now, she thrust at him, a careless move, for the next moment he had knocked the sword from her hand. He spoke in French, words she could not understand, but he made no move to put his cutlass through her, as she half expected. Instead he kept her pinned to the bulkhead, his weapon raised threateningly.

Francisca, turning her head, saw that Miguel, now bleeding from his sword arm, was fighting two men again. He can't keep it up forever, she thought in despair. *No quarter*, he had told her. He would fight until his last breath.

She began to pray, in fear and confusion mingling Catholic with Hebrew prayers, the Hail Mary with snatches from David's psalms. To no avail. God did not hear her. A few moments later Miguel lost his sword, and the curly-haired pirate gave him the coup de grace.

Francisca tried to run to him as he lay in a pool of blood, but was prevented by the brigand who guarded her. She wept then, wept openly, unashamedly, tears running down her dusty face, calling on him, sobbing his name. But Miguel did not answer. He would never answer her again.

Chapter XIX

The dead, along with the wounded, were flung overboard. When two of the buccaneers commenced hauling Miguel's body away, Francisca screamed and tried to get at him. She was restrained and forced to watch helplessly as they tossed Miguel into the sea.

The *Espíritu's* cargo and guns were shifted to the brigantine. Francisca, also considered part of the booty, was bound hand and foot and carried aboard the pirate ship. She was spared the horror of witnessing the slaughter of the remainder of Miguel's crew. The ship itself was put to the torch. The merchantman, slow and awkward, built for the endurance of long voyages, was of little use to the cutthroats, who relied on speed and maneuverability to hunt their prey.

Francisca was installed in a cabin that seemed to be the officer's mess. Still bound, she sat on a velvet-upholstered chaise impervious to her surroundings, too full of grief to care or to speculate about her future. It did not seem possible that life could end for such a strong, vigorous man as Miguel. But it had. He had been killed; for him it was over. But not for her. How could she go on breathing, feeling the beat of her torn heart, when he was dead? Why hadn't she been killed instead of Miguel? Of all the cruelties she had suffered, this seemed the worst. Had she been angry at him? Had they quarreled? Yes, there had been words, but she couldn't remember what had been said or why.

A shadow darkened the doorway, and a pirate in the cast-off coat of a British officer entered. He spoke in French, and when she made no response, he hoisted her from the chair, cut the rope from her ankles, and led her out on deck. The rank smell that emanated from his blood-encrusted clothing sickened her, and she shrugged out of his grasp. He laughed, a high, cackling sound, but made no move to touch her again.

The pirate stopped before another cabin door, knocked, then entered.

"La femme," he announced.

The curly-headed buccaneer who had killed Miguel rose and gave her a slight bow.

"Señora."

For a brief moment Francisca felt a hot surge of hate. Then it was gone, and the dullness of exhaustion and despair took over.

"I'm sorry we've had to inconvenience you." He spoke heavily accented Spanish, a tall, swarthy-skinned man with a gold earring threaded through his right earlobe. He had changed clothing and was now dressed in a claret-colored velvet coat over frilled spotless white linen. His cutlass and a pistol were thrust into a wide belt at his narrow waist. Black breeches tucked into high leather boots polished to a gleam completed his costume, one that contrasted sharply with that of the ruffian who had just escorted her.

"Permit me." He removed his cutlass and cut the remaining ropes from her hands. At his touch, she went rigid, but he did not seem to notice.

"Please sit." He indicated a carved-backed chair.

Without speaking, she accepted his offer, more to ease her trembling knees than to obey.

"Let me introduce myself. I am Jean Blanchard, captain and commander of this fleet. The ship you are on is *La Duchesse*." He paused. "And you, señora, are called . . . ?"

She did not answer.

He drew up another chair and sat facing her. "I realize that this may be an ordeal for you. I'm sorry about your husband, a brave man, but such are the fortunes of war."

She wanted to spit at him, but her mouth was so dry, she couldn't bring moisture to it.

"So you do not choose to speak." He looked her up and down, coolly, without desire, much as a man would assess the good points of a horse or a mule he has won as a prize. She was aware in a dim, dull sort of way that her grimy face and torn dress did not impress him, and she was glad. If hate could kill, he would have been dead by now.

"I see by your eyes that you are angry, and rightly so." Blanchard gave her a small smile. "But let me assure you that no harm will come to you. As soon as your ransom is collected, we will set you free."

Ransom? From whom? Who was left of her family to buy her freedom? No one, no one at all. The unreal nightmare of grief and terror she found herself in, capped by a polite request for ransom, struck her as insanely funny. And suddenly, as if a dam had burst, she began to laugh and sob, gripped by a hysteria she could not control.

The buccaneer struck her. His slap had the weight of a powerful arm behind it and snapped her head back on her neck. The laughter and the tears ceased abruptly. She sat still, eyeing him, her hand on her stinging cheek.

He rose and went to a cabinet and removed a bottle, pouring some of the contents into a chased Venetian glass. "Rum," he said, holding it out to her.

"I don't want it."

"Drink it," he ordered, pushing the glass at her.

She was too drained to argue. The rum burned her throat, and she coughed. He waited a moment, then put the glass to her lips again. "Finish it. *Please.*" She swallowed, closing her eyes momentarily as the raw liquor spread warmth through her body.

Blanchard put the glass aside. "Now we can talk in a more

civil manner. Please, what is your name?" He had a way, she noticed, of being civil, of saying "please," that carried with it an undertone of threat. He was courteous, but it was a courtesy that masked a ruthless will.

Gathering the tatters of her exhausted strength, she drew herself up, meeting his hard black eyes. "I am your prisoner, señor, and I suppose I have no choice."

"None. I think it would be wise if we understand each other from the beginning. You are called . . . ?"

"My name," she said with biting clarity, "is Doña Francisca de Silva de Diaz y Roche."

"And your husband, the captain—I assume he was the captain—of the *Espíritu*?"

"Don Miguel Velasquez del Castillo."

A flicker of interest passed across his face and was gone. "Then you were a passenger."

She did not correct him.

"And your husband, then, is . . . where?"

"He is dead."

"Your family?"

"They are either dead or in prison."

He leaned back in his chair, contemplating her again with cool appraisal. "It will gain you nothing to lie, señora. If you are no good to us for ransom, then I have no choice but to pass you among my men for their amusement."

Francisca felt her skin crawl She had seen enough of the pirates to know that they were a crude, barbarous lot. Hairy and unwashed, they had crowded around her, their eyes filled with lust, before Blanchard had ordered her transferred to *La Duchesse*. To lie stripped naked before them while each took his turn, panting like animals over her, was a horror she did not want to contemplate. If the buccaneer chose to kill her, she could accept death, but not mass rape.

She realized now the mistake she had made in telling the truth. If she had named her husband as ransomer, it would have taken months before the pirate's emissary traveling to and from Mexico City would have discovered Ruy was dead, months during which she might have attempted, and perhaps succeeded in, escape. But wait, she told herself; it might not be too late to invent a lie.

"Very well," she said after a few moments, as if she had given the matter weighty thought. "I have an uncle in Acapulco. He trades in goods from the Philippines and could well afford to stand my ransom."

"I see." He had eyes that seemed all of a piece, pupil and iris black and as hard as stone. "And you and this uncle are on good terms?"

"Yes. I am his favorite niece." Did he believe her? She couldn't tell.

"His name?"

"Don Alonso de Cardenas. He lives on the Calle de Flores, not far from the waterfront."

"I see."

She wished he would stop saying, "I see." She wished she could read those implacable features, the eyes that gave away nothing.

"Acapulco is a long way from here. It means sending someone across the isthmus on muleback, unless we chose to go round the cape. And then there is no assurance that your uncle would be forthcoming. It depends . . ."

Again the black eyes assessing her.

"You could put me ashore in Jamaica," she suggested.

He smiled, a smile that did not reach his eyes. "I am afraid I would not receive a hospitable welcome in Jamaica. I would say the same goes for Havana, if you are thinking of that."

"No."

"We might have had another alternative had you been a virgin." He shrugged, a movement of powerful muscles that rippled under the claret velvet. "There is a certain gentleman that pays fairly well for untried maidens—white, that is, and fairly young. But, of course . . ."

Again that smile that in the growing dimness of the cabin seemed sinister.

"Why don't you run me through with your cutlass and

have done with it?'' she asked wearily, irritated because she was forced to bargain in this manner with a scoundrel.

He leaned back in his chair, fingering the inlaid ivory and silver handle of his cutlass. ''You have spirit, I see, señora. But I make it a rule not to use violence against my female prisoners.''

''But you would have them raped?''

''Used, señora,'' he corrected. ''But . . .'' He leaned forward so that his velvet-clad knee touched hers. This time, oddly enough, she felt no impulse to shrink back. For a span of moments her irritation and dislike, lulled under his suave civility, gave her the false sense of dealing with a gentleman. ''I will consult with my men before I make a decision. In the meanwhile, I am sure you will want a fresh gown. And a bath—sea water, I'm afraid.''

She stifled the impulse to thank him. Why should she thank him for murdering Miguel, for taking her captive?

''You may use my cabin. I advise you not to venture too far from it since my crew is not always of the same mind as myself. There is a key to the door you may use for safety's sake.''

He rose, brooding down at her for several moments. ''It will be a long voyage for you, señora. Let us hope, for your sake, it is a successful one.''

While she waited, she had time to study the cabin, which was furnished more luxuriously than the *Espíritu's*. There were rich carpets underfoot, a heavily carved wardrobe against one bulkhead, and a bed, wide enough to be shared by two, hung with brocade and silk. Another chest, decorated with fruit and flower marquetry, was brought in by a tall, thin pirate, who gave her sidelong glances as if he had been warned not to look at her but could not help himself. When he had gone, she lifted the lid and found that it contained gowns of satin and velvet, in hyacinth blues and apple greens. In addition, there was silk underclothing, petticoats and shifts, minutely stitched with gossamer threads, and beautifully embroidered. And slippers of doeskin leather.

Booty, of course. From what ships had this apparel been stolen? Who had worn the gown and petticoats, and what feet had walked in these slippers? The furnishings in the cabin, the Venetian glass, the gold-knobbed press, the inlaid table, the bed itself, perhaps the rum, too, had all come by the sword, murder and pillage done with callous brutality.

And she was a prisoner of these men, bound to them, their possession until redeemed, an impossibility since there was no generous uncle in Acapulco. The thought of taking her own life as a way out of her dilemma flashed through her mind. With Miguel dead, what reason did she have to go on? But even as the thought occurred, she dismissed it. There was Jorge. For him alone she must survive; she could not surrender. As long as there was the possibility—even re-mote—that she and her child would be reunited, she would face whatever had to come. Perhaps, if God was with her, the *Duchesse* would be captured by a merchant ship whose sympathetic captain would set her free.

No one disturbed her while she bathed in a rusty tin tub, the sea water stinging her skin. Dressed and combed, she was silently served by the thin man, who brought in a supper of beef packed in vinegar, and rice studded with currants. After he had removed the tub and the tray, she locked the door. Then, fully clothed, she lay down on the bed and, finally giving vent to her grief for Miguel, cried herself to sleep.

In the afternoon of the following day Jean Blanchard knocked upon her door.

"Señora—" the same courteous bow "—may I come in?" His gaze took her in: the crimson gown with its clinging bodice, the slim waist aproned in lace, the white arms ex-posed from elbow to wrist. Something moved behind those black eyes, an unfathomable thought or emotion. Surprise? Male admiration? She could not tell.

"I can understand now where your uncle might be well disposed to pay the one hundred thousand pieces of eight," was all he said by way of noting the change in her appearance.

It was, at best, a left-handed compliment. Yet Francisca had to stifle the civil urge to thank him.

"I've come to tell you that we are bringing the *Duchesse* into a lagoon to careen and refit her. You will be transferred to one of the smaller ships until we are ready to sail again."

"Would it be possible for me to go ashore and stretch my legs on dry land?"

"No. I assure you, señora, that this particular island is uninhabited, if you are thinking of seeking assistance. Furthermore, the men will be dividing booty, then celebrating with drink and boisterous carousing. It could be unpleasant."

She wished he wouldn't smile that way. There was something in the curve of his lips, the steady, dark gaze, that inferred he might enjoy the unpleasantness himself. She did not like him any the better for it.

After a week the fleet set sail again, on the prowl, looking for the Spanish flota that was rumored to be on its way from Cartagena to Puerto Rico. A few days later in the early afternoon as they lay in wait in the Mona Passage, they caught sight of the fleet. Twenty-three ships, all heavily armed, with the snouts of their cannon poking out below the taffrails. Francisca, watching from the porthole, saw them sailing majestically by and thought, with a lift of her Spanish heart, that Blanchard's pirates would not dare to attack. She was right. The pirates kept their distance. But after the others had disappeared over the horizon, a laggard came along, a galleon alone and unprotected.

Francisca heard a cry go up. She went out on deck and watched while a pinnace, a boat with a single sail and eight oars, was made ready. It was launched after nightfall and joined by two others from adjacent barques. It was too dark and the Spanish galleon too far away for Francisca to see what was happening, and although she strained her ears, she heard no sound of shots.

The pinnaces returned toward dawn laden with booty. As Francisca learned later, it had been a bloodless capture. The man had scrambled up the poop and, surprising the officers over cards and brandy, had seized the great ship without firing a shot.

Two weeks later the pirate fleet dropped anchor in the harbor of Tortuga, their home port. Levasseur, the French governor of this tiny island off the coast of Hispaniola, acted as middleman, buying the cargoes the corsairs had captured, then disposing of them to his advantage at Port Royal, Jamaica.

Here on Tortuga, Blanchard had built his stronghold. Like the governor, the buccaneer had placed his fortified dwelling on a high, rocky promontory, reached by a series of stone terraces, each of which accommodated a battery of guns and ten men. The last thirty feet to the top was accessible only by means of an iron ladder which could be raised or lowered. Francisca, making that climb, felt her heart sink. Though she had a magnificent view of the sea and the mountains to the north, she felt just as imprisoned as she had been on the *Duchesse*. How could she possibly escape from this rampart, where the eagle eye of Blanchard's sentries could detect anything that moved along the face of the rock?

Yet she would not allow herself to despair. Some day, she told herself, an opportunity would come, how or in what guise, she could only imagine in fantasy. But she was determined that she would not surrender to apathy, that she would never permit herself to be reduced to a slave or used as a whore by Blanchard's thugs.

She was given a large, airy room, where sunshine poured in from windows framed in crimson velvet. The walls were hung with beautifully wrought tapestries depicting Aphrodite rising naked from the sea and Eros poised with bow and arrow. The bedposts, carrying out the love motif, were carved in the form of cupids. The chest containing the apparel she had used aboard the *Duchesse* was carried in. But there were more gowns hanging on pegs in a lacquered Chinese cupboard, lovely wide-skirted silks of gray, turquoise, and black.

Francisca wondered who had used this room before her, what woman had slept in the bed, fingered the gowns, stared out of the window. Another prisoner like herself? Or perhaps at one time Blanchard had had a wife or a mistress, a woman who no longer graced his island home.

He came the next day to inquire if she was comfortable.

"As comfortable as anyone confined against their will can be," she answered tartly.

"How you fare depends entirely on you." He was dressed in black velvet, the white of his shirt contrasting with his dark skin. Handsome, Francisca thought dispassionately, in a sinister sort of way. "You may have the run of the house, if you wish. And if I see that you have accepted your situation with grace, then you may go anywhere on the island you choose."

"You would trust me, then?"

"Tortuga is a small place, señora, eight leagues in length and two in breadth." He seated himself in a high-backed chair and stared at her with impassive eyes before he spoke again. "You may hide in the woods, perhaps, or swim to Hispaniola, but I doubt you would do either."

"Are you that certain?"

He shrugged. "We would find and bring you back, in any case. And then . . . well . . ." He spread his hands. "I shall leave it to your imagination."

She said nothing, her mind refusing to imagine.

"The governor dines with me tonight," he went on. "We should be honored by your presence."

She was on the point of refusing when it occurred to her that she might appeal to Levasseur for her release. True, he dealt in pirate booty, but he was an official of the French government and might be persuaded to negotiate or order her to be freed.

"I will be pleased to attend," she said, smiling sweetly, thinking that rancor had not accomplished much. Should the governor fail her, she might lull Blanchard into believing her docile, and thus make him less watchful.

She wore crimson, her skirt and low-cut bodice slashed over with cloth of gold. She had no jewels—the few she had received from Miguel had been taken from her—and her slender white throat rising from a creamy bare neckline cried out for the sparkle of precious gems. Yet gazing at her poised and regal reflection in the baroque-framed glass, she asked herself, what is vanity? If Miguel was not here to see her, what did it matter if she had no jewels? What did it matter if her cheeks glowed pink again, and the black hair he loved so well (worn tonight in a braided crown intertwined with a golden ribbon) had regained its glossy luster? It was for Miguel she wanted to be beautiful, and for no other.

The governor rose and kissed her hand, his small, slitted eyes going over her in a frank disrobing sweep. He was not alone. The woman with him was introduced as Madame Lenoir, obviously Levasseur's mistress. Madame, no longer young, with pale blue eyes, a painted face, and blond curls piled high on her head, gazed at Francisca with undisguised venom.

Francisca ignored her. Seated next to Levasseur at a table laden with silver and gold service, Francisca tried to engage the governor in conversation and found, to her dismay, that he did not understand a word of Spanish. What few French phrases she had managed to pick up since her capture were woefully inadequate to convey her message. Nevertheless, she smiled a great deal at him, and later, when they had retired to the *grand salon* for coffee and brandy, she managed a few moments alone with him while Blanchard was engaged in showing Madame Lenoir the recent acquisition of a marble statuette. By using her hands and what she believed were eloquent facial expressions, Francisca sought to explain her predicament. The governor, however, took her efforts as flirtatious, and covertly grasped her hand, guiding it to his swollen member.

She moved away from him quickly and seated herself in a chair across the room, where she remained until the couple bid their adieus.

After they had gone, Jean Blanchard gave Francisca his arm and escorted her back to her room. Instead of leaving her in the corridor, he came inside, closing the door behind him.

"I am very tired," Francisca began. "I would prefer—"

"I don't give a damn what you prefer. Sit down." There was cold fury behind those words, all the more intense because his face did not betray a sign of emotion. "Sit! *Por favor! Please.* That's better."

He towered over her, observing her with a cool malevolence. "What did that performance mean in there? And don't tell me you don't know what I'm talking about. You were batting your eyes and thrusting your bosoms at the governor like a prostitute soliciting a client."

She went red to the roots of her hair.

"So you can still blush. Did you have the mistaken notion that *he* would pay your ransom, or perhaps that by offering yourself as a bed partner, he would help you escape? Let me dissuade you. The man is venal. But not stupid. He knows better than to cross me."

"Then you own him, too," Francisca said, recovering from the insult, meeting his hard gaze with a determination not to allow this rogue to intimidate her.

"What I own is beside the point. We had an agreement, and you broke it."

"If we had an agreement, it was one entirely on your side."

He bent and brought his face close to hers, his dark eyes smoldering. "Liar!"

She drew back. The smell of brandy on his breath was

overpowering. He must have been drinking glass after glass
while she was sitting next to Levasseur in the salon.

"You're drunk," she said, her stomach clenching.

"Not too drunk to know a liar. But . . ." he said, straight-
ening, "it comes as no surprise. I've known for some time
how smoothly you can fabricate a story that is utterly false."

"I don't know what you mean," she said haughtily.

"Don't you?" He seated himself on the edge of a table,
swinging one booted leg, his eyes going over her, slowly.
This was not an indifferent assessment like the one she had
encountered when she first faced Blanchard, but an appraisal
deliberately stripping her bare, a narrow-eyed survey lingering on her white breasts with a frank sexuality that sent a
shiver up her spine.

"You can hardly blame me for attempting to use any means
to gain my freedom," she said reasonably, giving him a small
smile to hide her growing fear. "Wouldn't you do the same?"

"Let me warn you, señora, if you are thinking to appeal
to my better nature, I have none. Furthermore, I do not suffer
liars."

He walked to a cupboard where a supply of liquor was
kept. Sloshing rum into a glass, he came back, resuming his
seat on the edge of the table. "I drink to you, Doña Francisca
de Silva de Diaz y Roche. At least you gave me your correct
name. But for the rest . . ." He raised his glass to her, then
drained it.

Blanchard eyed her for several long moments. "Where
would you go if I did set you free?" he asked abruptly.

Francisca hadn't thought that far ahead. All she wanted to
do was to get as far away from Blanchard and his freebooters
as she could. Spain was out of the question now that Miguel
was dead and could not give her the protection she needed.
Nevertheless, she lifted her chin and answered. "Seville."

"Liar," he said softly, his voice silky smooth. "The Inquisition is waiting for you in Spain, isn't it?" Then roughly,
"Isn't it? Well, answer me!"

"Yes."

"And you have no uncle in Acapulco."

"But I—"

"He is fictitious, made up out of whole cloth. Am I right? Speak!"

"Yes." She wet her dry lips. Then, as he continued to glare at her, "How long have you known?"

"Oh, I suspected from the first. And my suspicions were confirmed by a certain attorney, representing the Holy Office, Señor Lopez. Does that name touch a chord in your memory? I thought so. He happened to be a passenger on the Spanish galleon we raided, and when it was mentioned that we had a compatriotess of his as prisoner, calling you by name, he wanted you turned over to him. And I assure you, if he could have paid your ransom, there would have been no hesitation on my part."

"Then why didn't you do it?" she threw at him bitterly, despising him. "Why didn't you hand me over to Lopez if you knew that I had no uncle—or family, for that matter—who could redeem me?"

"I never give anything away unless I have no use for it." Again his eyes rested on her breasts, traveling to her throat, to her warm, red lips. "You are a very beautiful woman and should be worth something in the marketplace. Perhaps one or two of my own men might bargain for you, share and share alike."

If he had thought to reduce her to pleading for compassion or mercy, he was wrong. Above all, she would not show fear, though her heart trembled and shook in her breast.

He got up and strolled aimlessly about the room, finally circling behind Francisca's chair. She sat rigid, not moving, hardly daring to breathe.

"I have been trying to make up my mind what to do for some time now." Casually, he placed his hand on her bare shoulder.

She suppressed a shudder. Of fear? Or was it something more? The strong hand resting on her flesh, its implied virile strength recalling another hand, perhaps?

For a long time he stood motionless in that pose, not speaking, while Francisca sat as if made of stone, wondering what he was thinking, yet afraid to turn her head.

Still behind her, he lifted her from the chair by the elbows and stood holding her, her back to him, the chair between them.

"Have you nothing to say on your behalf, señora?"

She tried to wrest free, but he shifted his hands to her arms, gripping them so tightly, she nearly cried out with pain. "You disappoint me, Doña Francisca. I would have thought you had some clever retort. Another.lie, perhaps."

She drew in her breath. "I refuse to give your insults the dignity of an answer." She was too angry now to be afraid. "You are nothing more than a beast!"

With a violent motion he booted the chair aside and whirled her around. His face was dark as thunder, his eyes burning into hers. "You are right. I am a beast and have acted the gentleman too long."

Slamming her against his chest, he caught her mouth in a brutal, ravaging kiss. She tried to arch away from him, but a steely arm brought her back, flattening her breasts against the cold, hard buttons of his coat. His tongue pried her stiff lips open, darting inside, pillaging her mouth. Then he was kissing her again, bruising her lips, moving with hot hunger to her cheeks, her throat, then down to the soft mounds of her breasts.

When he finally lifted his head, she could only say weakly, "Let me go."

He laughed, and his laughter was more chilling than his kisses. Still holding her with one arm snaked about her waist, he traced the outline of her breasts with a finger and smiled diabolically as he felt the nipples rise through the silken cloth.

"So you do not hate me as much as you pretend."

"I spit on you!"

He drew her back, sinking his teeth into her shoulder. When she cried out, he ripped at the neckline of her gown, tearing it down the front. Using the last of her reserve, she tried to struggle free, but his hand gripped and held the tangled mass of her hair while the other hand tore at her gown, stripping it away.

In a matter of moments she was naked, thrown across the bed, feeling his weight on her. She closed her eyes as he fumbled with his clothing, hot tears running down her cheeks, waiting helplessly for him to take her.

But nothing happened. He remained poised over her. She could feel the pounding of his heart, his heavy breathing. But he made no move to part her legs, no move to fondle her breasts, no move at all.

Cautiously she opened her eyes, round and luminous with tears. Resting on his elbows, he was staring at her with a look she could not fathom, a deep, dark gaze, pensive and brooding. Then he lowered his head and kissed her gently on the tip of her nose, on her bruised and swollen lips, brushing her cheek, her throat, her breasts, with a tenderness she found strange and, despite herself, moving.

"La Belle Francisca," he whispered. *"Tu es très belle."*

He made love to her slowly, with evocative lips and hands, taking great care to rouse her. She kept telling herself that she hated him, that he had killed Miguel. But she was of flesh and blood, young and vibrantly alive. Soon, despite herself, she felt a familiar warmth stealing through her body, drowning her in a treacherous sensual languor. She closed her eyes again, pretending it was Miguel kissing her, Miguel stroking her arms, caressing her breasts, Miguel's mouth trailing fire along her inner thighs, *his* tongue flicking and teasing until she found herself moaning with pleasure.

When the buccaneer separated her flanks and entered her, she responded, rising to meet him, matching wild passion for passion in a frenzy of mounting joy. And at the last, she cried out Miguel's name.

The buccaneer lay beside her. He had lit a cigar and silently puffed at it while he absently stroked Francisca's hair.

"So he was your lover," he said at last, "the captain of the ill-fated *Espíritu*?"

"Yes."

"Did you love him very much?"

"Yes. Very much."

He turned to her in the dark. "But he is dead, *ma chérie*."

"Yes, he is dead." She paused, adding softly, "But not for me. Never for me."

Chapter XX

Determined to have her forget Miguel and make her completely his, Blanchard showered her with jewels: emerald and diamond baubles from Brazil, bloodred rubies from Hindustan, and lustrous pearls from the fisheries of Rancheris. He provided her with silks and brocades from China, and set a gold, gem-encrusted coronet from Peru upon her dark head.

Yet he never declared his love, never once spoke a word that would indicate he had given his heart to her. Francisca often wondered if he did have a heart. She did not love him, would never love him. The kind of love she had for Miguel could only happen once in a lifetime. But she thought it odd that this man who could display such ardor, who could huskily whisper ardent French words of endearment in her ear, never once, even at the height of his passion, murmured *"Je t'aime."*

She knew almost nothing of his past. Whether his good manners had been inculcated by a genteel upbringing or whether he had come from plebeian stock and somehow had acquired a smooth patina of civility was a mystery. How or why he had fallen into piracy was also a secret he apparently did not care to divulge.

Yet he showed no reluctance in discussing the present situation, explaining the workings of his marauding fleet, its structure and method of operation, and sometimes in his cups, even boasting of his personal exploits. She knew that he, like all buccaneer captains, had been elected by the men and that they divided the booty according to a set of articles agreed upon before each voyage, the captain and the officers receiving a larger share than the ordinary seaman. The first man to spy out a ship's sail on the horizon, and the first man to board a prize, earned a bonus. There were five other captains besides himself, all subordinate, and all elected because of their bravery and their expert seamanship. Asked why, if the spoils were divided so fairly, he lived so luxuriously while the others seemed to get by in comparative squalor, he gave her a simple answer.

"I do not squander my ill-gotten gains, as those brutes do. They spend everything they make on wine and whores as fast as it comes into their hands. I've known some who will buy barrels of wine just to splash it on passersby in the street. After an orgy on Saint Kitts, you might find the prostitutes of the town wearing diamonds and sapphires. On the other hand, I've not only retained my gold and jewels, but have made some sound investments, which have paid handsomely."

"What sort of investments?" Francisca had asked out of curiosity.

"Various ones. There are always fools begging to be duped out of their money."

He was a scoundrel and gloried in it. He had no use for the English shopkeepers who fleeced his crew nor the French planters who lived off the backs of slaves. The Spanish he scorned the most.

The pirates, he told her, had no corner on brigandage or cruelty. When one thought of the plunder the conquistadors had taken from the Aztecs, their wanton massacre of thousands of Indians, how they had slowly worked to death thousands more in their mines and on their haciendas, Blanchard and his freebooters seemed like a band of light-fingered thieves.

As for the Inquisition, he could not think of a more nefarious and inane institution.

"I don't give a tinker's damn whether you observe the law of Moses or that of a Toltec's," he told Francisca. "What is hard for me to comprehend is why anyone would go through so much anguish for the sake of a creed. Wouldn't it have been simpler for you and your family to embrace the Catholic church?"

How could she explain that faith had not only bound the Judaizers to their God but to one another as well? She recalled with a lump in her throat the Sabbath eves at home, the glowing lights of the candled menorah, her father's voice, the soft, sweet smile on her mother's face, and the love that had wrapped them all in warmth.

"You would never understand," Francisca said. "A man without conscience, who is unprincipled and godless, could never conceive of the spiritual joy that comes in the belief of Jehovah, God of Israel."

"And I suppose your lover understood. Señor Lopez mentioned that he was a Roman Catholic who had committed the heinous sin of helping you escape the Inquisition's clutches. Very commendable. And even as a son of Mother Church, he accepted your adherence to Judaism?"

"Of course he did," she lied, remembering her last quarrel with Miguel. Now, in retrospect, the angry words they had exchanged seemed even more petty. She had loved him so much, what difference did it make if he wanted his sons to be Catholic?

"I suppose," Blanchard said casually, "he was a finer man than I gave him credit for."

"He was . . ." Francisca began, then suddenly found that, again, words failed her. She could not describe Miguel to a cutthroat ruffian like Jean Blanchard any more than she could describe her feelings for Judaism. Miguel was as strong, intelligent, and brave as Jean, but there the similarity ended.

While the buccaneer was motivated solely by selfish expediency, Miguel lived by a code of honor, a chivalric ideal which tempered violence with pardon. And the more she knew Blanchard, the more Miguel's luster brightened.

Soon she could no longer pretend to herself that it was Miguel making love to her. When she tried to resist Blanchard, he fought her with bruising relish, enjoying the struggle and his ultimate—always foreordained—victory. Unwilling to give him the satisfaction of bringing her to submission, Francisca endured Jean's caresses, never forgetting that hanging over her head was his threat to dispose of her in a way that would humiliate and degrade and, in the end, kill her. She was his possession, just as the gowns and the jewels she wore were his possessions, and she chafed under the knowledge, secretly despising him, waiting, hoping for an opportunity to break free.

He had told her that if her behavior warranted it, she would have the run of the island, but she was not advised to wander about alone. "Too dangerous," he told her. So he appointed a disabled freebooter, Pierre Barrot, to act as her guard.

Pierre was older than the general run of buccaneer, or perhaps it was his scarred face, from which one eye gleamed balefully, that made it seem so. In addition, he had lost both hands and wore iron hooks in their place, instruments that he used with chilling deftness. He made no secret of his distaste in being assigned to escort a woman about. And it was some weeks before Francisca learned that he spoke Spanish as well as French and English.

She made another discovery. He had no particular fondness for Jean Blanchard. Though he never spoke a word against him, Francisca sensed by a look or an occasional meaningful shrug or muttered curse that Pierre viewed his captain with a great deal less than respect. She stored this knowledge away, though how she would use it, she hadn't decided.

In the meanwhile, he performed his duties with maddening tenacity. She could not take a step outside the door but that he wasn't there. He was a constant presence, either over her shoulder or as a shadow on the wall, when she strolled the path that skirted the house. If she was to climb down the ladder, he was there above her. Some days, thinking to get away, she would select a horse from Blanchard's stable located at the edge of the town. Galloping over a stretch of savanna and through the woods, her hair streaming in the wind, she would head for the Côte-de-Fer, feeling that at last she had shaken Pierre. But before long a glance behind revealed him trotting doggedly after.

Blanchard and his fleet would be away for weeks at a time, plundering ships and sacking unprotected settlements on the islands of the Greater Antilles and along the coast of Panama and Venezuela. They would return to Tortuga, their holds filled with silver ingots, dyewoods, cloth, indigo, damask, and confiscated brass cannon. Then from the town below would come sounds of high revelry, shots, shouts, screams, and drunken laughter. But Jean rarely lingered in the taverns with his men. He would stride into the house, swing Francisca in his arms, throw her on the bed, and make hungry, passionate love.

Life was precarious and lived for the moment. No one cared about the future or who governed the island as along as they had a middleman who gave them a fair price for their goods. This indifference to local rule, combined with a callous disregard for human life, was illustrated by Blanchard's lack of concern when Levasseur was assassinated by his two adopted sons in a quarrel over Madame Lenoir's favors.

The adopted sons, Thibault and Martin, subsequently declared themselves joint governors of Tortuga. Not a soul, least of all Jean, protested or thought overmuch about it. That was the way the world went. Plunder was their business, not politics.

Francisca thought often of her family. She could not forget her mother's face as she lay dying. She wondered about poor,

mad Leonor, about the fate of her father and Aunt Juliana.
She agonized over the loss of Jorge, hoping he was alive, that
his captors were not treating him cruelly, and that someday,
praise God, she would see him again.

But it was her dreams of Miguel that disturbed her the
most, eerie nightmares in which he tried to reach her through
leaping flames as she stood tied to the stake. Sometimes it
would be he who was bound and she who was desperately
trying to bridge the fire and release him. One night she had
a particularly vivid dream. He was sitting in a circle of dark-
skinned Indians, dressed like them in a leather-fringed
breechclout, his face painted with blue and yellow streaks.
Suddenly he sprang to his feet. She could see his face
so clearly, the sapphire-blue eyes, the flaring nostrils, the
copper-colored beard. He spoke her name, ''Francisca.'' Just
her name, that was all. But spoken so clearly, she could have
sworn he was in the room and that his voice had awakened
her.

He wasn't in the room. The man sleeping beside her was
Jean Blanchard, not Miguel Velasquez del Castillo. But she
knew then just as surely as she knew she had a beating heart
and breath in her lungs that Miguel was alive. He was not
lying on the bottom of the ocean, a drowned corpse, half-
eaten by fish, but whole and alive. Logic told her that this
could not be true, that her own eyes had seen him run through
with a sword and thrown overboard. But logic and intuition
were not the same. In the very depths of her soul she *knew*
that somewhere, somehow, he lived.

From that day forward she began to think about escape,
not in a vague, nebulous way as she had all along, but weigh-
ing pros and cons, mulling over one possibility, then another.

Hispaniola lay only a few miles across the channel. If she
could reach it, or better still, the city of Santo Domingo on
its south coast, she would almost certainly find refuge. She
couldn't do it alone, of course. She would need at least two
men to row or sail a small craft. Surely among the few hundred buccaneers who were at Blanchard's command, there

might be at least a pair who were amenable to helping her escape if sufficiently bribed.

By this time Francisca was on a conversational footing with Pierre. Not that they talked much. Their topics of discussion usually consisted of the weather, the possibility of storms, the tides, and the interesting shells washed up on the beach. One afternoon while riding through a forest, they happened upon two hunters who had bagged a boar. After Francisca remarked on it, Pierre gave her a short history of the island, how it had once teemed with wild cattle, hogs, and horses, descendants of the domesticated animals brought over by the Spanish from the Old World. The men who had hunted these animals, dressing the hides, curing the meat, and selling them to ships that put in at the harbor, were French and English. But the Spanish, wishing to gain control of Tortuga, killed off most of the animals in order to drive the hunters away. Instead of disappearing, the hunters became buccaneers, the name itself, Pierre told Francisca, derived from the French *boucanier*, one who dries meat.

The subject threw Pierre into a curious reminiscent mood. He began to talk about his life as a hunter, about his comrades, a brotherhood of hearty souls who slept under the sky, using a nest of leaves for their bed, smoking their clay pipes and drinking their liquor neat around a roaring fire each night.

"We were free men," he said, a note of nostalgic regret in his voice. "Beholden to no one."

"And it all changed when you gave it up?"

"Yes."

"Your hands . . . ?"

"That came later. After I had taken to the sea."

She waited for him to tell her how it had happened. They were riding side by side now, following a trail that led past a cane field and through a stand of cedars. When they paused at the banks of a small stream to let the horses drink, he said, "Jean Blanchard cut them off."

She turned to him in shock. His mouth was twisted in bitterness, his one good eye gleaming with hatred.

"But why?" Francisca said, breaking the stunned silence.

"I was accused of stealing a leather pouch that contained a few pieces of eight."

She did not ask if he had actually stolen the pouch. Instead she said, "But surely the punishment hardly fit the crime." When he did not speak she asked, "Why do you stay?"

"Because I have no choice. I'm his slave. I have no money, nothing but two useless stumps. It is easier to stay than to run away."

"No!" her voice was sharp with denial. "Listen, my friend, I am just as much a slave as you. I will never give up wanting to get free of this island. I have the money, jewels worth a small fortune, enough to gain us both our freedom."

For one brief moment she thought she had spoken too soon. What if Pierre had lied to her? Suppose he was loyal to Blanchard, in fact, had been instructed to lead her on with a false tale of how his hands had come to be lopped off to test her? But no, that would have come months ago, early on in her captivity. She believed Pierre. She had to.

"We could get a small boat, a canoe or pinnace, and sail to Hispaniola," she went on eagerly. "We can do it while Jean and the fleet are away."

"Blanchard, as well as the governors, keeps sentries posted whether he's in port or not," Pierre said. "It won't be easy."

"But not impossible?"

"No. Though I think we should try for Santiago de Cuba instead of Hispaniola. And we should have another man, perhaps two."

They spent the next few weeks refining their plan. Pierre was able to enlist two other pirates who were more than willing to receive ample payment for a risk that seemed minimal compared to storming a village or ship. A pinnace would be hard to come by without attracting notice, so it was decided they would use a large canoe rigged with a single sail. With favorable winds and good weather, they should make the Cuban port in three to five days.

They waited until Jean and his pirate fleet took to the sea. The two renegades, Phillipe and Stéfan, respectively, had pleaded illness as their excuse for staying behind. The canoe was outfitted with several casks of water, some dried beef and fish, and a sack of plantains. There was some delay because of rough weather, but before dawn on a Wednesday morning, they stole out of the harbor while the sentry above was still getting the sleep out of his eyes.

Putting their backs to the oars, the men rowed out into the straits, where they hoisted their sail. Francisca, wrapped in a dark blue cape, sat in the prow. The wind was sharp and cold, colder than she imagined it would be, and she drew the hood of her cape over her head. If the wind held, they would be in Cuba in a few days. She smiled at the thought. She had no definite idea what she would do once she reached shore, but she would think of something. Though Cuba was Spanish, she hoped Santiago was too much of a backwater to be troubled by the Inquisition. With the money she received from the sale of what was left of the jewels after she paid the men, she would be able to organize a search for Miguel. Reason told her that it was foolish to embark on a quest over such a vast territory as the Antilles on the strength of a dream, but she would never be satisfied unless she tried.

The wind died completely in the afternoon of the second day, and the men were forced to go back to the oars. Pierre, with his iron hooks, could not row, and by evening there was some grumbling about how fortunate it was for some people to escape hard work.

The third and fourth day found them still becalmed. Their supply of water was dangerously low now. Phillipe and Stéfan objected to a ration of equal shares. They did most of the work and deserved a larger portion. The merciless sun beating down from a cloudless sky and reflected up from the glassy sea increased their thirst and shortened their tempers. Francisca, sitting under the shade of the limp sail, felt the animosity of the two men against Pierre and herself. The bag of jewels she carried next to her heart grew heavier and heavier. She realized that both Phillipe and Stéfan were armed. They could easily overpower Pierre, kill her, take the jewels, and throw them both into the sea.

A small wind rose on the fifth morning, then died. The men, tormented and weakened by thirst, gave up rowing, letting the current take them where it would. Pierre told Francisca he feared they were drifting east, beyond the Windward Passage, which divided Cuba from Hispaniola.

"Sooner or later we must sight land," Francisca said, refusing to despair. "There are many islands in these parts, and once we touch shore, we can replenish our water and take our bearings."

The next evening a sandy-beached coastline appeared on the horizon. The men, taking heart, rowed toward it. But as they neared the island, they saw huge rollers crashing in white foam on a jagged reef. It was too dangerous for even their shallow-drafted boat to cross without being knocked to kindling.

Under the hot sun, Pierre's face seemed to shrivel like a raisin. He never complained, hardly spoke at all. If he regretted this expedition, he made no sign. On the other hand, Phillipe and Stéfan cursed bitterly and loudly. Unable to quarrel with Pierre, who simply refused to speak, they quarreled among themselves, occasionally hurling an invective against Pierre or Francisca. She ignored them, just as Pierre did, straining her eyes on the skyline, praying for a landfall. She had faced thirst before, but never like this, with water all around, tantalizing aquamarine-blue water stretching in every direction, yet fatal to drink.

Soon the two men grew too ill and weak to quarrel. They lay sprawled against the oarlocks in a delirious semicomatose state, occasionally emitting a feeble groan. Watching them, Francisca clung to her own sanity with a tenacious ferocity. She had been through too much to give up. *This* was not the way she was going to die.

One morning Francisca awoke and noticed that Pierre had not shifted position since he had fallen asleep the night before. Crawling past the two men, she leaned over him. His face was the color of bleached bone, his skin cold to the touch. Sometime during the night he had died in his sleep.

Phillipe and Stéfan, fearing the corpse might attract sharks, debated whether to throw him overboard. But the sight of his dead body was unnerving, and soon, when the heat of the day was upon them, he would begin to smell. He had been a small man, and now shriveled and desiccated, he could not have weighed more than a child. Yet groaning and sweating, it took all their strength to heave him over the side. In a few minutes, true to their fears, they were surrounded by the sinister dorsal fins of a half dozen sharks. They sat watching in terror as the agitated waters turned dark with blood.

A half hour later the wind came up, the sail filled, and they began to move. Stéfan managed to get hold of the tiller, but soon his arms gave out and he sunk down in his seat, his body racked with dry sobs. Francisca, attempting to reach him, was almost there when she saw the tall masts of a ship in the distance.

It was *La Duchesse*.

Jean Blanchard, returning unexpectedly to port, and learning of Francisca's flight, had gone in search of her.

His retribution was merciless. First he had Phillipe and Stéfan's eyes burned out, and then, using his own cutlass, severed their heads.

Francisca's punishment was to watch this grisly procedure. When she tried to appeal to Jean to spare the men, saying that she was to blame, he said, "I don't look on it that way at all. My men are always free to go or come as they like as long as they do not steal anything that belongs to me. Rest assured, Francisca, their deaths could have been far worse, a lingering agony that could have gone on for days. I thought I showed great leniency."

She was taken back to Tortuga—while not in chains, it might as well have been so. She was no longer allowed the run of the island. Confined to the house and the perimeter of the platform upon which it stood, she was closely watched. Both the outdoor sentries and the servants within the house were changed every few weeks, so that Francisca would not have the opportunity to befriend or bribe them.

Otherwise nothing was changed. As before, Jean treated her with outward courtesy. Making love to her now, he told her, was more exciting than it had ever been.

"I sense that you are afraid, Doña Francisca, and fear always gives a fillip to a man's desire. Hate, too. I like that much better in a woman than mewling declarations of love. Hate shows that you are by instinct passionate. Just to my taste."

If a show of hate gave him pleasure, then she would never let him see the depth of hers. Nor would she let him know the slightest sign that the hope to be free was as strong as ever.

Chapter XXI

Tortuga had a new governor. The Chevalier de Fontenay, appointed to succeed Levasseur, landed on the island prepared to take over from Thibault and Martin, by force if necessary. But the two assassins, seeing they had little support from the islanders, quickly came to terms, receiving pardon for their crimes and full possession of their property.

To Jean the change meant little. De Fontenay, despite his illustrious title, was an adventurer, and had come to the Indies in search of his fortune. From the beginning of his tenure he and Blanchard established a mutually beneficial arrangement. The French governor went one step further than his predecessors. He issued a letter of marque to Blanchard. The so-called letter (a forgery, which de Fontenay had no authority to serve even if it were authentic) was an official patent which permitted Jean to attack foreign towns and seize foreign ships in the name of the French king. It had one advantage over the pursuit that Blanchard already enjoyed. If caught, his commission was security against a hanging.

"Fontenay fancies himself a lady's man," Jean told Francisca, "and boasts of his conquests. Not that I hold it against him. Conquests are a man's privilege. What concerns me is how he will perform if the island is attacked."

"Do you expect such an attack?"

"The possibility is always there. The Spanish would like to regain Tortuga and, no doubt, are waiting for the right opportunity. *I* am prepared for it. I'm hoping that de Fontenay is of the same mind."

Jean's words were more prophetic than he had anticipated.

At dawn on the morning of June 15 the people of Tortuga awoke to find five Spanish men-of-war anchored in their roadstead. Blanchard had just returned from a successful raid on the towns along the Mosquito coast, and his entire fleet, with the exception of one barque still at sea, had been commandeered during the night. Blanchard's ships had been easy prey. The crews, as was usual after a successful voyage, had been in the town celebrating their capture of several rich prizes in a drunken spree, and the few men left on board had been swiftly overpowered.

It was evident that the Spanish also meant to sack the town. Sobered by the sight of the armed galleons in their harbor, the pirates began removing their recent booty stored in warehouses along the waterfront, carrying it off to the woods beyond the port. The townsmen followed suit, loading their families and possessions on mule-drawn carts and making haste for the hills.

Jean ordered extra cannon and barrels of powder rolled out upon the platforms leading up the steep cliff to the house. To his satisfaction, de Fontenay proved to be as quick and determined to repel the attack. In addition to his own mounted cannon, de Fontenay had a picked squad of sharpshooters stationed on the roofs of the houses along the shore.

The Spanish rode anchor at the mouth of the harbor just out of gun range. They made no attempt at a landing, and Jean guessed they were waiting for nightfall, when they would send their longboats ashore. Deciding it would be suicidal to dispatch their own small boats out to harry the Spanish, Jean and de Fontenay spent the day reinforcing their defenses at points where the enemy were expected to land.

But the Spanish surprised them. They had managed to come ashore in a rocky cove some distance from the port, for at midnight a platoon of helmeted soldiers burst from the woods. Firing their muskets, they sent those townsmen who had remained fleeing for cover. Francisca, watching from her bedroom window, heard the rattle of musketry and the distant shouts of men. The Spaniards, carrying torches to light their way, were fighting, looting, and burning as they advanced. Flames darted and shot from shingled roofs and cedar-hewn walls, silhouetting the men battling hand to hand.

Greatly outnumbered, the defenders who had not been killed or wounded were forced to retreat to the fortifications on the rock. Some of Blanchard's henchmen, deciding that discretion was the better part of valor, simply disappeared, swallowed up by the night.

Daylight found the town a smoking ruin. To make matters worse, the Spanish soldiers—around four hundred, according to Blanchard's estimate—had mounted guns on the hills surrounding the fort. But Blanchard and de Fontenay were ready for them. All that day and the next, the guns spoke, acrid clouds of smoke sometimes obscuring foe from defender. Blanchard himself directed the fire, and when the nearest cannoneer was picked off by the Spanish, Jean took his place. An abortive attempt was made by the Spaniards to scale the rock. They were quickly brought down by a volley of shots. Jean, his face covered with soot, his impeccable linen dirtied by powder blast, seethed with rage. He swore his determination to kill every Spaniard who had dared come against him. Those who would not be killed outright would receive a slow and lingering death at his own hands.

Francisca's feelings were mixed. While she hoped against hope that the Spanish would emerge the victors, she was dismayed to see that these ships (except for a small barque, which flew no flag) displayed the official banners of the king of Spain. Officialdom meant the Inquisition, reminding her that its long arm was not as far away as she had thought.

Using a spyglass, she watched the fighting with trepidation mingled with flashes of optimism.

On the afternoon of the third day, peering through her telescope at a Spanish emplacement, she saw something that stopped the breath in her lungs. A tall figure with a head of red-gold hair! The man was not dressed as a soldier, but in pirate garb. From a distance she could not make out his face, and even though reason told her that any number of men might have the same coloring, she felt certain it was Miguel.

She kept staring at him, following him with the glass as he disappeared and reappeared again. A drift of smoke parted, and she saw his features more clearly.

It *was* Miguel!

Miguel here on Tortuga? She looked again, just to make sure. Yes, yes! Miguel! She wanted to shout, to fling her arms about and wave to him, to dance with joy. Did he know she was on the island? If only there were some way she could communicate her presence. Consumed with wild excitement, she tried to think of how she could get to him. But they were under siege. Anyone caught signaling the enemy or attempting to leave would be considered a traitor and shot on sight.

That evening Jean, sharing a hasty meal with Francisca, told her that he and eight of his men, under cover of darkness, would equip one of their barques as a fire ship. Sailing it close to the largest of the Spanish galleons, attaching it with grapples to her sides, they would set off the barque with an explosive. The flames quickly spreading to the man-of-war would distract the enemy. In addition, he would dispatch several more of his cohorts to climb the hills held by the Spaniards and throw grenades consisting of pots of powder fired by long fuses into the gun emplacements.

Francisca, hearing this, felt as though a cold hand had clutched her heart. In her mind she imagined the stealthy pirates snaking up the rock-strewn hill, the flare of tinder, and the airborne fire pot arching across the darkness. Her picture was so real, she could almost hear the explosion. And Miguel . . .

She had to warn him.

The moment Jean left to supervise the preparation of the fire ship, she hurried into the menservants' quarters, empty now since everyone had been pressed into service on the ramparts. Her eye went over the row of garments hung on pegs from one wall. She took down a stained pair of breeches and a coat she thought would fit her best. Back in her room she quickly exchanged clothing, thinking wryly of the times she had done this before and that if she ever came out of this episode in one piece, she would never don a pair of man's breeches again.

Observing herself in a mirror, she saw that the coat barely hid the swell of her breasts. But it couldn't be helped. Perhaps in the dark no one would notice. She hid her hair under a pirate's kerchief such as Blanchard's men wore and stuffed a cutlass in her belt. Carrying several of the gunpowder pots in a gunnysack, she went out. Calling to the sentry who guarded the ladder, she explained that she had been instructed to bring extra explosives in case the men attacking the emplacements should need them.

With this dubious excuse Francisca managed to reach the bottom of the cliff. The fired houses had burnt themselves out, and the town lay in blackness under the shadow of the mountain. The streets were as still as death, with not even a barking dog to break the silence. Francisca, stumbling about over the cobbles, began to feel that she might not be in time to reach Miguel's gun emplacement. Nevertheless, there was still the chance that Blanchard's men had been delayed, or perhaps that the fuses would go out before the gunpowder could be ignited.

Moving quickly, she was threading her way past the standing wall of a rubbled house when suddenly she was grabbed from behind. The oath *Madre María!* escaped from her lips a split second before a rough hand went over her mouth, stifling a scream.

The hand relaxed, then fell. She was turned about. *"Estás
español?"*

She could not see her captor's face. But the voice, the
touch—she would know it anywhere.

Chapter XXII

As she went into Miguel's arms, an explosion shattered the night, rocking the ground beneath their feet. Miguel pressed her close, holding her protectively while a series of thunderous blasts followed, lighting the sky in shooting rockets of flame.

"They must have hit a magazine on one of the ships," he murmured.

At the sound of running footsteps, he pulled Francisca through an open door of a charred house. Half the roof had been burned away when the town had been sacked, and they could see a bright orange glow, together with flashes of crimson and torrents of fiery sparks, above them, paling the stars.

"Will it come ashore?" Francisca whispered. Billows of gray-yellow smoke redolent of tar and pitch began to roll heavenward.

"I don't think so. It will burn itself out on the water." He closed the door. "For the moment we are as safe here as elsewhere."

So much to say, so much to ask. But for now it was enough to be held by Miguel again and to feel the beat of his heart under her cheek. She sighed, and then, suddenly not sure that he might be real or part of a dream she had dreamt so many times, she turned her face upward to look at him, devouring his features, staring into his smiling sea-blue gaze.

"Miguel . . . ?" she asked tentatively, her voice catching as she touched his cheek.

His lips met hers in a long, tender kiss, his mouth, his arms, and his solid chest telling her that this was no dream. He was real, he was here.

"I thought they had killed you," she said, leaning against him, speaking with difficulty past the painful contraction in her throat. "But then I had a dream—and I knew that you were alive and that . . . that someday we would be together again."

His mouth caressed the tip of her nose, the sweet, rosy lips, her cheeks wet with tears of joy.

"Francisca," he whispered, almost as unbelieving as she had been a moment before. He drew the kerchief from her head, running his hands through the dark, tumbling hair. "My Francisca." His arms clasped her tightly, their bodies melding in a long kiss, their hungry lips seeking to reaffirm the miracle that had brought them together again.

At last when they drew breath, Miguel spoke. "The thought of you was the only thing that kept me going, Francisca. I could have died several times over, but for you." He cradled her against him for a few silent moments before he went on.

"I had known Blanchard would take you to Tortuga long before I heard it as a fact from a band of buccaneers."

"You are with the Spanish warships?"

"Not exactly. I am one of a crew of the *Dolores*, a privateer whose captain has a grudge against Blanchard. We came along with the galleons for the promise of revenge and booty."

"You have been with the privateer all this time?"

"No. I will tell you what happened. Come, let us sit." He led her to a charred bench. Outside the fire still raged. Tall flames leaped up and receded, dying, then leaping up again. Somewhere a cannon was booming, but from the street beyond the door there was no sound.

"When they heaved me overboard from the *Espíritu*, I was barely conscious," Miguel began. "Blanchard's sword thrust was not lethal, thanks to God. The cold water must have revived me and somehow staunched the blood. After I came to the surface, I had enough strength in me to keep from going under again. Fortunately, I came across a floating plank, part of the debris the pirates had thrown into the sea. How long I clung to it, I cannot tell you. Thirst was my worst enemy, thirst and the blazing sun. I must have sunk into momentary black forgetfulness more than once, only to wake and find myself slipping beneath the waves."

Francisca held his hand tightly while he spoke, her eyes fixed on his face, half-hidden by shadow. His beard, grown to fullness, was peppered with gray. There was a scar on his right cheek she had never seen before. He looked older, harder.

"By the grace of God," he went on, "I was washed ashore. Indians searching for clams found me and took me to their camp. I later learned they were Calusa, whose habitat is southeastern Florida. To say they were unfriendly would be putting it mildly. Apparently their experience with the white man, especially the Spanish, had not been a happy one. They immediately began building a huge fire, and from their gestures I was made to understand that I would be torn limb from limb, each part slowly roasted over the flames."

Francisca, shuddering, slipped her arm around his waist, holding him protectively, as if to shield him from the pain of memory.

"I asked for water," Miguel continued, "the last wish of a doomed man. There was an argument between an old woman and a man I took to be their chief. A few minutes later she came forward with a calabash of water. It seems that she had seen me in a dream, a man with hair like the sun, a gift of the gods that spelled good fortune.

"They believed her—for the moment, at any rate. I was treated as an honored guest, nursed back to health, taught their language, and on numerous occasions, asked for advice. As luck would have it, this particular band did prosper, and the old lady's prophecy came true. However, I realized early on that I was also their prisoner. They were not about to let their live talisman go, and forestalling the possibility of my leaving, guarded their canoes.

"One morning, searching for a land route, I came across a band of buccaneers who had beached their pinnace for repairs on a creek that ran into the sea. I warned them that if the Calusa discovered their presence, they would be massacred.

"They left in a hurry, and I went with them. It was from them I learned that you were still on Tortuga. Six months later we joined up with the Spanish fleet who sailed on the king's orders from Santo Domingo with instructions to capture the island. Needless to say, I was happy with this turn of events, since I had been trying to persuade my buccaneer friends to put in at Tortuga from the start."

Francisca asked, "Do you think the Spanish will prevail?"

"Yes. De Fontenay is putting up a good fight, but I think he will eventually capitulate. But you and I are not going to remain to see that happen. We'll take one of the smaller boats, a pinnace or a ketch, whatever I can manage, and sail to Jamaica. The sooner we quit this island—and the Spanish, for I don't trust them—the better."

We. You and I. Were there happier words? Francisca nuzzled her cheek against Miguel's broad shoulder.

He smiled at her. "Tell me, Francisca, why you are dressed as a boy?"

"I saw you through a glass. I wanted to get to you, and it was the only way I could pass through the sentries." She explained about Blanchard's plan to blow up the gun emplacements.

"You were being held for ransom?" Miguel asked.

"Why . . . yes."

But her affirmation was too late. He had caught the hesitancy in her voice. He grasped her shoulders and held her away, his blue eyes blazing as he scrutinized her face. The fire's glow had died to a smoky red. But there was still enough light to see by.

"You were Blanchard's mistress?" His voice was hard, uncompromising. It was the voice of a man who, discovering infidelity, will never forgive.

"I thought you were dead, Miguel."

"That is no excuse."

"I had little choice. He threatened to give me to his men if I did not comply."

"You should have killed yourself first."

She looked at him in disbelief. "How can you say that? Do you think I wanted to die? Did *you* want to die?"

"It was different in my case."

"Then you hold your life more dearly than you hold mine."

"You don't understand." This was the woman he had risked all for, would gladly die for. Yet thinking of her in the arms of that dog, submitting to his foul caresses, made him want to tear her apart.

Yet he loved her. That was the simple, painful truth.

Francisca could sense the inner struggle going on in his mind. A proud man did not take lightly to the news of his woman bedding another man. But she wasn't any woman, she was his loved one, and she had given herself to Blanchard because there had been no alternative.

"It is you who do not understand." She shrugged out of his grasp, angry because he refused to see the dilemma she had been forced to face. "You never have! I could have lied to you, but I chose to tell the truth. I see now where you would have preferred the lie."

Was she right? He thought of the moments he had spent as a captive himself, his every move watched. Made to conform to village life, he had relied on the shaky goodwill of the Calusa chief and an old woman to keep him alive until he could find a way to escape. Surely Francisca's predicament had not been too different from his own?

The silence between them stretched on. Even the guns were still. The fire, except for a few spurts of flame, had almost burned itself out.

"We are quarreling," Miguel said finally, thinking, what did it matter? She had come to him chaste. He had been the first, her only love. "Ten minutes together and we are at it. I didn't want it to be this way."

"Nor I." She felt the sting of hot tears, but kept her voice steady. "Perhaps you should go on without me."

His fingers grasped her shoulders again, biting into the flesh. "Never! Don't say that even in jest." He touched a crystal tear trickling down her cheek, then kissed it away. "My beautiful Francisca," he said in a softer tone, drawing her into his arms. "Let us not contend. You are the one constant in my life. I have my faults. So be it. But my love for you is without blemish. If you had not been here . . . But we shan't speak of it. Whatever has happened is in the past. Now we must think only of the future."

Miguel found an untended shallop—a small open boat fitted with oars and a sail—beached under the shadow of the fort above. It was still night. The moon had gone in, and the only light was the faint gleam of embers from the ship still smoldering in the harbor. The cannoneers and those armed with muskets, unable to see their targets in the darkness, bided their time until dawn.

The shallop was stocked with a cask of water and a sack of dried fish, enough provender, Miguel said, to get them to Jamaica. Francisca would have liked to take her jewels, or at least a few of them, for Miguel had very little money, and they would need some when they reached their destination. But she did not dare return to Blanchard's house on the cliff. In any case, there was no time. Miguel felt they should be well away by daylight.

He rowed them out under the guns of the fort, past the

sinking masts of the fired galleon, past the anchor lights of the Spanish and the darkened pirate ships. It seemed to Francisca that the creak of their unoiled oarlocks could be heard from one end of Tortuga to the other. At any moment she expected to hear a voice shouting the alarm, followed by a fusillade of shots spattering across the water. But they made it to the open sea safely, and Miguel hoisted the shallop's sail. Guided by the light of the stars, he brought the little skiff about and pointed her nose toward Jamaica.

Toward evening of the following day they could see storm clouds gathering on the southeastern horizon, and presently the wind picked up. The waves swelled, the sky grew dark, and before Miguel could lower his sail, the storm in all its fury was upon them.

Angry blasts of wind tore the sail from his hands, snapping the mast in two, whipping the sea into a frothing rage. The shallop rode up one mountainous wave and down into a trough so deep, Francisca could see the white comber poised above them. But the little boat, shaking itself like a terrier, was lifted up again, only to sink once more into the dark green abyss. The winds increased in velocity, the sea sweeping over them in great battering waves. The rudder went; the oars were ripped from their sockets. Francisca, wet through, her hair plastered to her skull, clung to the sides of the boat.

With the rudder, mast, and oars gone, they were completely at the mercy of the storm. Miguel, crawling forward to where Francisca sat, shouted in her ear that they must bail. He pushed a bucket into her hands, and she began to scoop frantically at the rising water. Soon it was up to her knees. Each comber seemed to be larger than the next, crashing mercilessly down upon them. She could feel the seams of their vessel expanding, coming apart under the onslaught.

"We are foundering!" Miguel shouted.

He emptied the water cask and tied Francisca to it.

"No!" she screamed. She did not want to live if he drowned.

But the knots were tight, and though she tried, she could not undo them. Then a huge wave lifted her from the sinking boat. She saw the gray, pitiless skies, the boiling turmoil of the sea, felt the lashing rain, and then—nothing.

Sunlight beating on the side of her face woke her. She was on a calmed sea, still bound around the waist to the cask. She coughed, spitting sea water. Her lungs ached; her throat felt raw. Nothing was in sight, not a floating spar on the lapping waves, not a single flying bird, nothing but the blue sea and a cloudless sky. Limitless, lonely horizons stretched all around her, an emptiness that was terrifying as it was complete.

"Miguel?" Her lips formed his name, but no sound formed on her swollen tongue.

She closed her eyes against the blinding light reflected from sky and water. Fate had separated her from Miguel again. Fate, perhaps death. No, she wouldn't think of dying. She wouldn't think of the fathomless sea below her dangling legs or the sharks that roamed these waters. She would think only of possibilities, of . . .

A splashing sound brought her slitted eyes open. Miguel, buoyed by a section of the overturned shallop, was slowly kicking his way toward her.

She didn't know whether to weep or laugh, but was too exhausted to do either.

That afternoon an English merchantman, the *Sea Bear*, picked them up. The captain, after having been assured that Miguel, despite his dress, was not a shipwrecked pirate, had given them a tiny cabin and loaned them a change of clothing. Francisca's gown, donated by a female passenger, hung in unsightly folds about her. But she was so happy to be wearing it, so happy to be alive and reunited with Miguel, she did not much care how she looked.

To her astonishment, the captain informed them that the

de Bustos, former Christian friends of her father's, were aboard.

"Yes, Señora Castillo, they are also fleeing from the Inquisition." To avoid embarrassment, Miguel had claimed that Francisca was his wife.

"But they are good Catholics," Francisca protested.

"Someone—they think, perhaps an envious business rival—accused them of blasphemy and Protestantism, and they thought it best to leave at once."

"They have come recently from Mexico City? Then perhaps they have news of my family. Please take me to them at once."

Although she had once felt resentful toward the de Bustos because they had shied away from offering her family help when they were in jeopardy, she now greeted them like long lost friends. Their own plight brought them closer to her.

Their news was not good.

"We had heard the rumor that your father, mother, and husband died under torture," Doña Ana told Francisca. "They are to be burned in effigy in the next *auto*. Your aunt Juliana's fate is uncertain; whether she is alive or dead, no one can say. Your sister languishes in the convent of the Carmelites. They tell us she is quite mad. Of Jorge we know nothing. He and his foster parents disappeared from Mexico City some time ago."

In the past Francisca had hoped that at least her father's and Juliana's lives might have been spared, that they might have been let off with a prison sentence, an order to wear the sanbenito for a number of years. But now all had gone, either dead or possibly dead or mad. Only Jorge remained, living somewhere among savages.

The ship was bound for New Amsterdam, where Miguel proposed that he and Francisca settle. There was no question of returning to Spain, even briefly, where they risked being recognized. The continent of Europe, embroiled in disputes and wars, offered no peaceful haven. But New Amsterdam did. Of all the colonies on the north continent, Miguel said, this seemed to him the most promising.

He and Francisca were careful about the subject of religion, stepping around it with caution. Neither had realized that the events of the past year had changed them. They had become less narrow, less zealous in their beliefs and more willing to compromise. Then one afternoon as they were standing on deck discussing New Amsterdam, Miguel said, "We'll start a fresh life, Francisca. I still hope to get an annulment from my wife. We'll marry, have children, half-Jew, half-Christian. Let them decide when they are grown which or both."

From Miguel this was a concession Francisca had always hoped for. For a few moments she could only stare at him, her lips parting in a slow smile. Then she flung herself at him, kissing him again and again, overcome with joyful gratitude—the bridge had been crossed, and the last obstacle between them had vanished.

"Well!" he exclaimed, holding her at arm's length. "What is this all about?"

"Come, let me show you," she said.

The cot was narrow and lumpy, but the lovers hardly noticed. Naked, hip to thigh, they rediscovered all the places that thrilled to touch and kiss, their mutual passion lighting old fires that burned with a new flame. Had they been separated a day or a thousand years, it would have been the same, her black hair tumbling on his breast, the pink lips parted in gasps of ecstasy, the baritone murmurs of delight, the fierce, generous, all-consuming, passionate taking and giving of love. Together they soared into a world that was their own, a man and a woman whose love had been forged through pain and tragedy, losing themselves in each other for a handful of precious time. Later, lying spent in each other's arms, Francisca, looking up into her lover's face, saw a sudden shadow cross it.

"What is it, sweet?"

"I was thinking how like you Jorge looks."

Always that memory, always that shadow.

Ten years had gone by.

In New Amsterdam the del Castillos prospered. They were married now. (News of Miguel's wife Ana's death had reached them just as Miguel was about to set sail for Spain.) They had been blessed with three children: a boy, Pablo; his brother, Pedro; and a girl, Mariana, named after Francisca's mother.

It was after the arrival of the second boy that Miguel had taken passage to Tampico. Traveling the overland route on muleback to Zacatecas, he had gone in search of Jorge again, only to find that there had been a massacre of the Chichimecs in that area, and that Jorge was counted among the dead. Narrowly escaping a trap set by an agent of the Inquisition who had been informed that Miguel was in Mexico, he returned home, sadly resigned to never seeing his son again.

Through luck, skill, and a series of wise investments in profitable cargoes, Miguel had become master of his own ship, the *Doña Francisca*. He and his family lived in a large brick house with a tiled roof and true glass windows curtained in linen. The furnishings, from the Russian leather chairs and French nutwood cupboards (or *kastens*) to the paintings by Jan Steen (one of Francisca hung over the foreroom's fireplace), were similar to those to be seen in other well-to-do households.

When Francisca and Miguel, in his infrequent stops at home, entertained, or were entertained, Francisca wore gowns of silk, sarcenet, velvet, or satin, the detachable wristlength sleeves made of lacy Holland ruffles. Her wardrobe held dresses in colors that were fashionable for the day—scarlet, purple, fawn, and ash gray. She wore gold bodkins in her black, glossy hair, diamonds on her fingers and in her earlobes, and around her neck a gold chain with a chased locket bearing Miguel's coat of arms.

Meanwhile, New Amsterdam had become New York, with

the English taking over the colony from Peter Stuyvesant on orders from James I in a brash, bloodless move. The colony became even more heterogeneous, although there were still few Jews and Catholics. But Miguel managed to find a priest who conducted mass in a private home, and Francisca attended services—also in a private home—during the High Holidays, finding to her astonishment that the celebration in Mexico City had been only a faint echo of prescribed ritual.

They were a happy family. Miguel and Francisca were still very much in love. Because Miguel was out at sea for such long stretches, his homecomings were all the dearer, their lovemaking a turbulent, passionate reunion as if they were again bedding for the first time.

Only Jorge's death remained in their memories, the one small cloud in their sky.

One day Miguel arrived home from a voyage where he had taken on cargo from Bermuda. With him was a young boy of about sixteen. Miguel had found him working as a bound servant in Hamilton for a surgeon.

Francisca did not have to be told who the boy was.

Though he stood straight and tall, his expression was shy, a little bewildered. And Francisca, overcome with emotion, her eyes filling with tears, suddenly felt shy, too. Her baby, her little boy, grown almost to manhood! She looked at Miguel, whose eyes were also suspiciously moist, then back to Jorge, whose lips twitched as if he did not know whether to smile or to cry.

"Jorge," Francisca whispered. And with the sound of his spoken name, the awkward silence was broken. Through a veil of tears the mother reached out and embraced the son she had thought she had lost forever, taking him to her heart, holding and cradling him. "Jorge, oh, Jorge."

Did he remember her? "Oh, yes." His Spanish was halting. "And Papá, too."

It seemed that Jorge's Indian abductors had been killed in a Spanish raid when the boy was ten. The leader of the raid, having taken Jorge prisoner, had sold him to the captain of a ship, who in turn had bound him over to the surgeon on Hamilton.

"That is the bare bones of the story," Miguel said to a tearful Francisca and the other children who had gathered around to stare at their long lost brother. "There is more, much more."

"Ah, but loves," Francisca said, kissing each of her children and lastly Miguel, whose strong arm circled her waist, "we have a lifetime ahead for the telling."

A touch of romance... from Cordia Byers